The Hou

by

The Quay

Also by Elise Darcy

The Sunrise Coast Series

New Beginnings at the Harbour Inn
The Secret of the Summerhouse
The Cottage by the Sea
The Guest House at Shingle Cove
The Houseboat by the Quay
Return to Willow Tree Cottage
The Bookshop of Memories
The Beach House
A Summer to Remember

The Scottish Highlands Series

Winter in the Scottish Highlands
The Secrets of the Glen
Return to the Lake House
The Boathouse by the Loch
Summer in the Scottish Highlands
Coming Home to Aviemore

The Living Apart Together series

Living Apart Together
It Takes 2 to Tango
Dear John
Love on the Rooftop

Standalone books

Lola & The Man
A Mallorcan Affair
The Villa in Sicily
We'll Meet Again

The Houseboat by The Quay

A Novel

ELISE DARCY

ISBN 978-1-913147-15-0

"Sometimes, the biggest risks are those we take with our hearts." Anonymous

1

Lexi jumped at the sound of the fire alarm. 'Oh, drat! Not again!' A colleague rushed by, shouting, 'Everybody out, this is not a drill!'

Lexi sighed and instinctively reached for her handbag before she joined the throng exiting the building on Lexington Avenue. She stood on the pavement outside her place of work, nervously twiddling a strand of her dark hair between her fingers and staring up at the skyscraper, which dwarfed some of the original thirties-built New York skyscrapers.

She imagined that someone had burned some toast again in the office kitchen. What a palaver,' she commented. She was no stranger to the odd looks she got from her fellow Americans when she used such British colloquialisms.

Lexi was feeling quite blasé about the enforced morning break, until she realised she'd had no choice but to leave without backing up her work. She was a marketing manager at a publishing house in downtown New York and had just drawn up a launch strategy for one of the prime authors on their books. She swallowed, staring up at the building and praying for a false alarm. There was no billowing smoke, nothing to indicate a fire.

'So, how's things?'

Lexi turned around at the sound of a young guy's voice. They had worked together five years earlier when Lexi had started at the publishing house as an eager twenty-one-year-old intern. He had been an intern too.

'Are you still with Brandon?' he asked.

Lexi inwardly sighed before forcing a smile. He'd asked her out when they'd first started working together. She'd told him she was already with someone, but he was one of those guys who didn't like taking no for an answer. She had been relieved when they'd gone their separate ways within the company; he had become an editor, and she had gone into the sales side of the business.

The trouble for Lexi was just what her mother had warned her about: was he interested in her because she came from one of the wealthiest families in America? Thankfully, Lexi didn't need to find the answer to this question; she was still with Brandon, her soulmate, whom she had started dating in high school.

'So, did Brandon get that recording contract?'

The smug look on his face said he knew that her boyfriend hadn't.

Lexi shook her head. 'No, but he's still working on it.'

'Sure, I bet.'

Lexi frowned at him. She knew what he was thinking; that Brandon was just living off her money.

Out of the corner of her eye, she caught sight of a tall, blonde, leggy young woman waving from across the street. The woman weaved her way through the small crowd gathered on the sidewalk and linked her arm with the young man's. 'Honey, I got your text. Let's go for coffee.' She eyed Lexi suspiciously.

Lexi stared up at her. If this woman was his type, why had he been interested in *her*? She sighed. She guessed it was the same reason most guys thought they were attracted to her – her wealthy background. Lexi was five foot nothing, with dark, shoulder-length hair and green eyes. She still preferred to wear jeans, comfy jumpers, flat shoes and the brown leather jacket she'd found in a thrift store. Of course she couldn't wear those to work – she wore trouser suits. She wouldn't wear a figure-hugging dress and high heels like the young woman standing in front of her; she knew she wouldn't feel comfortable. And besides, she just didn't have the height to carry off that outfit.

She remembered the cutting remark the young man had made when she'd declined to go out with him. He'd said she was playing at being poor. He had just discovered where she shopped for some of her clothes.

She wasn't playing at anything. Lexi was trying to make her own way in the world, even though she wouldn't admit to anyone that she was still on the family's payroll, as her grandparents referred to it. It was the only way she could afford to live in an apartment in New York and work in her dream job in publishing. In reality, it didn't pay that well and had turned out not to be quite the dream job she'd imagined. It involved long hours, and the salary was low enough that despite not having to pay rent, she was often left short at the end of the month. It was expensive to support two people living in New York.

'Hey, aren't you the granddaughter of the Harringtons? I've seen your photo in magazines.'

Lexi frowned at the young woman. 'Yeah, I think that was way back when I was twelve.' Lexi had avoided any further publicity, trying to distance herself from her grandparents' real estate empire. Her little sister had joined the family business, but Lexi wasn't like her sister at all.

'Well, you haven't changed a bit.'

Lexi took the comment as it was intended – *not* as a compliment.

'Is your partner still trying to get a recording contract?'

Lexi shifted her gaze to her ex-colleague. They'd obviously been talking about her. 'Yeah – so?'

'How long has it been?'

Lexi stared at her. 'I'm going to find out if we can go back to the office.' She turned around and tried to walk away, but didn't have much luck making her way through the throng to get to the security personnel standing at the doors to the building.

Someone caught her arm. 'Just ignore them, Lexi.'

'Pardon?'

'Sorry, but I overheard the conversation.' It was the young intern, a woman fresh out of college, who was shadowing Lexi's role. Inevitably they'd chatted about their personal lives. Lexi had opened up about the difficulties she'd often experienced as a result of her background. Most people assumed her life was cushy, which it was financially, but like everyone else, she had other problems to deal with. Brandon being one of them. It was a sore point.

'Your boyfriend will make it – you'll see.'

Lexi managed a smile, even though the words were just an echo of Brandon's own. *I'll make it, you'll see.* She changed the subject. 'Look, I'm going to head off home.' She wasn't shirking; she could work from home on her laptop.

The young intern also looked about her, trying to locate their boss. 'Oh, look – he's over there.' She pointed at the middle-aged man staring up at their office as he chatted with a firefighter who had just exited the building. Lexi decided to hang around to see if they would be ushered back inside.

'Can I have your attention, folks?'

There was a hushed silence as the firefighter spoke. 'There's an electrical fault in the building, so you won't be returning to your offices today until an engineer has located the fault. If you need to go into the building to collect personal possessions, please do so.'

Lexi already had her bag with the keys to her apartment. 'I'm heading off home.' *Home.* It was good to think of it that way. She smiled, recalling the time five years earlier when she had left her original home, moving from Connecticut to New York for her work. Brandon had come too. It was when they had moved in together.

People milling around outside started to enter the building. Lexi was about to leave when she saw her manager waving at her, trying to attract her attention. She walked over. 'I've already got my bag, so I don't have to go back inside. I can work from home.' She wouldn't have been surprised if some of her colleagues were going to take the day off, but that wasn't Lexi's style. She wasn't about to use it as an excuse not to put in a days' work.

'Well, here's the thing, Lexi. I was going to call you into my office today.'

'Okay,' Lexi said slowly, staring at him.

'I know this isn't the time or place, but …'

She eyed him. 'But – what?'

'You heard that there's some cost-cutting exercises going on.'

'Yes.' Lexi shrugged, wondering why they were having this conversation right now, on the street corner. It wasn't anything she hadn't heard already. They weren't taking on new clients, and they'd let go some of their long-running authors who weren't making the company money.

'Look, the book you're marketing. I'm afraid we've decided to shelve that for now.'

Lexi couldn't hide her surprise. She'd assumed they'd want to market the book; how did they think it would sell unless people knew it had been released? She looked at him, bewildered. *Could they do that? Just drop a book like that after all the effort she'd put in to prepare for the release date?* 'But it's ready to be promoted.'

'I know. We gave the author a small advance, but we want to concentrate on the big players. There's a recession on the way, and unless an author is already generating a lot of interest, well, we need to stick with the safe bets right now.'

'So, do you want me to stop working on that?'

'Yes.'

Lexi didn't like leaving things unfinished, but if that was what her boss wanted, she didn't have a choice. 'So, what do you want me to work on now?'

'Well, that's the other thing.'

Lexi frowned. 'What other thing?

'We've had to make some changes.'

'Yes, you told me that already.'

He offered Lexi an apologetic look that she'd never seen from her manager before. That was when it dawned on her. 'You're letting me go?'

'I'm sorry, Lexi.'

'But I've been here five years, and I've built up all this experience.' And she hadn't had a pay rise in all that time, during which she'd seen well-known authors, for whom the company had put aside huge marketing budgets, being paid large advances – often several times her annual salary. Lexi glanced at her colleagues, who were filing past her. She realised they wouldn't let the interns go. They were working for nothing. But there were others in paid positions in the company with less experience. 'Why me?'

'Do you want me to be honest?'

'Hell, yes!' Although the moment those words came out of her mouth, Lexi feared what he was going to say. Was her work below par? How could that be when she worked so hard? 'It's my work, isn't it? You're not happy with the results.'

Her manager furiously shook his head. 'No! Look, this wasn't my decision. You are good at what you do. In fact, I wouldn't be surprised if one of these days you pump out a novel of your own.'

Lexi stared at him. That was the last thing she wanted to do. She'd seen the writers she'd been involved with, sweating blood to make deadlines, having no life outside of work, consumed with writing. She'd seen Brandon face the same issues with his creative endeavours, trying everything to get that coveted recording contract and the money and fame that would go with it. Life was just too short. She looked at him. 'Are you suggesting I write a novel for your publishing house?' she said in astonishment. This was not what she had been expecting.

He shook his head. 'No, not at all.'

'Then what are you saying?'

'I can offer you a good reference.'

'Wait – you're telling me this here, on the street corner?' Wasn't there a protocol for letting someone go? Didn't she have to be sitting in an office?

He sighed. 'Look, it's not my decision, Lexi. It's come from the top. We've just got to start tightening our belts and that means letting some of our authors and staff go. However, anyone who has not been given a notice period will receive sixty days severance pay and a redundancy package.'

That did not make Lexi feel any better. 'Who else is going, then?'

'I can't say.'

'Why me, then, if I'm so good at doing my job?'

He looked uncomfortable.

'I want the truth. I need to know.' If she was as talented at her job as he said she was, but she wasn't one of their well-paid staff who had been there for decades, then why her?

'We had to think about our employees' personal circumstances. Some of them have got children and big mortgages. The fact is, they can't afford to lose their jobs. It's nothing personal.'

Lexi stared at him, open-mouthed. 'You're letting me go because you think I'm rich? How can that not be personal?'

'You are rich.'

'I come from a wealthy family, but I'm making my own way.'

'Are you? How are you paying for that New York apartment? On my salary, I can't afford to live in Manhattan. We all commute across the river. Not you, Lexi.'

'This isn't fair!'

'Life isn't fair.'

'I could sue you for discrimination,' blurted Lexi. She wouldn't. It wasn't in her nature to go down the litigation route, even though she might have a good case.

'Try it, Lexi. I'll say it was your work or inexperience. I'm just telling you this rather than lying to you, so you know it's not about your professionalism or how capable you are at your job.'

Lexi breathed a huge sigh. 'Will you give me a reference?'

'Of course. The best.'

'You know that after this, I won't give you the rights to my bestseller?' she said, trying to crack a joke but realising she wasn't joking at all.

She noticed his smile slip. *So he does think I might write a bestseller one day*, she thought.

He offered her his hand. 'I don't want us to part on bad terms.'

I bet you don't, she thought, *if you think there's a chance I might write the next Harry Potter.*

She shook his hand. What else could she do? There was no point parting on bad terms. She would be professional to the last. Besides, what was done was done. She was grateful that he'd given her the position after her internship – few were kept on afterwards – and it had provided her with the opportunity to gain invaluable experience, and the freedom to leave home and pursue her own career in New York.

'So, I guess I need to go into the building after all.'

He nodded. 'I believe my colleague has already gone in ahead of you to start clearing your desk.'

Lexi noticed another colleague looking teary-eyed as he exited the building carrying a box. So, she wasn't the only one. Lexi recognised him. He was young too. She cast a sympathetic gaze in his direction.

'At least you don't have to worry about money, Lexi.'

Lexi frowned. 'Well that's as may be, but not all problems in life are solved with money,' she retorted. At that, she stalked off into the building. She met the security personnel coming down in the elevator with her box. They handed it over. She glanced inside. There were some files, books on sales and marketing techniques, a pencil case, and a mug that surprisingly they hadn't bothered to empty, let alone rinse out; there was still some cold tea in the bottom. But they had found her box of PG Tips in the shared kitchen – at least that was something. And her bar of Cadbury Dairy Milk had been retrieved from her drawer and added to her box. As long as she had her own mug, her PG Tips and her bar of chocolate, for which she'd had to make a special trip to the English shop she'd discovered in The West Village in New York, she really didn't care for anything else – apart from the folding photo frame containing a photo of her beloved late parents.

Lexi was going down in the elevator when she realised it was missing from her box. She turned to the security guards as the elevator came to a halt on the ground floor. 'Where's my photo?'

They exchanged blank looks.

Lexi managed to hold the box under one arm and rummage through the contents again. It definitely wasn't there. 'I had a silver photo frame – well, it was two frames attached by a hinge. It was sat on my desk – you couldn't miss it.'

'We cleared everything from your desk, your desk drawers and even anything from the kitchen with your name on it. If it isn't in the box, then it wasn't there. Perhaps you're mistaken.'

'How can I be mistaken? I look at that photo every single day.'

The elevator door opened. 'Ma'am, please step out.'

Lexi's heart sank. Of course she had other photos, but it was the thought that it might be found and just binned that brought tears to her eyes.

One of the security guards noticed. 'Hey, look – wait outside. I'll go back upstairs and take another look. Please, don't cry.'

Lexi stepped outside and stood looking around, biting her lower lip and hoping no one she knew spotted her standing there with a box. They'd know immediately that she'd been let go. It seemed to take forever for the security guard to reappear. She immediately spotted the small photo frame in his hand. 'Oh, thank god,' she breathed. 'Where did you find it?'

'It must have fallen behind the back of your desk when we were clearing out your stuff. I'm so sorry.'

Lexi said, 'It's okay. I'm just thankful you found it.' She glanced at the photo of her mum in one frame and her dad in the other. They had been taken years apart – her father's twenty years earlier, just before he died. Her mother's photo was more recent. It had been six months since she had passed away at forty-eight from an incurable brain tumour, but she was still the first person that Lexi wanted to call with the news that she'd lost her job. Six months was no time at all to come to terms with her grief. That was why she had needed this job; to keep her mind off such a terrible January.

Lexi picked up her mobile and scrolled through the phone numbers; her mum's was still in her contacts list. She couldn't bring herself to delete it. Her finger hovered over her sister's number. Lexi frowned. Her sister who was three years younger than her, was working in the family business as a realtor, and was getting married. She was ticking all the right boxes when it came to her grandparents' wishes – she always had. Lexi didn't fancy phoning her and letting her know that she'd lost her job; yet another thing in a long line of what her family classed as failures. She imagined her sister, Andrea, would be delighted; she'd always wanted her to go home to Connecticut and work in the family business. As far as Lexi was concerned, though, hell would have to freeze over for that to happen.

2

Lexi strode down the street and sat down on the first public bench she came to. She wasn't about to trudge home carrying a bulky box, so she emptied some of the contents into her shoulder bag. That left only empty files, blank notebooks, and her work mug, which she wasn't bothered about keeping. She dumped the rest in a bin on the sidewalk and decided to walk back to her apartment rather than take the subway, which would take no time at all.

She needed time to think, and besides, Brandon would still be asleep if she arrived home right now. A night owl, he worked on writing songs until late in the evening – when he was most creative – and then caught up with sleep late in the morning, briefly rousing to kiss her goodbye when her alarm went off at six.

She thought his music and lyrics sounded amazing. It was just a shame that no record label felt the same way. He had yet to secure a single recording contract after all his years of hard work, no matter how many demos he'd produced.

Lexi walked into a deli near their home and bought three takeaway coffees and bagels. She glanced at her watch while she waited for the coffee and thought that Brandon should be up by now. She wasn't looking forward to telling him she'd lost her job; he depended on her money. They both did. Apart from the use of the apartment, which belonged to her grandparents, she'd supported herself almost completely since she'd left college. She knew he'd just tell her to dip into her savings until she found another job. The problem was that supporting both of them and hiring a recording studio to produce demos wasn't cheap. Over time, his dream had used up all her savings as well as the monthly allowance she still received from her grandparents. Right now, she was technically broke, apart from the fifty-dollar bill she had in her purse. It was all she had until her next allowance hit her bank account.

Lexi handed over the fifty-dollar bill and took her change. 'Can you put one of the bagels in a separate bag, please?'

They did as she asked. She handed over the money, took her change, and picked up two bags of bagels and a tray with three coffees.

She paused outside the deli and gave a homeless man a coffee and the bag with the single bagel. Inside the bag, she'd slipped the change from the fifty-dollar bill. She couldn't afford to do that, but disappointingly, after working so hard to achieve some semblance of independence from her wealthy grandparents, she was feeling as though she was back to square one.

She smiled at the homeless man, realising no one would be empathetic to her situation. She had a safety net and always would, no matter what life threw at her. It might be uncomfortable depending on her grandparents for money, but her boss was right: she had nothing to worry about on that score.

Lexi stopped and let some pedestrians pass before she crossed the road, heading for one of the entrances to Central Park on the Upper West side. She walked through the park for around fifteen minutes, leaving through another entrance. Just across the road, near the American Museum of Natural History, was their apartment. It was an old red-brick pre-war building with striking features and an elegant foyer. There, she rubbed shoulders with celebrities and the movers and shakers of Wall Street.

She remembered that they'd got some odd looks when they'd moved in, as though they didn't belong there. She guessed it was because they were so young. She had started university in New York. She'd overheard one couple say, 'Do you think he's a rock star or she's an actress?' Lexi just smiled at the thought that they'd had no idea who she was.

Exiting the elevator, Lexi could already hear faint music. Brandon mostly worked wearing headphones so as not to disturb the neighbours, but sometimes, when it was late morning and their nearest neighbours were out at work, she knew he'd take the headphones off.

Lexi stopped outside the door to listen. She smiled. The music was good. He deserved a recording contract. She deserved for him to have one too, after all the support she'd given him over the years.

She unlocked the door and stepped inside the apartment. It was full of light from its floor-to-ceiling windows, which had breathtaking views over Central Park. Brandon was sitting with his back to her, playing his guitar, belting out a song. She stood there for a moment, watching him, recalling their time in high school. He'd joined a band there, and she had hung out with him and the other band members at recess. Lexi was about to cross the room and surprise him when the door that led to the bedroom opened.

She nearly dropped the paper bag with the coffee and bagel when she saw a young woman hurriedly getting dressed. Brandon spotted her. He stopped playing. 'Where are you going?'

'My husband just phoned. There's been a fire, well not exactly a fire, but the building where he works has been evacuated – some electrical fault, he said – but he's making his way home from work as we speak. So I must go.'

'Where does he work?' asked Brandon.

'The building on Lexington and Fifth,' replied Lexi.

Brandon whirled around in his seat so fast he banged his guitar on the coffee table in front of him.

The young woman who had been slipping on her shoes stared wide-eyed at Lexi. 'You know my husband?'

'Of course not,' Lexi said through gritted teeth.

'Lexi works in the same building,' Brandon said sheepishly.

'What a coincidence,' said the young woman.

Lexi grimaced. 'Yes, it is, isn't it?' Her gaze shifted from the woman to Brandon.

Brandon rose from his seat. 'This means nothing, I swear.'

The young woman threw her shoe at Brandon. 'Are you for real? Six months means nothing?'

'It was just a bit of fun. You're married, and I've got a girlfriend,' Brandon shot back.

Lexi's mouth dropped open. The woman, who was cheating on her husband, clearly knew that Brandon was with someone else too.

Brandon started towards Lexi. 'Look, I can explain …'

'How? What is there to explain?' Lexi's bottom lip started to tremble. She didn't need an explanation or an excuse for what she could see right in front of her eyes. Six months he'd been cheating on her. *Six months!*

She watched the young woman march over to Brandon. He recoiled as though she was about to hit him. She didn't. Instead she bent down, picked up her shoe, and strode over to the door. Lexi took a step to one side and watched her reach down and retrieve her other shoe.

The woman stopped in the doorway and turned to Brandon. 'Perhaps if you spent less time chatting up girls during your gigs and more time actually playing music, you might get somewhere!'

Lexi looked from her to Brandon. 'What do you mean by that?'

'I met him at one of his gigs, but I get the feeling I wasn't the first impressionable groupie he's been with.'

'Groupie?'

She looked at Lexi. 'When was the last time you went to one

of his gigs?' Lexi knew Brandon played in bars and clubs. Firstly to earn a bit of ready cash, but primarily to see if he might be talent-spotted by a record label. So far, that hadn't happened. The gigs were the reason he was often sleeping in until mid-morning – or so she had thought.

She didn't go to his gigs because she was working and couldn't burn the candle at both ends. Even at weekends, she was often too tired after work to go out much. Besides, going clubbing or to nightclubs or bars just wasn't her thing. Now she wished she had gone along. Perhaps she'd have found out what was really going on sooner. She eyed the young woman coldly. Just how many times had that woman been in and out of their apartment while she was busy working long hours in her job?

As the young woman brushed past her and left, Lexi stood there and stared at Brandon, who looked sheepishly in her direction. 'It's true what I said. It meant nothing, I swear.' His eyes shifted to the paper bag. 'Did you bring coffee and bagels?'

Lexi walked in and dumped the coffee and bagels on the coffee table. She skirted the large L-shaped leather sofa in the centre of the room, which faced the enormous TV screen mounted on the decorative red-brick wall that ran the length of the apartment. The furniture had all been paid for by her. She carried on through the door to their bedroom. She didn't want to go in there, where Brandon had obviously been having sex with that woman, but she had no choice if she was going to pack up her stuff and leave.

Brandon followed her into the bedroom. 'What are you doing?'

Lexi grabbed armfuls of clothes from the walk-in wardrobe and dumped them in her suitcase. She rummaged through drawers, extracting her belongings and dumping them in another small case. It was fancy luggage her sister had bought her one year as a Christmas present when she had planned to go travelling; something that had never materialised because Brandon hadn't wanted to miss a potential opportunity by leaving the country.

Now she wished she'd gone travelling on her own.

'Are you leaving me?'

Lexi zipped up her cases and turned to face him. 'Are you seriously asking me that question right now?'

'Where are you going to go?'

Lexi stopped and got her phone out from the back pocket of her jeans. Scrolling through her contacts list, she sighed at the long list of so-called friends who were not, in fact, her friends but friends of her charismatic rock-star-wannabe boyfriend. Lexi shook her head. She imagined them laughing behind her back, thinking he was just with her because of her money.

Lexi wheeled her cases to the door, Brandon hot on her heels. 'Look, I made a mistake, okay? Can't we get past this?'

Lexi stopped at the door. 'I've just found out you're cheating on me. How can I possibly get past that?'

Brandon wasn't listening. 'Where do you think you're going?'

Lexi looked back at the apartment – *her* apartment. 'You're right. Where am I going? This is *my* place.' Actually it wasn't. It belonged to her grandparents.

Brandon stared at her. 'Oh, right. God, I don't know what I'm going to do.'

'Perhaps you should have thought of that before you jumped into bed with … with …'

'Kimberley.'

Lexi really didn't need to know her name.

'I guess I'd better pack my things and go.' Brandon didn't make a move to do that. Instead he stood there, staring at her, giving her the puppy dog eyes. 'The thing is, I've got nowhere to go.'

Lexi stared at him. He knew she was aware of that. And he knew she didn't need this apartment.

'Look, I'll sleep on the couch. Just let me stay here for a bit longer. I know I'll get a recording contract. I feel it in my bones. I'll pay you back when I become, like, the biggest rock star ever.

You'll get half of everything, I swear.'

'Yeah – sure.'

How many times have I heard that before? she thought.

'I will, I swear it.'

Lexi knew she was the biggest soft touch. She didn't make a move to walk back into the apartment, but she found herself glancing towards the door that led to their bedroom. A horrible thought occurred to her. 'How many others have there been?'

He flicked his long, wavy, blonde hair. She hated it when he did that. It meant he had something to hide.

'Lexi …' He reached for her.

'Don't Lexi me. Just be honest with me. How many?'

She stood in the doorway with her suitcases, watching him sigh heavily, flicking his hair. He'd been on the gig circuit for years, following her from high school to New York when she'd left for university. She said, 'One?'

No reply.

'Two then.' She eyed him. 'Three?'

'Do we have to do this?'

'More than three? Five?' Lexi's mouth dropped open. 'Oh, my god. You've lost count.'

'Look, they just keep coming on to me. And besides, you were often working late on your, your … what is it you do, exactly?'

Lexi stared at him. 'How could I have been so blind? You strung me along for the money …'

'No, Lexi. I love you.'

'Well, you've got a funny way of showing it!'

'Lexi. Since your mum died, things have been …'

'Don't blame your infidelities on me!' She cut him off. 'You can stay in the apartment.' She couldn't live there now. It would just remind of her of him, and Kimberley, and however many other Kimberleys there had been.

'I lost my job.' She didn't know why she was telling him this now they were so obviously no longer together. It wouldn't matter to him if she'd lost her job. However, although she would still let him live in the apartment rent-free, she was no longer going to support him. She turned to leave.

'What will you do?'

'Are you seriously showing some concern for me now?'

'You'll be okay,' Brandon said. 'At least you don't have to worry about money.'

Lexi could feel her bottom lip quivering again. Why did everyone think money made everything okay?

Now she had two options. One was to go cap in hand to her grandparents who, she knew, would only say *I told you so.* They never had liked Brandon. The other was to phone her little sister.

Lexi walked down the hall towards the elevator, wheeling her two cases behind her. Since she was a little girl, the one person she'd felt she could always rely upon was her best friend, her soulmate. She cast a glance over her shoulder. Her supposed best friend was striding down the hallway towards her. He stopped as she reached the elevator. 'Lexi, please don't go. I've been an idiot. I made a mistake.'

Lexi stared at him. He hadn't just made one mistake. Even so, she said, 'Can you promise me it will never happen again?'

He opened his mouth, and in the split second he hesitated before he replied, she knew that was it. Their relationship was over; there was no coming back from this.

She managed to hold it together as the elevator doors opened. She stepped inside, turning around to face him. As soon as the doors closed, her knees buckled and she slid, with her back against the smooth interior, to the floor, crying uncontrollably for her job, for her apartment, for the life she had in New York, and for the future she'd thought she had with Brandon. But most of all for her best friend, the person who'd been a constant in her life since they started elementary school together. She felt such a fool. She'd insisted on going to the local high school rather than the fee-paying public school her sister Andrea was sent to, just so she could be with Brandon. Now she wished, in hindsight, that her mum had forced her to go to Andrea's school too. She hadn't had a good time at high school; she'd been singled out as the rich kid who didn't belong. Perhaps if she'd gone to another school, she would have made new friends, and met another guy, and be settling down, like Andrea, with someone who she would spend the rest of her life with.

3

The elevator counted down the floors. Fortunately for Lexi, it didn't stop until it reached the ground floor. She hastily scrambled to her feet and wiped her face with the sleeve of her jacket just before the elevator door opened. She had her phone to hand. As soon as she walked into the foyer, she dialled her sister's number. Curiously, it went straight to voicemail.

It wasn't like her sister to have her mobile phone switched off. Lexi didn't want to leave a message, so she phoned her sister's home number instead. Andrea didn't live far from their grandparents in Connecticut. If Andrea could put her up while she figured out what to do next, that would be great. She'd have to use her credit card to purchase a ticket to take the train, and then get a taxi from the rail station. The quickest way to get to her sister's from Manhattan was by car, but Lexi had never learnt to drive. There were no direct train routes from Manhattan to Hartford, which meant that the journey would take almost twice as long by rail as it would have done by road.

Just as she was debating whether to pay for a taxi for the two-hour road journey, she got through to her sister's home answering machine.

Hi, everyone, its Andrea – and Chad.

Lexi sighed at the sound of Andrea's fiancé butting in with his name. Andrea's voice on the answering machine continued. *As you may have guessed, we're not here. Chad has bought us a surprise pre-wedding cruise in the Mediterranean. So in case you can't get hold of me, us, you know where we are. See you soon.*

Lexi stared at her phone. *Was that it? No mention of when they would be back?* 'Damn! Now what?' Lexi was thinking that perhaps, in hindsight, it was for the best. Andrea was in love and engaged to be married. Her and Chad hadn't long moved in together. They wouldn't want her older, messed-up sister crashing on their sofa.

Lexi's phone rang, surprising her. She smiled, guessing it was Andrea already, realising she'd had a missed call on her phone. Lexi answered it immediately. 'Andrea – where are you? I didn't know you were going away.' It was a surprise, so clearly her sister didn't know either.

'I'm sorry, but this isn't Andrea.'

'Oh, right.' Lexi realised she should have checked the number first. It was a man's voice, and one that she didn't recognise.

'My name is Miles Lauder. I'm calling from Lauder & Irvine law firm.'

Lexi was taken aback to hear from them. She thought all the probate stuff with the family lawyer had been wrapped up months ago. It wasn't as though her mum had a lot to leave in her will. 'Is there a problem?'

'No. It's just that I have been doing a routine audit, and I found a … well, an irregularity.'

'An irregularity?'

'With your mother's probate.'

'What sort of irregularity?'

'There's something that was not given to you.'

'What is it?'

'I think we should arrange a meeting at our office.'

'In Connecticut?'

'Yes.'

Lexi sighed.

'Will that be a problem?'

'No, no problem. I was actually heading back from New York to Connecticut anyway.' She couldn't afford to book into a hotel in New York, and as she couldn't stay with her sister, she had no option but to head back to her grandparents' place in Connecticut. Her plan was to start applying for another marketing position in publishing straight away.

'Will you be able to come in to see me this afternoon?'

Lexi nodded. 'I'll make it back to Connecticut to see you today.'

'Shall we say the last appointment of the day at five, to give you time to get here?'

'Sure.' Lexi ended the call. The concierge at the front desk had obviously overheard her conversation. 'I'm sure there's a grey-hound bus to Connecticut.'

Lexi hadn't thought of that. She walked over.

He said, 'You can buy tickets online.' He swivelled the laptop around to face her. She'd assumed it would be quicker going by train, but the journey time by bus was a little under two and a half hours, saving her an hour. Lexi booked the tickets online using her credit card. The concierge kindly printed them out. She thanked the concierge and slipped the tickets into her bag.

'Off on holiday?' She saw his gaze shift from her suitcases to the elevator, looking for Brandon.

Lexi shook her head. 'I've moved out. I'm going home to my grandparents.'

'I'm sorry.'

Not half as sorry as I am, thought Lexi. 'Yeah, so am I.' She took a final look back at the elevator, expecting Brandon to make an appearance in a last-ditch effort to make her stay. But then again, he wouldn't do that. He knew her too well; once her mind was made up, that was it.

'Have a good trip.'

Lexi nodded. 'Thanks.' She left the building, wheeling her cases down the road towards the subway station. It was a forty-minute walk to the Port Authority Bus Terminal, which would have been doable if she hadn't had two suitcases. She looked for a taxi, but after a few minutes waiting by the kerb, she didn't want to wait any longer. She decided to take the subway instead.

There was an alternative; she could just phone her grandparents. They'd send a chauffeur-driven car to pick her up and take her straight home. She didn't want to do that, though. It was enough that she was heading home in the first place. She didn't fancy telling them over the phone that she'd left Brandon.

She sighed heavily. This was not how she'd envisaged her day would turn out when she'd woken up that morning. Not. At. All.

Lexi had just reached the subway station when her phone rang again. This time it was Andrea. 'Hey, sis – what's up?'

Lexi knew why she was asking that question; it wasn't like they were in touch every day, or even every week. The fact was that since Lexi had left for college in New York, they mainly spoke on major public holidays.

'I'm coming to stay at Nana's and Grandpa's for a bit.'

Lexi had stopped on the sidewalk to answer her phone; she could barely hear herself think with the trundling noise of her cases. 'Andrea, are you still there?'

'What's going on, Lexi? Are you okay?'

Lexi knew why she was asking that. It was the last thing Andrea expected to hear from her independent-minded older sister, who was always determined to go her own way.

Lexi sighed heavily. 'Let's just say it hasn't been one of my better days.' That was putting it mildly. 'I lost my job and …' Lexi looked about her. There were people on the sidewalk milling around who could overhear her conversation. 'I've left Brandon. I don't want to go into it over the phone, but I need to get out of New York.'

'Come and stay with us.'

'I thought you were on holiday?'

'On holiday?'

'Your answerphone message—'

'Oh, no, I forgot to change the message. We returned last week. My feet have barely touched the ground since Chad told me about the surprise vacation. I was going to tell you about it before we left, but there just wasn't time, so I thought I'd tell you all about it when we meet up next.'

'Did you have a good time?' Lexi asked.

'Yes, it was fantastic.' She paused. 'Sorry, but I was at work when you phoned, showing a client around a property. I had my phone on silent. So, will you come and stay?'

Lexi shook her head. 'No, but thanks for the offer.' She knew it wouldn't be fair. They were living in an apartment, but in the process of buying their first family home. She knew they were packing up their apartment to move, and imagined there were packing boxes everywhere. The plan was to move house once they were married, but the wedding wasn't for a couple of months yet, and it looked as though their move would happen a lot sooner. She imagined that now would be the worst time to have a house guest. Besides, it wasn't as though Lexi didn't have anywhere to go.

'So, are you returning to the cottage?'

'Yes.'

They both knew what she was referring to – the cottage in the grounds of their grandparents' estate where her mum had brought them both up after their father had passed away.

'Can I come round and see you after work?'

Lexi had it on the tip of her tongue to ask her why, but Andrea answered her question anyway. 'It will be a bit of a novelty to pop in after work, see my sister and have a catch-up.'

Andrea had told her once how she hated that she'd moved to New York, so far away. Lexi had said it wasn't that far, just two hours from their hometown, and they could always chat on the phone. She didn't add that it was far enough away that her grandparents couldn't stick their noses in and interfere with her life. 'Look, I've got an appointment with the lawyers in Hartford.'

'Oh, Brandon isn't going to—'

Lexi laughed. The thought of Brandon going after her money was laughable. 'No, of course not. Look, I don't know what it's about. I'll tell you all about it later. I'd better go, I've got a bus to catch.'

4

Lexi wheeled her suitcases into the lawyer's office and left them with the receptionist. The journey had taken longer than she'd anticipated. She'd just made it in time before they closed.

'Am I too late?'

The receptionist shook her head. 'I'll let him know you're here.'

Lexi glanced around the small room. The office was on the ground floor of a two-storey, flat-roofed red-brick building. It was typical of Hartford. With a café one side and a grocery store on the other, the family-run law firm had been a fixture in the small Connecticut town for decades.

Lexi couldn't imagine they made mistakes. She didn't particularly want to pay them this visit, though. The last time she had been there was for the reading of her mother's will. She hadn't envisaged that she'd be back.

'Ah, Miss Dawson. Please come in.'

Lexi followed the young man into his office. She was expecting to see the older gentleman who had dealt with her mother's will.

'I imagine you were expecting my grandfather,' the young man said.

'Your grandfather?'

'Yes – I believe he dealt with your mother's will.'

He gestured at the seat opposite his desk.

Lexi sat down and glanced around the office. It was just as she remembered it, with its old-fashioned, heavy oak desk and chair. Dark wooden bookshelves filled with law books lined one wall behind the desk. But that was where the similarity ended – there was no old gentleman sitting behind the desk.

'He retired for health reasons.'

'I'm sorry to hear that.'

'Thanks, but he was getting on a bit. It was high time he retired. My father didn't follow him into law, so that left me.'

She got the impression he hadn't been there long.

'So, I've been doing an audit, checking all the files while I familiarise myself with the cases. That's when I discovered something was … how shall I put it … amiss.'

Lexi looked at him, puzzled. For the life of her, she couldn't imagine what it was.

The young man opened a file on his desk.

Lexi leaned forward in her chair.

He got out an envelope. 'It's a letter.'

Lexi sighed. 'Ah, I already have mine.' She explained that both she and her sister had been left a personal letter from their mother in her will, although she knew he was already aware of that.

'It's not for you. Or your sister.'

Lexi threw him a questioning look. 'Then who?'

He handed her the envelope.

She glanced at the name written on the front in her mother's handwriting. 'Who is Margot Dorey?'

The lawyer shrugged. 'Apparently, your mother wanted you to find her and give her this letter personally.'

Lexi was about to take the envelope when he said, 'A word of advice. The letter came with certain . . . conditions.'

Lexi looked at him. 'Do you know the contents of the letter?'

He shook his head vehemently. 'No. All I know is that it came with this.' He handed her a paper wallet. Lexi took the wallet and looked inside. 'Oh.' Inside was a wad of English notes. 'What's this for?'

'I assumed you knew.'

Lexi rolled her eyes, thinking of the letter from her mother that she still hadn't opened. It was as if by not opening it, her mother's death wouldn't feel real. But that was only part of it. The other worry was what her mother might have written inside. Did she want Lexi to go and work for her grandparents, to abandon her dream of being independent from the family firm by working for a publisher instead? Did she want her to leave Brandon?

Lexi frowned, thinking that at least one thing was ticked off the potential list that might be in the letter.

'So, this lady is in England?'

He nodded. 'I presume so.' He passed her a hand-written note. 'There is also this. It's for you. Sorry, I read it because it wasn't in an envelope. It was in with the money. I had to open the wallet and see what was inside because it had been filed away. I randomly came across it.'

He breathed a sigh. 'This is difficult. As you are probably aware, my grandfather's firm has acted for your family for years. I spoke with my grandfather when I discovered the letter, surprised that something like this would have been missed and just filed away.'

Lexi was surprised too, although she wasn't about to make a big thing of it. She shrugged. 'It's just one of those things.'

'Well, the thing is, I get the impression that it wasn't just *one of those things*.'

'You mean it was withheld by your firm on purpose?'

'Look, my grandfather wouldn't have done that without specific instructions to do so.'

Lexi stared at him. 'So, are you saying my grandparents—?'

'I don't know for sure. It was my grandfather who dealt with the case, and he refused to answer my question. I'm afraid that the refusal in itself was answer enough for me.'

Lexi stared at him. 'So, you're saying that for some reason they don't want me to find this woman and give her the letter?'

He nodded solemnly. 'It would appear so.'

Lexi read the little note that had come with the English money.

'A word of advice. I would heed your mother's conditions – don't open the letter, and tell no one.'

Lexi was a bit put out by the implication that she would even consider opening someone else's mail.

'Sorry, I didn't mean to imply you would. I'm just duty-bound to read out the stipulations.'

Lexi took the envelope. She understood the 'tell no one' bit, if indeed her grandparents had had a hand in making sure she did not receive the letter. It meant, however, that her mother had been aware that her grandparents wouldn't approve of her trip to find this mystery woman.

Lexi had a question. 'How am I meant to find this lady if there's no address?'

'I assumed you knew her.'

Lexi shook her head. 'I lived in England with my parents, but that was a long time ago.' She had dual nationality because her mother was American, her father British. 'We moved here when I was six, after my father died.'

'I see.' The young lawyer nodded. 'But you don't remember a lady called Margot Dorey?'

'I don't think so. I haven't been back to England since I was a child.' That wasn't her fault. She would have loved to visit England again, the country of her birth, but her grandparents had strongly discouraged it.

'Well, isn't this the perfect excuse to return?'

Lexi frowned. 'I wish had more to go on.' She stared at the cash in the envelope. At a rough guess, it was a couple of thousand pounds, probably more. It was obviously cash for an airfare and hotel accommodation, but it would really come in handy as a deposit to secure a rental while she looked for a job. She could change the notes back to dollars. Lexi bit her fingernail. There was no rush to return to find this Margot Dorey right now.

'Has this lady been in touch at all?'

The young lawyer shook his head.

Lexi thought that if it was really that important, then surely they might have been in touch, or her mother would have had the address. It could wait until she had got a new job and sorted out her mess of a life. Lexi eyed the money in the envelope; she could really do with it right now.

The lawyer resumed his seat and typed something on his laptop. He turned the laptop around. 'Now, I'm not saying this is the same person. I don't know if that's even her real name, but it's kind of an unusual name. I'm thinking there can't be many Margot Doreys.'

Lexi stared at the screen. 'Why would you say you don't think it's her real name?'

'Look – here.'

'She's a children's author?'

'The article implies that she was a recluse and avoided publicity. She hasn't written anything since this series of very successful books, apparently.'

'Probably lives the life of Riley off the royalties,' remarked Lexi.

'What's *a life of Riley*?'

Lexi gave him a look. 'Never mind.' She got that a lot when she slipped into British colloquialisms. Although she had only lived in England until she was six, she loved it and was a proper anglophile. She knew why that was; she didn't remember England too well, but she had been born there, and her dad, whom she adored, had been English. It held a special place in her heart. She'd been determined to keep her British accent, and although that hadn't happened – she'd just been too young when they left – she still came out with British words and phrases from time to time, which tended to perplex people.

'So, there's still no private address for this lady,' said Lexi.

'No. But there is the publisher's address in London.'

'London?' A peculiar thought crossed Lexi's mind. *Perhaps they'd have an opening. I can't do that – can I? Up sticks and move back across the pond?* Then another little voice in her head said, *Why not?* She knew the reason she couldn't – her maternal grandparents. They wouldn't want her to move away to another country; they didn't even like the fact that she'd moved two hours down the road to New York.

Besides, she was getting ahead of herself. What made her think that the publisher in London would have an opening, let alone want to hire her? Even so, she still she couldn't get the possibility out of her mind of a fresh start in England.

'So, are you going to make the trip?'

Lexi stood up and took the letter and the wallet full of cash. She wasn't sure she wanted to thank him for this, although once again she thought the money would come in handy if she decided not to make the trip straight away. Lexi shrugged. 'Maybe.'

The young lawyer walked her over to the door. 'Remember, there were strict instructions to tell no one,' he reminded her before she left the office.

5

'So, why did Mum want you to find this lady called Margot Dorey?'

Lexi sat down at Andrea's kitchen table. The taxi had dropped her off at her sister's apartment. She'd texted on the way to her grandparents' house on the off-chance that her sister was home and she could make a little detour. It was late afternoon, and she hoped that Andrea had finished work. She was in luck.

Andrea frowned. 'So, let me get this straight. You've just seen the lawyer who said you're not to breathe a word about this woman and the trip to anyone, meaning your grandparents and me. That's what he said.'

Lexi pursed her lips and wished she hadn't mentioned the conditions. She didn't envisage that her sister would tell her off for doing exactly what the lawyer had told her not to do.

'I don't get why Mum just wanted you to go to England – and not even tell me.'

'Oh.' Lexi hadn't stopped to think that her sister would be put out when she found out, and – judging by her expression – upset.

'It's not a big deal. I've just got to find an Englishwoman and give her this letter.' The question remained, though – why her and not her sister?

'But why didn't she ask me?'

Lexi sighed. 'Maybe because you don't have much interest in

England or remember the country.'

'Oh, and you do.'

'Well – yeah.'

'So, you remember England, and where we lived?'

'Sort of.'

'That's not a definitive *yes*.'

'I remember things, okay. I remember a house.'

'Well, so do I. There was a large garden with tall trees, and an old house with cottage-style windows and shutters, and a driveway that led to double gates.'

Lexi stared at her. 'Those are *my* memories, not yours.'

'Don't be stupid!'

'Remember that time when I was about twelve, and you were nine, and always going through my stuff. You found my diary.'

'Yeah – so?'

Lexi cocked her head to one side and gave her *the look*.

'Oh, right. That was written in your diary?'

'Yes.'

'I could have remembered those things too.'

Lexi sighed. 'You were three when dad died and we left for America.'

Andrea changed the subject. 'What does it say – the letter?'

'I have no intention of opening it to find out.' That was not to say it hadn't crossed her mind. Lexi had turned the letter over in her hands on the way there in the taxi and had felt an impulse to open it, but she'd already gone against her mother's wishes by telling Andrea.

'I still don't get it. What's the big mystery? Why doesn't she want me or our grandparents to know about it?'

'How do I know?'

'Mum must have mentioned this person at some point, surely. I don't remember the name, but I would have thought she'd have said something to you, Lexi.'

'Why would she do that?'

'It's obvious – she chose you to deliver the letter.' She paused. 'And why has it just come to light now?'

Lexi decided not to tell her sister the probable reason the letter had been left on file; their maternal grandparents weren't happy about the letter or the instructions to take it to England. They'd been using the same small local law firm for decades, were its largest client, and were good friends of the young lawyer's grandfather. Lexi thought it was obvious that they'd taken advantage of that friendship. It was quite possible they'd requested that the letter was misfiled and didn't see the light of day.

There was no point mentioning this theory to her sister, who wouldn't hear a bad word against them. She imagined Andrea would tell her that the young lawyer was just trying to cover up a mistake. It was, after all, quite possible that his grandfather, who was of advancing years, had made a mistake and misfiled the letter by accident, rather than on purpose. But Lexi didn't believe that. Although it was never spoken about, she knew her grandparents weren't fond of England. Perhaps that antipathy arose from the fact that their only child had met an Englishman and moved there to live against their wishes. Perhaps they were afraid that if their granddaughter visited England again, she might not want to return to America.

Lexi sighed. It had occurred to her that there was a simple explanation regarding why their mother wanted her to deliver the letter. 'You know why she chose me, don't you?'

Andrea shook her head, frowning. 'Why?'

'She knew you were getting married. And you were buying a house and moving. She probably thought you had too much on your plate to do this right now.'

Andrea's frown softened.

'And I imagine this Margot Dorey is an old friend, someone she knew way back when we lived in England. I mean, I don't remember the name. It could have been from before we were born, before she even married.'

'Yes, you could be right,' Andrea said.

Lexi knew it still didn't explain why her mum had stipulated that she must not tell anyone, but she had a theory about that too. Andrea was very close to her maternal grandparents. If Lexi told her, it might get back to them, and they might attempt to stop the trip.

'So, when are you going?'

'I don't know. Now isn't a good time. I mean, I can't exactly drop everything.'

'Drop what?'

'I did have a career. It's not my fault I got fired.' Lexi sighed and told her the reason her boss had chosen to let her go rather than somebody else in the office who had children and who needed the money.

'That's just not fair.'

'I know.'

'Well, isn't this the perfect time to go?' Andrea suggested. 'I mean, you've got no job, and you're no longer with Brandon. It's not like you're engaged, or planning a wedding, is it?'

Lexi frowned at her sister for reminding her just how successful her own life was: a wedding to her high school sweetheart and a career in her grandparents' real estate business that she loved and earned good money from.

As if reading her mind, Andrea said, 'I'm sure they'll give you a job.'

'Andrea you know that's not what I want.' Lexi changed the subject. 'You do realise we're orphans now. Feels odd as an adult saying that, doesn't it?'

'But we've got our grandparents,' Andrea said.

Lexi wasn't as close to their grandparents as Andrea was, though. Perhaps it was the fact that she'd resented leaving England when their father had died and they'd had to move back to America. The fact that their grandparents owned a big house had meant they could go and live with them, but if it hadn't been for them, maybe Lexi, Andrea and their mother would have stayed in England. Lexi had loved her little primary school and the life they'd had. In hindsight, Lexi had realised that she hadn't just left England behind, but the family they had been before her father had died and everything had changed.

Lexi sighed. 'I've always dreamed of going back.'

'Back – where?'

'To England.'

'Oh, Lexi, not that again. We lived there years ago.'

'I know. I loved the seasons, and . . . and I just miss it.' She'd wanted to go to university in England, but that dream of returning had died long ago. Now, the letter had awakened that urge to return.

'Mum didn't want you to go.' Andrea was right: her grandparents had refused to give her the money, and so had her mum. It was like England was out of bounds; she would have struggled to afford to go to university abroad without her family's financial support. It just wouldn't have been feasible.

Lexi had guessed why her mother didn't want her to go; she hadn't wanted her daughter to move thousands of miles away from home. Lexi imagined that her mother's antipathy towards England also stemmed from the fact that it was where she had lost the love of her life. Returning to America meant leaving that hurt, that pain behind, if she could, and starting over.

Her mother, like her grandparents, hadn't supported her going there, not even for a holiday, which made all this rather strange. Why now, after she'd passed away, did she want Lexi to return to give some lady a letter?

'I'm surprised Mum didn't mention it.' Andrea stared at her. 'You have read your letter from Mum, haven't you?'

Lexi pursed her lips.

'You haven't read it?' When she got no response, she added. 'Why ever not?'

'I'm not ready.'

'Ready for what? It's been six months! Perhaps there is an explanation in your letter about this lady and why she chose you to deliver it.'

'Perhaps.'

'Oh, my god, you're still not going to open it, are you?'

'I will – I promise.' Lexi glanced at her sister. 'I take it you opened yours.'

'Of course. The day the lawyer gave it to us.'

'And?'

Andrea fell silent.

'Sorry, that was insensitive. You don't have to tell—'

'She wanted to be at my wedding and to see me walk down the aisle, and … and to hold her first grandchild. She told me to live my best life, and to look after Mitchell because she knew he'd be lost without her.'

Mitchell was their stepdad.

Lexi always thought it was weird that Andrea called him Dad. She'd said as much on many occasions. Andrea found it odd that Lexi didn't. 'They've been married for years,' Andrea had once said. 'We might not be related, but he's the closest thing I've had to a dad my whole life. And the same for you, Lexi – he's been your dad longer than our real father was.'

'Don't say that!' Lexi had shouted back.

That had been the first and last time they'd ever fallen out.

Lexi stared at her. She stood up and walked around the table, and gave her a hug. She wished they hadn't brought up the letters. Poor Andrea was in the throes of planning her wedding, and the last thing she'd expected was for her mum not to be there.

It made Lexi wonder what her mum had written in her own

letter. Lexi eyed her little sister and couldn't help but ask, 'What else did she say in your letter?'

'Oh, some other stuff.'

Lexi frowned. 'What stuff?' She hoped it wasn't about her. Andrea looked uncomfortable. Lexi raised an eyebrow. 'It's about me, isn't it?'

Andrea sighed. 'Look, she just wanted me to look out for you, y'know?'

'No, I don't know.'

'Honestly, she didn't say much, it's just . . . well your life hasn't exactly been on a straightforward trajectory like mine. Joining the family business, meeting *the one* at high school, marriage, hopefully babies.'

Lexi frowned. 'I've got a high school sweetheart. Well, I *had* one.'

'Brandon? Let's face it, he was never going to amount to anything.'

'Who said that? Was that Mum? Oh, no wait. That wasn't Mum – that was all of you.' She didn't know why she was defending him now they'd split up.

Her sister was on a roll. 'And of course, it's not like you chose the easy life. I mean, me and Mum, we chose to work in the family business.'

'Real estate.' Lexi let the words roll off her tongue like it was a job shovelling shit. She didn't add that they hadn't *chosen* to work in the family firm; it was expected.

'That real estate empire gave us the most amazing childhood, remember? We had ponies and wonderful holidays.'

Lexi grimaced. 'I never wanted a pony or holidays to Hawaii on luxury yachts.'

'Why not?'

She recalled those vacations when they were teenagers and her sister would spend virtually the entire summer in a bikini, showing off her athletic figure, bronze tan, and blonde locks. She took after their mother.

Lexi, on the other hand, covered up her slender, almost boyish frame and her fair, freckly skin, which went bright red at the first hint of sunshine. Her dark hair, which she often dyed with a streak of purple, made her look like something out of *The Munsters*. While her sister dived and swam in the sea she would sit, bored, on deck under a wide-brimmed hat, praying for a thunderstorm and wishing it wasn't so blasted hot. The climate just never suited her. Nor did the boredom of beach holidays; she had her head in a book most of the time. Her family didn't understand her – apart from her mum, who said she took after her father.

Lexi wondered what she'd meant by that. Was it just her appearance, or was it more than that? Would he have hated those holidays in the heat too? She would have thought so after living in England's lovely temperate climate.

'Will you promise me you'll read your letter?' Andrea asked.

Lexi nodded. 'Yes.' She just couldn't promise when that would be.

Thinking of her mum, she remembered something she'd said. 'Mum said that we didn't have relatives in England, but how can that be? Dad must have some relations.' She was keen to make the most of her trip and find some English relatives – if and when she decided to go.

'He was an only child. He didn't have any siblings, remember?'

'What about our other grandparents?'

Andrea shrugged. 'What about them? If they wanted to know us, they'd have been in touch, don't you think? Besides, they're probably dead.'

'What makes you say that?'

'Well, they'd have come to Mum's funeral, wouldn't they?'

'That's true.'

'Why don't you ask Nana and Grandpa? They'd know.'

Lexi thought that was a good idea, as long as she didn't give the game away about the letter and that she was considering a trip to England. There was one thing telling her sister, but she wasn't going to tell her grandparents. 'I would like to find out if we have any English relatives – like some distant cousin, twice-removed or something.'

'What does that even mean, *twice-removed*?'

Lexi laughed. 'I have no idea.'

'What do you think the big deal was with us not going back to England? Perhaps you could ask them that too, while you're at it.'

She shook her head. They both knew she wouldn't. 'I don't want them to suspect that's what I'm considering.'

Andrea nodded.

They fell silent again. Lexi said, 'I still don't think now is the best time to go. I mean, I just discovered Brandon has been cheating on me.'

'I was so sorry to hear that.'

'And I've lost my job. I feel all over the place. I'm not really in the mood for a holiday.'

'I can imagine. Look, why don't you stay with us? I've got extra bedding around here somewhere. I can make up the bed in the spare bedroom.'

Lexi followed her sister's gaze around the kitchen full of packing boxes. She shook her head. 'That's really lovely of you to offer, Andrea, but I can't intrude on you and Chad when there's a whole cottage I could crash in just down the road.'

'Chad won't mind, honestly.'

'I know.' Lexi got on well with Chad. He was easy-going and laid-back, and she felt it suited her workaholic, intense little sister to marry a guy who would encourage her to relax and try and smell the roses.

He did work hard as a site manager for their grandparents' real estate business, but unlike Andrea, he knew how to relax and climb down at the end of a work day. Lexi hoped it would rub off on her sister.

Despite the offer, and the fact that Lexi didn't want to return to her grandparents, she knew she'd feel awkward staying in their little apartment in such close quarters with a loved-up couple. And besides, she'd already nearly tripped over one packing box. Andrea could easily have lived in one of the cottages in the grounds of their grandparents' sprawling estate. However, although she worked for the firm, just like her big sister, she still wanted her independence. She wanted to feel she was making her own way, even if they did pay her wages.

Andrea asked, 'Are you okay for money?'

Lexi smiled. It seemed an odd thing to ask, but then Andrea was all too aware of how much money Lexi gave to Brandon to support him in his so-called music career – quite a lot of it from the *family payroll*, as her grandparents called it. Despite insisting that she didn't want her allowance once she'd left college and started work, the money didn't stop. It was just as well, because neither did Brandon's ever-increasing expenses, living and otherwise, in pursuit of that elusive record contract.

'Yes, I'm okay. I suppose in light of losing my job, it's good they didn't stop my allowance.'

'Yeah, I've still got mine. I donate a large proportion of it to charity.'

In hindsight, Lexi wished she'd done the same, rather than funding Brandon all these years. She sighed. 'I'm not looking forward to going home,' she said. It wasn't that she didn't want to see her grandparents, or to stay with them; it was what they would say when they found out her relationship with Brandon had fallen apart.

Perhaps she wouldn't tell them about Brandon's infidelity. But either way, she knew they wouldn't be surprised about the split. They'd be pleased; it was what they'd wanted all along. They never had liked him and were not backward in voicing that opinion.

'Why don't you go and stay with Dad instead?'

Lexi frowned at her sister. It always seemed odd to her, calling Mitchell *Dad*, but Andrea had only been five when their mum had remarried. Being so young, and having little memory of her real father, Mitchell was the only dad she'd ever really known. Chad reminded Lexi a lot of Mitchell – just a younger version.

Lexi shook her head at that suggestion. She knew her stepdad would love to see her, and for her to stay at his, but she wanted some time on her own in the cottage. She had yet to process what had happened with Brandon. She'd trusted him. She'd thought they were best friends, soulmates, but he'd betrayed her.

'Lexi – are you okay?' Andrea asked softly. 'Sorry, that was a really dumb thing to say. Of course you're not okay.'

Lexi managed a smile. 'I'll pop in and see Mitch – I promise.' He lived in Connecticut too, not far from her grandparents. 'I'm going to head off to Nana's and Grandpa's first.'

'I can drive you.'

'No, it's fine.' Lexi phoned for a taxi.

'Won't you at least stay for dinner?'

'No, thanks all the same. I'd rather get this over with.'

They both knew what she was talking about. She hadn't contacted them and told them she was heading home. She'd decided to put off the embarrassment of telling them she'd split up from Brandon until she arrived.

She picked up her bag and wheeled her suitcases over to the door. 'Right, well the taxi is only going to be five minutes, so I'll head off now.'

Andrea followed, giving her sister a big hug at the door. 'You will tell me, won't you, when you're going to England?'

'But I haven't decided if I'm going.'

'Oh, you'll go. I know you will.'

Lexi smiled at her sister. You wouldn't believe, to look at her, that she was half-English. Unlike Lexi, growing up here had suited her.

Lexi's phone buzzed with a text. The taxi had arrived. 'I had better go.' She frowned at the thought of a lecture from her nana about Brandon. 'Wish me luck.'

'Good luck.'

6

'Are you here for a job? My wife works in this street, cleaning houses. Nice job if you can get it. Better than driving a taxi.'

Lexi stared out of the window at the familiar wide, tree-lined street as they passed gates that led up drives to expansive homes, some not visible from the street. She thought about the taxi driver's words and shifted her attention to her thrift store clothes. She imagined he would be surprised to learn that she had grown up there. She didn't respond.

The taxi driver turned the car into a driveway and stopped outside the high metal security gates. 'Are they expecting you?'

Lexi shook her head.

'Ah.' He turned around in his seat to look at her. 'Do you want me to wait in case it doesn't work out?'

Lexi thought about it for a moment. It wasn't a bad idea. In fact, she was quite sure it wouldn't work out, but stranger things had happened. However, right now she didn't have anywhere else to go. 'No, it's fine.'

He nodded. 'Okay, I'll just press the buzzer.'

'No need,' said Lexi. She got out of the taxi, skirted the front of the car and walked up to the little silver box.

'They gave you the code already?' he said through the open car window as Lexi punched in the code.

She shook her head. 'I know it off by heart.'

'Really?'

'I should do. I grew up here.'

She caught the taxi driver's look of surprise before she got back into the car. She obviously wasn't quite what he imagined sprang from these parts. Some of her grandparents' neighbours were celebrities – models and actors. Others with long-established, successful businesses like her grandparents had grandchildren who were social media influencers and had huge followings.

She realised that with their backgrounds, they had no impetus to work for a living – not in the ordinary sense of the word. But Lexi's family had never really moved in those circles, and it was a credit to her mother and Mitch, and her grandparents, that although they had grown up privileged, they had never been spoilt. And there had always been the expectation they would stay in education and then work for a living, ideally in the family business.

The trouble was that their grandparents had a narrow-minded view of what work was. It was business, or a nine-to-five job, rather than acting or modelling or something on social media – not that Lexi felt inclined to do any of those things. Or writing songs and getting a recording contract, even though all those things could earn much more than an ordinary job. That was one of the reasons they had taken a huge dislike to Brandon. That and the fact that he'd encouraged her to do what she'd always wanted to do with her life, which was move away from Connecticut and work in publishing.

Her mum had worked in publishing before being widowed and moving back to America. Lexi had always loved books. She had wanted to work either in a bookshop, in a public library, or in publishing. Although her mum had been supportive, her grandparents had not. She knew they wouldn't support anything apart from her deciding to work in the family business like her sister. 'Well, that's not going to happen in a month of Sundays.'

The taxi driver heard her talking under her breath. 'What do you mean, a month of Sundays?' he asked as the gates slowly opened and they started up the long drive.

Lexi rolled her eyes. She hadn't meant him to hear that. 'It's nothing.'

'Nice house!' he exclaimed at the sprawling mock Tudor property. 'My wife would love the grounds.'

Not if she had to pay for the upkeep, thought Lexi. She didn't know how many gardeners her grandparents employed to keep it watered and pristine.

'If I'd grown up here, I'd never want to leave,' he remarked.

Lexi frowned. She kept her mouth shut, thinking of the times that she and her sister had wanted to play in the grounds, to run around playing tag and hide and seek, but had been confined to the cottage and patio and the small garden that came with it. Andrea didn't remember the house where they lived in England, with the garden full of wild flowers and a weeping willow tree where they had played hide and seek. But Lexi did.

She remembered the loss of freedom after they moved – not just within the gated complex that belonged to her grandparents, but outside, where they were ferried around in big cars, taken to and from school; they were escorted everywhere. It was only at university, when she'd moved to New York, that she had begun to recapture that feeling of being truly free.

She sighed, picked up her bag and handed the taxi driver her fare. She watched him get out of the car and open the trunk, then wheel her suitcases over to the passenger door.

Lexi stared up at the house. She hesitated before she got out of the taxi. She should have gone to stay with Mitch.

He followed her gaze, staring at the impressive house. 'Are you sure you don't want me to wait?'

Lexi guessed he had noticed her reluctance to go in. 'No, thank you.' She reluctantly got out of the car.

She looked up at the house. No one had come out to greet her. Perhaps her grandparents were out? She couldn't tell because they didn't leave their car on the driveway.

She glanced at the triple garage next to the house. If Nana was out, her grandpa would doubtless be too busy working in his study – they didn't believe in retirement or doing 'idle things', as they called hobbies.

For some reason, the thought that she'd never had a pet when she'd come to live at her grandparents' house came to Lexi's mind. She'd always wanted a dog, but she imagined her mum had been worried that it might ruin the pristine lawn of the big house, as Lexi called it, if it got out of the cottage garden.

Lexi stood on the driveway and watched the taxi turn around and head back down the drive. She turned around and looked up at the impressive house. With five bedrooms, most of them en suite, and as many reception rooms, a house this big meant the occupants inside wouldn't necessarily hear a car turn up outside, depending on where they were in the house. The study was at the back of the house, along with the conservatory, where Nana enjoyed spending her time reading when the weather was inclement.

Lexi turned from the house and decided to head to the cottage, thinking that perhaps this was for the best; she'd rather settle in first before she had to tell them why she was there.

Lexi turned to her left and trundled her suitcases down a narrow flagstone path that snaked through the garden at the side of the house to a single-storey red-brick building. It had previously been the pool house, but her grandparents had converted it to a three-bedroom home when Lexi and her mum and sister had come to live there. There was plenty of space for them in the main house, but her mum had wanted their own little family home. It was just as well, because quite soon after they had returned, Mum's old friend, Mitch, had moved in, and their little family of three had become four again.

Lexi trundled the cases up to the door. She still had a key. Both she and Andrea had kept their keys when they moved out. Lexi opened the door and walked in, slipping her shoes off at the door. She wheeled her cases along the wooden floor into her childhood bedroom.

The cottage was kept pristine; the cleaner and gardeners still looked after the property as they did the main house. The cottage was painted white and had wooden flooring and shutters, which suited the style of the property but wasn't to Lexi's taste or her mother's. She was sure her mum would have loved to redecorate and furnish it in her own style, with some more colour, some rugs, vibrant cushions, and pictures on the walls. Even though they lived there, it had never really felt like their home.

Lexi sat down on the double bed. She couldn't believe she was back. She looked at her cases but didn't feel inclined to unpack right now.

Staring around her bedroom, her gaze settled on the letter from her mother. She hadn't told Andrea that during the wake, which had been held at the cottage, she'd left her letter on the dressing table in her bedroom, thinking she'd read it in the privacy of her room when everyone had gone. That had never happened. She felt guilty about it now, that she'd left the letter behind when she'd returned to New York with Brandon. She hadn't been back here since.

Lexi got up from her bed and walked over to the dressing table. Perhaps Andrea was right, and there was an explanation in her letter about the English lady. Lexi sat down at her desk and picked up the letter. She'd left it long enough. She was about to tear open the letter when she heard a knock at the door.

She put the letter down and walked out of her bedroom. Even though the front door was made of frosted glass, she could see it was her nana. She knew it was her anyway because she'd knocked. If it had been her grandfather, he would have walked right in.

Lexi opened the front door and smiled at the diminutive lady standing on the doorstep. With coiffed grey hair, a grey pencil pleat skirt, crisp white shirt, and patent black shoes, she looked dressed for an evening out rather than a day at home. But that was Lexi's nana. She had always been the same.

Lexi shifted from one foot to the other, feeling as she'd always felt under her nana's gaze – as though she was being scrutinised. She wished she hadn't worn her trademark brown leather jacket from the thrift store, even though she was still wearing the trouser suit she'd worn to work. It occurred to her that her little sister looked more like their grandmother every day. She wore the same sort of clothes – always formal, always meticulously turned out.

Lexi slipped off the leather jacket and hung it on the coat stand by the door. She caught Nana eyeing the jacket disapprovingly as she walked in.

Lexi sighed and did as she'd always done – offer an excuse for her appearance. 'I find that old jacket nice and comfy.' She looked sheepishly at her grandmother.

Nana said, 'I thought someone had arrived.'

'Only me,' said Lexi, wondering when to tell her grandmother that she and Brandon had split up. She wasn't looking forward to a lecture about Brandon, along the lines of *we all thought he wasn't right for you.*

Lexi followed her down the hallway.

'We've been expecting you.'

Lexi stopped. 'You have?' she said in surprise.

Her nana glanced over her shoulder. 'Andrea phoned.'

Lexi glared at her nana's back. 'She did?'

Nana abruptly turned on her heel, catching Lexi unaware, and spotted her expression. 'Don't blame your sister.'

Being told not to blame her little sister was nothing new. Why hadn't Lexi learnt by now that anything she told Andrea in confidence would go straight back to their grandparents?

She wondered what else Andrea had told them.

'I phoned Andrea about the wedding – just a detail I wanted to check regarding the flower-arranging.'

Lexi didn't miss the subtle dig about not getting involved in her sister's wedding. She had declined the invitation to be a bridesmaid. She didn't want to wear one of those long ball-gown type dresses that Andrea had chosen for them. She wouldn't feel comfortable. With her height, or lack of, she felt she just wouldn't be able to carry it off. She knew she would look odd in the wedding photos, standing among her sister's statuesque friends.

'During the conversation with your sister, she said you were on your way home.'

Home? The problem was that it didn't feel like her home, and never had. She often thought Andrea was the lucky one; she didn't remember their real home back in England. If Lexi was honest, her memories from when she was six were hazy, but it was less about what she remembered – more a feeling of belonging.

Lexi followed her nana into the living room and rolled her eyes when she said, 'Andrea told me you and Brandon have split up. Is that true?'

Lexi had only just arrived. She hadn't even put the kettle on. 'Do we have to do this now, Nana?'

What she would have preferred was a hug, and Nana offering to make her an English breakfast tea with a dash of milk and plenty of sugar before telling her to settle in and talk about things when she was ready. But Nana wasn't one of those demonstrative grandmotherly types. Or the type to back down. 'Yes, we have to do this now.'

'I'll just pop the kettle on.'

'Stop stalling, Lexi.'

'I'm not stalling. I want a cup of tea.' Lexi left her inquisitive, demanding nana sitting stony-faced on the sofa. Lexi stood in the kitchen and filled the kettle. She stared out of the window. She wished she hadn't come back. She should have taken Andrea's advice and gone to stay with Mitch. At least she wouldn't have been given the third degree, and she'd have gotten a great big bear hug for her troubles.

'Damn! Why did I come back here?' she said under her breath. Now, she was worried what else Andrea had told their grandmother. As the kettle boiled, she knew she was about to find out.

7

Lexi took her time making two cups of tea. She would have to go out and buy groceries, but she had a small supply of tea, coffee, sugar and milk she'd brought with her, knowing there would be nothing in the cottage. No one had lived there for some time.

She carried the cups on a tray into the lounge. Nana perched on the grey, L-shaped sofa. Lexi handed her a cup and took a seat on the sofa too. She turned to face her grandmother. 'Brandon cheated on me.' There. She'd said it. No use beating about the bush, as her real dad had always said when she was naughty and had to own up to something. She cherished those memories.

She wanted to get the conversation with her grandmother over with. 'That's why I've come back. I left him.' Lexi sipped her tea, avoiding eye contact. She knew it was just what her grandparents would want to hear; that they were right in what they'd thought about him over the years – he was a waste of space.

It would be easy to think Lexi had gone out with Brandon just to cheese her grandparents off – that was what Andrea had said when they were teenagers. But that wasn't true. He was her best friend. What was she going to do without him?

She took a deep breath and tried to hold it together. Her grandparents were old-school. The British had a very apt phrase for it: 'the stiff upper lip'.

Lexi sat there waiting for a gloating, *I told you so.* She stole a glance at her nana.

'Lexi, I always thought he wasn't right for you. I told you that on numerous occasions.'

Here we go, thought Lexi, rolling her eyes. 'Yes, I know, Nana.'

'I can't say I'm surprised, Lexi. Brandon had a roving eye. When you were here last I saw the way he looked at your sister.'

'Nana!' Lexi nearly spilled her tea. 'That's just not true! That's ridiculous.'

'Is it?'

Lexi thought of the woman he'd caught Brandon with before she fled the apartment. 'You know what? I don't want to have this conversation. You were right all along. What else is there to say?'

'What are you doing here?' Nana asked. 'I thought you wanted to live in New York?'

'I left him, I told you. I had nowhere else to go.' That wasn't strictly true. She reminded herself again that she could have stayed with Mitch.

Margot Dorey and that letter came to mind, along with the envelope full of money her mother had left her for the trip. Perhaps she should have taken a taxi straight to the airport and got a flight to England. She tried to push it out of her mind as she avoided eye contact with Nana. She still didn't know whether her sister had mentioned the letter during her conversation with Nana.

'What I meant, Lexi, was what about the apartment? Presumably you kicked him out.'

Lexi studied her fingernails.

'Oh, Lexi, don't tell me you let him stay—'

'I couldn't kick him out. He'd have nowhere to go.'

'But that's not your problem.'

'I know.' Lexi sighed. She and Brandon had known each other since they were little. Despite what he'd done, she couldn't see him out on the streets. He didn't have a back-up plan or family like Lexi.

He had his mum, but she'd sold up and bought an RV, and was travelling around the country. There might be space to accommodate him in the RV, but how would he get a recording contract if he was on the road or on the other side of the country in Arizona or somewhere off the beaten track? She'd heard that his mother was parked up with a community in the desert.

Lexi made the mistake of voicing her thoughts as she finished her tea.

'Lexi, that is none of your concern now. You are such a soft touch. I think that's been the problem all along.'

Lexi picked up a rich tea biscuit that she'd bought from the British shop on Hudson Street in Manhattan's West District. She offered her nana one. She almost recoiled when Lexi told her what they were. 'I prefer American cookies.'

Nana continued, 'If you want God's honest truth ...'

Lexi stared at her, thinking, *Do I have a choice?* Whenever Nana spoke a sentence containing the words *God's honest truth,* it meant she was about to say something that Lexi didn't want to hear.

'If you hadn't been propping him up all these years, I bet he would have dropped this silly dream of becoming a famous pop star—'

'Rock star,' corrected Lexi. She quickly added, 'He was never after fame or fortune.'

'Why doesn't that surprise me? It's not as though he needed a fortune when he had your money – or should I say *our* money – to live off.'

Lexi sat drinking tea while her nana delivered her monologue on her failed relationship. Then she put her teacup down. She'd had enough of the lecture. 'You know what? I did not come here to get a lecture on Brandon or our relationship.'

'I bet.'

'Can't you at least be a little bit sympathetic? I know you didn't like him, but I just lost my boyfriend, so it has not exactly been the best day.' She knew it was quite the understatement. She hadn't expected her nana to throw her arms around her, give her a hug, and let her cry on her shoulder. She could never imagine Nana, ever the practical one of her grandparents, doing that. Grandpa would although he'd still have had an *I told you so*, but at least she'd get a hug from him.

Nana's expression changed ever so slightly. 'All right, Lexi. I understand.'

Actually, you don't, thought Lexi. Nana had married her soul-mate, and they had been together forever. She had no clue. Lexi breathed a huge sigh. 'Is it okay if I crash here for a bit while I figure myself out?'

'Of course.'

'Great.' Lexi had only asked out of politeness. This was her childhood home, after all. There would be no reason not to let her stay. It wasn't as though anyone was living there.

'I'm sure it will be fine.'

Lexi looked at her. 'Okay,' she said slowly, a little surprised by that comment.

'I'll have to check with your grandfather.'

Before Lexi had a chance to ask what she was checking, Nana was already making a move towards the door. 'In fact, I'll ask him now.'

Lexi would have preferred her not to, but it wasn't as though she had a choice. She gathered up the two mugs and heard the front door click shut. Her grandmother passed the kitchen window as Lexi walked into the kitchen.

She stood watching her walk along the paved path that snaked through the garden up to the main house. A memory resurfaced of a garden, not dissimilar to this one, but smaller, wilder. She was playing hide and seek with her sister around a weeping willow tree, having tremendous fun. Then a lady with a wide-brimmed straw hat, trousers and a colourful blouse came outside carrying a tray with two tall glasses of something fizzy. She remembered that because her mum had never let them have fizzy drinks.

Lexi stared after her grandmother. She realised it couldn't have been here and it couldn't have been her. 'Was it my other grandmother?' she said out loud, as if by saying it, the memory would become clearer and the answer would come to her. 'I can't remember,' she uttered, disappointed.

She recalled what Andrea had said to her about asking Nana if her maternal grandparents were still alive. She'd asked her mum many times, over the years, angling for a trip back to England to visit relatives, but her mother had just said they were gone. Lexi had always presumed she'd meant they were dead.

She was just putting the cups in the small dishwasher when she heard the front door. She knew it would be her grandfather. She stepped out of the kitchen and nearly walked straight into him. Tall, slim, and slightly stooped now, he still cut a suave, gentlemanly figure, his once-dark hair now snow-white. Bright blue eyes regarded her for a quick moment before he put his arms around her. Lexi, who was determined not to get emotional, suddenly started sobbing.

'Now, now.' He gently patted her back. 'I know you don't want to hear this, but I'm going to say it anyway. It's for the best. There's someone special out there for you, and it is not Brandon.'

Lexi had heard it all before; her grandparents had tried to convince her to split up with Brandon when they had first found out they'd become an item in high school.

In between sobs, Lexi said, 'Please don't tell me *I told you so*.'

Her grandfather drew back and offered her one of his monogramed handkerchiefs.

Lexi wiped her face and blew her nose. She handed it back. 'Sorry, I've got a tissue here somewhere.'

'No matter.' He screwed it up and popped it in the pocket of his slacks. He looked at her. 'What now?'

'I was hoping I could stay here for a bit while I sorted myself out. Nana said she'd have a word with you.' Lexi hoped it wouldn't be a problem. 'That's okay, isn't it?'

'Of course.'

Lexi breathed a sigh of relief. As far as she was aware, the cottage hadn't been used since they'd all moved out.

'However ...'

Lexi looked up sharply.

'Brandon will have to vacate the apartment in New York.'

Lexi knew Nana would tell him. 'Why? It's my apartment. You gave it to me.'

'Yes, that's the point. It's *yours*. I don't get why you still want to help him.'

Neither did Lexi. She shrugged and walked off into the living room. Her grandfather followed. 'Look, I think I can help.'

Lexi slumped down on the couch. 'What is it?' She was relieved that it didn't appear that Andrea had mentioned that letter or her late mother's instructions for her to return to England to find a certain Margot Dorey. She looked up at him standing by the fireplace.

'I have a proposition for you.'

She knew what that meant. When it came to her grandparents, everything came with strings attached. Even New York. The apartment had come with a caveat.

And now he was here to collect.

'What is it you want?'

'It's less what I want, and more what I can do for you.'

Lexi folded her arms.

'Remember we said we'd let you have the New York apartment for as long as you needed, to see if your career in publishing took off?'

She remained silent, realising she hadn't told them that she'd also lost her job. Had Andrea told Nana that too?

'Now, I heard that you really haven't had a good day. You lost your job too.'

Lexi rolled her eyes. They knew. She stood up. 'Look, do we have to do this now? It's been a really long day.'

'Sit down, please. Just hear me out.'

Lexi reluctantly took her seat.

'Look, living in New York, working in publishing, wasn't going anywhere really, was it?'

Lexi frowned. She could tell immediately that this conversation wasn't going to end well. She was thinking that it was just as well she hadn't unpacked her suitcases. There was no point arguing with him. That was his opinion. It had been all along. He had just been waiting for her to fall flat on her face. *Why was that?* She eyed him. *Why did they want her to fail?*

'This is your home. You know there is always a job here, a house ...' He cast a gaze around the cottage. You could meet someone. We have lots of friends, with lovely grandsons.'

Lexi had met them growing up. That was one of the reasons she had opted for a public school, rather than fee-paying, so she wouldn't have to see them every day of her life. That wasn't her only motivation, but it was certainly one of them. If she didn't like those boys at twelve, what could she possibly see in them when they were older and even more entitled?

Public school had been quite a change from her private elementary school. Her grandparents rued the day they let their grandchild choose. They had no idea her real motivation wasn't some lofty ideal regarding not believing in private education; that was what she'd told them. She knew that would swing it and they'd agree. She knew them. They were impressed by her independence of spirit, her belief that she could go it alone, coming out of her cosseted, small independent school straight into the lion's den of a massive public high school.

She remembered they said they'd give it a week and she'd be

begging to go to the private girls' school they had lined up for her. If they'd known one of the motivations for her choosing that school, they would never, ever have let her go. *Brandon.*

He had been lined up to go to the boys' private school across the road, and they had planned to meet up at lunchtime and after school, but then his father had died suddenly and everything had changed. Lexi had the most stupendous idea when she'd discovered that he was going to the local high school. She'd decided that she was going too.

At first, he wouldn't hear of it. He didn't want her to forgo the sort of opportunities the fee-paying school could provide. But then she told him it wasn't just because of him. She'd decided that she did not want her grandparents paying for her education any longer. She wanted to make her own way in life, even though at twelve there were limited ways she could do this; she was a child, her grandparents were supporting her. But this could be the start.

Whether she would have still gone through with it if Brandon hadn't gone to the local high school too, Lexi wasn't sure.

Some of Brandon's dad's life insurance money had been set aside with the intention of privately educating him, but Brandon wanted his mum to invest the money for his future. In the event, she did neither, frittering away the insurance money on nice cars, luxury holidays, boyfriends and helping out her friends until there wasn't a dime left. Lexi knew that the money would have really helped him out over the years. The sad thing was that the private school had a particularly good music department with a recording studio and a renowned music teacher with contacts in the music industry. It might have given him an advantage. Instead, almost a decade after leaving high school, he was still chasing that dream.

Lexi couldn't just turn her back on him – not now, not when he had so many songs to perform, if only someone would listen to his demo. Although she hated what he'd done, she knew she could never hate him.

'We have a job for you.'

Lexi was immediately snapped out of her reverie back to the here and now, and the reality that her life was coming full circle straight back to where her grandparents wanted her – and where she didn't want to be.

'How about it? Why not give the job a try? You never know, you might like it.'

'I'll think about it.' She didn't have to ask what the job was; it would be working in some capacity in their real estate business. She knew she didn't want the job, but she couldn't sit on her behind all day; it would just be a stop-gap while she looked for another marketing role.

'Well, don't think about it for too long.'

Lexi frowned at him. 'How come?'

'We're not getting any younger, and we want someone to take over the family firm.'

Lexi stared at him for a long moment. 'Wait, you don't mean me – do you?'

'Of course. Why not?'

Lexi was stunned. She had thought that they had always been more interested in her little sister. 'I assumed that Andrea would take over.'

'What made you think that?'

Lexi thought it was obvious. 'Where to begin? She's been to private school, got a better education than me, and more experience in the firm – she's worked for you forever.'

'You are my first choice.'

Lexi was stunned. 'But why on earth would you choose me?'

'You're independent-minded. You've got spirit. And you don't just do as you're told.'

Lexi stared at her grandfather. Andrea would not want to be a fly on the wall right now. She had done all the things in life to please her grandparents, and had worked hard for the privilege.

Lexi frowned at the audacity of his request. So, if she wanted to use the cottage, she had to return to work in the family business. Oh, and Brandon had to get out of the flat.

She knew that going back there had been a mistake.

8

'We think you're more cut out for the job, Alexandra.'

Lexi frowned at him. She'd left that name back in England. No matter how many times she told them her name was Lexi, they always came back with, 'It isn't your given name.'

Since she'd lost her dad and they'd moved to America, her grandfather's insistence on calling her by that name had just reminded her of home – of England and her dad, and that happy, carefree childhood before he died and her world changed.

'Anyway, I hope that's not going to be for a while yet.'

Lexi looked at him curiously. 'What?'

'Me stepping down from running the company.'

Lexi hoped so too because he would be in for a huge disappointment; she had no intention of stepping into his shoes. Hadn't she made it plain enough when she'd left for New York that she wasn't coming back? And yet here she was. Her frown deepened.

'Right, well, I'll let you settle in. And when you're ready, come up to the house. I will be in my study. We'll discuss your new job.'

Lexi watched him walk out of the living room. She sighed heavily and shook her head. She'd known that if she came back, they'd want something in return. Nothing was ever a free ride when it came to her grandparents. Her privileged upbringing had always come with the understanding that, despite the generous allowance, they were expected to work. Lexi didn't think was a bad thing at all. As her grandfather always said, *work maketh the man* – or the woman, in her case.

Lexi wasn't sure whether that was a proverb or something he'd made up. But in any case, the problem arose if you didn't want to work in the family business. It made her wonder about her mum; when she returned to live in this cottage, what exactly had she had to give up in order to return to the family fold? Unfortunately, her mum had rarely talked about the life they'd left behind in England.

'You'd be following in your mother's footsteps. Don't you want to do that?'

Lexi knew he wasn't talking about her mother's life in London; she'd worked in a publishing house. It was where she'd met Lexi's dad.

'You've got nowhere else to go, Alexandra. Think carefully about your future. All this could be yours someday. Publishing could be a hobby – hell, write a book. But do it in your spare time.'

She tried not to glare at him. She was aware they had her best interests at heart. But it rankled her that she knew how they had always viewed her career – as a hobby.

Lexi followed him to the door. She had to be honest. 'Look, I wasn't expecting a job offer straight away. I mean, I've only just arrived.'

'No time like the present,' he said, smiling.

'Yes, well, it's a bit too present for me. I've literally just lost my job today. I was hoping for some time here in the cottage to—'

'Kick back and relax?'

'Absolutely not!' She frowned. 'That's the furthest thing from my mind, right now. I was intending to apply for jobs.'

'Now you don't have to.'

'I meant jobs in publishing.'

'So, do that in your spare time.'

Lexi heaved a sigh. Her grandfather was smiling from ear to

ear. She knew that expression; he was not going to back down on this one. It was a done deal.

'I'll see you in the morning.' He turned to go.

'What if I decide to go back to New York in the morning?' Lexi blurted. She hadn't meant to say that.

'Well then, you had better contact Brandon and kick him out of the apartment. In fact, talking of whom, you just reminded me – I want him out!'

Her grandfather was no longer smiling.

Lexi stared at him. *Trust me to open my big mouth and remind him*, she thought.

'Did you hear what I said?'

'Yes, of course I did.'

'Good. That's settled then.'

Lexi wasn't about to argue. New York was a long way from Connecticut; she'd find a way round it without them knowing Brandon was still there.

'Right, I'll leave you to unpack.'

Lexi wasn't feeling inclined to unpack now.

'Do you want dinner with us this evening?'

Lexi didn't want to hurt his feelings, and it had nothing to do with being railroaded into a job; she was just so tired. She yawned. 'I'll order some take-out if you don't mind.'

'Well, it's your insides. There's a nice home-cooked meal instead, if you change your mind.'

I won't, thought Lexi. She didn't say that. 'Okay, but I'm pretty sure I'm just going to order pizza and get an early night.

'Suit yourself.'

Lexi shut the door behind him and rolled her eyes. 'God, I definitely should have gone to stay with Mitch.' The problem was that now they knew she was back. It wouldn't have done any good going straight over to Mitch, because her stupid little sister had already let the cat out of the bag and told them she was back in

Connecticut. Lexi got out her mobile phone, intending to call Andrea and ask why she had done that. Then she changed her mind. She put the phone back in her pocket. She was too tired to get into an argument with her sister over the phone.

Lexi was just striding back down the hall when there was a knock on the door. She did an about-turn. 'I haven't changed my mind about dinner up at the house,' she said, opening the front door.

'That's just as well, because I bought pizza!'

Lexi looked at Mitch. 'How did you know I was back?' Even as she was asking the question, she was thinking of her sister.

'Andrea texted me.' He hovered in the doorway. 'She insisted I stop by.'

Lexi guessed that Andrea was worried about her, and thought her staying there wouldn't work out. She wasn't far wrong.

'Are you okay, sweetheart?' he asked, then shook his head. 'That's a dumb thing to say, isn't it?'

'Yeah, you could say that.' She smiled nonetheless, keeping up the brave face that she wished she'd had for her grandpa. She didn't think it had fully sunk in, losing her job and splitting up with Brandon all in the space of one awful morning. She thought about how you just never knew what surprises life was going to throw at you when you thought you'd woken up to another perfectly ordinary day. Who would have thought she'd find herself back in Connecticut?

'Come in, Mitch. I never say no to pizza. In fact, I was about to order one. Your timing is perfect.' She had thought that she wouldn't want company, but she was pleased Mitch was there. The reality of sitting on her own with a pizza, staring at four walls, had suddenly hit home.

He gingerly stepped inside, gazing around the hall. Like Lexi, it wasn't a place he had ventured since her mother had died.

The moment he stepped inside, she guessed that it brought

back vivid memories of the wake, as it had for her.

He said, 'You know, you don't have to stay here.'

'I know. It's kind of you to—'

'I'm sure your grandparents wouldn't mind you staying at the house. They've got plenty of spare bedrooms.'

'Oh, right. Sure.' Lexi felt a bit embarrassed that she had assumed he would offer for her to stay with him. Andrea had planted the idea in her head. She looked at the pizza. 'I'll get some plates.'

Lexi fetched some plates from the kitchen, and walked into the living room. She put the plates down on the coffee table as Mitch opened the pizza box. Lexi looked at the pepperoni pizza. 'Hey, that's my favourite.'

'I know.'

Lexi sat down on the sofa next to Mitch and gave him a hug. She picked up a large slice of pizza. 'So, I guess Andrea told you about Brandon.'

Mitch put a slice of pizza on his plate. 'Yeah. Just as well he's in New York, otherwise I'd—' He stopped short.

'You'd what?' Mitch wasn't the type to harm anyone. But she imagined he might have stormed over to the apartment and given Brandon a piece of his mind.

'I've seen this coming for years, Lexi. The writing was on the wall.'

Lexi put her slice of pizza down. 'Why is that? Because he wants to be a rock star, and all famous songwriters have groupies and sleep around?'

Mitch shook his head. 'No, not at all. That's not what I meant.'

'Then what do you mean? That he was never good enough for me because he didn't come from money?'

Mitch sighed. 'It's got nothing to do with your background, Lexi.'

'Then what?'

'He's just not right for you. I could see it. Everyone could.'

Lexi didn't have to ask who he meant by *everyone* – her grandparents. 'Mum liked him,' she said in a small voice.

'Yes, she did. She just wanted you to be happy. But she felt the same way too.'

'She told you that?'

'Yes. She thought there was someone else out there for you. But as long as you were with Brandon …' he trailed off. Although he did add, 'I think it's for the best that you found out about his roving eye before things got serious.'

'Serious?' Lexi thought *what part of being together since high school wasn't serious?*

'I meant, you know, before you got married.'

The problem was that they had been together so long it felt they were married in all but name. He was her best friend. How could there be anyone else?

Lexi wanted to change the subject. Or at least think about something else. She wished she hadn't gone to Andrea's first and told her about Brandon. She was wondering what else Andrea had told him. Had she mentioned her visit to the lawyer and that letter?

It occurred to her that she didn't have to ask her grandparents about Margot Dorey. Mitch had known her mother for years. Would he know who this woman was?

Lexi bit her bottom lip, debating whether to ask. It would mean telling him about her unexpected call from the lawyer who dealt with Mum's will, and again going against the strict instructions to tell no one. She eyed the man that her mum had been married to for nearly two decades. When her mum had stipulated, *tell no one*, that couldn't have included Mitch, surely. He'd have no objections with her returning to England – would he?

Lexi thought she'd test the waters. She picked up another slice of pizza, and said, 'I've been thinking ...'

She watched Mitch undo the plastic wrapping from the six-pack of sodas he'd also brought with him and open one.

'I was thinking that as I'm now in between jobs ...' Lexi chose not to mention that she had already been offered a job, no doubt starting the next day, although she wouldn't have been surprised if he already knew. She willed herself to hurry up and get to the point. 'I was thinking of going away, on a little trip.'

Mitch put his can of soda down on the coffee table. 'A trip? Sounds like a marvellous idea, Lexi. I think that would be just what you need, rather than hanging round here.' He glanced around the room.

'You do?'

'Absolutely. In fact, I was thinking of taking a few days off work myself. If you want the company. I was thinking we could head up to one of the state parks. I could hire an RV.'

Lexi stared at him. 'Er, that wasn't exactly what I had in mind.'

'Oh, no – of course not. You'll want to go with people your own age.' He caught her expression. 'Or perhaps on your own.'

'No, it's not that. Well, it is kind of. I was thinking of going a bit further afield.'

'Ah, yes – I remember you wanted to go to Mexico. Or was it Hawaii?'

Lexi shook her head. She didn't recall that. Perhaps it was something Andrea had mentioned as a child. 'I was thinking of Europe.'

'Europe. That far?'

Lexi nodded.

He eyed her. 'Whereabouts, exactly?'

Lexi chewed her bottom lip. 'England.'

The word was hardly out of her mouth before her stepdad was on his feet, spilling his can of soda down his shirt. 'What do you want to go there for?'

Lexi was surprised by his reaction. What was the big deal? Anyone would have thought she'd said she was going to Outer Mongolia. Lexi calmly answered his question. 'I miss England. I haven't been back for years, since I was little. I just thought I might never get another chance.'

'Is there any particular reason you want to go now?'

Lexi thought about the letter, looked at Mitch, and said, 'No.' She could have sworn she heard an audible sigh of relief.

'So, your mother didn't ask you to go back there?'

Lexi stared at him. 'Why would she do that?'

'No reason.'

Lexi caught him look at her sheepishly, his bushy eyebrows raised. She noticed he'd said *no reason* pretty quickly.

Lexi asked, 'Did Mum ever mention anything about relatives back in England.'

'Nope. Absolutely not.'

And there it was again, thought Lexi, a quick response – just too quick. He was lying, she was sure of it. Lexi persisted. 'I'd like to go and find out if my paternal grandparents are alive.'

Mitch reached for another slice of pizza. He took a bite, avoiding her gaze.

'Are they?'

'Are they what?' he said with a mouthful of food.

'Still alive?' She waited for him to finish chewing the pizza. 'Well?' She leaned forward in her seat.

'I don't know a thing.'

Lexi stared at him. 'What does that mean?'

'I meant, I don't know anything about your paternal grandparents.'

Lexi didn't believe him. 'Do you know a lady called—'

'Wow, is that the time? I'd better make a move. Dolly won't be pleased I've been gone this long.'

Lexi stared at Mitch as he rose from his seat. She folded her arms. 'Really? You're going to use Dolly as an excuse to leave?'

'She doesn't like being left on her own for too long.'

'Dolly is a cat.' Lexi had seen the little black and white moggy.

She was very sweet. He'd bought her not long after Lexi's mother died as a bit of company. Even so, she didn't warrant him leaving this early.

Mitch started for the door.

'But you haven't finished the pizza.' Lexi stood up.

'I'm fine. I could do with losing a bit of weight.' He patted his stomach, which had once been flat; that youthful figure had disappeared long ago. 'You, on the other hand Lexi, could do with putting on a bit of weight. You're all skin and bone.'

'I am not!' Lexi would be the first to admit that she'd never had her sister's full figure. Andrea had never been overweight, but she had one of those athletic, toned figures that Lexi, who had always been diminutive and small-boned, could never hope for. 'What am I going to do with the rest of the pizza? Don't you want to take it with you?'

Mitch opened the front door and turned around. 'No. Perhaps you could invite your nana and grandpa in for dinner.'

'For a takeaway pizza and a soda from a can?' *Like that was ever going to happen.* Lexi looked at him as though he'd gone barmy.

Mitch caught her expression and chuckled. 'I can't imagine it either.'

Lexi shook her head at the ludicrous idea.

'You know, I don't think they've eaten takeaway food in their life. Would be funny, though, wouldn't it? To see the look on their faces.'

Lexi laughed. 'Yes, I suppose it would.'

Mitch stepped outside.

She stood in the doorway. 'Are you sure you won't stay?'

'No, I've got a cat to feed.'

Was it something I said? Lexi felt like saying.

He turned to go, then did an about-turn on the doorstep. 'This business about going to England ...'

'Yes?'

'I don't think it's a good idea.'

Lexi shook her head in frustration. 'Yeah, I think I got that.'

'So, will you reconsider?'

'Why isn't a good idea?'

'It's a long way to go for nothing, Lexi. I mean you've seen the sights when you used to live there. London, and Trafalgar Square, and all that.'

'It was a long time ago. Besides, there's more to England than London.'

'What makes you say that?'

Lexi frowned. 'I remember the sea, and a river, and a house—'

Mitch suddenly grasped her by the shoulders, taking her completely by surprise. 'No.'

'I beg your pardon?'

Mitch slowly released his grip. 'Sorry. Sorry.'

Lexi rubbed her sore shoulder, too shocked to say anything more.

'Look, they weren't memories. You lived in London. You didn't go anywhere else. Do you understand?'

Lexi stared at him. He wasn't suggesting, he was telling her. In that moment, she made a decision. She would return to England, and wouldn't share the reason she was going with Mitch or her grandparents. Did it have something to do with Margot Dorey, or was it something else, the reason her mum had instructed that she should tell no one? Whatever it was, there was something Mitch and her grandparents were hiding from her and her sister, and she knew the answer lay in England.

9

'I thought you weren't coming to dinner.'

Lexi stood at the door to her grandparents' house. 'I'm not. But thanks for the invitation.'

'Come in. Don't dawdle on the doorstep.'

'No, I can't. Can you give Grandpa a message?'

'He's in the study if you want to tell him yourself.'

Lexi felt she would rather not. 'I've decided to return to New York.'

'Really?' Nana gaped at her. 'But you've only just arrived.'

'I know. Tell Grandpa that I'm going to throw Brandon out and spend the next month looking for a job. If I don't find one then I'll come back and take up Grandpa's offer of a job.'

'Okay,' Nana said slowly.

Lexi avoided her gaze. Nana wasn't stupid. She was highly perceptive, certainly when it came to Lexi telling fibs. For that reason, Lexi wanted to keep the conversation short and sweet. 'I've organised a taxi to take me to the station in the morning.'

'You don't have to do that, sweetheart. We can take you. In fact, I'm sure Grandpa has some business in New York next week. Why can't you wait until then, and you can both drive up there together? It would make the perfect little road trip.'

Lexi stared at her. That was the last thing she needed. 'I want to get back as soon as possible. I can't wait for his business trip.'

The thought of him going to New York had dampened her enthusiasm for what she had thought was a good plan. What if he called in on her at the apartment? She'd have to say something right now to stop that from happening.

'Look, I'd rather he didn't just pop round when he is in New York. I might be in an interview online or something. If he could call me first? You've got my mobile phone number.' Lexi knew that if he did phone her, she'd just fob him off, delay his visit for as long as she could.

'Of course. I'll be sure to let him know to do that. You'll be busy job-hunting. He'll get that. In fact, I think he will be rather pleased.'

'Really?' Lexi didn't think he would be. If she did find a position then it meant she would turn down his job offer to join the firm.

'Oh, yes. It's best not to mope around.'

Lexi nodded in agreement, although she had no intention of moping around, or looking for a job in New York – not right now. Instead, Lexi was heading off on a little holiday that they would know nothing about – as long as her sister could keep her trap shut.

'So, if things don't turn out, and you don't get a job, you'll come back?'

'Of course, Nana. Why wouldn't I? It's not like I've got anywhere else to go, is it?' she said sullenly, thinking she wished she had. After her trip to England, Lexi was intending to return to New York to look for a job, but of course, if that didn't work out, she'd be back. She turned to go.

'Good, good. So, when will you be back?'

Lexi did an about-turn and blurted, 'Are you saying I won't find another job?'

'I meant for a visit.'

'Oh. Right. Sorry.' Lexi hadn't meant to snap at her grandmother. She still couldn't believe she'd lost the job that she'd worked so hard for. Next time it would be wise to keep her wealthy background to herself. That was easier said than done when their name was so well-known. Of course, that wasn't the case in England. Lexi raised an eyebrow, wondering why that had crossed her mind.

Lexi leaned in and gave her Nana a kiss goodbye. 'I'm leaving early, so I won't have a chance to pop in and see you before I go.'

'All right.'

'I will come and visit. I promise.'

'That sounds a bit final.'

Lexi frowned. She hadn't meant it to sound like that. 'I'm confident I'll find another job in publishing.' *When I get back from England*, thought Lexi. She just had one thing to do before she organised her trip.

❖

As soon as she returned to the cottage, Lexi phoned her sister. 'I'm going to England.'

'Really? When?'

Lexi was already on her laptop, looking up flights. She hoped there was a seat on a flight tomorrow, or the day after. She'd just have to stay at an airport hotel overnight. She told Andrea her plans.

'I knew you'd decide to go. But why so soon? I thought you said it wasn't a good time, what with Brandon and losing your job.'

Lexi admitted, 'I've had a job offer already.'

'Well, that's brilliant news. When does it start?'

'Tomorrow.' At least Lexi assumed it would.

'Huh? So why are you jetting off to another country?'

Lexi fell silent.

'Grandpa offered you a job, didn't he?'

When Lexi didn't respond, Andrea squealed down the phone, 'Oh, Lexi, you've got to take it! Just give it a try. I know you were always dead-set against working in the family business, but just imagine—'

'Yes, just imagine,' said Lexi flatly. She didn't want to sound ungrateful. Many people would give their right arm to be handed an opportunity like this – a job with a six-figure salary and a house. It would be some people's dream come true. But not hers.

'Just imagine you and me taking over the reins when Grandpa retires.'

Lexi decided not to burst her sister's bubble and repeat what her grandpa had said. She changed the subject. 'You can't tell them I'm going to England. You know that – right? Promise me.'

Andrea went quiet. 'Did something happen when you returned?'

Lexi decided not to bring up what had happened during Mitch's visit when she'd mentioned England, nor the fact that she'd been annoyed that Andrea had told Nana about Brandon. 'No, but you just need to promise me you won't breathe a word.'

Andrea sighed down the phone. 'I promise. Why do you think they hate England so much?'

Lexi had her own theory. She knew the story of how her mum and dad had met when her mum was travelling and working in England. She imagined her nana and grandpa hadn't wanted her mum to marry an Englishman and live in England. But that didn't explain Mitch's antipathy towards Lexi visiting the country.

Lexi sat at the kitchen table while she was on the phone, staring at the letter she had to deliver. She still thought that perhaps Margot Dorey may have been a good friend from her mother's past that she'd lost touch with over the years. A famous but reclusive children's author, she hadn't been seen for twenty years.

That was what the lawyer had googled and discovered – if it was the same Margot Dorey she had to hand-deliver the letter to.

Lexi told Andrea what the lawyer had told her.

'She's a children's author?'

'Yes. The article online said that she was a recluse and avoided publicity. She hasn't written anything since this series of very successful books, apparently.'

What connection *did* her mother have to this woman? And why couldn't Lexi just post the letter? Why did she have to travel to England and hand it over personally?

'Lexi – you still there?'

'Ah, yes. Sorry. Look, there's something else I need to tell you.' Lexi knew Andrea would get cross when she told her that she'd lied to Nana.

'I can't believe you're letting Brandon stay in the apartment.'

Lexi shook her head. 'Never mind that. The fact is, I knew they'd want to know where I am, so I told them that I'm returning to New York to look for a job.'

'But he doesn't have to be there.'

Lexi bit her lower lip. 'I can't just throw him out.'

'Then I'll do it.'

'No!'

There was an uncomfortable silence. Lexi thought Andrea had hung up. Eventually, Andrea said, 'Okay. But he can't stay there indefinitely. They'll find out sooner or later. You know he's never going to get a recording contract. He'll just have to do like the rest of us and get a job, get his own place, and pay his own way. Besides, what happens when you return from England?'

'Who says I will?' blurted Lexi, wondering where that had come from.

'Pardon?'

Lexi quickly backtracked. 'I meant, who says I'll want to return to New York afterwards?' Lexi imagined her sister smiling down the phone at that comment.

'If you come back and work for our grandparents, it will give

Brandon as much time as he needs to stay on in the apartment.'

'I thought you didn't agree that Brandon should stay on? Besides, didn't you just say he needs to get a job and a place of his own?' Lexi said sarcastically.

'Well, actually, perhaps it's not a bad thing.'

Lexi frowned. 'You mean, if I don't return to New York after my trip.' It wasn't a question. She knew Andrea really wanted her to return to Connecticut and stay there for good.

'Please think about Grandpa's offer while you're away before dismissing it. You won't have to search for another job. It's a good life, Lexi. It's a perfect life. Job security, plenty of money. And we're working in our own business that we can pass on to our kids.'

She'd had this conversation before with Andrea when she'd made up her mind to go and live in New York and start a career in publishing. Andrea couldn't understand why she'd want to do that.

'Look, you've explored other avenues, Lexi. You've proved you can live independently. Now, it's time to—'

'What?' Lexi was getting cross. Andrea sounded like their grandparents. What was she going to say – that it was time to stop playing around?

'All I'm saying is that I'd love for us to work together. Just take some time to consider it. It will be fun working together. I know I'm being selfish, but I'd love my big sister to live just down the road, so I can pop round. As things move on and we both have children, wouldn't it be great for them to grow up together?'

Lexi heaved a sigh. She'd just split with Brandon. Just then, having a family and settling down couldn't be further from her mind. 'Look, I've got to go. I've found a flight.' Lexi had been surfing the net. There was an international flight to London from JFK leaving tonight.

'Have you even got a new passport? I haven't renewed mine.'

That was where she was in luck. Lexi had wanted to take a

holiday in England with Brandon for years, but it had just never happened. What they'd both done, though, a few years earlier, was apply for passports.

'Yes, I've got a passport.'

'Oh.' Andrea sounded disappointed. 'You will let me know when you arrive safely?'

'Of course I will.'

'And if you find Margot Dorey? I'd like to know who she is. I mean, apart from being some famous – well, once-famous – reclusive writer. Perhaps you'll find out why it was so important to Mum for one of us to find her and hand her that letter.'

It wasn't one of us, thought Lexi, *it was me. Why was that?* She supposed if she could find her, she'd find out.

'I wonder what's inside the letter ...' She trailed off.

Lexi knew Andrea was after her opening the letter. It's not as though the lady would know. All she had to do was put it in another envelope and write her name on it. But she couldn't. It wasn't right opening someone else's mail. And it was a felony.

However, that wasn't really what was stopping Lexi. If the contents of that letter had been meant for her and Andrea, then her mother would have told them. Whoever the lady was, it was something personal between them. Lexi respected that. Besides, for some reason her stomach churned when she thought of what was written inside. It was an absurd thought, but could this letter, this woman, be the reason her grandparents – and Mitch as it turned out – did not want her to return to England?

She could confront them and tell them she was going to England. What could they do about it? She was an adult. She could do what she wanted.

Yeah – right, thought Lexi. Why had her mum left her cash to pay for flights and accommodation? She knew the reason; and it was the same reason she couldn't afford to tell them, not just when she'd lost her job; they'd stop her allowance.

'How long will you be gone?'

'I'm not sure.'

'You are booking a return flight – aren't you?'

Although they had both been born in England, Andrea had given up her dual nationality years earlier. Lexi, on the other hand, had not. Andrea knew that. It meant she had two passports. Lexi didn't tell her that she'd made sure to renew both.

'Of course I'm booking a return flight. I was thinking of booking a flexi-ticket in case I need a few more days, or I can't find her and decide to come home early.' Lexi knew she couldn't be away indefinitely, but at least this would give her some flexibility.

They fell silent for a moment.

'Can you do something for me while you're over there?'

'Yes – anything.'

'Can you find where we lived and take some photos. I'd like to see if I they help me remember our time there when I was little.'

Although Lexi smiled – it would have been nice to share some memories of those early years in England – she knew that the task wouldn't be easy. She had memories of a detached house in gardens with a weeping willow tree. She thought it might have been near the sea. But that was all she had. Any paperwork, or photos, or anything else related to their life in England was gone.

She'd yearned for some photos of her dad, but her mum had said they'd all been lost in the move to America. Was that true, or had she left those behind, dumped them along with her past life in England when she left?

'Did Mum ever talk to you about England?'

'No.' Trying to broach the subject with their mum and talk about their childhood there had felt off limits. There weren't even any photos of them in England; it was as though their past had been erased. It was little wonder she had scant memories, and her sister virtually none. There was nothing to jog their memories.

'That's disappointing,' commented Andrea.

Lexi guessed her mum hadn't talked to her sister either, although Andrea hadn't shown much interest in the time spent living in another country she barely remembered. Not until now.

Lexi frowned. How would she find where they used to live? Lexi didn't want to disappoint Andrea by telling her she thought it was doubtful she'd bring home any photos.

'You'd better go, Lexi.'

'Yes. I'll phone you when I arrive in London.'

There was a pause. Lexi knew there was something else on her mind.

'Look, about Brandon. Have you told him you're going to England?'

'Why should I?' Lexi heard Andrea breathe a heavy sigh down the phone.

'He is living in your apartment. If Grandpa finds out that he's still there when you said you were returning to New York, intending to chuck him out ...'

'He won't.'

'But what if Grandpa wants to pay you a visit?'

'I've been living in New York for years, and he never visited us once.' Lexi knew that he'd been to New York on business trips, however. Lexi would rather not think about that conversation in which Nana had told her that Grandpa had some business in New York next week. She hoped Nana remembered to tell him that she might be too busy to meet up and that he should phone first. She added nonchalantly, 'Why would he start now?'

'Because he might be worried about you living in New York all on your own. He'll probably try and persuade you to come home. He obviously wants you to start work with the business.'

You mean run the business, thought Lexi, still flabbergasted that he'd asked her and not Andrea. She felt relieved when she realised that Andrea need never know. It might cause a rift between them after all the work and sacrifices she'd made.

Lexi wasn't the only one who'd had a dream. Andrea loved interior design. A small part of her job as the head of sales was overseeing the interior design of new builds and the furniture packages that were used to set up show homes. She knew her sister would have liked to be more hands-on in that department, but she was management, and it wasn't to be.

'How long do you think you'll be away for?'

Lexi couldn't decide how long she'd need to be away. That was the problem. How long would it take to find Margot Dorey? 'Andrea, I don't know how long it will take to find her.'

'How long do you want to go for, Lexi?'

The word *forever* crept unbidden into her mind.

'I know you're booking a flexi return ticket, but you can't stay away forever.'

Lexi raised her eyebrows. Of course she was right. Lexi sighed. 'I know. I was thinking two or three weeks.' She might even stretch to a month but thought best not to tell Andrea that just yet.

'That sounds like a plan. You could be lucky and find her in a few days, or not at all, no matter how many weeks or months you search. At least you would have tried.' Andrea paused. 'And then there is the other possibility ...'

'What other possibility?'

'I don't want to throw a spanner in the works.'

That made Lexi smile, recognising the English phrase. Although Andrea had scant memories of England, she did come out with some very English phrases from time to time. Whether she'd heard them from their dad or from her big sister, Lexi didn't know, but it made her smile all the same, until Andrea said, 'What if she's passed away?'

Lexi fell silent.

'You haven't thought of that, have you?'

'No.' Lexi heaved a sigh. 'This might be a pointless waste of time.' She wanted to meet this woman. Perhaps she had known both Lexi's parents. Maybe she could tell Lexi things about her mum and her life in England. Unless she could find any relatives in England, Margot Dorey was her only link to their past. 'This trip might be a pointless waste of time if she's gone.'

'Not at all, Lexi. You've wanted to return to England for years. If it wasn't for Brandon and losing your job, you wouldn't be booking a flight to London. This is your opportunity. Go, Lexi, before you change your mind.'

10

'I've done it, Andrea. I've booked my flights.'

'That's great, Lexi. I just wish …'

'What is it, Andrea?'

'I wish I could come too.'

Lexi smiled. 'Me too. There'll be another time.' Even as she said it, she knew there wouldn't be. Andrea was getting married, but it wasn't that. Chad would be up for a trip to England. It was their grandparents. It always had been.

'Do you think she might know why Mum wouldn't talk about her time in England after she left, and why returning to England was off limits?'

'So, you think that too? That there's a reason we've always been discouraged from returning to the country of our birth?'

'I've thought about it often.'

'Really?' Lexi had felt it was just her.

'Yes.'

They fell silent.

'Lexi, I'm really sorry about Brandon.'

'Look, I'd better go.' Lexi didn't want to be reminded about him.

'I think this has turned out for the best, having a chance to get away and focus on something else.'

Lexi agreed. She looked at the time. 'I really have to go.'

'Okay. Well, good luck. Safe journey. Text me when you arrive.'

'I will.'

'I hope you find her. Do you know where you'll start?'

Lexi had an idea. 'I'm heading to London to visit her publisher. I know it was years ago that her books were published, and from what I googled, they're a small publisher, but it appears they're still in business, so perhaps there's still someone there who remembers her.'

'Let's hope so. Hey – maybe they'll have a job for you.'

Lexi didn't respond.

'It was just a joke, Lexi. You're coming back to work in the family business. I can't wait.' She paused. 'Lexi, are you still there?'

'Yes. Look, I really have to get a move on now.' She'd stayed on the phone far too long, and now the conversation was veering into awkward territory that Lexi would really rather not get into. 'Bye, Andrea. Remember what I said. I've returned to the apartment in New York to look for a job.'

'Okay, Lexi, although I still don't think it's a good idea not to tell—'

'Bye, Andrea. I'll text when I arrive.' Lexi ended the call and slipped her phone into the back pocket of her jeans. She threw the remains of the pizza into the trash and washed up the mugs, leaving them on the draining board to dry. She stood for a moment, staring out of the kitchen window. She could see her grandparents' house through the trees, the lights on downstairs. She wouldn't be surprised if her nana came calling with a hotpot of food, leftovers from dinner.

She rummaged through the kitchen drawers and found what she was looking for – a small notepad and pen. She'd told them she was leaving in the morning. She imagined they'd pop in to say goodbye.

In hindsight, she was glad she was leaving tonight. It would avoid a conversation about returning to New York, and Grandpa trying to twist her arm to return with him.

She looked at the notepad. She scribbled a note to let them know she'd left tonight instead. She added that she'd be too busy to catch up with Grandpa in New York, but that when she had a spare moment, she'd be sure to get in touch. That was a lie, but how else was she going to get round him just dropping by?

She called for a taxi and trundled one of her cases to the door after she'd had a quick sort-out of which clothes she wanted to take for her trip. She left a suitcase behind full of mainly work clothes that she wouldn't need while she was away. She switched off the lights before stepping outside and walking down the cobbled path to the front of the house.

She started walking down the drive, throwing backward glances over her shoulder to check if she'd been spotted. Their kitchen and dining room were at the back of the house, so she doubted it. Even so, she hurried down the drive, hoping the taxi hadn't arrived before she got there. She'd told them over the phone not to ring the buzzer outside the gates when they arrived, and hoped they had done as she asked.

Lexi ran the last hundred yards when she spotted the taxi outside the gates. A man got out of the car. 'Did you call for a taxi?'

'Yes, that was me,' Lexi replied, sounding breathless. She caught the taxi driver casting her an odd look. 'I could have driven up to the house.'

'I know. It's fine.' Lexi punched the number into the keypad and waited impatiently for the gates to open. She cast one last furtive glance up the drive. It wasn't as though her grandparents had any clue she was leaving that night. Even so, she breathed a sigh of relief when no one followed.

Lexi walked through the gates to the waiting taxi. The cab driver opened the trunk and placed her suitcase inside while she sat in the back and found her purse.

As soon as he got in the driver's seat, she said, 'Bradley Airport, please.' She had been lucky to get a seat on a flight from Bradley International Airport in Connecticut to London. She guessed if she'd been flying from New York, it might have been tricky organising a flight at such short notice. Although she imagined there were more flights between London and New York, there would also be a lot more tourists heading back and forth between London and New York, rather than New England.

New England. When she was a child and discovered that they were leaving England to live with her grandparents in New England, she'd said to her mum that she preferred to stay in Old England. Lexi didn't understand that New England was a region in the north-eastern United States, not a country. And there was no such thing as *Old* England.

When they'd moved to Connecticut, it was their very first visit to America. Her mum had tried to explain that Connecticut was one of six states in New England, and they would be living near the capital, Hartford. Lexi had replied, 'Will I like the capital of New England? I like London. Do you think the capital of New England is like the capital of Old England?'

Lexi sat in the back of the cab and smiled. She didn't exactly remember that conversation; it was something her mum had told her on that rare occasion she'd talked of their old life.

'Going on vacation?'

Lexi looked at the cab driver as he backed the car into the main street and set off for the airport. He glanced at her in his rearview mirror as she nodded.

'So, where are you going?'

'London.'

'London?'

'Yes.'

'Never been abroad myself.'

Lexi glanced out the window and sighed. 'I was born there.'

'Really? Are you visiting family?'

Lexi shook her head. 'No.'

'Friends?'

Lexi didn't want to get into the ins and outs of her trip. Instead, she said, 'I'm doing some sightseeing.' She wasn't telling a complete fib. She did intend to do some sightseeing while she was in London. Lexi's eyes went wide when she thought about the reason for her trip. In her haste to leave, she couldn't remember what she'd done with the letter. Was it still on the kitchen table where she'd been sitting with it in her hands when she was on the phone to Andrea? *Oh, god, have I left it behind?* she thought.

The cab driver caught her frantically emptying her handbag on the back seat. 'Is everything okay? Did you forget something? I could turn the car around.'

'Oh, thank god!' exclaimed Lexi as soon as she put her hand on the letter at the bottom of her bag.

'Did you find your passport?'

'No, that wasn't it.' Lexi held up the white envelope. 'I have to deliver a letter. For a moment, I thought I'd left it behind.' She frowned. She hadn't intended to mention it.

'Seems a long way to go to deliver a letter. Can't you just post it?'

'Apparently not.'

Sitting in traffic as they entered the city, the taxi driver turned to look at her, raising his eyebrows.

She sighed. 'It's a long story. I've got to find the recipient first.'

'Ah, okay. Well, I hope it all works out.'

'So do I.' Lexi wondered what she would do if she couldn't find this woman. She looked at the envelope. Then she'd have to open the envelope and see what was written in the letter; perhaps the mystery that was Margot Dorey would be revealed.

11

Lexi stared out of the small cabin window at the large grey clouds and the rain drops splattering the window. She smiled even though she was feeling a mixture of emotions she hadn't expected when the plane landed at Heathrow Airport.

It had been two decades since she was last there. It was hard to believe that the last time she had sat in a plane on the runway at Heathrow was when she was six years old, clasping her mother's hand tightly, missing her father dreadfully, full of trepidation over what New England and the grandparents she'd never met would be like. She wondered when, if it hadn't been for the letter, she would have returned.

A loud *ping* interrupted her thoughts. She looked up to find that the seatbelt sign had been switched off. Suddenly, everyone in the cabin sprang to life, getting up from their seats and opening overheard compartments to find their carry-on luggage. Children chattered and a baby was crying.

She overheard the two young English children sitting in the seats behind her asking their parents if they could have a McDonalds on the way home. She'd spent the plane journey listening to their incessant chatting, and arguing, but it hadn't bothered her in the slightest. It had just made her think of her and her sister's first ever plane journey all those years ago.

She stood up and turned around, smiling at the two children, a girl and a boy, who looked like twins. She guessed they were around seven or eight years old.

'I am so sorry they have been loud the entire journey. I kept telling them to keep it down.'

Lexi had heard their mum telling them to be quiet and to stop kicking the seats in front of them. The young couple who had been seated next to Lexi had vacated their seats and were already moving down the centre aisle to exit the plane.

Lexi smiled at the children's mum. Wasn't that the English way? Always apologising. Lexi suddenly felt inexplicably happy to be back on English soil, despite only spending six years of her life there. 'Really, you don't have to apologise.'

'Ah, you're American.'

Lexi frowned. She wished that she'd kept her English accent, but then who was she kidding after twenty years abroad. 'I've lived there for years, but in actual fact I was born in England, and spent the first few years here until—' Lexi clammed up. She didn't know why she hadn't thought about it until that moment, but while she was there she wanted to buy some flowers and visit her father's grave.

'Until you moved to America?'

'Yes.' Lexi didn't mention her father.

'Are you staying in London?'

Lexi nodded. She'd booked a hotel for just one night in central London. She hoped that it was a wise decision. She intended to visit the publisher first, see whether they still had an address for the author who had once been on their books, and find out whether they were willing to give it out. She was hedging her bets; what if Margot Dorey didn't live in London? It would be a waste of money to book more than a night if she had to travel to a different part of the country to find her. For some reason, Lexi had a feeling that might be the case. She had no idea why.

'Well, you must see the sights. A lot has changed in twenty years. There's the London Eye, and the new Docklands Light Railway – that's worth a look at along with Canary Wharf. There are still the old haunts too. You must see the Tower of London and the museums in London. We always enjoy a visit to the Natural History Museum and the Science Museum. There's the British Museum too – that's always worth a visit.'

Her husband interrupted. 'They're free, you know.'

She turned to her husband. 'I'm sure she knows that. I was mainly mentioning the new things she might not be aware of.'

'Yes, dear, I get that but—'

'Mummy, Daddy, stop arguing!'

'Sweetheart, we are not arguing.'

Lexi stared at them all. Was this how things had been when she was a child, before she lost her dad? Had her parents bickered like this family? She tried to remember, but disappointingly, she couldn't.

She smiled at the couple. They were being so helpful to a stranger. 'I'm sure I will check out the old stuff and the new.' Lexi had been so young when she was last there that she doubted she'd notice any difference. And it wasn't as though they had lived in London the whole time they'd been in England. Lexi raised her eyebrows. *How did I know that? We used to get two trains. There was a little train with three carriages that we weren't on for long, then a big train that seemed to take forever.*

'Are you all right?' The young mother touched Lexi's hand, which she'd rested on the headrest of her seat as she waited to get out into the aisle.

'Oh, yes. It's the strangest thing. I just had a childhood memory.'

'What was it?'

'I think we moved out of London when I lived here as a child. We used to get two trains to London.'

'Hmm. Two trains.' She looked at her husband. He shrugged. She turned to Lexi. 'Sorry, can't help you there. You could be going in any direction from Heathrow.'

'Of course.' Lexi hadn't expected them to know.

'Can't you ask your parents?'

'They've both passed away.'

'You're not going to die, are you, Mummy?' The little girl's big blue eyes went wide with fear as she started up at her mother. They were younger than Lexi thought – perhaps the age she had been when she flew to America.

'No, of course not, sweetheart.'

'But that lady said her mummy and daddy are dead.'

'Sorry,' said Lexi, staring at the children's worried faces. She hadn't meant to blurt it like that.

'I'm sorry for your loss.'

Unfortunately, Lexi could tell that was the end of their conversation.

'Come on now, children. Make sure you've got everything. Look, someone is letting us out into the aisle.' They quickly moved out of their seats. 'Well, have a good trip,' the young mother said. 'Hope you find what you're looking for.'

Lexi cocked her head to one side, wondering what she had meant by that. Evidently, the woman's husband had thought the comment was strange too. She heard him whisper, 'That was an odd thing to say.'

'Are you calling me odd?'

'Of course not, I just wondered what you mean by that.'

So did Lexi. She was straining to hear the woman's reply as she joined the queue in the aisle to disembark, with several people between her and the family.

'I think she's not just here to see the sights. There's more to her trip.'

'What makes you say that?'

Lexi caught the husband briefly cast his gaze in her direction. She looked around the cabin, avoiding eye contact, as though she hadn't heard a thing.

'Well, her parents are gone, so she's come back for a reason. Perhaps there's a long-lost relative who was in their will and she's trying to trace them. Maybe her parents left them something in their will and she's trying to track them down and give it to them. Remember my uncle. We had a devil of a time trying to find my cousin, who it turned out had moved—'

Lexi was stuck behind someone getting a bag down from an overhead compartment. The couple with the children had moved ahead, their conversation drowned out. Lexi stared after them. She thought of the letter in her handbag, addressed to a stranger. Did this mean Margot Dorey was in her mother's will? Had she left her something? If so, what? The lawyer hadn't mentioned anything. All he'd given her was the letter. Was it money? Was there a cheque inside?

Lexi resisted the urge to tear open the letter and find out. She wouldn't have begrudged her mum leaving someone money. It was hers to do with as she wished. But it still bothered her that her mum had failed to tell either her or Andrea anything about this woman, who was obviously important to her.

As Lexi exited the plane, she was looking forward to finding Margot Dorey and unravelling the mystery of just who she had been to her mum. But the clock was ticking. Although she'd booked a flexi return flight, Andrea was right: she couldn't stay away forever. She'd also had the presence of mind to book the return flight to New York rather than Hartford. On her return, Lexi intended to look for another job.

She'd told Brandon he could stay in the apartment. That had been on the spur of the moment. Now, Lexi had changed her mind. She'd decided to give him two weeks, three weeks tops, to vacate the New York apartment before she returned. She had yet to tell

Brandon the new plan. It wasn't long, but he had a girlfriend; what was the problem with him moving in and sponging off someone else for a change? Although Kimberley was married, they'd just have to figure it out.

During the flight, and the seven-and-a-half-hour layover in Washington, where she'd booked into an airport hotel thinking she'd get some sleep before the international leg of the journey from Dulles International Airport to Heathrow, Lexi had hardly slept. Instead she'd had plenty of time to mull things over. And she'd come to a decision; despite her initial reluctance, she now wanted Brandon out of her apartment. Andrea was right, in fact they all were. She'd been completely blind to how he'd been using her. How could she have been so stupid? She'd thought they weren't just soulmates but best friends, and he'd never use her or go behind her back and cheat on her.

Then there was the other thing on her mind that had woken her up when she'd finally dozed off; what would her impression of England be? All this time, she'd pined to return, thinking she'd love it, that she'd feel she was coming home, but perhaps she wouldn't feel that way at all. Maybe she had left that little English girl behind for good, and she'd just feel like a fish out of water – a tourist with no connection to the country of her birth and, worse still, to her British father.

Lexi walked down the aisle of the plane, holding her British passport, and stepped outside into the bracing morning air. The wind and rain lashed her face. She paused for a moment behind the slow-moving line, walking carefully down the metal steps to the tarmac runway below. Lexi closed her eyes and breathed in the chilly morning air. That memory stirred again of a garden and her sister hiding behind the branches of a weeping willow.

'Excuse me.'

Lexi opened her eyes, to find people brushing past her. The line of people was moving again.

'Oh, I'm so sorry.' Lexi smiled. 'Sorry,' she apologised again.

'I'm sorry. Do excuse me,' said a member of the cabin crew as he brushed past her.

'Oh, excuse me,' a lady said, stepping to one side.

'So sorry – my fault,' another passenger said when the member of the cabin crew walked into her suitcase.

Lexi's smiled broadened. She'd been on many other flights over the years, both within the US and to the Caribbean, which had been full of other nationalities who didn't appear to have heard of the word *queue* or have that very peculiar British habit of feeling the need to apologise at every turn.

Lexi's smiled broadened as she watched the flight attendant apologising and excusing her way down the stairs carrying two walking sticks for an elderly lady who'd just reached the bottom.

Lexi could feel tears welling up. 'I'm home,' she breathed.

12

'Miss. Miss!'

Lexi could feel someone gently clasp her shoulder. Her eyes shot open. 'Where am I?' For a split second she was disorientated.

'You fell asleep, miss,' said the taxi driver.

Lexi wasn't surprised. Perhaps she would have been better off taking a night flight and sleeping on the plane, but the only flights available from Hartford had a stopover, and unsurprisingly the one with availability had the longest stopover.

It was a shame she'd hardly slept in the airport hotel in Washington, even though she'd arrived there at ten in the evening after the two-and-a-half-hour flight, checked in at eleven and gone straight to bed.

Her flight out of Dulles International Airport was at six-thirty the following morning. It had landed eight and a half hours later at Heathrow. By the time she'd got her luggage and gone through passport control, she was exhausted.

'We've arrived at the hotel.'

Lexi looked at him in surprise. *We're here already?*

She remembered the dream she'd been having – or was it a memory? She had been on a boat – no, it was a houseboat. There had been faded curtains at the porthole windows, and the sensation of the boat moving gently up and down in the water, and a girl around her own age falling, falling into the cold, murky water. She had reached for her, but the girl was gone.

Lexi shuddered. *Was that a dream or a memory?* If it was a memory, then where was the houseboat, and who was the girl? And what happened to her after she fell in? Lexi got out of the cab, thinking that if it was a childhood memory and not just a dream, why was she recalling it now, after all these years?

She looked up at the entrance to the hotel, a Georgian-fronted building overlooking gardens in London's Bloomsbury, not far from the British Museum. She immediately wished she'd booked more than one night. But when she had made the booking, her thinking had been that if she were to find the address for Margot Dorey, and it was in another part of the country, then she'd rather head off and give the lady her letter. Then she'd be free to return to London before she returned to America, and do the tourist things that the lovely couple on the plane had mentioned.

Lexi rubbed her eyes and texted Andrea that she'd arrived in London safely, something she'd promised her she'd do. She slipped her phone in her bag and found her purse to pay the driver. He was unloading her suitcase from the taxi. She'd chosen this part of London to stay in because the company that published Margot Dorey's children's books was located in Bloomsbury.

Lexi asked the taxi driver, 'Do you know where Gower Street is, by any chance?' She knew it was walkable; she just didn't know in which direction.

The cabbie smiled. 'Of course.' He stood next to Lexi on the pavement and pointed down the street. 'You want to head down there, turn right past Russell Square gardens and keep walking. When you come to the next street, turn left. It's a fifteen-minute walk, if that.'

Lexi knew she could have taken the taxi straight there, but what would she do with her luggage? She wanted to check in first.

As she approached the three concrete steps up to the entrance, a young doorman dressed in a grey uniform approached to help her with her with the suitcase. He took her suitcase and opened the door of the hotel. She followed him into the carpeted entrance lobby, looking about her at the ornate wooden panelling and the wide curved staircase as she approached the reception desk.

Lexi had booked a suite. It was expensive, but it was the only room available at short notice. It had eaten into a fair bit of the money her mum had left her for the trip, but Lexi had already found alternative, much cheaper, accommodation in London if she needed to stay on or when she wanted to return. There were rooms in university halls of residence in London available because the students had gone home for the summer. It meant she wouldn't necessarily have en suite facilities, but the accommodation for London was very reasonable and included a cooked breakfast.

She walked up to the reception desk. 'I've got a room booked for tonight.'

'What name please?'

'Lexi Dawson.'

Lexi watched the young man on reception turn to his computer screen. He passed her a room key and told her the floor where she'd find her suite. 'The lift is over there.'

'Lift?'

'Ah, I believe you call it an *elevator* in America.'

Lexi glanced around the plush entrance hall as she made her way to the lift with her key card to the suite. She had changed some of the larger British currency into smaller ten- and twenty-pound notes for her taxi fare from the airport, put the remainder of the two thousand pounds worth of cash in the paper wallet they'd given her, and tucked it in her handbag. She planned to leave the money in her room when she went out. She didn't like carrying around that amount of cash. What if she lost it? She had a thought.

She retraced her steps back to the check-in desk. 'Would it be possible to pay for my room now rather than when I check out tomorrow morning?'

The staff were accommodating, although a little taken aback when they reached for the card reader and discovered she was paying in cash. Lexi stood at reception and counted out the notes in front of a receptionist. She stopped halfway through when she caught him staring at her. 'You do accept cash – don't you?'

'Or course, madam.'

Lexi guessed by the look on his face that this was most unusual. She continued counting it out. She had a master suite, with views over the gardens and a separate sitting area. The double or twin rooms had sold out, along with the junior suites. If it wasn't for the location, she would have booked elsewhere.

Even so, she couldn't really justify this sort of expense just for the convenience of walking down the street to the publishers. She finished counting out the notes for the two-bedroomed master suite, deciding that tonight was going to be her little indulgence. Apparently, the room came with canapes. She was looking forward to a little snack before setting out to find the publishers.

'There. I think that does it.' Lexi had used some of the smaller notes too, so now the wallet wasn't bulging. She'd just handed over a little under a quarter of the money for one night's stay.

The receptionist took the money and gave her a receipt. He clicked his fingers at a young man standing by the stairs who took Lexi's suitcase to the lift and asked for her room key. Lexi handed it over. They rode up the lift in silence. Lexi was looking forward to a coffee and canapes in her room.

Two floors up, they exited the lift. Lexi followed the young man as he trundled her suitcase along the thickly carpeted hall to the end, where there was a white door with brass door furniture. He swiped the key card and handed it back to her before taking her case into the suite. When he turned around, Lexi already had a ten-pound note to hand.

He looked at the note, but didn't take it. *Was it too much*, she wondered?

Lexi frowned. 'Do you take tips?' She was used to tipping in America.

The young man glanced at the door and gingerly took the note.

Lexi got the impression this wasn't the 'done thing', as the British liked to say. She watched him stuff the note in his pocket before showing her round the suite. She didn't know if that was what they usually did, or if it was just because she'd slipped him a tip, but it wasn't necessary.

'And the minibar is here,' he said, opening a small fridge inset in a mahogany dressing table.

Lexi loved the sitting room. There were two comfortable high-backed chairs positioned in front of a large Georgian window overlooking a very English garden with tall trees, shrubbery, and creeping ivy that came up to her window. She adored the outlook over the gardens and the views to the back of more tall majestic Georgian buildings that fronted another street in Bloomsbury. 'I love it,' Lexi exclaimed. She looked about for the canapes.

As if reading her mind, he said, 'Would you like the canapes now?'

She could order room service, but she'd paid an extortionate price for the suite, even if it was rather lovely, so she decided she'd have a free lunch of the canapes. It had taken over an hour by taxi from Heathrow to the hotel in Bloomsbury and she was starving. At least it saved dipping further into her money.

She hadn't waited long before she heard a knock at the door. Lexi crossed the room. It was the young man again with a tray. He set it down on the coffee table between the two chairs by the window. Lexi smiled at the pot of coffee.

He hovered in the room, staring at her.

'Oh, er … of course.' Lexi offered him another note. She wasn't sure that was what she should be doing, and wondered if he was taking advantage of a young naïve American tourist. He grinned at her and left the room. She heard the door to the suite close behind him.

Lexi frowned. The young man reminded her of Brandon.

She took a seat, poured a cup of coffee and chose a canape. The combination of cream cheese and fresh smoked salmon was delicious. There was a variety of canapes, but the smoked salmon ones were her favourites. Lexi opened her handbag and looked at her phone. Andrea had texted back, sounding relieved she'd finally arrived.

Lexi had forgotten to mention the long layover when she'd booked her flight, so Andrea had been anticipating a text hours ago. Now Andrea wanted to know what she was doing, where she was staying, and how she was feeling now she was back in England.

Lexi texted back, keeping it brief. She avoided mentioning the dream she'd had and how she'd felt when she'd landed that she was coming home. She also chose not to mention the memories that were resurfacing – if that was what they were. Instead, she sent Andrea a photo of her hotel suite and the view from the Georgian window.

Lexi popped another canape in her mouth, took a sip of freshly ground coffee, and stared at her phone. She desperately wanted to tell her best friend all about her trip. She desperately wanted him here, with her. She looked around her lovely suite. She had never felt so lonely.

It hadn't taken long for the euphoria of arriving in England to dissipate. She was still happy to be here, but not like this, all alone. The reality of her situation hit her as she sat staring out of the window. As much as England felt like home, she realised home wasn't a street, a city or even a country; it was family. *It was* – Lexi could feel tears rolling down her cheeks – *Brandon.*

Lexi texted her sister, *I feel homesick already.*

Her sister wasted no time texting her back to say how relieved she was to hear that. *I thought you wouldn't come back.*

Oh, I'll be back, Lexi replied, *don't you worry about that!* Lexi regretted booking that return flight to New York rather than heading straight back to her grandparents' house in Hartford.

Thinking of New York, Lexi knew she had to get in touch with Brandon. If her grandfather did try to call in on her when he was in New York – even though she'd given Nana a message to pass on to him not to do that – she needed to tell Brandon what was going on. She had to tell him to pack up his stuff and leave. He had two weeks.

However, she just couldn't imagine hearing his voice down the phone; she knew she was liable to burst into tears. She'd text. Just not right now. He'd want to call her – she knew he would – to find out why she'd changed her mind. She'd told him he could stay in the apartment. The problem was that her grandfather might turn up and discover she'd lied. If Brandon was there, but it looked as though he was packing his stuff and moving out, and he was prepared to tell a little white lie and say he had moved out and was just back to collect some of his stuff, that could work.

Lexi poured herself another strong black coffee. She felt drowsy. She wasn't surprised after going a night without much sleep. They didn't call it jet lag for nothing.

'I have to stay awake.' Lexi wanted to visit the publisher that day before they closed. She didn't know their opening times but hoped they kept normal office hours. If she finished her coffee and left the remaining canapes until later, she'd have time to walk there, perhaps get a little lost, and still make it in plenty of time to turn up unannounced and wait to have a word with someone who may know the whereabouts of Margot Dorey.

Lexi made the mistake of walking into the bedroom and trying out the double bed.

13

'I see you're checking out this morning.'

'Have you got any vacancies for tonight?' Lexi asked the receptionist. She had already eaten breakfast, but still had two hours before she officially checked out – time enough to visit the publisher and return to the hotel to check out of her room.

She had been annoyed with herself for falling asleep and wasting the afternoon in bed – until she realised that she hadn't done so at all. She had been so tired after she'd landed that she had forgotten the time difference; her phone had still been on flight mode, so it hadn't automatically updated to the new time zone, and she hadn't put her watch forward five hours. Because it had been so light out when she'd arrived at the hotel, she'd had no clue that it was far later than she'd thought.

If she'd flown into London at another time of year, when the evenings drew in earlier, she would have realised, but it was summer, and still completely light out at that time in the evening. It meant she needn't have beaten herself up over falling asleep early in the afternoon – it was, in fact, getting on for ten at night. The publishers would have closed hours earlier.

Now she felt much better after a night's sleep, and discovering that she had not wasted an afternoon. After losing her job and losing Brandon in the course of one horrible Monday, and taking her first long-haul international flight on her own the following day, she wasn't surprised that the events of the last couple of days had caught up with her. And with the addition of jet lag, it was little wonder she felt exhausted and disorientated on arrival. She realised she shouldn't be too hard on herself, under the circumstances, for forgetting the time difference.

That morning, Lexi had changed the time on her watch and switched off flight mode on her phone. She was definitely now on London time.

After a lovely breakfast, and a good night's sleep, Lexi was feeling far more positive about things than she had the previous day. She'd felt elated upon waking up in London. She still couldn't quite believe she was there.

'Let me see if we have a room available for you. One moment.'

Lexi waited, biting a fingernail. She would much rather enjoy her day knowing she was returning to this hotel and not having to worry about finding somewhere else for that night.

If she could stay there, it would make her day so much easier. She'd visit the publisher, then, depending on what came out of that, she'd either plan her onward journey that evening, but take in some sights in London, or she'd find alternative accommodation for the remainder of her stay in London. Either way, staying at the hotel was preferable to having to spend her morning organising another hotel.

'Ah.'

Lexi stared at the receptionist, praying that it was a positive *ah* rather than an *oh dear, I'm afraid you're out of luck*, with a very big, British apology. 'If you are happy to shift rooms, then I can put you in a junior suite on the same floor.'

'Really?' Lexi was incredibly happy. Not only did they have a room, but she imagined the junior suites were less expensive.

The receptionist said, 'It has one bedroom, so it's smaller than the master suite you're currently in.'

And cheaper, thought Lexi. 'I'll take it.'

'Would you like to pay now?'

Lexi looked at the receptionist. It was the same lady with whom she'd stood and counted out the money yesterday. However, today she was keen to get off and find the publisher. 'I'll pay for the new suite when I check out tomorrow. If that's okay.'

'Of course. Now, I'm afraid you'll have to check out of your suite today. You could leave your luggage with us at the reception desk until the junior suite is ready. 'Can I come back and check out of my room at twelve?'

'Of course.'

'Perfect.' Lexi planned to find the publisher and then spend the afternoon at the museum, by which time her new suite would be ready. She turned to go, then had a thought. 'Will I still get canapes with the junior suite?' She felt the colour rise in her cheeks for asking, but they had been delicious.

'Yes, of course, madam.'

Lexi grinned. Her first day in London was turning out better than expected. She'd slept so well, had a great breakfast, and had already organised another night in the lovely hotel in Bloomsbury. She hoped her luck continued when she visited the publisher.

Lexi turned from reception and headed towards the hotel entrance. She stepped out into bright sunshine and smiled. It wasn't even raining. Lexi decided that today was going to be a good day. She'd swept thoughts of Brandon and looking for a new job out of her mind and was focused on her surroundings.

I'm in Bloomsbury, London, she said to herself as she walked down the long tree-lined Montague Place and came to Russell Square gardens. A public square with trees and park benches, its perimeter was fenced with black railings. *How lovely*, thought Lexi, taking in the leafy crescent of tall Georgian buildings lining the streets on all sides of the square.

She felt that Bloomsbury seemed familiar somehow. That

wasn't surprising. They had lived in London. She had been born there. She imagined they must have visited the British Museum close by when she was a child. She wasn't sure where in London she'd lived or where her father was buried, which was a shame because she did want to visit her father's grave. She wished she'd had certain conversations with her mother before she died. She felt she would always regret not having done so. Time had passed and the meaningful things she now wanted to ask her were lost forever.

Lexi sighed. She tried not to think about that, saying to herself *today is going to be a good day.* She continued to follow the directions the cab driver had given her the previous day. Fifteen minutes later, she turned a corner into Gower Street. Tall, imposing red-brick buildings, some with plaques on their walls, lined the street. It was not dissimilar to Montague Place, where the hotel was located. However, there were no hotels in this street; instead there were several faculty buildings belonging to University College London.

The area reminded her of back home in Connecticut, around the campus of Yale University. She'd visited there, as her grandparents had been keen for her to go to Yale. Lexi's first choice had been to become an international student and attend university in London, but she'd bowed to their wishes for her not to go because they'd held the purse strings and wouldn't have funded her if she had.

Some students got loans, and part-time jobs, and made things work. Lexi glanced up at one of the university buildings and regretted not having had the confidence to at least try to go it alone. Although she had liked Yale, she had refused an offer of a place just because it had been where her grandparents and her mother had wanted her to go. In the end, she had settled for New York. It hadn't been her first choice, but it had at least been a choice she had made for herself, against their wishes – which at the time had somehow made sense. She had never returned to live in Hartford after that.

Lexi breathed a heavy sigh and wondered what her grandparents would do if they found out she'd returned to England. *Cut you off,* was her first thought. She shook her head and smiled. They were her grandparents; they wouldn't do that.

She stopped in front of an impressive building with the number 37 emblazoned on the door. There was a plaque that listed several business names in gold lettering, one of which was the publisher, located on the third floor. Lexi took a deep breath and tried the door. It was locked. Below the inscription she noticed a button and a small metal grill. She pressed the button and expected to be buzzed into the building. Instead, a crackly male voice said, 'Good morning, do you have an appointment?'

'Well, er, no – but I'm here to see someone in Grosvenor Publishing.'

'One moment, please.'

There was a loud crackle before another voice, a woman's this time, said, 'Do you have an appointment?'

Lexi rolled her eyes, 'No, but I'm here to see someone about—'

'I'm afraid no one can see you without an—'

'— appointment, yes I get it!' Lexi shook her head. 'Well, when can I have one? I'm free all day.'

'One moment, let me consult the diary.'

Lexi stood awkwardly on the step. It was quite frustrating trying to bend down and have a conversation with a little metal box on the wall. Why couldn't they just buzz her in, then she could explain why she was there face to face?

'Right, our next free appointment is in two weeks' time.'

'Two weeks! Look I'm only here a few days.'

That wasn't strictly true. She had two weeks, possibly three. She'd even be prepared to stay for a month if that meant she'd locate Margot Dorey, but she wasn't intending to spend all that time sitting on her hands, or sightseeing. Besides, she wanted to find out if Margot Dorey was alive or dead, and where she might be today, not in two weeks' time.

'Take it or leave it.'

Lexi frowned at the rude lady. 'Okay, I'll take it.' She sighed. At least it was better than nothing.

'Can I take your name, please?'

'It's Lexi Dawson.' Lexi thought she heard some typing in the background.

'That's all booked in for you. Make sure you have your submission inquiry and one chapter only of your work.'

Lexi rubbed her forehead. 'Oh, I'm not here to get an agent or publisher.'

'So, you are just making an inquiry.'

'Yes.' Lexi was hopeful they might fit her in for another appointment a lot sooner now they knew she wasn't here to plug a book.

'Fine, we'll see you in two weeks.'

Lexi exhaled a sigh, heavy with disappointment. She thought of the letter in her handbag and felt stupid for having thought it was going to be a good day. Now she just thought the opposite; after a lovely stay in Montague Place, everything would be downhill from now on.

'It's a shame I have to wait all that time when all I had was a quick question regarding Margot Dorey,' commented Lexi, more to herself. She turned and walked back down the three concrete steps to the street, wishing she had checked out of her room that morning, which would have saved her the walk back to the hotel when the museum was just around the corner.

'Wait! Wait! Are you still there?'

Lexi turned around. She thought she heard a voice coming from the metal box. Lexi returned up the steps and spoke into it, 'Hello?'

'Is that you, the lady I was speaking with a moment ago?'

'Yes.'

'Did you say you know Margot Dorey?'

Lexi hesitated. 'Er, yes.'

She immediately heard the sound of a buzzer and a click. The large black front door opened a crack.

'Come straight up the stairs in front of you. We're on the third floor. There's no lift. Please close the main door behind you.'

'Okay.' Lexi pushed the heavy door open and made sure it clicked shut before she started up the wide wooden oak staircase before her. Three floors up, she reached a door with a plastic sign – *Grosvenor Publishers.* She thought they sounded quite distinguished.

Lexi opened the door and immediately spotted a middle-aged lady sitting behind a small desk in the cosy reception area. It was just as she would have expected a publisher's reception to be, with tall bookshelves lining the walls, comfortable green leather chairs, and writerly magazines strewn over the coffee table between two green leather sofas that looked like something out of a Hitchcock film.

It was all very old-fashioned, Lexi thought, drinking in the room. Would Margot Dorey have entered this building and stood right in this spot decades ago, hoping to get what would become children's classics into print? She thought so.

'Are you the lady—?'

Another woman, older than the one on reception, flung open a door, interrupting. 'Heather, is this the young lady you spoke to a moment ago?'

'Yes.'

The older women scrutinised Lexi. 'You know Margot Dorey?'

Lexi took a deep breath and glanced from one woman to the other, both looking at her wide-eyed. She nodded.

'Come through, please.' The older women beckoned her into an office before she had a chance to explain. 'Here, take a seat.' She quickly tossed some books and a newspaper off the upholstered chair, and placed them on her cluttered desk.

Lexi gingerly sat down. The office was small, and the bookshelves, like the desk, cluttered. The woman, whom Lexi guessed was in her sixties, took a seat behind her desk. 'I'm Hazel. And you are ...?'

'Lexi.'

'Okay, Lexi. So, how do you know Margot Dorey?' She stared at Lexi intently as she leaned forward in her chair.

'Well, er … ' Lexi opened her handbag and got out the letter. 'I have this.'

'She sent you a letter? Are you a relative?'

'Ah, no she didn't send me anything. My mother gave me this letter to give to her.'

Hazel frowned. 'That's all very interesting. So, you're going to see her?'

Lexi nodded. 'I hope so.'

'Good. Good. Can you give her a message when you see her?'

Lexi grinned. 'Absolutely.'

'We want her back on our books, as you must appreciate.'

Lexi didn't, but she had an idea what Hazel meant; they wanted what she imagined must have been their most profitable writer back working with them. She cast her gaze about the office. Although there was a lot of paperwork, a lot of manuscripts, she wondered how many letters sitting on the desk were rejections.

Hazel must have caught her staring at the desk. 'All these?' she held up numerous letters. 'They're rejection letters. I'm afraid most people just don't cut the mustard. What I mean is, they just aren't good enough.'

'I know what cut the mustard means,' said Lexi.

'I see. Well, in any case, most of these … ' Hazel picked up a manuscript, held it up over a waste paper bin and dropped it in there, 'are just no good at all. I'll have to remember to delete them from my inbox too. I like to glance through them on paper, just in case I have missed something. Most times they're just as bad on paper, probably worse.'

Lexi was so glad she had no aspirations to be a writer. She'd lost count of the number of people she'd worked with in publishing who aspired to writing the next bestseller. She shuddered at the thought of all the blood, sweat and tears, the years of angst trying to write a literary masterpiece. She stared at the mountain of manuscripts littering the desk and said, 'I'm a marketing manager.' She didn't think she'd need to explain what her role entailed in a publishing company. She imagined Hazel knew all about the need for an experienced marketing manager to promote and sell books.

'I'm in between jobs. I have excellent references.' Lexi had built up a fair bit of experience in marketing and had an excellent track record collaborating with authors, editors and other sales staff. 'Would you have an opening?'

Hazel frowned. 'So, you're here for a job.'

'Er, no. I just saw all that and thought …' She trailed off. It had been at the back of her mind, when she visited here, that she might ask. Not that she had any intentions of staying. She'd told Andrea when she was booking her flight that she'd be back. But as she had walked through Bloomsbury this morning, she had felt rather different.

14

'Although you're right, I could do with help, I'm afraid I can barely pay myself and my PA out there,' said Hazel. 'I had to let the other member of staff go, so I'm afraid although there is technically a vacancy, I couldn't pay you a bean. So unless you are an heiress or something and want to work for free – or, as you Americans call it, *be an intern* – then no, there is no vacancy.'

Lexi bit her lower lip. She wasn't exactly an heiress, but unbeknown to Hazel, she did have a generous allowance to live on, courtesy of her grandparents. As much as she would have liked to take the position, there was no way her grandpa was going to pay for her to live and work in London. Lexi frowned.

Hazel caught her expression. 'I thought not. Well, back to Margot Dorey. So, you'll give her my message? If she's even thinking about writing something, then I need, er, want her back. Once again, we'll promote her work and get her into the bestseller lists in no time.'

'But she hasn't published for years,' said Lexi.

'Ah, you're not familiar with how the UK publishing business works. Our readers have long memories. Those books still sell very well today. It's the only way my little publishing house in Bloomsbury has survived all these years. But even so, I'm afraid sales are not what they once were.'

Lexi guessed that Hazel was looking for her next Margot Dorey but hadn't had much luck.

'So, if you can give her the message, that would be appreciated.'

'Of course I will. There's just one thing ...'

'And that is?'

'The reason I'm here. I need her address.' Lexi held up the envelope. Apart from her name, the envelope was blank.

'I don't understand,' said Hazel. 'I thought you said you knew her?'

'Er, no. Not exactly. I know of her. My mother left me this letter in her will with instructions to deliver it to Margot personally. I think it's the Margot Dorey that wrote those children's novels.'

'You *think* it is?'

'Yes, but to find out for sure, I need her address. So I was hoping—'

'You're here to find her?'

Lexi nodded.

Hazel sat back in her chair, looking deflated. 'Oh, child, we've been talking at cross purposes.'

'Huh?'

'I thought you knew where she was – that's why I wanted you to give her a message. I have no clue where she disappeared to.'

'Did you just say *disappeared*?'

Hazel sighed. 'I take it your mother knew her?'

'Yes – at least I assume so.'

'There must be something very important in that letter for your mother to want you to ensure it reaches her personally.'

Lexi agreed.

'Have you read it?'

Lexi was shocked that she would suggest it. 'Of course not. It was given to me sealed.' Lexi had a question. 'Do you know why she stopped writing?'

Hazel leaned forward in her seat and placed her elbows on the table. She stared pensively at Lexi. 'She became a recluse.'

'How come?'

'I think something happened to her family. The last time I spoke with her she said it was a tragedy. She wouldn't go into detail, but she said that she couldn't write anymore. She didn't see the point. And that was the last I heard from her.'

Lexi frowned. 'Do you have her last known address?'

'I'm afraid not. She was very private. Rarely did interviews. I spoke with her on the phone occasionally in the past, and we corresponded by post. All her mail was sent to a Post Office box.'

'What does that mean?'

'Ah, basically it means correspondence is delivered to the post office for you to collect rather than direct to your home address.'

'So, it's a way of keeping your home address private.'

Hazel nodded. 'That's correct. I haven't heard from her in an age.'

'Do you think she's ... dead?'

'Who knows.' Hazel breathed a sigh. She leaned back in her chair and opened a drawer, rummaging inside. 'I paid her a visit once.'

Lexi leaned forward in her seat. 'You did?'

'It was strange.'

'How so?'

'Hold on, I just want to see if I can find ...'

Lexi wondered what she was looking for.

She opened several drawers in her desk. 'Now, where did I put it?'

Lexi sat with bated breath, hoping she had an old address.

'I wonder if it's in one of these ...'

Lexi watched Hazel stand up and peruse the bookshelves behind her. She held up a finger, then reached for a book. 'I knew I'd kept it!' She turned around with a book in her hand. Lexi saw the name of the author on the front cover – it was Margot Dorey. Lexi noticed something poking out of the top. It wasn't a bookmark.

Hazel resumed her seat. 'This is one of her books.'

Lexi nodded. She watched Hazel open the book and take something out.

'Is that her address?'

'As I said, she became something of a recluse. I think she was always a bit ... eccentric.'

'Okay,' said Lexi slowly, wondering where this was leading.

'This is where she lived.'

Lexi grinned. 'So, you do have her address.'

'Well, no, not in a manner of speaking. Here, this was where she was living when I met up with her once.'

Lexi looked at Hazel as she passed her the photo that she'd found in one of her books.

'I don't have the address, but I do have this. It's a photo of her and the houseboat.'

'She lives on a houseboat?' Lexi stared at the photo.

'I can't guarantee she'll still be there, but at least it's something. Sorry, I'm not the best at taking photos. It didn't help that she moved when I snapped the picture, so she's a bit of a blur. I do remember she didn't want her photo taken. I promised it was just a keepsake for me, and that it wouldn't go anywhere.'

Hazel reached for the photo.

'No, wait!' Lexi moved it out of her reach. She got out her phone and took a picture. She looked up at Hazel as she passed it back to her. 'Technically, it hasn't gone anywhere.'

'That's true.' She smiled at Lexi.

Lexi stared at her phone. Margot Dorey was standing on the towpath. Behind her was a houseboat. It was narrow, painted in dark green with little port windows. There were flowers in pots on the roof, and something written on the side in swirly red writing.

'What sort of boat is that?'

'It's called a narrowboat. They used to transport coal and

goods up and down the canal waterways in Britain up until the seventies. Some of them were converted into homes for people to live in, like this one. You can rent them for a holiday too, in different parts of the country, and travel up and down the canals.'

'Where was this taken?'

'Walberswick.'

'Walberswick? Where's that?'

'It's on the Suffolk Coast.'

'Suffolk?'

'Yes. Lovely part of the world.'

'Is it far from London?'

'Not at all. I think it's a gem of a county, overlooked by Londoners, who tend to head down to Brighton and places like that. They don't know what they're missing.'

Lexi was a little lost with the conversation. She had no idea where Brighton was.

Hazel shook her head. 'Sorry, you have no idea what I'm talking about. But my point is, the Suffolk Coast is stunning. Fifty miles of coastline designated an AONB.'

Lexi looked at her blankly.

'Ah, that means it's an Area of Outstanding Natural Beauty. There are amazing heathlands to walk and little seaside towns like Aldeburgh, Southold and Thorpeness nearby along the heritage coast. It's got everything. I love it so much, I'm planning to retire there.' She smiled. 'Look, even if you go there and can't find her, I'd recommend it for a holiday in any case, as a change from London. How long are you over here for?'

'A fortnight, give or take.'

'Well, there you go. You must visit and stay for a week. You won't regret it.'

'How do I get there?'

'Take the Greater Anglia service from London Liverpool Street. You can get to Liverpool Street on the tube, the Central

Line. Then it's about an hour or so to Ipswich. Remember to change at Ipswich for the little train on the East Suffolk Line.'

Lexi stared at her. 'Little train?'

'That's what I call it. It's a train with just two or three carriages.'

Lexi raised her eyebrows. 'Two or three carriages?' That was what she'd remembered when she had been talking to the couple with the two children on her flight. She suddenly had a memory of a train journey that sounded peculiarly like this one.

'Yes, but don't let that put you off, it's a very scenic train journey through some beautiful unspoilt Suffolk countryside all the way to the Victorian seaside resort of Lowestoft. Be sure to look out of the window, you'll be rewarded with lovely views of rivers and estuaries – not to mention heath and woodland,' said Hazel, enthusiastically.

Lexi got the impression that Hazel had taken the little train many times.

'The train calls at Suffolk market towns like Woodbridge, Saxmundham and Halesworth. The train journey does go on to Beccles where the route crosses the Carlton Marshes Nature Reserve, but you won't be going that far.'

'What station should I get off at?'

'I'm afraid there isn't a train station in Walberswick. If you get off the train at Halesworth then you can get a bus or taxi from the station. Sorry, I'm not sure what bus you get, although I believe there is one every half an hour or so that connects with the train, but with luggage it's probably best to take a taxi. In a little over two hours you'll be there.'

But where was *there* exactly, thought Lexi. 'How do I find the houseboat?'

'The easiest way to find the quay where the houseboats are moored in Walberswick is to walk from the neighbouring larger town, Southwold. I'd get a taxi there if I were you. The quay is right next door, just the other side of the river. Walk through the town, along the beach with very pretty beach huts, and keep going. It's not far. You'll come to the small working harbour with fishing boats and a rather nice pub. Just cross over the footbridge and there you are. Just the other side is the pretty little village of Walberswick and the quay where the boats are moored.'

'Thank you.' Lexi frowned. 'Will I have a problem finding somewhere to stay, do you think?' She was aware that it was the school summer holidays in England, and she imagined, by the sound of the area, that it would be popular with tourists.

'Ah, that's why I suggested that you head to Southwold rather than Walberswick. I recommend staying in Southwold. It's larger and there will be more holiday accommodation. It's a lovely place, by the way. There are several hotels in the centre of the town. There's bed and breakfast accommodation too, and holiday cottages for rent. I wouldn't be surprised if there's even a houseboat you could hire on the quay in Walberswick.'

'Oh, I don't think I'll do that,' Lexi blurted. Her dream – or rather her nightmare – suddenly came to mind; she was in a boat, and she was desperately holding out her hand, trying to save someone from drowning, but they had disappeared under the water. In her dream, Lexi couldn't see their face, but she knew it was a child, and that she had been a child too. She shuddered.

Hazel noticed. 'Lexi, are you okay?'

'Oh, yes. Sure. I was just thinking, do you remember the name of the houseboat?' Lexi glanced at the picture on her phone. Try as she might, the image was blurry, and she couldn't make out the name.

'Ah, yes. It's pretty hard to forget.' Hazel held up the book in her hands.

Lexi read the book title. *The Hideaway*.

'It was her first book.'

'She named her boat after her book?'

'That's an interesting question. I don't know which came first.

You'd have to ask her, if she's still there.' Hazel looked at the book in her hands. 'Here. I want you to have this.'

'Oh, I couldn't possibly ...'

Hazel smiled. 'How funny, you sounded very English all of a sudden.'

Lexi grinned. 'Did I? I was born here, but I left to with my mum and sister to live in America when my father passed away.'

Hazel said, 'Oh, I'm so sorry, Lexi.'

'Yes, so am I. I didn't want to go.' She sighed heavily. 'That's all in the past now.'

'Is it?' Hazel asked. Then she thrust the book at her. 'Take it. Your mum obviously had a connection with the writer. I know it's a children's book, but it's set on the Suffolk Coast. I think it would make interesting reading. Even if you don't enjoy the story, it will give you some idea of what to expect when you arrive. Her descriptions of the Suffolk Coast are quite spot on.'

Lexi took the book and leafed through the pages. She had been expecting large print, and more pictures that words, not a full-blown novel. She looked up in surprise.

'Yes, it's the length of a Harry Potter novel. A lot of adults used to read her books – still do.'

Lexi noticed the book was illustrated with beautifully drawn pictures at the beginning of each chapter.

'You've got a two-hour journey ahead of you. Give it a go. You might enjoy it.'

Hazel got out of her seat too. 'As I said, it's been years. I can't imagine she's still there. But if you do find her, you'll be sure to give her my message? We'd be over the moon to work with her again.'

Lexi nodded. 'I will.' She turned to go.

'There's something else.'

Lexi turned back.

'If she does have a manuscript, I'll give you ... let's call it a finder's fee if she agrees to write another book for us.'

'Okay.' Lexi would rather a job at a publisher, but she didn't want to come across as ungrateful. 'Thank you, Hazel. And if a job were to come up here ...' She wasn't sure what she'd do if one did. But as Hazel had said, there was no chance that would happen.

'Well, we'd certainly need more hands on board if we were getting our star writer back.'

Lexi stared at her and grinned.

Hazel tempered her enthusiasm when she said, 'She wasn't happy when I just turned up. That was when that photo was taken. It was her birthday. I wanted to give her a surprise. It didn't exactly work out. As I said before, she's a bit of a recluse, so don't expect a warm reception if she is still living at the houseboat by the quay when you turn up out of the blue.'

Lexi frowned, aware that it was exactly what she'd be doing.

15

'Excuse me. Have you got the time?'

Lexi had been walking down the street when a young woman stopped her.

'Oh, yes – sure.'

She'd just got out her mobile phone to check the time when a young man bumped into the woman, sending her careering into Lexi.

Lexi's handbag went flying.

The young woman bent down and picked up her bag. 'Here – I'm so sorry.'

Lexi smiled. 'No harm done. It's eleven-thirty by the way.'

'Oh, er … thanks.'

Lexi glanced at the young woman, who took off at a pace down the street. Lexi guessed she was late for something. She shrugged and slipped her phone into the back pocket of her jeans. 'God, is that the time?' She had chatted to Hazel at Grosvenor Publishers for longer than she'd realised. She had to get back to the hotel to check out of her room and leave her luggage with reception.

Lexi quickened her pace. It was only a ten-minute walk. She'd been heading back that way, taking her time looking at the amazing architecture in Bloomsbury, when the young woman had stopped her to ask for the time. She did think it a bit odd. *Who doesn't have a phone?* she thought. *Perhaps her battery had died.*

Lexi retraced her steps back to the hotel as she mulled over what the immensely helpful Hazel had told her. Lexi had discovered she couldn't phone or email this lady at her houseboat. It meant a visit out of the blue. By the sound of things, if she was still there – which Lexi doubted – she imagined she would not get a warm welcome. She really didn't care. All she wanted to do was fulfil her mother's wish to deliver the envelope. It didn't matter whether the lady was welcoming or not, as long as she had the opportunity to put it in her hand.

As she walked, Lexi recalled that Hazel had mentioned a PO box. If she couldn't find Margot Dorey, then she already had a Plan B in the making. She decided she'd have to call on Hazel again and ask if she still had that PO box address so that she could post it. She could put the publishing house as a return address on the envelope in case it wasn't delivered. She was sure Hazel wouldn't mind, considering that Margot might have closed down the PO box in the years since she last wrote a book, or might have passed away.

The only thing was that if she didn't meet her, she wouldn't have the opportunity to find out who she had been to her mother, or what was so important about that letter. It did occur to her, though, as she skipped up the stone steps of the hotel, that Margot Dorey might not tell her a thing, even if she did meet her. By the sound of what Hazel had said, she most likely wouldn't be that approachable. Why would she divulge the contents of a personal letter to a stranger, even if that stranger was the daughter of the woman who had written to her, and had travelled so far to find her? Andrea came to mind. She felt like calling her and telling her about the visit to the publisher that morning, and what she had found out so far. She knew what Andrea would say: *You always overthink things. Just go and see if you can find her first.*

Lexi took the lift up to the next floor. She wouldn't phone Andrea, not now. It was only about six-thirty in the morning back in Connecticut. Besides, she didn't have time to make the call because she had to vacate her room.

Lexi had hardly unpacked, so it took her no time at all to gather her things and wheel the case out of her room. She pulled the door to with her foot. It clicked shut.

Lexi threw her coat over her arm and her handbag over one shoulder. Pulling her case behind her, she walked down the corridor to the elevator. She had to remind herself that in England it wasn't an elevator but a lift. A moment later, she was back at reception. She handed them her room key. 'Can you store my luggage, please? I have a different room booked for tonight.' It was a different receptionist at the desk.

'Of course.' He smiled as he walked around the desk to fetch the luggage. 'We have a room back here.' He pointed to a door behind reception with a keypad entry.

'Thank you.'

With her luggage safely stowed behind the locked door, he returned to the front desk and looked at the computer screen. 'I see you have a junior suite booked for tonight. Check-in time is three, but if your room is ready earlier, we can contact you. We have your mobile phone number.'

'Thank you. I'll pay when I leave,' said Lexi. There was a queue behind her of people wanting to check out, and she didn't want to hold them up while she counted out all those notes. Besides, it was all rather embarrassing. Tomorrow morning she'd just use her bank card.

'Of course.' He smiled again. 'Is there anything else I can help you with?'

'I just had a quick question. Could you also book me a ticket on a train from Liverpool Street Station to Halesworth in Suffolk for tomorrow, if there is any availability?' Lexi assumed that she would only need one ticket for her entire journey, even though there was one change. 'And can you add that to my bill?'

'That will not be a problem. Is there any particular time you would like to travel?'

'Say around ten?'

'A wise choice. It will be more expensive travelling before nine, and busy with commuters.'

Lexi hadn't thought of that. 'Thank you.'

'Would you like a single or return?'

Lexi hadn't thought of that either, but she would need to return to London to catch her flight from Heathrow. 'A return ticket please.'

'I'll leave it in an envelope on reception.'

'Oh, that's very kind of you, but I can collect the tickets when I check out and settle my bill.'

'Okay, but if you change your mind, I will get them booked today and leave them here.'

'Fine.' Lexi smiled at the extremely helpful receptionist. She peered at his nametag. She'd be sure to leave Emmanuel a generous tip before she left. 'Just one more thing. Can you point me in the direction of the British Museum?'

'The main entrance to the museum is on Great Russell Street or there is an entrance on Montague Place, both are close. Would you like a street map?'

'A street map would be really helpful,' Lexi replied.

The receptionist reached below the counter and found a tourist map of London which he handed to Lexi. 'Do you know that the British Museum was the first public national museum in the world?'

Lexi shook her head. 'No, I did not.'

'Yes, it's got one of the most comprehensive collections in the world, some eight million artefacts. You won't be disappointed.'

Lexi smiled. 'Thank you for the map.'

'You're welcome.'

She picked her handbag off the desk and walked out of the hotel. This time she walked through Russell Square gardens, cutting straight across the gardens diagonally to exit through a gate on the other side. Five minutes later, she passed some tacky souvenir shops and saw the grand entrance to the huge museum. There was a long queue snaking down the street.

Lexi sighed and joined the queue. It wasn't like she had anywhere else to be. As she waited, she thought about catching the train tomorrow. She couldn't wait to see the Suffolk Coast. From what Hazel had described, the county sounded like one big holiday area.

As much as she was enjoying her time in London, it was still a city, like New York, like Hartford in Connecticut where she had grown up. This didn't particularly feel like a holiday. She was going to take Hazel's advice and have a holiday at the British seaside, seeing some of the little towns and villages dotted up the coast. After all, when she returned home she'd be straight into job-hunting, and if she failed to find a position in New York, she'd return to Hartford and join the family business. Her grandpa would expect her to start work straight away.

Lexi frowned at the thought. Her mood lightened when another thought occurred to her. What if she could find Margot Dorey and persuade her to write another book for Hazel? Wouldn't that just be the best, if she could get a finder's fee, like Hazel promised, and even be taken on at Hazel's company as a marketing manager or whatever Hazel wanted her to do? She wouldn't be picky. Even if it was just temporary, she thought that would be okay.

Despite feeling a mixture of emotions since she'd arrived in England, being elated, then starting to feel homesick and lonely the previous night, she'd felt entirely different in the morning after a good night's sleep and a hearty breakfast. So much so that she felt she would welcome the chance to stay in England longer.

She suddenly felt she had nothing to return to America for. She and Brandon were over. She didn't want to return to New York and that apartment. It held too many memories. What she needed, she realised, was a fresh start. She looked about her and wondered whether England could be her fresh start.

16

'Did you have a good time at the museum, madam?'

Emmanuel was still on reception when Lexi returned. The museum had been better than she had expected. The building alone had been worth the visit, the exhibit halls well laid out. She hadn't expected there to be so much to see. She could understand why people might return time and again. She'd focused on just two galleries, chosen at random.

One in particular had drawn her in because the artefacts had been discovered in a place called Sutton Hoo in Suffolk. Lexi spent some time reading about how Edith Pretty, a landowner, along with an archaeologist called Basil Brown, had uncovered some spectacular treasures dating back to early Anglo-Saxon England. Over a coffee in the restaurant, Lexi had done a Google search on her phone to see if the place was anywhere near Southwold, as she felt she would like to make a visit. Although only forty-five minutes away from Southwold, it would mean a special trip. She decided she wouldn't fit it in on this trip.

Lexi had entered the museum from Great Russell Street. As soon as she stepped inside and saw the Great Court, with its massive domed ceiling and the helpful information points, café and bookshop, she remembered the museum. She'd been there before. It didn't surprise her. Both her parents loved culture and had always taken them to museums, art galleries and the theatre. Her mum had continued to do this when they had moved to Hartford. Of course, the museums weren't like this, Lexi thought as she'd walked through the galleries. She remembered one particular visit, just her and her father. She imagined that the trip stood out because it had just been the two of them, and he'd probably bought her too many sweets and spoilt her rotten.

She recalled that her sister was a toddler at the time, so Lexi imagined she would have been around four or five years old. It was no surprise that they would have left her mum and sister at home, on occasion, and come together. Maybe it wasn't just that Andrea was younger. Perhaps it was because Lexi was his favourite, and so he had taken her out on adventures in London. At least, that was what Lexi liked to think. Although she imagined that their dad had most likely spent just the same amount of time with Andrea, if he had, her sister would have been too young to remember.

She stopped at the reception desk and replied to Emmanuel's question. 'Oh, yes. I had a wonderful time, thank you.' It was in part due to the fact that childhood memories of her time there were resurfacing.

'Well, that's just wonderful.' He reached under the desk. 'Oh, here.' He passed her an envelope. 'These are your train tickets. You are booked on the ten-thirty train on the Greater Anglia service from Liverpool Street. There is one change, though, at Ipswich. I bought you a return ticket. I hope that was correct.'

'That's just perfect.'

'It's an open ticket, so you can travel back to London when you want.'

It hadn't occurred to her that she'd need to decide when she would return to London. Lexi grinned. 'You've thought of everything.'

Lexi was about to reach in her bag for her purse. 'I must give you a tip.'

He shook his head. 'I'm afraid we do not accept tips here.'

'Oh, okay.' Lexi tried not to let it spoil her day that the young man who had helped her with her luggage had not mentioned that. Perhaps he didn't want to hurt her feelings. Maybe he needed the money. Or he had sniggered behind her back, thinking, *stupid American tourist.*

She glanced over her shoulder and happened to make eye contact with the same young man, who was helping another guest to the lift with their luggage.

'Is everything all right?'

Lexi saw him staring at her. She caught his anxious expression. He was no doubt afraid that she might mention the tip. Lexi turned back to the man on reception. 'Everything is just fine, thank you.'

Lexi had no idea what it was like to depend on a wage. She'd always had her allowance to fall back on. But that didn't mean she couldn't put herself in the young man's shoes. She expected that one word from her could mean the end of his job there. She wouldn't do that. But she knew some people would have no such qualms.

She imagined that young man had been thinking that twenty pounds was nothing to someone who had the money to pay upwards of four hundred pounds for one night at a swanky hotel. It was probably more than he took home in a week.

'Thank you for the tickets.'

'I've added them to your bill.'

Lexi smiled. 'Excellent. Thank you.'

'You're welcome. Here's your room key for one of the junior suites on the third floor. I'm afraid this one doesn't overlook the gardens, and it is a little snug compared to the master suite.'

'I'm sure it will be absolutely fine.'

'Good, good. We've already had your luggage taken up to your room.'

'Great, thanks.' Lexi was relieved she wouldn't run into the young man again. Although she had the cash, and access to her allowance, she didn't particularly want to part with another ten pounds. She wanted to save some of the cash to buy her sister some souvenirs.

She hadn't bought anything at the British Museum, not even lunch. Lexi hadn't been hungry after such a huge breakfast. And the souvenirs she'd wanted to purchase could wait until she returned to London. It would mean less to carry on her travels.

Lexi returned to her room to change for dinner. Her trip, so far, was going better than expected. Although she didn't have a residential address for Margot Dorey, she had found out her last known address – even though it wasn't quite what she expected. She had not anticipated that a wealthy author would live on a houseboat.

From what Hazel had said about the eccentric writer, Lexi thought her living arrangements actually made sense. She couldn't wait until tomorrow to find out if Margot Dorey was still there.

17

Lexi woke early the following morning in the junior suite, which she liked better than her previous room. It was small, but cosy. The moment she woke up, she wanted to call her sister and tell her how things were going, and where she was off to that day.

Lexi momentarily forgot the five-hour time difference. She reached for her phone and knocked it and her handbag off the bedside table. She rolled her eyes as she got out of bed and discovered the contents of her bag were littering the floor. She picked up her phone and tossed it on her bed, remembering that it was around two in the morning in Connecticut. She scooped up her lipstick, eyeliner, two pens, a comb, a small pack of handwipes, and her travel-sized hand gel. She cursed under her breath as she continued to pick up stuff littering the carpet, wondering why she carried around so much crap in her bag.

Lexi retrieved the letter addressed to Margot Dorey, which had almost disappeared under the bed. 'That wouldn't do at all,' she commented at the thought that she might have lost it. She tucked it safely in her handbag. 'That's odd.' She looked about her. She glanced inside her handbag, looking for her purse.

She got down on her hands and knees and glanced under the bed. Her purse was brown; it would be easy to overlook on the brown carpet, especially if she'd inadvertently kicked it under the bed as she picked up her stuff. It wasn't under the bed.

That wasn't all she couldn't find. The paper wallet containing all her cash was missing too.

Lexi stood up, thinking, *They were in my bag just a moment ago … weren't they?*

After a thorough look all around the room and a frantic search through the pockets of her coat, her backpack, and inside her case, Lexi realised they weren't anywhere in the room.

She sat back down on the bed and tried to remember the last time she had seen her purse and the wallet containing the cash. It didn't take long. 'I was in Hazel's office yesterday morning. That's right. I showed her the letter.' Lexi spoke out loud as she recounted the events. She recalled it was annoying that the letter had been right at the bottom of her handbag and she'd had to shift her purse and the money out of the way to reach it.

'So, I had my purse and the cash when I left Hazel's office.'

Lexi continued to backtrack over the events of the previous day when it suddenly dawned on her. 'Oh, no.' She put her hand to her mouth, shocked. 'I've been mugged.'

At first she couldn't believe it. The young woman who had asked her for the time had seemed so innocent and polite. Then a man had bumped into the young woman, and Lexi recalled her handbag flying out of her hands. But as far as she had been aware at the time, nothing had fallen out of her bag.

She hadn't looked in her bag since the young woman had kindly picked it up and handed it back to her. But her back had been turned for a split second – time enough for the young woman to undo the clasp and grab her purse and the wallet full of cash, but not enough time to do the bag back up properly. Lexi raised her eyebrows. That explained why, when she'd just pushed it off the bedside table, the contents had all spilled out. Lexi had kept her phone in her back pocket. There had been no reason at all to look in her handbag yesterday.

'Oh, no,' she said again. Lexi could feel her heart pounding in her chest. Nothing like this had ever happened to her before. 'Now what am I going to do?'

She tried to remain calm and collect her thoughts. She had a hotel room to pay for. And she'd booked her onward accommodation in Southwold in Suffolk, in a lovely little bed and breakfast on the sea front. A bit of a change from the grand London hotel in Bloomsbury, but the guest reviews had sounded wonderful.

She shook her head. *How am I going to pay for all this?* She remembered to breathe slowly. She looked at her phone. There was nothing to worry about. Although she had no bank cards and no cash, one phone call to Andrea was all it would take. Andrea could pay for the hotel stay over the phone. Hopefully, under the circumstances, if Andrea paid more than the room rate, they would be able to give her the difference in cash to tide her over for a few days.

'Problem solved!' she said out loud. *There's nothing to worry about. All I have to do is get in touch with Andrea*, she thought. She knew she had to contact the bank to cancel her cards, but first she quickly dialled her sister's number. Andrea would be really concerned when she found out her sister, who was thousands of miles away, had been mugged and had no access to money. She knew that her sister would sort things out straight away.

As soon as Andrea answered her phone, and she'd explained the situation, she'd quickly get dressed and high-tail it down to reception where she could pay the bill and, fingers crossed, arrange some cashback. Right now, it was the only solution, otherwise she didn't know what she'd do. Lexi sighed. She'd have no option but to go to the American Embassy for help. Or phone her grandparents.

'Oh come on, Andrea – pick up the phone!'

18

Lexi wasn't feeling very hungry. When she hadn't gone down to breakfast, the concierge had rung her room and insisted they send up a breakfast tray. Under any other circumstances, if she'd been unwell, or had slept in late, she would have welcomed their attentive concern – but not today.

Lexi sat moving the scrambled egg around her plate. With bread, cheese, fruit, yoghurt, little cakes, and croissants, she decided to make up a sandwich and take the fruit, little yoghurt pot and all the other items, including the little butters, jam and sachets of and sugar with her. It would come in handy as she couldn't buy herself lunch.

She frowned as she buttered two slices of bread and slapped two slices of Edam cheese in between. *What a ridiculous situation to find myself in, abroad, thousands of miles from home, with no access to money*, she thought. And her sister wasn't answering her phone.

She wasn't failing to answer the phone on purpose. Lexi knew that. It hadn't gone to voicemail, so the phone couldn't have been switched off. She imagined that Andrea had left it downstairs when she went to bed the previous night and hadn't heard it ringing. Lexi cringed. Perhaps it was just as well. Once again, Lexi had forgotten the time difference. It was the early hours in Connecticut, and her sister would have been fast asleep. Lexi knew she'd have to wait until midday or thereabouts until Andrea woke up and discovered the missed calls from her sister.

Lexi frowned. She really didn't want to phone her grandparents. She looked at the time. It was only nine in the morning. She was checking out early so that she would make it to the train station in time for her train. She considered her options. She'd left a message on her sister's mobile phone but, forgetting the time difference, had been cagey about what she'd said in case Andrea was showing people around a property, or she was with Mitch, or her grandparents or even Chad.

It was all too embarrassing to spell out in a phone message. And no one knew she was in England except Andrea. So Lexi had just said, 'I've run into a problem, and I really, really need you to call me when you get this.'

Lexi decided she was not phoning her grandparents for the sake of waiting for Andrea to pick up on her message and give her a call. She stared at her phone, scrolled through her address book, and stopped at Mitch. After his reaction when she'd mentioned her intention to go to England, she discounted him immediately. That left Brandon.

Lexi shook her head. 'No, way!' He was the last person she'd want to contact. Besides, what made her think he'd have the money to pay her hotel bill? She'd given him five hundred dollars just the other week to help clear his credit card, only a few days before she'd found out he was cheating on her.

She didn't have anybody else, besides family, to phone. She imagined most people in her shoes might have a best friend to call, another young woman whom they could confide in. But Brandon was her best friend, and his group of friends had become hers. Over the years, since leaving school, nothing had changed. She'd met other students at university, but not formed the sort of close relationship she'd had with him. She hadn't thought what that would mean if they ever broke up. The possibility that they wouldn't be together forever had never entered her head.

Lexi swallowed her pride and rang his number. She didn't know how he could help, but she desperately wanted to speak to him, to tell him what had happened. Although her sister wouldn't be awake, Lexi knew her ex-boyfriend might – he might be at a gig or writing another song. Or shagging his new girlfriend.

Lexi's eyes went wide. She immediately ended the call.

A moment later, her phone rang. *Andrea!* That was her first thought. Perhaps she'd got up in the night to use the loo and had checked her phone.

Lexi frowned when she realised it wasn't Andrea. 'I might have known.' She took a deep breath, and despite her misgivings, answered her phone.

'Lexi? Did you just call me?'

'Yes.'

'Is everything all right?'

Lexi stared into space. What a stupid, dumb question was that? Her soulmate was gone, and he had the bloody cheek to ask her *Is everything all right?*

'Oh, sorry – look, that was a really dumb thing to say.'

'Yes, it was.' Lexi wiped a tear from her cheek. It was so good to hear his voice. Too good. It was hard to believe they'd split up. She'd only been gone three days, but it seemed like forever since they'd spoken. *I miss you*, was on the tip of her tongue.

'What's wrong, Lexi?'

Tears rolled down her face. *You found someone else, that's what's wrong.*

'Who are you talking to, Brandon?'

Lexi swallowed when she heard a woman's muffled voice, and the sound of someone moving around under sheets.

'It's no one. Go back to sleep.'

Lexi's hand flew to her mouth as she stifled a sob. She ended the call immediately and threw her phone across the room.

Fortunately it hit an upholstered chair, bounced off a cushion and landed on the carpeted floor. That would be all she needed – to smash her phone.

Lexi stood up and walked over to pick it up. As she reached for it, it rang. She knew who was on the end of the line. Lexi switched it off and returned to the little table in the sitting room of her suite. She opened her handbag to slip her phone inside and saw the envelope with her train tickets inside.

She sat back down at the table and got out the return tickets. Scrutinising them, she discovered Emmanuel had not only booked her a return ticket on the mainline Great Anglia service, but there was a separate ticket for the London Underground. Lexi could have cried. She had all that she needed to make it to her next destination, including lunch.

There was still the issue of paying for the hotel bill. Lexi glanced at the clock on the wall. By the time she arrived in Walberswick, Andrea would be up, and she would have checked her phone and got her message. If Lexi had the number of the hotel to hand, then all her sister would have to do was contact the hotel and pay the bill by card over the phone. It meant Lexi wouldn't get to have any cash on her – assuming they would have given her cashback if her sister had overpaid the bill – but that could be arranged when she arrived at the bed and breakfast in Southwold. It meant she'd have to walk out of the hotel without settling the bill, but she knew that was her only option under the circumstances.

Her sister would be in touch and would pay the hotel bill that day, so it wasn't as though she would technically be skipping town without paying. It would just have to be paid later in the day. *But would they accept that and let her just leave?* She doubted it. Lexi looked at the train tickets. She really wanted to catch her train that day.

She walked into the bathroom, ran some cold water and sluiced her face. She caught sight of her reflection in the bathroom mirror. Her eyes were puffy from crying. Lexi went to fetch her makeup bag and used a concealer pen to hide the black rings under her eyes. It was a start. She hadn't had a good night's sleep. There was nothing wrong with the bed. It had been just as comfortable as the one in the master suite.

The problem wasn't the bed, but her dreams. One dream in particular had felt so real that Lexi could still recall what it was. She blamed it on the conversation with Hazel about the blasted houseboat. It was the same dream she'd had when she'd nodded off in the taxi on the way from the airport. The one she'd recalled when she'd been sitting in Hazel's office.

She brushed it aside for now, returned to the breakfast tray and packed up all the food she hadn't eaten into her backpack. Grasping the handle of her suitcase, she popped on her coat and with one last glance around the room got ready to leave. She was not looking forward to this.

Lexi was counting on the reception desk being busy. The hotel was full. Surely, with only one or two receptionists manning the desk, there would be a queue. Would they notice her stealing past and out of the door? Emmanuel might. He'd remember booking her train tickets. But would he be working this morning? She hoped not.

19

'Well, here goes.' Lexi opened her door and looked up and down the hallway. She was about to step out when she looked at the key card in her hand. Normally, she would have handed it in at reception when she checked out. She had a thought. Rather than just leaving without paying, wouldn't it be better to leave a note explaining that her sister would phone later in the day and settle the bill? At some point that morning, when they looked on the system and realised she hadn't checked out, someone on reception would phone her room. When they got no answer, they'd send someone upstairs to knock on her door.

Lexi found the little notepad and pen on the bedside table and hastily wrote a note. She looked about her and decided to leave it on the small table in the sitting room area with the key card. Either the reception staff or the cleaners would come across it.

She felt much better now about leaving. It occurred to her that they probably wouldn't mind her hanging about in one of their lounges for the morning until her sister phoned and paid the bill. The train tickets could be reorganised for later in the day. She didn't want to waste half a day of her holiday effectively under house arrest until her bill was paid, but that was Plan B if she couldn't sneak past reception. Lexi glanced over her shoulder at the note and checked she had everything, because once the door shut behind her she wouldn't be able to access the room. She stepped out into the hall and hurried towards the lift. Her heart pounded in her chest as the lift took her down to the ground floor. She prayed that there was a queue at reception and that Emmanuel wasn't working – or that if he was, he'd be too busy to notice her as she walked past.

Lexi took a deep breath as the lift doors opened. Her eyes darted to the reception desk. There was a queue. 'Oh, thank god!' Lexi murmured. She'd just stepped out when the young man who had taken her suitcase up to her room appeared.

'I don't need any help,' Lexi said, thinking, *please go away.* She averted her gaze when she heard him speak. 'Look, about the tips. I shouldn't have taken them. It's against the rules. I don't want to get into trouble.'

Lexi caught one of the receptionists, who was busy with a guest, briefly glance her way. *Damn.* But it didn't appear that Emmanuel was on reception. Who was to say she hadn't settled up already?

She turned to the young man, who was still following her. She stopped. 'Look, it doesn't matter. I won't tell anyone.'

'Okay, but I'd just feel a lot better if I gave you the money back.'

Lexi opened her mouth, about to refuse the offer, when it occurred to her that she had no cash whatsoever or access to any until her sister phoned. And when she did, they'd have to work out how to get her some money. Which reminded her – she really had to contact her bank and cancel her cards. She still hoped that she could get some cashback when her sister paid for her next stay at the bed and breakfast in Southwold. Failing that, Andrea would have to post out some travellers' cheques. That wasn't ideal; they would take too long to arrive. At least she had her plane ticket home, and it was a flexi-ticket. Not that she wanted to cut her trip short.

There was another option. She thought of what Hazel had said about a finder's fee. If she could find Margot Dorey and persuade her to write another book, then the fee, whatever that might be, would be hers. She knew that she was getting way ahead of herself, but it was a nice thought. If she could have a job too, that would be even better.

Lexi suddenly noticed they were attracting attention from other guests passing by the lift. She looked at the notes the young man had thrust at her. He was attempting to give her money back. In any other circumstance, Lexi would have refused. She felt terribly embarrassed taking the money, even though she now realised he'd taken advantage of her.

Lexi stuffed the notes in her coat pocket. 'Thanks.'

'Can I help you to the taxi with your bags?'

'Er, no. I'm not taking a taxi.'

'Okay. Well, let me help you to the door.' He reached for her suitcase.

'No, really. I can manage myself.'

'It really is no trouble.'

Lexi could envisage a tussle breaking out and very reluctantly gave in. But she distanced herself from the young man wheeling her suitcase out of the door. He was quick about it. Lexi followed at a discreet distance, glancing about her, ignoring the young man with her luggage.

It was a silly ruse because at least one of the reception staff, and some of the guests milling about in the foyer, had clocked her talking to him. But she did it anyway in the hope that it wasn't obvious she was leaving and that she looked like just another guest going out for the day.

She avoided glancing at anyone on reception, but with the hotel full and a queue at the desk, she doubted they'd remember without checking the system who she was and when she was due to leave.

Even so, despite reassuring herself she wouldn't get caught, her stomach churned all the way to the door. It seemed to take forever to get there, even though it was a matter a seconds before she was standing outside with her case.

She had the sudden impulse to give the young man the money back. Instead, she compromised and gave him half, leaning forward to say thank you and slipping a ten-pound note into his jacket pocket as he turned to go. She had a feeling he'd still refuse, and she didn't fancy attracting attention with another altercation on the front steps. She just wanted him to take the money and go.

She still had ten pounds. It wouldn't go far, but she had her tube and rail fares, and a hotel booked with an evening meal to look forward to. And she had a packed lunch for a picnic on the beach when she arrived. She knew she shouldn't, but she thought she'd treat herself to a takeaway coffee on the train.

Lexi suddenly realised she was standing on the front steps and could be seen by the reception staff inside.

She took her case down the steps to the street. 'Now, which way to the tube station?' Lexi wasn't sure, but she couldn't hang around there any longer. It was check-out time, and they'd soon discover that one of their guests was nowhere to be found.

Lexi walked at a pace in a random direction. She stopped a passer-by and asked for the nearest tube station. Russell Square tube station was in the other direction. Lexi had to walk back the way she came. She avoided the hotel and walked down a street parallel to Montague Place. The station was exceptionally busy, but she still looked over her shoulder, expecting a member of the hotel staff, or the police, to turn up any minute. The trouble was that Emmanuel had bought the train tickets for her onward journey. She'd only feel relaxed when she was on the Greater Anglia train, by which time she hoped her sister would have called and arranged to settle her bill.

20

Lexi finished the last of her takeaway coffee, which was now lukewarm. She brushed the crumbs from her lap. The croissant she'd just eaten that she'd brought from her morning breakfast tray had been delicious.

Lexi stared out of the train window. The London suburbs had given way to rolling countryside some time earlier. She hadn't expected the hour-long train journey to Ipswich to be so scenic. Apart from a couple of stops in Chelmsford and Colchester, the rest of the journey took in rolling fields, scenic little towns and even a lake – or perhaps it was a reservoir. There was a lovely little town beyond the lake in the distance that Lexi would have liked to visit, although she had no idea what town it was. She spotted a church spire and honey-coloured brick houses in the distance, but the train didn't stop there.

She turned from the window and looked at her phone. She frowned. Very soon the train would pull into the next station, where she would get the little train to Halesworth. So far, Andrea had not phoned her back. Lexi did a quick mental calculation, working out the time in Connecticut. Although it was Thursday, a workday, would Andrea be up yet?

Lexi had held off phoning her again while she was waiting to board the train at Liverpool Street Station. It was noisy and crowded, and she doubted her sister would hear her even if she answered her phone.

She had intended to try her luck and phone on the train, but now she had the opposite dilemma; it was way too quiet, even though the carriage was packed. Everyone would hear her private and rather embarrassing phone conversation, not to mention the fact that she'd have to spell out that she'd skipped town without paying her hotel bill.

Lexi shook her head and put her phone away. There was an announcement that the train was approaching Ipswich Station. She got up from her seat. Her case was stored in a little compartment opposite the toilets.

Lexi took her case from the rack and joined a queue near the doors. When she stepped out of the train, she noticed some people who were on her train were running down the platform. Lexi raised an eyebrow. What was the rush? Unless your connection was leaving in ten minutes, and was sitting on the platform across the tracks.

'Oh, crumbs!' exclaimed Lexi sounding very English all of a sudden. She flung her backpack over her shoulders, held her handbag tightly in one hand, grabbed the long handle of her suitcase and started towards the stairs that led up to the pedestrian bridge that crossed the tracks. They had alighted at Platform 3, and the connecting train was at Platform 1. There was a queue for the lift. Lexi decided to carry her case up the stairs.

People were bustling past her on both sides.

She was struggling up the stairs with the case when a middle-aged man wearing a suit and carrying a briefcase said, 'Here, let me help you with that.' Lexi watched him grasp the case and take the stairs two at a time. He pulled up the handle in time for Lexi to arrive and wheel it over the bridge, heading for the stairs on the other side. 'Thank you, so much,' said Lexi after he'd insisted on carrying it down the other side.

'Are you a tourist?' he asked.

She couldn't hide her accent, no matter how many times she said she'd been born in England and lived there until she was six. Lexi kept her mouth shut and just nodded. He couldn't be getting the little train because he wasn't running down the platform.

'Well, I must dash,' said Lexi, 'my train is going to depart any minute.'

'Enjoy your holiday. Or should I say vacation!'

Lexi offered him a weak smile. She didn't know why it hadn't occurred to her just how American she sounded until she arrived in England. 'Well, thanks again,' Lexi replied before she dashed down the station platform where a train consisting of just three carriages was waiting, and due to set off at any moment.

Lexi was relieved the helpful man wasn't getting her train. It was kind of him to help her with her luggage, but she could just imagine the next hour spent sitting next to him, telling her all the places that he'd recommend visiting in Suffolk. She would have welcomed the advice, but she had something urgent she must do – phone her sister.

Although she wasn't keen on the thought of speaking about her little predicament in front of an audience on the packed train to Lowestoft, she'd now decided that she really didn't want to arrive at her next destination with the bill from the last hotel still outstanding.

Lexi put her case and backpack on the seat next to her and got out her mobile phone. There were no missed calls. She had hoped Andrea had tried to call and she hadn't heard her phone amongst the chaos of people running to catch this train. Lexi rang her number. There was no answer. Worse still, it went straight to voice mail. Lexi left another message. 'I'm off to a place called Southwold on the Suffolk Coast in the east of England. I've booked a room at a small bed and breakfast on the sea front. Look, I really need you to phone me as soon as possible, please, Andrea.'

Lexi ended the call and waited several minutes to see if she rang back. A minute later, the small train jerked forward and began its journey. Once they left Ipswich behind, the route was once again scenic.

The first stop was Woodbridge. Lexi's nose was almost glued to the window; she was quite surprised at what she was seeing. On one side of the little station was The Station Café through a green door with little leaded windows either side. She could see it was equally old-fashioned inside, and the clientele appeared to be mostly retired people. But it wasn't that side that surprised her; it was the other side of the station. She could see a river, and a boatyard. There were sailing boats out on the water and she could hear seagulls in the distance. And was that the faint sound of buoy bells?

Lexi raised her eyebrows, wondering how she even knew what buoy bells were. It wasn't as though she came from a boating family. Apart from the private, crewed yachts her grandparents rented in the summer in Rhode Island, she had no clue.

She shook her head as the train pulled out of the station. She had just settled down with her sandwich, courtesy of the Bloomsbury hotel, when her phone buzzed. It was a text message. 'Oh, thank god.' She had been starting to wonder why Andrea wasn't answering her phone.

Lexi's wide grin faded when she saw who the text was from. *Brandon. Why does it have to be from him?* She stared at it. *Does that mean he still has feelings for me and misses me?* thought Lexi. *Does it matter, even if he does?* She wouldn't have him back – would she? Lexi was surprised that the idea had even crossed her mind. She didn't want to, but she read his text: *Is everything okay? Tried to call you back, but your phone when straight to voicemail.*

'That's because I don't want to speak to you,' mumbled Lexi. Suddenly, Andrea came to mind. The stupidest thought entered her head – was Andrea avoiding her? Of course she wasn't, she was just busy, or charging her phone, or having a lie-in. There were any number of reasons why her sister hadn't been in touch, despite Lexi phoning that morning and leaving several voice messages.

Lexi looked at her uneaten sandwich. She had suddenly lost her appetite. She wrapped it back up and put it away in her bag.

She decided to put her phone away too and just wait for her sister to reply. 'She'll call,' Lexi mumbled to herself as she stared out of the window. At least the scenery didn't disappoint. Rolling countryside, small villages nestled in a patchwork quilt of farm-land, tall steeple church towers, and little train stations with old-fashioned waiting rooms to shelter from the rain, some even with colourful hanging baskets. It all made the journey a delight.

It sounded stupid, but although she'd been in Suffolk for hardly any time at all, she was already falling in love with the county. It was definitely familiar. As Lexi stared out of the window, she just knew that she'd been on this little train before.

21

Lexi had arrived at the bed and breakfast, which was in a street behind the seafront in Southwold. She'd spent her last five pounds on the taxi to get her from the station to the centre of town. She'd checked every taxi before she'd found a driver who would accept cash. He'd asked her how much money she had.

Lexi had never felt so embarrassed in her life. She'd got the impression that the fare was more money than she had, but he'd obviously taken pity on her. Around her grandpa's age, he'd even taken her suitcase into the bed and breakfast and deposited it at the reception desk. Then he'd refused her fare. Lexi had said, 'No, please. I want to pay you for the trip.'

'I'll tell you what, if I see you out and about, perhaps you can buy me a coffee when I'm next in town.'

Lexi said, 'All right,' knowing it was highly likely she would. Southwold wasn't a very large town, from what she'd seen from the taxi. There was the main high street, off which branched streets with pretty cottages painted white or pastel shades of blue and pink. Along the high street was a hotel, coffee shops and cafés with little tables and chairs on the pavement outside, a bakery and two small grocery stores. With bunting strewn across the high street, it wasn't the sort of place you could forget in a hurry. 'I've been here before,' said Lexi to the older lady who ran the bed and breakfast from her two-storey, double-fronted red-brick house a stone's throw from the pier and the beach.

'Well, that's just marvellous my dear,' the older lady commented. 'Now, how will you be paying – cash or card?'

'Ah. I didn't know I had to pay on arrival.' Lexi bit her bottom lip. 'Here's the thing ...' She launched into what had happened yesterday, getting mugged in London. She told the lady she had money, but her cards had been stolen too, along with her purse and all her holiday cash. She explained it wasn't a problem because her sister in America was wealthy, and would have no problem paying the bill – when she got in touch.

'We're wealthy heiresses, in fact – well we will be when my grandparents pass away. Not that I want them to do that.' Lexi let out a nervous laugh. She didn't know why she'd said that. Nerves, she guessed. 'But the thing is, we both have generous allowances – I just can't access mine right now, obviously. But as I said, I'm just waiting on her call.'

'Really.'

'Yes.' Lexi caught her sceptical look.

'Where were you yesterday?' the lady asked.

'In London, staying in a lovely hotel in Bloomsbury.'

'And how did you pay for that?'

Lexi fell silent.

'Hmm?'

'Well, here's the thing ...'

❖

Lexi wheeled her case down the street and sighed. She realised that booking into a small bed and breakfast had been a mistake under the circumstances. She'd spotted a hotel called The Crown in the town on the way through and thought she'd try her luck there. She guessed it would be expensive, as it was situated in the heart of the town, a short walk from the beach and the pier.

She didn't have far to walk. There was a small street of cottages that fronted a green beside a footpath that led down to the beach. Around the next corner was the high street where The Crown was situated.

Lexi made a little detour across the small green. So far, she hadn't even seen the sea. She stopped on the path and looked down at the pastel-coloured beach huts below. They fronted a wide concrete boulevard, beyond which was a sandy beach and the sea. There were lots of families with children on the beach. Some had little tents to change in, and others had picnic rugs and folding camping chairs to sit on.

The path above the beach to her left gently sloped several hundred yards down to the pier. There were steps down to the beach too.

Lexi turned to look in the other direction. The path continued past cottages and a pub, and further on she imagined it sloped down to the other side to the beach.

Lexi breathed a sigh. After a cloudy start, it had turned out to be a beautiful day with blue skies and sunshine. But the weather did not match her mood. She stood on the path and looked at her phone. Andrea still hadn't phoned her back. Lexi had lost count of how many messages she'd left. It was getting embarrassing. How many times did she have to beg her to get in touch?

She turned around and walked back past the small green and the cottages. She had to navigate around a large queue in front of a fancy ice cream parlour, taking care not to knock into anyone's legs with her suitcase.

A little further along, she came to The Crown. She stood for a moment outside, admiring the hotel. She'd read about it online when she was searching for a place to book before she left London. It was every bit as grand as the photos she'd seen online. She loved the Georgian building with the sash windows. She expected the rooms were as luxurious as those in the London hotel she'd stayed in. Lexi hesitated before she stepped inside. It was now two o'clock in the afternoon and she hadn't spoken to her sister, which meant her second night's stay in the Bloomsbury hotel was still unpaid. What if she booked in here and still couldn't contact her? She couldn't keep moving around and absconding without paying the bill. *But I have to stay somewhere.*

There had to be a logical explanation as to why her sister hadn't answered her texts or phoned her back, despite her increasingly desperate messages. *One stage at a time*, thought Lexi as she tried to ignore the feeling that something was wrong. *I'll just get another room booked.*

She walked into the hotel. It looked very upmarket – the sort of place she'd love to stay – although the other guests who passed her on their way out, two older couples, made her wonder if the clientele were mainly retired. That wouldn't stop her staying there, but it might mean that the hotel staff, used to their older, well-heeled guests, would ask her to pay upfront.

The first thing out of Lexi's mouth when she approached the ornately carved oak reception desk was, 'Can I pay on departure?' She winced, aware that it was an odd question to ask when you have just arrived.

'Of course.' The receptionist didn't seem bothered by the question.

'That's great. I'd like to book a room.'

'When would you like to book one for?'

Lexi looked at her for a moment. She thought it was obvious as she was standing there with her suitcase. 'Er, tonight.'

'We haven't got any vacancies tonight. However we do have one room available in two weeks' time.'

'Two weeks?'

'Yes, I'm afraid we are fully booked.'

'What about other hotels in the town?' Lexi had realised too late she'd made a big mistake by booking the bed and breakfast and would have been far better off booking another hotel. But finding a room in August had been difficult as it was. And she didn't really want to ask her sister to have to fork out too much money. The London hotel had been pricey enough. Now it looked as though she didn't have much choice where she stayed. She just had to find a vacancy. 'Can you recommend another hotel in the town?'

'Yes, I can.'

'Oh, thank god.'

'But they won't have any vacancies for tonight. There's a show at the local theatre which tends to attract a lot of visitors, so the hotels get quite booked up in advance. But I can recommend the little bed and breakfast around the corner.'

Lexi frowned. She didn't mention that it was where she'd just come from. 'Thanks.'

Lexi turned on her heel. She was about to walk out of the door when she had a thought. 'Do you mind if I wait in the lobby? Perhaps you'll get a cancellation.'

The receptionist nodded. 'I guess that's ok. Stranger things have happened.'

Lexi frowned at that. She got the feeling that a cancellation that night was highly unlikely.

22

Lexi was staring out of the window, watching people going in and out of the shops and sitting at tables outside the cafés across the street, when the phone at reception rang. She listened intently.

'No, I'm sorry. We haven't any vacancies.'

Lexi silently cursed. Every time she heard the phone, she thought it might be a cancellation – but there was no such luck. All she wanted was a room for one night. She knew that if Andrea hadn't phoned by later in the afternoon, there would be no alternative but to phone Nana. It was a last resort, but she'd have no choice.

Lexi scrolled through the messages on her phone. She had expected her sister to get in touch with her straight away. Brandon had tried to call again. He had also sent several text messages.

Lexi breathed a heavy sigh. She really wished she hadn't phoned him in the first place. It had been a stupid idea to think she could ask him for money. Whatever money she gave him just disappeared. The takings at the late-night gigs he did at bars in the city barely paid for a drink for him and his band members at the end of the night.

Lexi texted him back just to shut him up and make him go away. *I'm fine. Just forget I phoned, alright?*

She got an immediate reply. *Where are you?*

Lexi stared at the message. When was she going to tell him that he had to vacate the apartment in New York in less than a fortnight? Not now. She had far more pressing things on her mind, like where she was going to stay that night.

She breathed a sigh and debated whether to phone Andrea again. It crossed her mind to phone Mitch or Nana just to check that Andrea was okay. The trouble was that she might have to explain why she was asking that.

'Things just couldn't get any worse – could they?' Lexi muttered to herself.

'Is everything ok?'

Lexi looked up. The receptionist must have seen her sitting there shaking her head. She added, 'I'm sorry, but I don't think there's going to be a cancellation tonight. You could try a hotel or B&B further up the coast in Aldeburgh.'

'What about Walberswick?' Lexi had found the picture on her phone that Hazel had given her of the houseboat. A hotel in Walberswick would be perfect; it would be closer to the harbour.

'Let me find out for you.' She lifted the phone receiver. 'There are two in Walberswick. They're not hotels but pubs. I'll give them a ring. Perhaps they'll have vacancies.'

'Do they accept payment on departure, do you think?'

This time the receptionist threw her a suspicious look. She slowly lowered the phone and put it back in its cradle. 'Why don't I give you their phone numbers and you can give them a call and find out for yourself?'

Lexi stared at her.

'Perhaps it's time you left.'

Lexi wasn't surprised she was being kicked out. She walked over to the desk as the young woman looked at her computer and scribbled down two phone numbers. 'Here.'

Lexi took the notepaper. 'Thanks.'

The receptionist looked towards the door.

Lexi got the hint. 'Can I leave you my phone number in case there's a—?'

'Of course.'

Lexi noticed the receptionist made no effort to write it down as she reeled it off. As she turned to go, she had a thought. 'Wait … can you tell me the quickest route to the harbour, and the footbridge across to Walberswick?'

'By taxi.'

'Is it walkable?'

'Well, yes.'

Lexi caught her eyes roving to her suitcase as she gave her the directions.

Lexi headed for the door.

'Are you going to try your luck when you get there?' asked the receptionist.

She glanced over her shoulder. 'Something like that.' She stepped out of the hotel and paused to look at the photo of the houseboat on her phone. Lexi stood for a moment, staring at the picture. Would it be so bad if she found the boat and asked Margot – if she was still there – to put her up just for one night?

Failing that, Lexi decided she'd have to phone her grandparents. If there were no vacancies in Walberswick, she'd head back to the bed and breakfast and her grandparents could pay for her stay over the phone, after she'd explained exactly what she was doing in England. They wouldn't be pleased, and she wasn't looking forward to *that* conversation, but they would bail her out of a sticky situation – she could guarantee it.

Lexi hadn't eaten the sandwich she had packed, nor the fruit, yoghurts or cake – that was all for lunch. *Maybe I will stop for a picnic lunch on the way*, she thought, feeling more reassured by Plan B.

She enjoyed the walk through the coastal town, along the street opposite The Crown which opened out on to a large green. Lexi followed the path around the corner, past a pub. She could see the path that ran along above the beach. If she turned left, passing some cottages, she'd arrive at the spot where she'd stood before heading for The Crown. Lexi turned in the other direction, following the path that sloped downwards. In a couple of hundred yards she came to the beach. There was a café on the beachfront which looked busy; there were several families sitting on the benches outside with drinks and ice-creams.

Lexi paused and turned around. The wide concrete boulevard fronting the beach stretched the length of the town, reaching right to Southwold Pier, which she could see in the distance. Large pastel-coloured beach huts sat on the boulevard at the near end of the beach. Beyond were more beach huts sitting directly on the beach, and behind them were sand dunes.

Lexi frowned. 'Now where?' She didn't want to walk back the way she had come, up the path that led to the town high above the beach, or along the wide concrete boulevard in the same direction that led to the pier. She wanted the harbour. The receptionist at The Crown had given her directions, but she couldn't see the path that was meant to lead to the harbour.

She started walking up the concrete drive, away from the beach and the café, and stopped at the top. The road gently curved around to the right, where there were more cottages and another green on the fringes of the small town. Lexi could see a lane at the top of the green, which she imagined led back into the high street at the other end of town where the taxi had driven into Southwold.

Lexi sighed. She really wished Andrea had been in contact and she was now settling into her room in the lovely bed and breakfast.

On her left was a path that led in the other direction – to the harbour, she hoped. She started down the path. The surface was rough, and it was hard work pulling her suitcase along the surface. Parallel to the beach, it soon came out onto a wide track with wooden huts, fishing boats, a car park and a pub on the harbour. She could already see the bridge and a small town just the other side – Walberswick. She sighed in relief. Lexi glanced at The Harbour Inn and wondered if there were guest bedrooms and vacancies. Although she was tempted to find out, she looked across the bridge and thought she spotted the houseboat from the photo. She made up her mind to visit the houseboat first and find out if Margot Dorey was still there.

Lexi crossed the small footbridge over to the other side and took the path to her right along the riverside. There were houseboats on the near side of the small river inlet. On the other side were fishing boats moored on the quay.

The houseboats there weren't all like the narrowboat in the photo; they ranged from large barges to small fishing vessels converted for living in. There was even a proper houseboat with a wraparound porch; the sort of thing she'd seen in the Florida Keys once, like a floating wooden house.

An older chap, perhaps in his sixties, sat on the porch reading a book. He looked up as she approached and offered her a friendly wave. Lexi offered a tentative wave in return as she passed by. She paused to look at the photo on her phone, and wondered if the man knew a woman by the name of Margot Dorey. Was she possibly his neighbour? She turned around, intending to retrace her steps and ask him, when she discovered that he had gone inside, leaving the book he'd been reading on the chair.

Lexi sighed and glanced at the photo once more; the houseboat in the photo looked cared-for, with pots of flowers on the roof, an old-fashioned bicycle with a wooden handlebar basket propped up on the front deck, and a small table and chairs. But this photo had been taken years earlier. She imagined the houseboat wouldn't look the same after two decades. But then, as she passed the narrowboat next door to the large houseboat with the wraparound porch, she stopped in front of the next boat and held up the photo on her phone in amazement. How was it possible that two decades on, the houseboat looked the same? It must have been well cared-for over the years. There were flowers in pots on the roof, and a small wooden table and chairs on the little deck outside the door to the cabin. The bike was different; although it had a basket on the front like the one in the photo, this one wasn't very old.

She recognised the style that had been quite fashionable a few years earlier, with high handlebars and a comfortable saddle. It was pastel blue. There was no doubt in her mind that someone lived there. The question was, would it be Margot Dorey who answered the door when she knocked?

Lexi checked in her handbag for the letter. All she had to do was hand it over. Then she was free. But free to do what? Lexi rolled her eyes. If Andrea didn't get in touch soon, she really would have to phone her grandparents – unless Margot Dorey would put her up for one night. She knew it was a big ask. They didn't know each other, but she had travelled all this way to hand-deliver a letter. Whatever was inside that envelope must be important.

Lexi didn't see the harm in trying her luck. She gingerly opened the wooden gate and stepped on to the gangplank. It was wide and sturdy with a railing either side. She anticipated someone might see her from one of the windows and come outside to greet her.

By the time she had stepped aboard, lugging her case over the lip of the boat and plonking it down beside the table and chairs, no one had appeared. She put her rucksack on the table and turned to knock on the cabin door. She stepped back in anticipation, hoping someone was home.

No one answered the door. Had she really thought it would be that simple? She decided to take a seat and wait. She thought she'd use the opportunity to try and contact her sister again. She got out her mobile phone and discovered there was no reception. 'Oh, you have got to be kidding me!'

Lexi's eyes roved to the little American-style post box on a wooden pole attached to the gate. She left her suitcase and bags on the houseboat and returned along the gangplank to the gate. Lexi looked about her. The closest houseboat was another narrowboat right next door. Was anyone home? Would the occupant see her looking in their neighbour's post box? She didn't see any curtains twitching in the houseboat next door or a face in the window.

That houseboat appeared brand new, as though it had been completely refurbished or even custom-built. It was wider than *The Hideaway* and was painted a vibrant green. Nobody appeared on deck to tell her off for nosing in someone else's post box.

Lexi opened the flap and discovered there was something inside. She looked about her before she picked it up. She was surprised to find the box wasn't locked, and imagined that all the neighbours were trustworthy. But what about a stranger opening the lid and reaching her hand inside to take out the letter?

For the first time all day, Lexi was in luck. There was no address or stamp on the envelope, but there was her name, Margot Dorey, in black and white. 'Oh, my god. She's still here!'

Perhaps a friend or neighbour had missed her and popped it in there for when she arrived home.

Lexi bit her bottom lip, debating what to do. She glanced at her watch. Who knew when the lady would be back?

Lexi stepped back onto the boat. She knew she'd feel guilty not waiting. After all, she'd come all this way to put the letter in her hand. What if she left and missed her by a few minutes? Lexi thought of her mum and the conditions about delivering the letter personally, and decided that as she was there, she might as well wait – just for a bit.

Lexi had barely sat down on the chair on deck when she heard a crack of thunder that made her jump. Then it started raining. Lexi looked up at the sky and frowned. 'Seriously?'

She'd only brought a light raincoat. Her umbrella was at the bottom of her rucksack.

It began to pour. Lexi looked across the river at The Harbour Inn. Even if she made a run for it, which would be a bit difficult with her case and bags, she'd still get soaked. But perhaps they'd have a room, and she wouldn't have to pay upfront.

Lexi was just trying to navigate her case around the chair when it slipped on the wet deck and careered into a flower pot by the door, knocking it over. Fortunately the ceramic pot didn't break. Lexi was just kneeling down to pick it up when she noticed a little plastic bag underneath. Inside was a key.

She took the key out of the bag and looked at the cabin door. 'No way. Who leaves a spare door key under a flowerpot?' She shook her head. 'Old people.' Lexi was about to put it back in the bag, and place it where she'd found it under the pot, when she had a thought. *I'd only need to step inside for a moment, out of the rain – just until it stops.*

Lexi put the key in the lock and turned it once. The door opened. Before anyone saw her, she grabbed her bags and made it down the small flight of stairs, awkwardly heaving her suitcase down in front of her. Lexi closed the cabin door behind her and stepped off the stair into the cabin.

She took off her wet raincoat and stared about her. It was cosy inside, with white curtains with a small daisy pattern at the windows. There was a light-brown woven rug covering the wooden floor, and a beige sofa with a white throw. It had a yellow daisy pattern that matched the curtains.

A trunk sat in front of the sofa, acting as a coffee table, and in the corner of the narrow room was a small wood burner. A table and two chairs were positioned under one of the windows. Behind the sofa was a kitchenette.

Although it was very small, Lexi liked it – a lot. She felt like being nosy and looking beyond the cosy sitting room. There was a door at the end of the room which she guessed led to a bedroom and a bathroom.

Lexi hung her raincoat on a little hook behind the door. She walked over to the window and glanced outside. She could see The Harbour Inn. Raindrops pelted the window. Lexi turned around and walked over to the little kitchen. The window on the other side of the houseboat looked out on to the riverside path.

She discovered there was tea and coffee in one of the kitchen cupboards, and some unopened long-life semi-skimmed milk. She put the kettle on, knowing it was cheeky of her to help herself to coffee and milk, but she had some change in her pocket, which she'd leave on the counter. Then she rolled her eyes, thinking that it would give the game away that someone had been there.

Lexi walked over to the sofa while she waited for the kettle. She sat down and closed her eyes – just for a moment.

23

Lexi woke up with a start. She could hear raised voices. She sat up and accidentally kicked over her suitcase that was on the floor by the sofa.

'Oh, no. I can't believe I fell asleep!' She looked at the time. 'It can't be!' She'd been out like a light for several hours. It was now almost seven o'clock in the evening. And it was still raining. Lexi rushed to the window. She guessed why she had fallen asleep in the middle of the afternoon. Even though she'd had two nights in the hotel in London, she'd missed a night's sleep on the flight, and her body clock still hadn't adjusted to the time difference.

It wasn't just that, though. Lexi rubbed the sleep out of her eyes as she stumbled to one of the cabin windows. She'd had that dream again – but it wasn't just a dream, it was a nightmare; someone was drowning, and she just couldn't reach her. She held out her hand, but the other child's fingers slipped through hers and she disappeared under the water.

Lexi didn't have time to think about that, though. Her thoughts were consumed with who was on the towpath outside. She could hear footsteps. Had Margot been out for an evening meal and returned?

Lexi threw on her coat and was about to switch on the light in the cabin and step outside, making her presence known, when she heard a child's voice saying, 'I don't want to stay here!'

Lexi paused with her finger on the light switch. She left the cabin in darkness and hurried to the window. She moved a net curtain to one side to see a young man and a child, a girl no more than nine or ten, arguing on the footpath. He put two suitcases down and roughly grabbed her by the shoulders. 'We're staying here, young lady, and that's the last I'll hear of it!'

'But Daddy, I don't want to!' she shouted back.

Lexi was about to rush out and intervene – she didn't like the way he was treating the child – when she saw him kneel down and speak to her, but this time so softly that no words carried. Lexi saw the little girl nod her head. Then they hugged before he stood up and picked up their cases, one in each hand. He had a backpack on his back and a laptop case flung over his shoulder.

Lexi's eyes went wide when they approached the gate to the houseboat she was on. It hadn't occurred to her that despite the letter addressed to Margot Dorey in the post box, she might not actually live there. It hadn't occurred to her that it could be a holiday rental.

'Oh, crap.' She backed away from the window and knocked into the wall. Her elbow struck a light switch. The ceiling light switched on immediately, bathing the cabin in a soft white light. Lexi held her breath.

'See? I told you it's not that one,' she heard a child's voice, the girl, shout out. 'There's someone in there. It's the one next door.'

Lexi remembered to breathe. She approached the window to close the curtain and saw the young man and his daughter walking down the gangplank towards the houseboat next door.

The young girl spotted her at the window. She waved.

Lexi waved back at the little girl with mousy hair, freckles and a cheeky grin. The girl's father caught sight of Lexi at the window, frowned at her, turned around and grasped his daughter's arm. 'Come on. We are not here to make friends.'

Lexi frowned. *What a horrible man*, she thought, although he wasn't horrible to look at – not at all. Lexi dismissed that thought, which had popped into her head. The trouble was that now she was starting to think of another good-looking young man – Brandon. She missed him dreadfully. Right now she wanted to talk to him, ask him what he thought she should do. Should she hang on to see if Margot turned up, or deposit her letter in the post box and be done with it?

The trouble was that the couch was awfully comfortable, and the houseboat cosier and more welcoming than some hotel rooms. Lexi couldn't believe she was contemplating still waiting until she turned up. A thought occurred to her. 'Perhaps she's away, staying overnight somewhere.'

Lexi bit her lower lip and sat down on the sofa. She turned the main light out and switched on the little sidelamp on the bookshelves to one side of the log-burner. She'd closed the curtains and now wondered if the light on in the cabin could be seen from outside. She was thinking of the neighbours. What if they knew Margot was away? Would they wonder who was in her houseboat? Would there be a knock on the door from a nosy neighbour?

Lexi was beginning to wonder if she should give up on waiting for Margot and just leave. She decided to do just that. She stood up, walked over to the window, drew the curtains and looked outside. It was still raining. She'd be soaked by the time she reached The Harbour Inn. Would it be worth the walk if they had no vacancies? Lexi shut the curtains, crossed the room and sat back down on the sofa with her back to the towpath. There were two cabin windows that looked out over the river to the bank on the other side, with a lovely view of the old Harbour Inn. The lights were on, and people were arriving, no doubt for an evening meal. Perhaps Margot was over there. Lexi frowned. If she was, she might be some time.

Lexi stared at The Harbour Inn on the other side of the bank and imagined that even if they rented rooms, they were probably fully booked by now. She decided to take her chances where she was. She got out the letter. Perhaps when Margot arrived home to this letter, she'd take pity on the messenger who'd flown all the way from America to deliver it.

She frowned at the letter, realising that she was making a lot of assumptions. What if whatever was in the letter was not what Margot wanted to hear? She must have known Lexi's mum. She'd be sad at her passing. Lexi started to feel confident that she'd let her crash on the couch for just one night. Unless there was another bedroom. Lexi stood up again. She felt bad, but she fancied snooping around the houseboat, and she needed to use the bathroom. It was a good excuse to find out what was behind that door.

She opened the door to a small lobby with a cubby hole of a shower room on the right, with a tiny sink and loo. Beyond that was another door. She opened it to find that at the other end of the houseboat was a small bedroom, just big enough for a double bed and an inbuilt wardrobe. You had to crawl across the bed to get to the wardrobe. It was the smallest bedroom she'd ever seen. However, it did answer her question; there was only one bedroom.

Lexi shut the bedroom door, used the bathroom and returned to the lounge. She made herself a cup of coffee, resumed her seat on the comfy sofa and found the packed lunch she'd taken from the hotel that morning. Apart from a cup of coffee and a croissant on the train, Lexi hadn't eaten since breakfast.

She fetched a couple of plates from the kitchen and laid out the sandwiches, fruit, yoghurt and cake on the trunk in front of the sofa. *If Margot walks in now and finds me sitting here eating, then so be it,* thought Lexi. She was starving.

She tucked in, unwrapping the sandwich that she'd put in a paper napkin. She leaned back in the sofa, kicked off her shoes, and put her feet up on the coffee table. She stared at the twinkling lights across the river in The Harbour Inn. *Perhaps if I'm lucky, I'll stay there tomorrow evening, having dispensed with this final errand for Mum.*

She wiped her fingers with a couple of paper napkins that she'd found in one of the kitchen drawers and then picked up the envelope. She couldn't hold out any longer. Despite her best intentions not to open the letter, every fibre in her body telling her it was wrong, she put her finger under the seal. She was about to prise it open when there was a loud knock on the door.

Startled, Lexi dropped the letter. She bent down to pick it up and held it in her hand as she nervously approached the door. She knew it couldn't be Margot Dorey – why would she knock on her own front door? Lexi could feel her stomach churning. This was exactly what she'd been expecting; a busybody neighbour come to see who was in the houseboat.

Lexi walked up the steps and opened the door to find a young woman standing outside wearing a bright yellow visibility jacket.

'I have a parcel for you.'

'Oh, right.' Lexi frowned. She supposed she'd better take it in. She was just reaching for it, when the lady said, 'Actually, it's not for you – it's for a guy called Ray.'

'There's no one here by that name.' At least, Lexi thought there wasn't.

'I think I've got the wrong houseboat.' She looked about her. 'Can you take it in for me?'

Lexi shook her head. 'Sorry, I … er … I'm new here. I don't know my neighbours. I'd try the houseboat with the wraparound porch. You must have just passed it.' Lexi pointed in the direction of the large houseboat just the other side of the boat next door that the young man with the child were renting.

'Okay.'

'I saw a guy on that boat as I was passing by. It might be the person you're looking for.'

'Great, thank you. Cool houseboat, by the way.'

Lexi thought so too. She looked about her, up and down the

path, but there was no sign of anyone else making their way along the path towards the houseboat. Lexi returned to her meal, but her appetite had waned.

She put the letter back in her handbag, packed up the remains of the food and found the fridge in the compact integrated cabinets under the worktop. Apart from an unopened pint of milk and a jar of pickles, the fridge was bare.

Lexi place the remains of her lunch inside and shut the door. She turned around. The place was spotless. She only just noticed it now, but there was nothing of a personal nature, no photos, no little mementos or keepsakes from a holiday. How odd.

She returned to the sofa. This time she didn't feel relaxed. She sat there quite rigid, waiting for Margot to turn up. She had a feeling this was going to turn into a long evening.

24

Lexi reached for her phone. She had a job finding it as it had slipped down the back of the sofa. Lexi was surprised to discover it was seven in the morning. She'd fallen asleep again, but this time she'd slept through the night. And nobody had turned up.

Lexi stared about her. Had Margot Dorey gone away? Perhaps this was just a holiday home? *That would make sense*, thought Lexi. It might explain why there was nothing personal in the houseboat.

She'd had a further nose about last night, once it had got so late that she realised Margot was not likely to turn up. She'd then curled up on the sofa with the book the publisher in London had given her – the first in the trilogy of Margot Dorey's children's novels.

It seemed somehow familiar. Perhaps she'd read the story when she was a child, or someone – maybe her mum or dad, or grandparents – had read it to her as a bedtime story. Maybe it had been made into a film; she'd never thought to ask the publisher if that had been the case.

The book was on the floor. It must have fallen out of her hands as she drifted off to a fitful night's sleep. It was that dream again, about someone drowning, that had given her a disturbed night. Lexi rubbed the sleep out of her eyes and wished it would stop.

She was surprised she'd slept on the boat; she had no fondness for boats. It wasn't the boats themselves she didn't like; she remembered the yacht her grandparents had rented off the coast of Florida when her and Andrea were teenagers. It was gorgeous. White leather seats, a large al fresco dining area on a wooden deck at the back, and spacious comfortable bedrooms with en suites on the deck below.

Although the houseboat was quite different, she loved the cosy feel. She just wished it was on dry land. For as long as she could remember, Lexi had had an aversion to water. She'd never ever questioned why. She'd just thought swimming and water wasn't her thing. Now, with these dreams she'd never experienced before setting foot back in England, she was beginning to wonder if something had happened in her childhood.

Lexi frowned at the thought that she couldn't ask her mum. She raised an eyebrow. Perhaps Mitch would know? Thinking of Mitch, her thoughts turned to her sister. Lexi checked her phone for any messages or missed calls. There was nothing. And at seven in the morning, it was too early in Connecticut to try her luck phoning Andrea again.

Lexi had barely woken up and her heart was already pounding in her chest with worry. She was anxious about money, something she'd never experienced before in her life, along with the unpaid hotel bill. She had a flexible return flight, and an open train ticket back to London Liverpool Street, but she didn't have the taxi fare to the airport. It had been a stupid oversight on her part, spending money on the train on an expensive coffee she couldn't afford.

But it wasn't just the thought of how she was going to cope that was making her stomach churn; it was the worry over why her sister hadn't contacted her. Had something happened? Lexi resolved to phone her grandparents if she couldn't get through to Andrea today.

She opened the curtains hanging at the windows that fronted

the river and drank in the early morning scene. She'd never seen anything so beautiful and peaceful first thing in the morning. She was used to living in New York, and the constant background noise of the city. This was a whole new world. And for someone who would not naturally choose to live near water, Lexi loved the tranquillity. The river was calm. An early morning mist hovered just above the water, giving it an otherworldly, almost ethereal feel.

She imagined that when the mist cleared, it would be a beautiful day. Through the mist, she could just make out the contours of The Harbour Inn. A hazy yellow light emanated from a couple of the upstairs windows.

She left the view for a moment to switch on the kettle, returning to the sofa with a steaming mug of tea and a croissant – the last of the breakfast she had pilfered yesterday from the hotel in London. There were a couple of text messages, and a voice message, all from the hotel, asking her whereabouts and noting that she hadn't paid her bill. She'd left her phone on the coffee table, and was surprised the messages had come through, as the reception was patchy.

One message said that her card had been declined. Lexi rolled her eyes. Of course it had; her purse had been stolen and she'd contacted her bank in America to cancel her cards. Someone had clearly tried to use her bank card.

For a split second, she had a scary thought that the hotel staff could track her phone to the houseboat on the quay. Lexi laughed at that absurd thought. But it didn't stop her googling if it was possible.

'Crumbs – it is!' exclaimed Lexi in surprise. But it turned out she'd need the GPS switched on. She felt a bit silly. Would a hotel really go to such extremes to track her down for the cost of one night's hotel booking? Was it even legal for someone to track someone else's phone? Would they really bother?

Lexi didn't know, but she didn't particularly want to find out.

She erred on the side of caution and googled how to switch off the location GPS on her phone. It would have been quite straightforward if she hadn't kept losing her phone reception. But after a few clicks, she managed to turn it off and breathed a sigh of relief. She drank her tea, ate the croissant and sat enjoying the view, wondering what the day would bring.

After breakfast, Lexi opened her case, took out a fresh set of clothes, and quickly showered in the little shower room, with one ear out for anyone turning up. It wasn't very relaxing. But then what did she expect? Lexi knew she was effectively trespassing. 'But I've got the letter,' she said to her reflection in the mirror as she was applying a bit of makeup. She shook her head, knowing that delivering the letter still did not excuse this – crashing in someone's place.

Lexi dried herself using a white fluffy towel in the bathroom. She found a small hairdryer in a cupboard in the bathroom, and blow-dried her hair. She was going to unpack her own travel hairdryer but thought the better of it. If Margot turned up, which it was likely she would after a night away, unless she was on holiday, then at least if her suitcase was still packed, she could mention the weather and that she'd found the key and needed to step inside just for a bit out of the rain while she waited for her to arrive.

Lexi cringed. She walked back into the sitting room and looked out of the window. The mist was clearing. It wasn't raining. There was no excuse to hang around inside the houseboat. She had a thought. She could put the key back under the flowerpot and sit outside on the deck. Perhaps she could ask a neighbour if they knew when Margot Dorey would return?

Lexi thought of the towels she'd just used. They were damp. She returned to the bathroom, set the hairdryer on a high heat and dried them as best she could. She folded the towels and placed them back in the cupboard. The bathroom had steamed up too. Lexi found a cloth in the kitchen and wiped around the shower room, leaving the door open to dissipate the steam. She glanced around the houseboat just to make sure that nothing was amiss and there was no evidence anybody had been inside the place. She tried not to think of the damp towels and the condensation she'd noticed had built up in the tiny shower room already.

She picked up her small rucksack. She could only carry one thing at a time up the little flight of stairs and out onto the deck. She intended to leave her suitcase until last. Lexi took a last look around the little houseboat, wishing she could stay there for her entire holiday. Although she wasn't keen on boats, she wouldn't have to go in the water or sail the thing. It was securely tied to the quay, or anchored – she didn't know which, and didn't care as long as it stayed put.

She stared wistfully around the comfy, cosy lounge. Then she spotted something out of place. 'Oh, god!' She'd left Margot's letter on the coffee table. She ran over and scooped it up, feeling the boat rocking beneath her feet.

Lexi stood for a moment until the rocking sensation had stopped. She put the letter in her handbag, returned to the foot of the stairs and walked up, gingerly opening the cabin door. She hoped Margot hadn't chosen this moment to return, just in time to catch her leaving the houseboat.

Lexi opened the door and deposited her rucksack on the deck. No one was about. She breathed a sigh as she started down the steps. That was when she heard somebody.

'Hello, there.'

Lexi froze. She walked back up the stairs, faked a smiled, and said, 'Oh, hello. You're the guy from the houseboat next door but one.'

She remembered the tall older man with the full head of wiry grey hair. He'd offered her a friendly wave from the deck of his houseboat as she'd passed by the previous day. He'd been sitting reading a book. She guessed he was retired.

'Settling in okay?' he called out.

Lexi tried to keep the fake smile plastered to her lips. Of all the times, he had to walk past just as she was leaving. There was no point denying it. She thought up a whopping lie on the spot. 'I'm … er … houseboat-sitting until she returns.'

'Well, that is a grand idea.' He came closer, opened the gate and took a few steps down the gangplank, presumably so he didn't have to shout. Lexi didn't mind. She'd rather he didn't tell the whole neighbourhood she was there, although she knew they would find out soon enough.

'Houseboat-sitting – I like it,' he chuckled.

Lexi had no idea why she'd said that.

'I'm Ray.' He drew closer and held out his hand towards Lexi.

Lexi stepped past the table and chairs, leaned forward and took his hand. 'I'm Lexi.' She shook it, casting a nervous gaze along the riverbank path, expecting to see a lady called Margot storming down the path, gearing up to tell her to get off her boat. So far she hadn't seen a soul, which reminded her to ask, 'How long is Margot Dorey away – do you know?'

'Didn't she tell you?'

Lexi realised too late her gaffe. She shook her head. 'You know what? I've clear forgotten.'

Ray smiled. 'Now, when you get to my age, becoming forgetful is par for the course, but you should have a memory as sharp as a pin, young lady – there really are no excuses. Unless you didn't listen ...'

Lexi nodded. 'Guilty – I'm afraid.' She looked at him sheepishly.

'I've heard that she goes away for the entire summer. Spends the time with her grandkids in London, apparently.'

'Her grandkids?'

'Yep.'

Lexi frowned. But from what Hazel had said, Margot Dorey

was a recluse. Hazel had also mentioned that she had no family. So where did she go? And why would Margot lie to her neighbours?

'What's she like – Margot Dorey?'

'She makes me laugh. She comes out with the funniest things sometimes; she's rather good at telling jokes. We call her 'The Colourful Lady', because she does dress a bit ... eccentric.'

'Maybe that's the writer in her. I wonder if she wrote her books on the houseboat.'

'Did you just say *writer*?'

'Yeah – she wrote a trilogy of children's books some years ago that were very popular. They were set here on the Suffolk Coast.'

'Well, I never. She never mentioned that.'

Lexi wasn't surprised. She'd stopped writing. I have a copy of the first book – it was called *The Hideaway*, set on the Suffolk Coast.'

Lexi got the impression by his wide-eyed expression that he was familiar with the books – just not the fact that Margot had written them.

'I used to read them to my son. He's not that much older than you, I reckon. I still have the dog-eared copies that I read to my grandson, William. Did you read them as a child?'

'I don't remember, to be honest. I may have.' Lexi didn't mention that the publisher had given her a copy. She'd started reading it and the story did seem familiar.

'A writer. Well, I never.' He shook his head. 'You know I never put two and two together with her name, and that of the author of the books. I suppose I should have, but I would have thought she'd have said something. I wonder why she never mentioned her books?' mused Ray.

Lexi had a good idea from what the publisher had said. 'Perhaps it's the fact that she hasn't written a book in quite some time.' Hazel mentioned a tragedy. Lexi wondered if she had lost family in some sort of tragic accident.

'I imagine that she doesn't want people asking when her next book is coming out if she's having some issues writing.'

Ray nodded. 'I see. That is true. You know, you have a very wise head on your shoulders.'

'I wouldn't say that.' She was thinking of the episode in London when she'd had her purse and money snatched. She was way too gullible. That thought brought Brandon to mind and the young lady who'd been in the apartment when she'd turned up unexpectedly. She was tanned, slim, and looked like a model, thought Lexi miserably.

Ray steered the conversation back to Margot and her houseboat. 'I must say, though, that when you catch Margot unawares, there's a melancholy side to her, as though the public persona, what you see, is different. I could say there are times she comes across as quite sad.'

Lexi nodded.

'Anyway,' said Ray, 'it's lovely to meet you. I didn't expect her houseboat to be occupied all summer. From what my neighbours have said, Margot doesn't normally have someone stay in her houseboat while she's away.'

Lexi bit her lower lip.

'I think it's not a bad idea, not bad at all. When a property is left empty, even if it is a houseboat and not bricks and mortar, you don't know who could happen along and break in.'

Lexi wanted the ground to swallow her up.

'Don't you think?' Ray peered at her.

For a moment, Lexi was lost for words. 'Oh, yeah – for sure.'

'Mind you, as my neighbours joke, there's nothing to worry about, as there's now a retired police officer in residence.'

'Who's that?' Lexi said, swallowing hard, trying not to feel alarmed.

'Why, that's me!'

'Oh, really?' said Lexi, aware her voice suddenly sounded a little too high-pitched.

'Yep, but my detecting days are behind me now. I do run a little business from my houseboat.'

'Oh, okay.' Lexi stared at him.

'I find people.'

'You find people?'

She felt like adding, *In that case, can you help me find Margot Dorey?*

'Well, that's the gist of it. I help locate long-lost relatives who may not realise they are beneficiaries of a will.' He looked at Lexi. 'You sound American. Are you over here visiting relatives?'

Lexi thought of the letter. 'Not exactly.'

'Just doing some travelling?'

'Something like that.' The trouble was that Lexi had no money – an issue that wasn't far from her mind. Ray ran a business. His time wouldn't be free of charge if she wanted his help. Lexi sighed. It was a good idea while it lasted. However, there was one thing he might be able to help her with right now. 'I don't know if you could give me some advice ...' She hoped it was free.

'Fire away.'

'Could you help me find my paternal grandparents?' she blurted.

Speaking to Ray, who could be around their age, made her think of them, and what they might be like. And whether they were still alive. 'I haven't been back to England since I was a child.'

'If I were you, I'd consider joining a website like AncestryDNA. Some of those sites offer a free trial to get you started.'

Lexi smiled. She could do that, although she would need the internet. Using her phone to get on the internet for lengthy periods of time to do some research on a site like that would be useless.

Ray said, 'There's a public library in Southwold. They can set you up on the internet.'

'For free?'

'Yes.'

'Great. Thank you, Ray.'

'You're welcome, Lexi. Have a great holiday in the houseboat. You are lucky! What a job.'

Lexi offered up a weak smile.

'You'll be here all summer then, as apparently she doesn't return until the children go back to school at the end of the holidays. She's lucky that she's not involved in the school run – I'm assuming her grandchildren are still at school.'

Lexi nodded, staring at him. Once again, she wondered why Margot would lie to her neighbours – unless it was the publisher who had got it wrong.

'Something the matter?'

'No, er, not at all.'

'It's good you're houseboat-sitting. I'm sure they won't mind.'

'They?'

'The others who live here. It's a nice little community, but I get the impression they're not keen on people buying up these boats as second homes, or – heaven forbid – holiday homes that are rented through places like Airbnb.' He sighed. 'I can understand their sentiments. Southwold is full of holiday homes and rentals. If you were here out of season you'd discover it can become a bit of a ghost town, and places where that happens can lose their sense of community. When I first came here – I'm the newbie, the newest addition, by the way – they thought I was a second-homer because I came from London.' He grinned. 'You're the newbie now.'

'Actually, not to split hairs, but that will be my next-door neighbour. They arrived after me.' Lexi raised her eyebrows at what had just come out of her mouth. Next-door neighbour? Anyone would think she'd moved in. She cast a gaze at the houseboat next door.

He paused and looked at the boat next door to Margot's too.

Lexi pursed her lips. She imagined the young dad and his daughter were there on holiday. She doubted they owned the houseboat. For a moment, when she'd seen them arrive, they'd seemed confused over which one was theirs. But she didn't want to 'out' them as holidaymakers and cause any bad feeling, although she doubted Ray was the type of person who would take offence – unlike his neighbours. She knew people would soon realise she and her neighbours were newbies, but not in a good way; not as permanent residents like Ray.

She gave her next-door neighbour's boat a sideways glance, wondering if the young guy and his daughter were in. She imagined at this time in the morning they would be. She hoped they couldn't hear the conversation from inside their boat. She doubted it above the gentle noise of the lapping water against the boats, the cry of seagulls overhead, and the chug, chug of a small fishing vessel entering the quay. She'd even heard a foghorn in the distance.

She wasn't accustomed to all these strange noises where she lived in her apartment in New York. She couldn't say she missed blaring sirens waking her up at stupid o'clock in the morning, or the late-night clubs open at all hours, or even Brandon's rock music when he unplugged his headphones and played a song on his electric guitar. It wasn't that she didn't like his music; it was the fact that at the weekends, after a long week, he always chose the moment when she fancied a lie-in to beg to play her his new song. The thought of that, of him, made her miss him even more.

'Well, I'd better let you go. I'm sure you're busy settling in.'

'Pardon?'

'Settling into your new home for the summer.'

The mention of the houseboat reminded Lexi that she had another question. 'Um, sounds a stupid question, but do you know *exactly* how long the summer holiday is in England? The agency was a bit vague.'

Lexi still wanted to have some idea of how long Margot might be gone.

'Six weeks.' Ray rubbed his chin. 'But if you want to know

exactly how long Margot is away during the summer, I can ask around.'

'Oh, no don't do that. I'll, er, call the um … agency and ask.' Lexi winced at another lie. She hoped he didn't ask the name of the agency that she was apparently house-sitting through. She could come up with some fictional name on the spot, no doubt, but this was a former police officer she was talking to. How many lies could she spin before she was caught out?

'That's probably a good idea – best to talk to the agency direct.'

Lexi nodded and remembered to breathe. She definitely didn't want him to ask around. That would be all she needed: for word to spread in the houseboat community about Margot's boat-sitter. Lexi intended to keep a low profile – although, looking at Ray, she realised she hadn't exactly made a good job of it so far.

'She hasn't done this before, then, rent out her houseboat?'

'No, not from what the other houseboat owners have said.'

'That's good.' The last thing she needed was for someone else to turn up for the key.

'Well, I'd better, er …' Lexi glanced down the short flight of stairs to the cabin below, where her suitcase was sitting at the bottom of the stairs. She guessed she wasn't leaving after all.

'Yes, you get on with your unpacking. I'm in the houseboat with the veranda, next door to your neighbour. Just call on me if you need anything.'

Some money, food, a job, thought Lexi. 'Thanks,' she said. She surreptitiously grabbed her rucksack and took it back down the stairs, closing the cabin door behind her. She stared around her. She thought about what Ray had said about Margot spending the summer with her grandchildren. She thought again about Hazel, the lady at the publishers, who had said that Margot Dorey had no family.

So where did she really go? And why did she need to lie?

25

Lexi couldn't believe she was contemplating staying on the houseboat. *Why look a gift horse in the mouth, as the British are fond of saying?* thought Lexi. Whatever reason Margot Dorey had for spending summers in London, the fact was that as soon as the summer holidays were over, and the children went back to school, she would return.

There was no point going back to London to try and find her. The publisher wouldn't have a clue where she might be. And if she'd lied about her reasons for spending the summer in London, perhaps she'd lied about that too, and she wasn't even in London. Perhaps she was abroad somewhere or in another part of the country.

Thinking of what Ray had said about the little community not welcoming second-homers, it made her wonder if Margot Dorey had a property somewhere else in the country, and she didn't want them to find out.

Lexi had decided that the best bet was to wait it out. She had a flexible return flight. Even so, she was considering another idea; enjoy a vacation here on the Suffolk Coast and rather than wait for Margot Dorey to return – she could just leave the letter in the post box, do some sightseeing, and then catch a flight home. It would be better than having to look the woman in the eye after staying in her houseboat all summer without her permission. There was just one glaring drawback to the whole plan. Lexi had no money. She sat down on the sofa, got out her purse and emptied the change from the ten-pound note on to the coffee table. It would buy some cheese and a loaf of bread. If she could afford a cheap tub of margarine, all the better. She sighed. 'I can't live off bread and cheese for the next few weeks if I stay on for the summer.'

There was another option: leave now. Deposit the letter in the post box and go home. It was the far easier option, especially as Lexi was worried about her sister. But Lexi knew she was never one to take the easy option. Besides, despite the thought of leaving the letter in the post box, Lexi did not really want to do that. Something was niggling away at her. She recalled her mother's wishes for her to hand the letter to Margot personally. Who was Margot Dorey to her mother? She'd only find that out by meeting the woman.

And there was another, more personal reason for her to stay; something she'd wanted to do for years – buy some flowers and visit her father's grave.

Lexi frowned at the change on the coffee table. When she'd contacted her bank during her train journey and they'd cancelled her cards, they had said they were sending her a new bank card through the post – which would have been all well and good if she had been at home in New York. But she wasn't. Lexi sighed.

Lexi walked over to the kitchen and peered out of the window that overlooked the path along the riverbank. As far as she could see, there was no one about. She walked back up the stairs and opened the cabin door. Lexi stood out on deck, holding up her phone for a signal. She'd got a signal earlier in the houseboat, but now her phone wasn't playing ball.

She'd just sat down in one of the chairs on deck, feeling deflated, when her phone vibrated with a message. But it was just an automated message from the bank with confirmation that her new card had been sent out. She sighed. She supposed that was one good thing. At least her bank card would be there when she arrived back in New York.

Lexi scrolled through her contacts and found her sister's number. She didn't care what the time was in Connecticut; she was just anxious to hear Andrea's voice and know she was okay.

'Why are you phoning me at this time in the morning?' Andrea said in a hushed voice. 'It's four o'clock!'

Lexi breathed a huge sigh of relief when she answered. 'I need to speak to you. Didn't you get my messages?'

'Hold on.' 'I need to speak to you. Didn't you get my messages?'

Lexi could hear rustling of sheets, then a door closing. She imagined her sister had got out of bed and gone into the bathroom so she didn't wake Chad. Lexi sat there nervously chewing a fingernail, hoping her phone signal didn't drop.

'Yes, I got your messages.'

'Oh, my god, Andrea. I was so worried. Why didn't you reply?'

Lexi expected her to say that she'd been trying to reply but that there had been a problem her end receiving international calls and texts. Lexi frowned when she remembered that she hadn't had a problem receiving Brandon's texts and calls. Even so, she said, 'Perhaps there's a problem with your phone.'

Andrea went quiet.

Oh no, have I lost my signal already? Lexi looked at her phone but that didn't appear to be the case. 'Andrea, are you still there?'

'Yes.'

Lexi frowned. She knew her sister. It wasn't like her not to reply to her texts of voicemails, especially when she'd said it was super-urgent, and most especially as she was abroad on her own. 'What's going on, Andrea?'

'I'm really sorry, but Nana and Grandpa found out.'

Lexi shook her head. 'I don't understand – found out what?'

'That you're in England.'

Lexi lifted off. 'Oh, my god, Andrea. Why did you tell them?'

'I didn't – I swear!'

'Then, how—?'

'Brandon.'

'Brandon?'

'Apparently, he phoned our grandparents – he said he got these texts, and was worried about you.'

'Oh, no.'

'Then obviously it came out that you hadn't been to New York to kick him out of the apartment, like you said you would.'

Lexi groaned.

'How come you thought they wouldn't find out?'

Lexi ignored her sister. 'I still don't get how they found out I was here.'

'It wasn't me, I swear, Lexi.'

Lexi didn't feel inclined to believe her. 'Then who—?'

'Dad.'

'Mitch?'

'Yeah.'

'I've been meaning to call you,' admitted Andrea.

Lexi understood. She didn't want to tell her sister what had happened. 'The thing is,' mused Lexi, 'I didn't tell Mitch where I was going.'

'Yeah, doesn't it occur to you that you didn't have to. He knows us too well.'

Lexi pursed her lips. Andrea was right. She shouldn't have opened her big mouth and mentioned England and the idea of taking a trip abroad in the same breath when she had seen him at the cottage in Connecticut. Even though she hadn't overtly said that was what she was thinking of, she might as well have.

Lexi said, 'I bet Nana asked you, even if it had come from Mitch.'

'I couldn't very well lie after it was all out in the open. Besides, you know Grandpa; he'd see straight through a fib.'

Lexi knew all right. That was why she'd insisted on speaking with Nana about returning to New York before she left Connecticut. 'Okay. What's done is done,' said Lexi, expecting an earful when she did return. But there wasn't a lot she could do about it just then. She had something more pressing on her mind – namely money. 'Look, about the reason for my call. I've got myself in a bit of a bind, as you may have gathered. I need some money.'

Lexi wasn't exactly sure how Andrea would physically get the money to her. Although she did have an idea. 'I'm in a place called Walberswick in Suffolk, an hour or so from London. It's just a little village, really, but there is a town, Southwold, which is walkable distance. I could go into Southwold and open a bank account.' Lexi had a British passport, so there was no reason why she couldn't open an account.

'I'll pay you back if you can just deposit some money into my account when I sort it out today.'

'No.'

Lexi frowned. *Did she just say no?* 'Er, pardon me?'

'I'm sorry, Lexi, but I can't.'

'You can't – or you won't?'

Andrea's silence answered Lexi's question. 'You are joking – right?' She couldn't believe her sister wouldn't help her out. 'Why ever not?' It wasn't like Andrea didn't have the money. 'Not to put too fine a point on it, Andrea, but I'm kind of destitute right now.'

'Where are you staying?'

'Well, that's beside the point.' Lexi would much rather not tell her she was squatting in Margot Dorey's houseboat.

'Look, Lexi, I understand you've got yourself in a bit of a predicament.'

'Oh, ya think!'

Obviously Andrea ignored that sarcastic tone, and continued.

'But all this can be resolved with a single phone call.'

Lexi fell silent. 'It's them, isn't it? They've told you not to give me any money.'

Andrea's silence said it all.

'You told them about my calls and texts – didn't you?'

'I told Dad.'

Lexi rolled her eyes. How could she have been so stupid? Of course Andrea would tell their stepfather. He hadn't been in touch either.

'I was worried about you.'

'If you were that worried, why didn't you just answer my calls?'

'Sorry.'

Lexi sighed. 'So, what have you been told to tell me?'

'Grandpa has booked you a flight home.'

'I've got my own flight home.'

'When's that?'

'I told you, I was thinking of staying maybe two or three weeks, although I booked a flexi-ticket in case it took a bit longer to locate Margot. When is the one they've booked for me?'

'Tomorrow.'

'Tomorrow?' Now Lexi knew why Andrea hadn't answered her phone straight away. She was probably gearing up to giving her the news that everyone knew where she was – including their grandparents.

'They've made a hotel reservation for you at Heathrow Airport tonight. It's all paid for. They've also got a cab company on standby who will pick you up wherever you are and drive you to the airport today. So, you see, your money worries are over. It's all been sorted.'

'Has it now?'

'What does *that* mean?'

Lexi wondered why Nana or Grandpa hadn't contacted her. Lexi already knew the answer – she was in their bad books. She raised her eyebrows. It was ridiculous. She was a grown woman. She could go on holiday where she fancied. And she fancied being there, in England. So nothing had been sorted as far as she was concerned. She said as much.

Andrea said, 'I don't know why they haven't been in touch themselves. All I know is that if you want that offer of a job to stay open, and you want to stay on the family payroll ...' She trailed off.

'Oh, my god. Are they threatening to cut me off?'

'I'm afraid so, Lexi. I can't believe it either.'

Lexi stared at a fishing vessel chugging past the houseboat. 'What *is* the big deal with me coming here?'

'I did ask that question. Well, I didn't ask, I kind of argued your corner. I thought exactly the same – what's the big deal?'

'You did?' That surprised her. Andrea never talked back to their grandparents.

'Anyone would think, by their bizarre behaviour, that they were hiding something – I mean, what is it they've got against England?'

'What did they say?'

'They didn't. They just said to make sure you get the message. I was going to phone you today.'

'The message about the flight, or the one about cutting me off?'

Andrea giggled. Then she realised that Lexi was being serious. 'Oh, sorry, Lexi. Yes, I see your point.'

Something occurred to Lexi. 'Did you mention the letter I came to personally deliver?'

'Of course not.'

'Good.'

The situation wasn't good, though, Lexi thought, especially given what the young lawyer had discovered; Lexi still hadn't told Andrea that the letter and her mother's instructions had been misfiled, and that the lawyer suspected that her grandfather had found out about the letter and told them to make it disappear.

Grandpa must have seen the name on the envelope, although he didn't know the contents; the lawyer was adamant that the envelope had not been tampered with. But that wasn't the point. Her grandfather did not want her to go to England, and Lexi knew she might never get another chance to find out what all this was about if she didn't stay and wait for Margot Dorey. The more they all pushed for her to return, the more she felt inclined to stay.

'You're not going to catch that flight tomorrow, are you?'

Lexi fell silent. She wondered whether, if she didn't make the flight, they would really cut her off.

'What are you going to do for money? You're going to run up a big bill at the hotel.'

What hotel? thought Lexi. Andrea's comment immediately made her think of the hotel in London. She'd paid for the first night in cash, which in hindsight, the hotel must think was a bit odd. She still had the second night to pay for. It wasn't as though she had accommodation to find at the moment. She just needed some cash for the basics and some money to pay for the that night at the London hotel, which was still worrying her immensely.

She stared across the river at The Harbour Inn. Would they have any job vacancies? Nothing fancy, just a bit of waitressing – something Lexi had done in her student days. Even though she hadn't had to work while at university, she'd enjoyed the first taste of earning her own money. She could do that again now. She'd even put her hand to some dishwashing, if it was cash-in-hand. Perhaps a bit of cleaning.

This wasn't how she envisaged spending her time in England, but what could she do? She knew the answer to that; get the private taxi to the airport, stay in the five-star hotel she knew her grandpa would have booked, and travel back to Connecticut, first class all the way.

But after everything that had happened, Lexi was determined to hand this letter to Margot Dorey in person. In fact, she felt like opening it to find out what was inside.

'Lexi?'

'I'm not coming back right now.'

'I can't help you out, Lexi. I'm getting married soon. Everything – the wedding, our new house, our livelihoods – depend on our grandparents. I can't afford to be cut off.'

'They wouldn't do that.'

'But you don't know that for sure.'

No, Lexi thought, *I don't*. What she did know was that once Grandpa had made up his mind, that was it. She swallowed. Was it worth risking everything just to meet this woman and find out who she was?

Andrea voiced her thoughts. 'Is it worth it, Lexi? What if you don't even find her?'

Lexi glanced about the houseboat. But I have, kind of. She hadn't told Andrea that. Although the damage would be done if she didn't return on that flight tomorrow, Lexi didn't feel inclined to give Andrea any more details about her trip in case they got back to Mitch and her grandparents.

'Don't worry about me.' Lexi sounded braver than she was feeling, but something was compelling her to stay – her mother's wishes.

26

Lexi scooped up the loose change on the coffee table and put it in her purse. She'd counted out how much she had to the penny, and hoped that it at least bought her lunch and perhaps some cheap breakfast cereal.

She could feel her heart thudding in her chest, her anxiety building at the realisation that she was really on her own. This wasn't a game – not like before, at university, and when she'd started her new life in New York. She'd always depended on her allowance. She had never really been independent of the family money, no matter how much she'd kidded herself that she was.

She thought of what her grandpa had said when she'd returned to Connecticut; they'd wanted her to take over the business when he retired. She realised that living in the apartment in New York and doing her job wasn't real – and that they knew that too. She'd got the impression from her grandpa that he'd mapped out her future but had indulged her in the little game she was playing – working at a publisher's on a salary that didn't pay enough to enable her to rent an apartment in New York – especially not a swanky apartment on Fifth Avenue.

Just like for Andrea, the allowance came with strings attached. How long did she think she could continue that game before she was expected to pay her dues and return to Connecticut for a life she didn't want? Lexi knew that if she didn't find work quickly – find some way of supporting herself over the next few weeks – then she'd have to get that flight home tomorrow. She hadn't told Andrea that. Her grandparents would know soon enough if she was heading home; she'd phone Andrea back and tell her the 'good' news.

Right now, she didn't want to think of the implications if she didn't catch that flight. She still couldn't believe they'd really cut off their granddaughter and virtually turn her out on to the streets. She tried to convince herself that it was just a threat, despite knowing her grandpa did not make empty threats.

Lexi put her purse in her handbag and headed back up to the deck. At the top of the stairs, she opened the door and checked that nobody was around before she exited the cabin.

Although Ray had said that the other houseboat neighbours were friendly, she got the impression they might not take kindly to another newbie, and would be curious as to why Margot had suddenly decided to have someone living in her place while she was away.

Ray hadn't asked too many questions, but she didn't know how inquisitive the other houseboat owners would be when they heard her accent; they would wonder where she came from and exactly how she came to be living on Margot's boat.

Under the circumstances, considering that she was squatting, Lexi wanted to keep a low profile. She quickly shut the cabin door and locked it. For a moment, she debated whether to put the key back where she had found it, under the flower pot. She didn't see the point. She expected no one knew it was there.

Lexi raised her eyebrows. That was actually a good reason to pop it back there. It was a small key, and it could really do with being on a keyring. She could just imagine losing it if she took it with her when she was out. Then she really would have a problem, with nowhere to live, and no other clothes besides what she was wearing – her suitcase was now locked inside the houseboat. She put the key in the plastic bag and tucked it out of sight under the flowerpot. She felt reassured that she'd done the right thing and that she wouldn't have to worry about mislaying it.

Lexi's first stop was The Harbour Inn on the quay in Southwold. She hurried along the footpath past the colourful houseboats and crossed the footbridge over to the other side of the quay. Passing wooden huts, one selling fish, the other with a fishing boat inside that looked as though it was undergoing repairs, Lexi stopped outside the large white building with mullion leaded windows.

She looked up at the large pub sign above the entrance porch. She didn't see any adverts in the window; she had been hoping for one reading something like *Help wanted, apply within.* Although the pub wouldn't be open until midday, she noticed that the door was ajar. She could hear voices inside. She opened the door and stepped inside. The pub had atmosphere and a quaint bar. She decided it wouldn't be a bad place to work – not at all.

A young woman was wiping down the oak counter at the bar. She looked up, her gaze shifting to the open door. 'I'm sorry, but we're closed. We open at twelve.'

Lexi approached. 'I just wanted to enquire whether you had any vacancies?'

'Vacancies?' She shook her head. 'I'm afraid we haven't got any rooms free. We are fully booked over the summer.'

'I'm not here for a room. I meant if you have a job vacancy like waitressing.' She trailed off, not wanting to sound desperate if she mentioned washing dishes too.

The young lady shook her head. 'No, I'm afraid not. We have a student who returns to work here during the summer months.'

Lexi's smile faded. She wasn't surprised. She wouldn't be lucky enough to walk into a part-time cash-in-hand little number just across the bridge.

'You might want to try the Co-op or Tesco in town.'

'You think they might have a vacancy?'

'I don't know, but they sometimes have small ads in the window. If you're looking for temporary summer work, you might find an ad in the window for help wanted – like cleaners or dog-walkers.'

'Dog-walkers?' Lexi liked the sound of that. She'd always wanted a pet. She loved dogs. 'Well, thank you very much.'

'There's the public library too, which might have information on job vacancies or where you could find them.'

'That's really helpful. I'm heading there now. Can you give me directions to the library?'

Lexi stepped out of the pub and followed the helpful young lady's directions past the quay and through the town. The library had recently moved. It was now housed in the old cottage hospital, a single-storey red-brick building that had been renovated and converted to house it.

After stopping at the local grocery store, Lexi arrived at the library. She didn't notice any job adverts on the information board as she entered. There was a lost cat advertised, and a second-hand car for sale. Someone was offering music lessons. But there was no ad for cleaners or dog-walkers. 'Yeah, I wouldn't be that lucky,' commented Lexi under her breath, starting to feel anxious again.

The young lady had also mentioned going to the job centre. There wasn't one in Southwold. That would involve a bus or taxi ride, or even catching a train, none of which she had the money for.

'Can I help you?'

Lexi turned around to find a middle-aged lady sitting at a reception desk. Lexi forgot her job-hunting for the moment. 'My father passed away some years ago, and I'm trying to locate his grave. A neighbour suggested a visit to the public library.' Lexi did wonder if it was even worth visiting a library on the Suffolk Coast for help, as they had lived in London at the time of his death.

'Do you think it was reported in the paper – the funeral?'

Lexi hadn't thought of that. 'I don't know. I can't imagine it would be a local paper, as we lived in London.' She wasn't sure when or how she'd get to the cemetery in London, if that was where he was buried, to lay some flowers. *First things first*, thought Lexi. She had to find the grave first.

'Okay, well do you know when he passed away?'

Of course Lexi knew. That day had been etched on her memory forever, the large cemetery, the short funeral procession of two cars, the black hearse, the squishy sodden boggy grass underfoot ruining her new black patent leather shoes.

It had rained that morning. It had rained all day. They'd stood under big black umbrellas watching her father's coffin being lowered into the ground.

Lexi reeled off the date like it was yesterday. It was the day after her birthday. She should have been playing with her new toys. She might have been playing with her dad if he hadn't had a heart attack at a ridiculously young age. She remembered he'd been complaining of feeling unwell, which wasn't like him. In her young life, he'd never had a day's sickness. In hindsight, that should have set alarm bells ringing. But she had been only six. None of them could have known that his sudden ill health was a harbinger of what was to come – a massive heart attack.

'We used to hold old newspaper records on microfilm to view on our microfiche machines, but now they are all stored digitally. They can be accessed on the internet. You can use one of the library computers.' She got out of her seat. 'Let me show you.'

Lexi sat down in a comfortable office chair in front of one of several computers in a row at the back of the library. The lady turned on the computer, punched some keys, and brought up an archive of old photos, memorabilia, and news articles with obituaries from around the date Lexi had given. The librarian said, 'An obituary with the funeral details would be the quickest way for you to find what you're looking for. Failing that, I would search the public records database which holds records of births, marriages and deaths.'

Lexi nodded.

'There is a website called *Find a Grave*. It's a database online of cemetery records, a free resource to locate someone's final resting place. You can search by city and then it will bring up a list of cemeteries. Each cemetery will have a list in alphabetical order of the information they hold regarding tombstone entries. Although without the name of the cemetery, that's going to prove quite a task – and that assumes they hold information on your late father's whereabouts. I'd start with the obituaries if I were you.'

Lexi didn't have a clue how to search public records. If the newspaper articles didn't yield a clue, then she'd have to ask the librarian or Google that website she'd suggested.

Twenty minutes later, Lexi hadn't found any mention of her father in an obituary in any national newspapers, nor an announcement of his death in the Classified Ads section, where the librarian had suggested she'd find personal announcements of births, marriages and deaths, including messages of condolences and funeral arrangements.

Lexi sat back in her chair, staring into space.

'Excuse me – is this computer free?'

A teenager, whom Lexi guessed was a student, stood by her chair with a large A4 folder and some textbooks in her arms. *She must have noticed me sitting there staring into space*, thought Lexi.

Lexi turned around and glanced at the library entrance where the librarian was seated. She appeared busy looking up something on her computer for an older guy standing in front of her desk. Lexi got out of her seat and smiled at the student, offering her the computer. She would have to wait to ask the librarian for help with accessing the public records database. She looked around, wondering what to do with herself while she waited. In one area of the library, there were a couple of people sitting in some cushioned chairs around a table. She noticed there were a few newspapers on the table. She walked over and picked up a local paper, The *East Anglian Daily Times*. Perhaps she'd find some job adverts inside.

She took a seat, opened the paper and found the recruitment ads at the back. There were a few temporary summer jobs on offer, but they weren't in Southwold. It meant she'd have to travel to another town by bus to do a cleaning round or bar work in pubs in the evening. She'd be dependent on buses, which might not be practical for getting to those sorts of jobs or working unsocial hours.

Lexi turned from the ads to glance at some of the latest news in the local area. Something caught her eye. There was a news story about graffiti found on some headstones at a cemetery in the area. The headstones had been vandalised with black spray paint.

Lexi shook her head, wondering what the world was coming to. There was a photo of the cemetery. It was quite large, with an abundance of established trees and flowers. The grass was neatly cut, not overgrown.

Lexi stared at the photo, idly wondering whether this could be the place where her father was buried. She remembered walking along one of the paths as they followed the coffin through some wooden gates and towards the far end of the cemetery, where there was a bench under a tree. A red-brick wall ran around the perimeter, just like the one in the photo. Lexi raised her eyebrows when she thought she remembered something else about that day; she recalled hearing seagulls and seeing the sea. Was she getting the memory of that day mixed up with a visit to the seaside?

Lexi frowned. That must be the case. She would have thought he was buried in London. That was where they had lived until he died. Although this area, the town and the beach, was definitely familiar;

she had been there before. Then there was that dream that seemed so real, the drowning dream. Was it a memory that had been triggered by returning to England? The dream had been quite vivid the previous night, while she was sleeping on the houseboat. 'It's just a dream,' Lexi said under her breath.

Lexi returned her attention to the article in the local paper. Even though she was quite sure that it couldn't be the same cemetery – she couldn't think why he would have been buried in a coastal town in Suffolk – she typed the name into her phone: St Peter and St Paul's Church, Aldeburgh.

'How are you getting on?'

Lexi turned in her chair and looked up at the librarian. 'There wasn't any mention of my father in any of the obituaries in the newspapers online. I thought I recognised this cemetery, though.' Lexi pointed at the news article in the local paper.

The librarian must have read the headline. She shook her head, echoing Lexi's sentiments when she commented, 'What is the world coming to?'

Lexi nodded in agreement.

'Did you say you recognised it?'

Lexi sighed. 'To be honest, I was six at the time. I'm sure this cemetery probably looks just like so many others up and down the country – and in London.'

'But if it is the one, then you've been searching through the wrong newspapers. It might be worth looking through old copies of local newspapers – like that one.'

Lexi looked at the paper in her hand. 'The *East Anglian*?'

'It's worth a try.'

Lexi stood up and put the paper back on the table. The computers weren't free. Her face dropped.

'Come with me,' said the librarian.

Lexi followed her over to the front desk.

'I've got some books to put back on the shelves. In the

meantime, you can use my computer. Let me just log in for you and pull up the archives for that date.'

'That is so kind of you.' Since she'd arrived in Suffolk, everyone had been so friendly and helpful. Although she couldn't imagine Margot Dorey would extend the same sort of welcome if she discovered her living on her houseboat.

27

'Here we are. You can look through these and see if there's a mention of your father in the obituaries or personal announcements sections in the local papers. I've pulled them up for you.' She got out of her chair and motioned for Lexi to take a seat. 'Good luck.'

Lexi smiled. 'Thanks.' While she had the librarian's attention, she asked, 'I don't suppose by any chance you have a job vacancy at the library? Even a bit of cleaning, starting immediately?' *I'm sounding desperate,* thought Lexi.

'Looking for summer work?'

'Er, yes.'

'Are you an American student studying in England?'

At twenty-six, and five foot nothing, Lexi realised that she could still pass for a student in her late teens or early twenties. She could lie, but staring at the sincere lady who had been so helpful, Lexi felt compelled to tell her the truth – some of it. 'No. I've got a degree in marketing. I worked at a publishing house in New York. I was good at my job, but they let me go.'

'Oh, what happened?'

'They were restructuring and wanted to cut staff. They chose me because—' Lexi suddenly stopped. She really didn't want to get into this family rift over her returning to England. If she said she was part of one of the wealthiest families on the East Coast, the librarian would wonder why she needed a job and couldn't just ask them for some money.

'I was the last to be taken on for a post.' It wasn't a lie. She had been one of the newest members of staff in the marketing department.

'Last in, first out.' The librarian sighed. 'It's so frustrating when you just get your foot in the door and want to gain some experience.'

Lexi got the impression that she'd experienced the same at some point in her working life.

'So, you've returned to England to see what opportunities might be here?'

Lexi decided to run with it for the time being. 'Yes, sure. It might not be a bad idea, having a fresh start. You know, when I touched down on British soil for the first time in twenty years, I felt like I'd come home.'

The librarian smiled. 'I'm not surprised. I couldn't imagine living abroad. I couldn't imagine living anywhere else but on the lovely Suffolk Coast.' She looked at Lexi. 'What brought you home, exactly? Just a holiday?'

'No.' At first, Lexi wasn't going to share the real reason, but she thought *why not?* 'My mother left a letter in her will to hand-deliver to someone in England.'

'Oh, I'm so sorry for your loss.'

'Thank you. She passed away six months ago, and this letter has only just come to light.'

Once again, Lexi didn't want to get into her family issues and the possibility that it had been misfiled on purpose.

'So, the letter is for a relative in England?'

Lexi shook her head. 'No, I think she must be an old friend, but I won't know for sure until I find her. I don't even know if I've got any relatives alive here.' She doubted it.

'You could join one of those sites like AncestryDNA.'

'My sister did that a while back. Her fiancé bought her membership as a gift one Christmas. It's a bit of a thing in America. He knows that we were both born here and hold dual nationality – well, I still do; my sister gave hers up. Anyway, my point is that he thought she might be interested in finding some English relatives. To be honest, she wasn't, but she joined the site, posted her details and did a DNA test because I wanted to know if there were any relatives here.'

Lexi didn't know why she was telling her all this, but she seemed interested.

'What happened?'

'Nothing, actually.' *Apart from Mitch going off on one when he found out.* Lexi thought at the time that his reaction was uncharacteristic; Mitch was normally so laid-back about everything. He'd been a breeze to grow up with as a stepdad; whenever they'd wanted something, all they'd had to do was ask Mitch, even if Mum had said no. Lexi had normally got her little sister to use her puppy dog eyes on Mitch, and that had always done it. As the baby of the family, and the only one of the two of them who had called him Daddy, Andrea had always had him wrapped around her little finger.

'Well, you might have some distant relations here. I've got an idea. I can put you in touch with a lovely gentleman who lives locally. He runs a business tracing relatives, often where someone has died intestate – without a will. But I'm sure he'd help you out.'

'You're not talking about Ray, by any chance? He suggested joining AncestryDNA too.'

'You know him?'

'Yes, he lives next to—' She had it on the tip of her tongue to say, *me*. 'To Margot Dorey. She's the person who I came here to find.' Lexi got the letter out of her handbag and showed her the envelope with the name.

'Your mum knew the writer, Margot Dorey?'

'Yes, I guess so. She must have met her when we lived in London. I was born here and have dual nationality. I have a British passport. My mum wanted me to hand-deliver a letter to her, but I understand she spends the summers in London.' Lexi looked at her. 'You know of her?'

After almost twenty years with no sign of another book, according to the publisher, it surprised Lexi that people still remembered the author and her books. Although perhaps it wasn't a surprise that a librarian knew of a well-known local author.

'She came here to read each book in her trilogy to local children when they were first published. Not here, but where the old library used to be.'

'Really? Were you working there at the time?'

'Yes, I'd just started – I was nineteen and had just left school. I can't believe I'm forty this year. Where does the time go? I'll tell you what, there's no time to waste doing things you don't want to do in life.'

Lexi thought of the job Grandpa had set his sights on for her, taking over the company. Was that what she really wanted? She didn't even have to ask herself that question. The librarian was right: there was no time to waste on jobs that weren't for you.

Or relationships, thought Lexi. She was thinking of all those years since high school that she'd spent with Brandon. Perhaps if they'd never got together, she'd have met her soulmate, like Andrea, and be engaged to be married by now. Perhaps she'd even have a family of her own or be looking forward to starting one.

'I have some photos somewhere of the last book-signing for that famous trilogy, and what would turn out to be her last published book. I kept them when we moved from the old library – I don't know why. Would you like to see them?'

'Oh, yes!'

Lexi watched her open a drawer and rummage through until

she found a paper envelope.

'Ah, here we are.'

As she watched the librarian get out the photos and put them on her desk, Lexi recalled what the publisher had said about Margot Dorey's refusal to do any publicity for the books. This must have been the one and only time she had. Although you couldn't exactly call it a publicity shoot – a young librarian taking personal photos, and an author reading her books to children in the local library. Lexi guessed that these must be the only photos of the reclusive writer.

'She looks older now, obviously.'

'You've seen her?'

'Of course. She pops into the library for a book from time to time. She keeps a low profile, though. I pretend I don't know who she is. I get the feeling she wants to keep it that way.' She handed Lexi the photos. 'I imagine it's because she was a three-hit wonder and never wrote again.'

Lexi picked up the photos and started to leaf through them. 'That's because she had a family tragedy and just stopped writing.'

'Really? Where did you hear that?'

'The publisher. They've offered me a finder's fee if – when I discover her whereabouts – I can persuade her to write another book.'

'Sounds as though that might be a bit of a challenge – persuading her to write again if she'd stopped due to a family tragedy.'

Lexi agreed. She turned her attention to the photos. The author was sitting on a stool in the children's book corner of the library. There was a group of children in school uniform sitting crossed-legged on the floor in front of her.

One photo caught her eye; it had a particularly clear image of Margot Dorey's features. She had dark hair in a curly bob framing her round cheeks, a straight angular nose, and large brown eyes. The photo had just caught a moment in time when she had looked up from reading her book and was smiling at the children gathered on the floor in front of her. She could only see the backs of the children's heads in this photo, but one child had turned to the girl sitting next to her, the photo catching her in profile. Lexi had a peculiar feeling when she looked at the child. She seemed familiar somehow.

'What year were these photos taken?'

'I wrote it on the back.'

Lexi turned the photo over. She looked at the date. She would have been six; it would only have been a short time after her father died. 'What school was this – do you know?'

'It's the local primary school here in Southwold. The school is still here but the uniforms have changed over the years. They wear white polo shirts and sweatshirts, instead of blouses and cardigans or jumpers.'

Lexi stared at the photo.

'Is something the matter?'

Lexi shook her head and leafed through the other photos, but all the children had their backs to the camera. Deep in thought, she gave them back to the librarian, who put them back into the drawer.

28

'So, you sound as though you've had a good education, and you've got work experience. You're keen to find work.'

'Oh, yes, very.' At some point in the conversation, it had dawned on Lexi that this felt a little bit like an informal job interview. She stopped slouching in her chair, sat up straight, shoulders back, and gave the librarian plenty of eye contact as she answered her questions, in case this *was* an informal interview. For what position, she hadn't a clue, but she remembered the extra classes she had attended at university to prepare for applying for jobs and to learn interview techniques. Of course, it could just be a friendly chat. She was American; maybe the librarian had time on her hands and was just a little bit nosy. Lexi had just decided that this must be all it was, when the librarian said, 'We have an apprenticeship.'

'I'm sorry, I don't know what that means.' *Is she offering me a position?* thought Lexi.

'They're government-backed schemes whereby businesses, charities, and the public sector can take on apprentices to teach them the ropes, and at the end of the apprenticeship, if they do well, they can be offered a permanent position.'

'Okay,' said Lexi slowly. 'Are you offering me one?'

'Would you be interested in changing career and becoming a librarian?'

Lexi felt like she would do almost anything for money, although that wasn't to say she wouldn't consider a change in career, and a slower pace of life. Working in a little local library and walking through town at the end of her day to cross the little bridge to a houseboat where she could watch the sun set over the water; what was not to like? Except it wasn't real. The houseboat wasn't hers and she could already guess the catch with the apprenticeship.

'It's like an internship – isn't it?' Lexi was familiar with those. It was how she'd started at the publishing house in New York. You were trained on the job but paid nothing as an intern. She could afford it when she was being bankrolled by her grandparents – but not anymore.

Lexi was interested, but she had to be honest. 'I really appreciate the offer, but I can't accept.'

'Why not?'

'I can't afford an unpaid position. I'm guessing it's similar to an internship?'

'Yes, and no.'

'Yes *and* no?'

'You do get paid, but it's a very basic wage while you work towards a librarian qualification. Your marketing skills would come in handy. There's a misconception that all we do all day is walk around with a trolley and put books back on bookshelves.'

Lexi gave the wooden trolley a sideways glance.

'But there's more to the role – much more. We get involved in the community, invite local authors to readings, hold book clubs, knitting clubs, all sorts of things take place in our community rooms. There's so much more to being a librarian. You'll find out if you take the position. But you'll have to work full-time for basically a pittance.'

Lexi listened with interest. It was something she had considered once, years ago. She'd either wanted to write, or work in a local library.

She loved books, but her mum had persuaded her to get a degree and aim high.

Was she particularly happy or fulfilled in her high-flying job in marketing for a publishing company? She'd thought she was, in the beginning. After all, it was what she'd worked hard for. But then she had started to have doubts over whether it was what she really wanted to do forever.

She'd admitted as much once to her mum, who had replied that she thought that was what Lexi wanted – to work in some capacity in publishing. Lexi remembered thinking at the time, *I don't know where she got that idea from*. She wasn't even sure it had been her own idea.

Lexi asked, 'How much is the pittance?'

'One hundred pounds per week. It's not nearly enough to live on, I'm afraid, but you just fall into the cut-off age-wise, at twenty-six, for me to be able to offer you the position.'

'That's more than enough. I've got my accommodation sorted—' blurted Lexi without thinking. She cringed, hoping she wasn't asked where she was living.

'Well, that great. So, would you like the job?'

'Oh, yes – absolutely.'

'And you wouldn't mind the hours?'

'Not at all.' Lexi was used to working full-time. She had no problem with that.

'To be honest, I don't know if we've got enough work for you to do full-time, but those are the stipulations of the apprenticeship scheme.'

Lexi could already see a fly in the ointment. 'I guess it will take some time, with paperwork and references before I can start in the position. I have my former employer's phone number. They said they'd provide excellent references.'

The librarian smiled. 'Perfect. Have you got a passport, some form of ID?'

Lexi got out her British passport.

'Great. You would just be pushing that trolley around to begin with and putting books away.'

Lexi didn't mind that at all. 'Fine by me. So, does this mean I can start straight away?'

'Yes. Now all we need is your National Insurance number so you can get paid.'

Lexi smiled faded. 'I'm sorry, what is that?'

'It's issued to anybody who has a right to live, work or study in the UK, and takes around four weeks to process.'

'Oh.' Lexi knew there'd be a problem somewhere.

'Chin up. Don't worry. It won't impede you starting with us. You can apply online. I will call up the website and you can fill in an application while you are here if you like.'

'That would be so helpful – thank you.' Lexi relaxed as another hurdle appeared to be overcome.

'Also there's a government fund we can dip into, to pay your wages in the meantime. Weekly, is that okay?'

'Weekly. Like the end of next week?'

'That's right. Payday will be a Friday, so this time next week.'

Lexi glanced at the plastic carrier bag full of shopping by her feet. That would mean making her bread, apples, and cheese last for an entire week, but she couldn't complain. At least it wasn't monthly. She did have thirty pence left. She'd seen a basket in the local Co-op with cheap food past its sell-by-date going for ten pence. She'd picked up a loaf of bread, two Belgian buns, and a packet of apples. That basket might come in handy later in the week before payday.

She'd felt guilty taking the cheap food away from people who might need it, but right now she was one of those people. She was literally counting the pennies. She had never thought she'd find herself in such a position.

She'd had to pay full price for the cheese and margarine, but those and the box of breakfast cereal had been from a cheap value range and had cost a pound each. After buying those and the few items for ten pence each, she felt she might just get by. Fortunately, she'd found some teabags and a jar of coffee on the boat, along with a pint of long-life milk, which she'd opened. That would last a few days.

She knew that this apprenticeship was all well and good while she was living rent-free on the houseboat, but what if Margot came back soon, or someone else discovered her there?

'How long is the apprenticeship before it pays a proper wage?' Lexi couldn't believe she was thinking of staying on in Southwold.

'Twelve months.'

Lexi thought of her grandparents; would they really cut her off if she didn't go home tomorrow? She couldn't survive for months if she had to pay a rent.

Lexi didn't want to think about that right now. She just wanted the position – and not just for the money. What if this was what she still really wanted to do? She wouldn't find out unless she tried.

Lexi's enthusiasm waned when something occurred to her. 'You must have other applicants. I wouldn't want to deny anyone else the opportunity, especially if they are young, right out of school.' Lexi was aware that she was older, she had a degree, and that she'd had opportunities and clear advantages in her life.

'We've been advertising the position for some time. We have a feeling that the government might withdraw the librarian apprenticeship, so this might be the last opportunity. But no one locally seems to be interested.'

Lexi grinned. 'Then I would like the position very much, if you'll have me.'

'Oh, most definitely.' The librarian walked over to the trolley full of books. 'I'll just pop these books back on the bookshelves, then I will sort out the paperwork for the position. We can submit your application for your National Insurance number today too.'

Lexi could not believe her luck, although she imagined they were keen for someone to fill the position because it meant an extra pair of hands but without funds coming out of their budget as it was paid for by the government.

'I'll just need to take some details down for the applications, like your current address.'

She felt bad that she hadn't mentioned the return flight she had booked for the US, and that her accommodation was not guaranteed – certainly not for twelve months. Lexi knew she had no choice but to give her current address – Margot's houseboat by the quay. Despite her desperation for a job and money, she just knew she would not have taken the opportunity away from someone who could commit to twelve months. But she was the only one interested in the position.

Lexi didn't know where she'd be in twelve days' time, let alone twelve months, but right now she didn't want to think about that. All she could think about was one hundred pounds in her pocket come the end of the week, and the next week, and the week after that – although the first thing she was going to do with her wages was to set aside as much as she could and pay what she owed to the hotel in Bloomsbury. But as well as the money, she would have somewhere to go, and something to do, so she wasn't sitting on a houseboat all day staring at four walls. She was used to working.

When she had first flown to London, she had imagined her days would be filled with galleries and museums and seeing the sights. But she knew she would soon tire of those things; it was what she had done for the past five years, living in New York. The fact was, returning to Connecticut had made Lexi realise she was already looking for a change. A change of pace, a change of scenery, and a change of job – but that didn't mean that working in her grandparents' business or staying in Connecticut was what she was after.

Suffolk was not that different to Connecticut in some ways.

There were beaches, and scenic little seaside towns, and walks in the countryside – but she was in England, the place of her birth. After New York, if she was going to consider a fresh start, then she couldn't think of a nicer place to make it.

'Don't forget to look through the old local papers online for your father's obituary, or an announcement by your family. You might find one, you never know.'

'Oh yes, right.' With all the talk of jobs and Margot Dorey, she'd forgotten what she'd gone to the library for in the first place. However, there was something she wanted to do before she looked through those newspaper articles. 'The photos in your drawer,' she said. 'Would it be okay if I took a photo on my phone of a couple of them? You see, I didn't really know what Margot Dorey looked like before seeing the photos, and it would be really helpful to have it to jog my memory.'

The librarian smiled. 'Of course, go ahead. You know where they are.'

'Thank you.'

Lexi photographed the picture she wanted and then turned her attention to the computer in front of her. She started to scroll through the personal ads in the local papers around the time of her father's death. She wasn't expecting to find anything. She didn't see why her father would be buried—

Lexi suddenly sat forward in her chair. There, in black and white were the details of the funeral arrangements for her father, and where to send flowers.

'Did you find anything?' The librarian asked as she pushed the trolley over to a bookshelf near the reception desk.

'Yes, I did. It was the cemetery in Aldeburgh that was in the news article I read.'

'St Peter and St Paul's churchyard?'

'Yes, that's the one,' Lexi said excitedly. She couldn't believe she'd found it. 'Is Aldeburgh far?'

'Aldeburgh is a seaside town along the coast. You can catch a bus from here. Hold on, I'll look up the details.'

Lexi moved to let the librarian sit down in front of the computer. She printed off some timetables. 'There are two options; you can get a bus, which takes around three hours as it's not a direct route, or you can take a taxi, which takes thirty minutes. Were you planning to go today?'

Lexi felt she would like nothing more than to go that day, but she didn't have the money for the fare, let alone a taxi. 'No, not today.'

'Why don't we get this paperwork filled in? Then you could officially start tomorrow. I know it's a Saturday, but we are open six days a week, including Saturday and Sunday. We're closed on Monday. Are you okay starting tomorrow, or did you have plans?'

Lexi shook her head. 'I don't have any plans.'

'Great. Let's get your application in for your National Insurance number. In the meantime, we can pay your wages from the library funds until we get you on the payroll system, if you are okay with it in cash? I would need to draw it from the account.'

'Oh, yes.' Lexi breathed a sigh of relief although something just occurred to her. 'Do I need to open a bank account?'

'You will need one for your wages to be paid into. There are a couple of banks in Southwold – Barclays and Lloyds Bank.'

She didn't know what she would do with the rest of her day, but she would open an account.

'They may need a small deposit to open an account.'

'I see.' That scuppered that plan, at least until she had some cash. 'What time would you like me to start?'

'We open at half-past nine tomorrow, so why don't you pop along at ten? Then we'll have a chat about the days and hours you work. You won't be expected to come in six days a week or every weekend.'

'Okay.' Lexi didn't mind what hours she worked.

'What are you going to do today – any plans?'

Lexi shook her head. 'I'm going to visit the cemetery at some point.' *When I have the bus or taxi fare*, thought Lexi.

'You could call Ray to see if he could help with tracing some relatives. I have his number somewhere.'

'Oh, yes – that might be helpful.' Lexi didn't need his phone number. She could just call on him when she returned to the houseboat, but of course she couldn't mention where she was living. Lexi waited for her to find the number. It was nice of her to go to the trouble, but Ray ran a business, and she didn't have the money to pay him at the moment.

'Oh, and if the writer, Margot Dorey, returns and pops in the library, I'll be sure to let you know.'

Lexi stared at her. If she did return soon, then her plans to spend the summer in this beautiful part of the world, and work at the library, would be scuppered. *Where would she live?* Lexi had momentarily forgotten the reason she was here in the first place – to hand Margot Dorey the letter.

29

Lexi took the shopping bag down the stairs and put the box of cheap cereal and loaf of bread away in a kitchen cupboard. She stocked the fridge with the margarine, cheese, and bag of apples.

She left the Belgian buns on the kitchen counter to have one with a drink. She had visited the grocery store on the way back from the library and had spent another ten pence on a packet of custard cream biscuits that were also past their sell-by date.

She'd just reached for the kettle when she heard a door slam and a child shout out. 'I don't care!'

Lexi heard a man reply, 'Come back inside and go to your room, young lady.'

'No! You can't make me! And it's not a room – it's a cabin.'

Lexi guessed the voices were coming from the houseboat next door. She stifled a laugh at the little girl's smart retort. She remembered those days when she was young, fast approaching her teens, and the uncooperative little minx she'd turned into.

'Right, well if you're not going to do as you're told and go to your room, you can sit here and take some time out. And when you are ready to apologise ...'

'I will not!'

Lexi heard another door slam. This time, she imagined it was the girl's dad slamming a door. What happened next wiped the smile off Lexi's face; she could hear the girl crying. Lexi took a few steps up the stairs and popped her head outside. The houseboat next door was larger than Margot's little narrowboat, with a wider deck. She could see the girl sitting on a garden chair on the wooden deck, in a recliner with soft, cushioned seats. But she wasn't sitting there enjoying the sunshine. Dressed in blue dungarees and a white tee-shirt, her thin spindly arms were wrapped round her legs, her chin touching her knees. Tears rolled down her face. It wasn't easy to gauge her age. Lexi guessed she was around nine or ten. Her mousy brown hair was tied up in ponytail.

Lexi called out, 'Hello.'

The girl suddenly stopped and looked about her. 'Who said that?'

Lexi walked up the steps and emerged out on deck. She glanced at the houseboat next door, expecting the girl's father to appear and tell her off for talking to a stranger.

The young girl wiped her wet cheeks with the back of her hand.

'I'm Lexi.'

'My name's Charlie. Well, it's Charlotte, but I prefer Charlie.'

Lexi smiled. 'Hey, we've got something in common. My name's Alexandra, but everyone calls me Lexi. I much prefer it.' Although it was true, she did like her shortened name, that wasn't the only reason she preferred it. Her father had always called her Alexandra, and it just brought back memories of him and made her sad when she heard her name.

She saw Charlie offer her a tentative smile in return. Her big blue eyes stared at Lexi. 'Can I come over and see your houseboat?'

Lexi had it on the tip of her tongue to say, *I don't think so, I don't want to get you into any more trouble.* But Charlie's dad was obviously busy doing something and hadn't heard their conversation. She reckoned Charlie could come over, see inside, and be back before he even noticed she was gone. 'Okay.'

'I'm not meant to talk to strangers,' said Charlie, 'but you're a neighbour, so that doesn't count.'

Lexi smiled at her as she stood up and peeked in through one of the windows to check her father wasn't watching before she crept off the boat. She ran the few paces along the towpath to Margot's gate. She stopped and looked at her houseboat. So did Lexi. There was still no sign of her dad.

Charlie opened the gate, walked down the gangplank and stepped aboard.

Lexi's first thought was that Charlie was younger than she had first imagined.

'Lexi, how old are you? I'm ten.'

Lexi tried not to look surprised. She didn't look ten. She smiled. Kids were so obsessed with people's ages. 'I'm twenty-six.'

'I wish I was a grown-up. Then I could do what I liked, and I wouldn't have to move house if I didn't want to.'

Lexi glanced at the houseboat. 'I thought you were here on your summer holiday?'

Charlie shook her head vigorously. 'We live here now.'

'Ah, so it's a rental.'

Charlie shrugged. 'I guess.'

Or he could have bought it, thought Lexi. In that case, he'd fit right in with the neighbours. She looked at Charlie and guessed she was not that enthusiastic about the move. That was probably why she and her father were having words.

'So, are you starting a new school in September?' Lexi expected that was tough, to start again with making new friends. But she was only ten; it meant she would make friends and go up with them to high school. Lexi frowned. Unfortunately, that thought brought Brandon to mind.

'I don't go to school.'

Lexi couldn't hide her surprise.

'I'm home-schooled.'

'Oh, I see.' Lexi didn't, not really. Why not send her to school? She'd miss out on so much, socially. Lexi wasn't completely against home-schooling. She imagined that in some places, certainly in America where families might live vast distances from schools, it was the only option. Even when it was just personal choice, though, she imagined that it suited some children to spend less time in formal education and more time learning through doing – be it visits to museums, helping out on a farm, or creative pursuits.

School wasn't for everyone. Lexi wouldn't have minded being home-schooled – as long as her sister was too. She couldn't imagine being on her own all day with just a parent; that would be boring and a bit lonely. And what about friends, and romantic relationships when she got older?

Once again, Lexi's thoughts turned to Brandon. He was the reason that she didn't have a best friend from high school. He *was* her best friend.

The trouble was, when other girls had first started high school, forging what would turn out to be lifelong friendships for some – besties, as they used to call them – Lexi and Brandon were already an item, and had been since they were twelve. When she looked back on it, that had been a mistake. Although they hadn't started a physical relationship until they were sixteen, Lexi regretted that she hadn't made the effort to make more friends.

It had not been easy for her, though. The other girls were jealous that she had a boyfriend at such an early age, even though, in those early days, he wasn't a proper boyfriend; he was just a boy she hung out with because he was her best friend.

Lexi glanced at the door to the cabin. She hadn't just invited Charlie over because she felt sorry for her, sitting out there all on her own. Lexi felt a little guilty for being selfish and thinking of herself; she wanted the company. However, she did glance at the houseboat, wondering when Charlie's father would notice her absence. Perhaps he was busy working?

30

'So, Charlie, does your father work from home?' Lexi thought that he must do if he was home-schooling her.

'Can I see inside now?'

Lex wasn't sure if her young visitor was avoiding the question, or just acting like kids often did, in their own little world, their attention easily diverted. 'Of course.'

Charlie opened the door and scooted down the small flight of wooden steps to the cabin. 'Wow, this is so *old*.'

Lexi smiled. She imagined it was quite different to the modern rental next door.

Charlie turned around and winced. 'Sorry, that was rude.'

Lexi laughed. 'There's nothing to be sorry about. I wasn't sure what I thought about it at first. But it grows on you.' Lexi was the same – she was used to modern, updated places, not this, old and chintzy.

'I like it, though,' said Charlie. 'I like the pictures hanging on the walls, and the rugs and cushions.' She ran over and jumped on the sofa. 'I think it's—'

'Cosy?' Lexi suggested.

Charlie grinned as she grabbed a big cushion and hugged it. 'Oh, yes. And colourful. It's not like our place.' Charlie's expression soured. 'Our houseboat is so ... beige.'

'Is it?'

'Oh, yes. Beige walls, beige carpet, beige sofa, beige curtains, beige *everything*.'

Lexi tried to stifle a grin.

Charlie settled her gaze on Lexi, 'So, this isn't your houseboat?'

Lexi shook her head. 'I'm afraid not.'

'Who does it belong to?'

'A lady called Margot – she's a writer.'

'What's she like?'

'I don't know.'

'You don't know?'

Lexi came to join her on the sofa. 'I'm houseboat-sitting for the summer.' She hated lying, especially to a child, but she didn't know what else to say – she could hardly tell Charlie that she had broken in.

'I hate our houseboat. I like yours much better. Can we swap?'

Oh, to be ten, thought Lexi, *when life appears that simple*. 'I'm sorry, Charlie, but we can't.'

'I hate moving.' She hugged the cushion close to her chest.

'Did you move here because of your daddy's work?'

Charlie shrugged. 'I don't know.'

Lexi was about to ask the question again about what he did for a living when Charlie said, 'I'm hungry.' She cast her gaze over to the kitchen.

'Oh, right, yes.' Lexi glanced at the clock on the wall in the kitchen. It was lunchtime. 'Would you like a sandwich?' It was all Lexi had to offer, besides the apples, Belgian buns and a packet of value custard cream biscuits – the ones Lexi remembered having as a child. She'd looked for them in New York, and had asked in the English shop she often visited. They had said they'd order some for her, but the biscuits had never materialised. If it had been a choice between the healthy apples and the biscuits, she'd have bought the custard creams.

'Yes, I'd like a sandwich. Have you got white bread? I only eat white bread.'

Lexi nodded. It had been the only loaf on offer in the shop. Lexi usually chose the healthier option – brown wholemeal.

'I only like cheese.'

'Okay. Cheese I can do.'

'And I like crisps.'

'Oh.'

'But that's okay because I have some here.' Charlie had an old, worn shoulder bag that looked as though it had seen better days. Lexi guessed it might have come from a charity shop. 'I bought some crisps and sweets with my pocket money.'

'Great.' Lexi added, 'I have some apples.' She saw Charlie's nonplussed expression. 'I have custard creams.'

'Really? I love those.'

Lexi stood up and walked into the kitchen. She opened the fridge and got out the cheese, margarine and loaf of white bread. It didn't take her long to whip up the sandwich, especially as it turned out that Charlie preferred the cheese sliced rather than grated. *The girl knows what she wants,* thought Lexi.

'Do we have to eat at the table?'

Lexi looked at the small table under the window. 'I'd rather sit on the sofa.'

'Me too!'

Lexi smiled. 'That's settled then.' She brought over a plate of sandwiches each and two apples, hoping to tempt her with a healthy option as part of lunch.

'Where's the custard creams?' asked Charlie as she opened a big bag of crisps.

Lexi returned to the kitchen to fetch the biscuits. She was going to bring over the packet but thought better of it. Instead, she laid out two biscuits each on a plate.

'I need a drink.'

Lexi sighed. Of course you do, and I've got no juice. 'Sorry, Charlie, but I've only got water.'

'What about tea?'

'Tea? You'd like a cup of tea?'

'Yes, please. Milk and two sugars.'

Sugar, thought Lexi, returning to the kitchen. She didn't have the money to buy a packet of sugar, although she did like sugar in her tea. 'Ah, here we are.' She knew there was a small packet of Tate & Lyle white sugar in the kitchen cupboards. It was unopened. Lexi hesitated. She hadn't planned to open it, but now Charlie was here, she thought she might as well. She'd just have to replace it, along with the teabags and milk she'd used.

Lexi waited a minute or two for the kettle to boil before she brought over two mugs of tea. Although she didn't mind a cup of coffee on occasion, she could understand the English obsession with tea. Lexi couldn't live without her PG Tips.

'Here we are.' Lexi had added extra milk to cool it down. She put it down on the coffee table in front of them.

Charlie peered at the mug of tea.

Lexi looked at her expression. 'Did I make it okay?'

Charlie picked up the mug and took a sip. She nodded. 'Ahh, that hit the spot.'

Lexi stifled another grin. 'Well, I'm glad it meets with your approval.'

Charlie lowered the mug. 'For an American, you make rather a good brew.'

'A brew?'

'A cup of tea.'

'Ah. A brew. I like that.'

Lexi had been wondering when Charlie would comment on her accent. 'I'm half-English, actually. My dad was English.'

'Okay,' said Charlie.

'Where did you hear the word, brew?' Lexi thought it was quite old-fashioned, along with the phrase, *hit the spot.* It was funny hearing someone so young talk as though they were in their seventies or even eighties.

'TV.'

'Where's your mum?' Lexi immediately regretted asking that question. Perhaps, like hers, she'd passed away.

'Mum lives with her new husband. She's having a baby.'

'So, you'll have a little brother and sister soon? Do you know if it's a boy or girl?'

Charlie shrugged. 'I don't know. I don't see her.'

'Oh, right. So, how do you know about the baby?'

'She's on Facebook. There's a photo of her with her new husband,' Charlie grimaced. 'And a kid.'

'I see.' Lexi got the picture. Or, more to the point, Charlie was out of the picture.

Lexi watched her take a handful of crisps and dump them on the side of her plate, then open up one of the halves of her cheese sandwich and crunch some of the crisps inside. She picked it up in both hands and said, 'He goes to a nice school.'

'Who?'

'Her other kid.' Charlie bit into the sandwich. She said with her mouth full, 'I saw photos on Facebook. He's not her boy – must be her new husband's.'

Lexi nodded and ate her sandwich while she listened to Charlie. *Poor kid,* she thought. She must miss her mum, but by the sounds of things, it didn't cut both ways. Her mum had obviously remarried, started a new family, and cut Charlie out of her life. What a shame for all concerned.

She couldn't imagine what it would have been like if her parents had split up and her mum had found someone else and left them behind with their dad. *But I would have loved to grow up here, in England,* thought Lexi. *I would have loved for my dad not to have died.*

Lexi smiled at Charlie. At least she had her dad. And perhaps in the future she could reconnect with her mum, if that was what they both wanted. Lexi kept her thoughts to herself. Charlie was ten. She wouldn't see it that way. She wouldn't see anything positive about her situation; not now, at any rate. All she'd see was the family she'd never have.

'I used to go to school and live in a nice house.'

Broken relationships. Divorce. Lexi knew that unfortunately, it often was the children that paid the price. She was just relieved that when it came to her relationship with Brandon, at least they weren't married.

It wasn't the thought of going through a divorce that bothered Lexi – although it was, of course, far simpler just splitting up – it was the thought of what it would have been like if they'd had children. Lexi didn't envy Charlie's dad. It must be hard being a single parent.

'Have you told your dad that you would like to go to school?' Lexi gently asked. She didn't know how long it had been, but it was obvious that Charlie missed school.

Charlie finished her sandwich and picked up the mug of tea. She shook her head and frowned.

'Does he know how you feel?'

She shrugged.

'You must tell him.' Even as she said it, Lexi had a feeling there was more to it than Charlie was letting on.

'It wouldn't do any good.'

'Why do you say that?'

'Can I tell you a secret?'

Lexi put her plate down on the coffee table and gave Charlie her full attention. 'Sure.'

Charlie furrowed her brow and stared into her large mug of tea. 'This is going to sound weird.' She looked up, fierce blue eyes staring at Lexi intently. 'You can't tell my dad I told you this.'

'Cross my heart and pinkie swear.'

Charlie frowned at her. 'What's a pinkie swear?'

Lexi held out her little fingers to showed her how you did a pinkie swear. She clasped her two little fingers together. 'It's like shaking hands, but shaking fingers. That's a pinkie swear.'

She had done it all the time with her sister when they were younger, especially when she got older and snuck out of the house to meet Brandon. Somehow, her sister had always managed to catch her in the act when she was meant to be in bed, fast asleep. Lexi made her swear not to tell. Of course, it wasn't actually that which had kept her mouth shut – it was buying her sweets when she was little, or not telling on her when she had started dating Chad and started sneaking out herself.

Lexi held out her pinkie.

Charlie put her mug of tea down and wrapped her little finger around Lexi's.

Lexi said, 'I pinkie swear to keep whatever you are about to tell me, a secret.'

Charlie smiled. 'Good.' She turned to face Lexi and sat crossed-legged on the sofa. 'I think my dad is in some kind of trouble, and we're—'

Lexi stared at her. 'You're *what*?'

'On the run.'

'Charlie!' came a male voice from outside.

'Oh, no. It's Dad.'

Lexi quickly got to her feet.

'Can I come back again?'

'Charlie!' came the voice again.

Lexi noted how cross Charlie's dad sounded. 'Of course you can, but next time you'd better ask your father first.'

Charlie reluctantly stood up. Lexi followed her to the door and up the stairs.

As soon as Charlie opened the door and stepped outside, Lexi heard her dad say, 'What the hell are you doing over there?'

Lexi appeared behind Charlie out on the deck. 'It's my fault. Don't blame her. I saw her out on deck, upset, and invited her over.'

That explanation elicited just the reaction she was expecting. She watched Charlie's dad turn to her and say, 'What have I told you about talking to strangers?'

'But she's not a stranger, she's our neighbour.'

'We don't know her.'

'I do.'

Lexi stepped forward, thinking *you do now*. 'I'm Lexi.'

She saw him hesitate before responding. 'I'm Scott.'

Lexi felt surprisingly uncomfortable under his gaze. Besides Brandon, she couldn't say she'd met any other guys that she'd felt an instant attraction to; all that had bypassed her because she'd already known Brandon for years before they'd got together.

Lexi swallowed and wished her neighbour with the suspicious, grumpy expression wasn't so good-looking – tall and broad-shouldered, with close-cut blonde hair, an angular nose, high cheekbones, and piercing blue eyes. She noticed he had a tan, as though he had been abroad in the recent past. She guessed he was in his early thirties.

'We both arrived the same day,' Lexi blurted. 'I'm houseboat-sitting.'

He stood on the deck of his houseboat, staring at her. 'You were watching us when we arrived?'

Lexi frowned. 'Well, no – I just happened to see you when I was, er …' – *hiding behind the curtain thinking it was the owner who'd turned up* – '… at the kitchen window, washing up.' *Was that a bit of anxiety in his voice*? Lexi was thinking of what Charlie had said about being on the run. She had initially thought that it must be Charlie's overactive imagination, but now she wasn't so sure.

'My daughter won't bother you again. Charlie. Get back here. Now!'

'She wasn't bothering me. She's lovely. We had a nice chat.'

Scott had turned around to go back inside. He quickly did an about-turn. 'What about?'

'Girl stuff,' said Lexi. She didn't say any more. She caught Charlie smiling.

He looked at her a long moment. 'Come on, I'll make lunch.'

'I've had lunch. Lexi made me my favourite – cheese sandwiches.'

'Oh, okay. Well come back inside now – you've got some school work to do.'

Charlie sighed heavily. 'Bye, Lexi.'

Lexi smiled at her and watched her step off the houseboat. She glanced at the water lapping around the boat, and called after her, 'Don't run – it might be slippery. You don't won't to fall in!'

She watched Charlie walk back and the two of them step inside their houseboat. Scott closed the door.

Lexi sighed, wondering what she was going to do with the rest of the afternoon. She knew there was something she could do – open her letter from her mum and finally read the contents. She stood on the deck, contemplating going back inside and doing just that.

31

'So, how are you finding your first day?' Jill asked.

Lexi looked up from the desk, where she was busy dealing with a pile of returned books, scanning their bar codes on the computer before she put them all back on the trolley and wandered around the library to return them to the bookshelves. She'd done that several times already.

It wasn't her first *full* day – that would be on Monday. It was Saturday morning. Lexi had sat with Jill while she spent time filling in necessary paperwork for Lexi's new role and given Lexi a brief induction. Then Jill had given her a tour of the library. It didn't take long.

Lexi smiled at Jill, and said, 'It's great.' If she was honest, she was a little bored, but it beat being run off her feet waitressing. She'd also seen an advertisement in the library for a vacancy in a nursing home in Southwold. The care home looked quite lovely – like someone's large summer home by the sea. From the photo in the advert, the property looked as though it was located high up in one of the streets beyond the town. It probably had spectacular views of the sea. Even so, she still preferred her job in the library.

I've got nothing against old people, thought Lexi, *unless they are an American couple who live in Connecticut and have cut me off because I've refused to come home.* She brushed that thought aside. She knew she'd have to face the music when she returned to the US.

It had taken her no time at all to walk to the library that morning, but she had been early. Jill, the librarian, hadn't arrived to open up yet, so Lexi had wandered around the town. She had happened to glance in an estate agent's window and had been so surprised at the exorbitant cost of properties in the area. It wasn't what she had expected. She supposed it was possible to commute to London from there, for people who didn't mind a two-hour journey each way into the office.

Perhaps some people were in the fortunate position of working from home in well-paid jobs. However, she imagined it wasn't commuters who lived there. She got the impression that Southwold was full of second homes, retired people and holidaymakers. She had noticed some cottages advertised as holiday lets. It was little wonder that Margot had bought a houseboat, considering the extortionate cost of property in the area – even though she was a best-selling author.

'I hope we haven't bored you to death,' said Jill.

'Oh, no – not at all.' Lexi fibbed. 'I'll be back on Monday.' That wasn't a lie. She needed the job. However, even on a proper full-time salary at the library, Lexi didn't know how she'd afford to remain living in Southwold, or the surrounding areas, once Margot Dorey returned at the end of the summer and she had to leave the houseboat.

That was her main problem. She didn't have a partner, like Jill, with an income to share the costs. She looked at Jill. She was married, with two grown-up children at university. She'd told Lexi she wanted to retire early and go travelling while she was still young. She wanted to train a replacement. Someone with a bit of vision; someone she would be confident could take over the reins of running the library.

Apparently, she had her sights set on Lexi. She had suggested that Lexi could move from the internship if she was willing to do a postgraduate qualification in librarianship and look at becoming a senior librarian, like herself. By the sounds of it, she was on a decent salary.

'Look, I know this is all a bit boring, and rather dull to begin with, but remember there's a lot more to running a library than putting books on bookshelves – you'll see.'

Lexi had been on the internet to look up the role of the librarian in English public libraries. It did not sound boring. It sounded varied, and rather interesting. So Lexi had no intention of dismissing it, although still in the back of her mind was how long it would take to become a senior librarian, and how she'd survive without her allowance. She'd never been without it before.

'Not you again!'

'I see you've met the cat,' commented Jill, smiling.

Lexi stroked the black and white cat that had jumped on her desk, startling her. White paws padded across the computer keyboard, causing all sorts of weird and wonderful things to happen on the screen in front of Lexi. He even managed to renew a book Lexi was in the process of returning. 'Hey – that's my job.'

'You know, he doesn't make friends easily. He can be a bit standoffish when he wants to be. I take it as a good sign that he wants to make friends with you.'

Lexi rubbed the soft fur under his chin and got a loud purr in response. 'Is he your cat?'

'Oh, dear me no. We have no idea where he comes from. He may belong to someone in the town, but then again he could be a stray. I think that's likely. He spends so much time at the library that he practically lives here. Although we do feed him, so that might be it. We don't know his name, so we call him Library Cat. LC for short.'

Lexi smiled. 'I like it. Hey, LC, are you going to help me with my work?'

LC purred.

Jill said, 'So, did you visit the cemetery in Aldeburgh and find your father's grave?'

Lexi frowned. 'Not yet.'

'I thought you were really keen to go? I would have thought you'd have gone yesterday afternoon as soon as you left here.'

'I'm waiting until payday. I haven't got a car, and getting a taxi would be expensive.'

'I'll say. Why not take the bus like I suggested? Aldeburgh really isn't that far down the road, although it will take much longer by bus.'

'Well, um, as I said, I'd prefer to wait until payday.' She avoided eye contact and continued to stroke the cat. She hoped the librarian didn't tell her that the bus was only a few pounds return. It would be really embarrassing to admit that she couldn't afford it.

'I'll tell you what ...' Jill reached behind the desk for her handbag. She took out her purse. 'You've got to sort out a bank account, so I imagine that there will probably a bit of a hold-up transferring funds from your bank account in America. So here, take this. The bus costs about five pounds return.'

Lexi was poised to say an immediate *no*.

'No arguments. It will tide you over until the end of next week and payday. I won't take no for an answer.' Jill handed her a note.

Lexi looked at the note. It was Saturday. She'd been wondering how she was going to get through a whole week until next Friday. She gingerly took the money, and then realised how much it was. 'Fifty pounds? I thought you said the bus was only five pounds return?'

'Thereabouts, I should imagine, but I haven't got anything smaller. Perhaps you'd like to buy some lunch in Aldeburgh while you're there.'

Lexi thought of the cheese sandwich she'd made for lunch. That was what she'd had last night for dinner as well as lunch with Charlie. She'd love something other than cheese. Even so, she looked at the money, and said, 'Oh, I really couldn't.'

'Yes, you really could.' Jill offered her an affectionate smile. 'You can reimburse me when you're paid.'

'All right.' Lexi felt much better at the thought that she would pay her back from her wages.

'The weather is gorgeous. I suggest you head on over to Aldeburgh this afternoon. Go and visit your father, buy some flowers, and don't forget some lunch. Make an afternoon of it. You won't regret it. The little seaside town of Aldeburgh is lovely this time of year. Fish and chips on the beach, that's what I enjoy in the summer when I visit.'

'You can buy fish and chips on the beach?'

'Er, no, in the town. It's just one long street behind the promenade that runs alongside the shingle beach. You'll love it – the fish and chips *and* the town.'

'What time does my shift finish today?' Lexi was aware that the library closed at one on a Saturday.

'Why don't you pop off at twelve? Just log out of the computer. I'll lock up the door.'

'Thank you so much.'

'Of course. And make sure you open that bank account.'

LC settled himself down on the keyboard.

Jill looked at the cat. 'Well, I'll leave you two to get more acquainted. Remember to go at twelve. I hope you find what you're looking for in Aldeburgh.'

Lexi understood what she meant. It was a bit awkward saying, *I hope you find your dad's grave.* 'Thank you, Jill.'

'You haven't got long to go.' Jill's gaze shifted from her watch to the trolley full of books to return to the bookshelves. 'Don't worry about those. Just leave the trolley there and they'll be done tomorrow.'

Lexi was surprised when she saw the time. It was ten to twelve. She couldn't have been that bored. The morning had flown by.

32

Lexi caught the time on a clock on the wall in one of the charity shops and realised she'd spent far too much time browsing, knowing that this time she had fifty pounds in her pocket. It was meant to last her all week, and buy flowers and a return bus ticket to Aldeburgh. She hadn't intended to visit the shops on the way to the bus stop.

However, it wasn't the four pounds she'd spent in the charity shop that bothered her – she had treated herself to a couple of blouses, one pink and the other a pale blue to go with her jeans to wear for work. It made a change not to have to wear office attire for work. It was the time she'd taken looking through all the racks of clothes and trying some on that was the problem. She realised now, as she walked through the town in the direction of the bus stop near the quay, that even though it was only early afternoon, she'd left it too late for the round trip to Aldeburgh by bus.

As she crossed the bridge and started down the path to the houseboat, she said to herself, 'What a shame. I'll have to do it another time.'

'What will you have to do another time?' a familiar voice asked from behind her.

Lexi stopped and whirled around.

Ray looked at her apologetically. 'Sorry, I didn't mean to startle you, coming up behind you like that. I just nipped into Southwold for some provisions.' He held up a shopping bag.

Ray's expression turned serious. 'I didn't mean to listen in on your conversation.'

Lexi looked at him sheepishly, feeling embarrassed.

'Ah, I thought you were on the phone,' he said.

Lexi shook her head. 'The mobile reception around here is rubbish. The fact is, I was talking to myself.'

Ray put her at ease. 'Well, I do that all the time.'

They exchanged a smile. 'But seriously,' said Ray, 'Now, I want to know,' he joked, although he did stare at her intently.

Lili sighed. 'Finding my father's grave.' She saw Ray's eyebrows shoot up.

'Sorry, I didn't realise you'd lost your father.'

'Thank you. It was years ago now. My father was English.'

'I lived here until I was six.'

'Is your father laid to rest in Southwold?'

Lexi shook her head. 'A town called Aldeburgh.'

Ray smiled as they fell in step, walking along the path together. 'I know it well.'

'You do?'

'Oh, yes. That's where my ex lives. She's got an apartment on the seafront. I used to run a little shop in a place called Cobblers Yard just off the main high street in the town. It was an arts and crafts shop, just a hobby, really, when I first retired and moved out of London.'

'That sounds nice. Why did you stop – if you don't mind me asking?'

'Not at all. I enjoyed it, but I was finding it a lot of work, and with my other business too, it was getting too much.'

Lexi nodded. She imagined he did not need the money on a police officer's pension either.

'If I'm honest, I didn't really know what I was getting myself into when I signed the lease for the shop. I was a silly fool.'

Lexi smiled at him. Ray was no fool. She did empathise though. 'The trouble is, until you try something, no matter how much you read up on it, the reality doesn't always live up to your expectations.'

Lexi was talking from experience. She was thinking about her job in New York. Although she had been shocked when she was given the push, and had been intending to dive headlong into applying for a position at another large, prestigious publishing house, the time and distance from her job had given her a bit of perspective. She had been overworked and underpaid, and hadn't enjoyed it half as much as she'd thought she would. In fact, she wouldn't admit to herself that her wonderful career, and her life in New York, was anything but.

'I'll tell you why I was a fool, Lexi. I only took on the lease because my soon-to-be ex-wife had bought a shop on the opposite side of the yard, and it was the only way I could think of to see her every single day.'

'Couldn't you just pop in to see her on the pretext of buying flowers?'

'I did that too.'

'You must have bought an awful lot of flowers. I bet your houseboat smelled lovely.'

'Well, no, actually. I didn't buy them for myself.'

'Ah.' Lexi grinned. She got the picture. 'What did she think of you buying her flowers every day?'

'She called me a silly old fool. Which I suppose I was. But I thought I'd win her back, you know. What I discovered, though, was that smothering her was having the opposite effect.' He shook his head. 'Isn't hindsight a wonderful thing? I followed her around when I should have given her some space. When I gave up the shop, and did just that, that's when things changed.'

It was very forward of her to ask the question, but Ray seemed so nice it did make her wonder. 'Why did you split up?'

'It wasn't any one thing in particular. Nothing dramatic happened, like one of us having an affair. We drifted apart when our son left home – classic empty nest syndrome, I guess. But I think we had drifted apart years before that; we were just working all the time, our jobs all-consuming, which left little time to spend with each other, and when we did we were just too exhausted to enjoy our free time together. Since we split up and went our separate ways, the big irony is that our relationship had gone from strength to strength.'

He shook his head. 'It's very strange, but I'm delighted. I'd like us to move back in together. But then again, if living apart is what works for Sarah, then I can live with that, as long as I can rip up the divorce papers now.' He chuckled. 'Absence makes the heart grow fonder. I rather like that saying. In our case, it was so true.'

Lexi thought about Brandon. Could that happen to them? Was there a chance they might get back together? Lexi couldn't get that woman she'd discovered in their New York apartment out of her mind. And it had been going on for months. How could she come back from that? Ray and Sarah's relationship was quite different. They didn't have to contend with the fallout of a betrayal.

'Lexi, when you go to Aldeburgh, you must go to Cobblers Yard. It's like something out of The Old Curiosity Shop.'

Lexi looked at him curiously.

'Old-fashioned store fronts, like something out of Dickens. A Christmas Carol.'

'Oh, yes, right.' Lexi got the picture. 'I will.'

'There's the flower shop called The Potting Shed where you can buy some flowers. Just mention my name and Lili, the owner, will give you a preferential price, I'm sure.

'Lili?'

'My wife sold the shop. She wanted to retire properly. She lives on the seafront and spends a lot of her time now on her hobby, painting, when she's not looking after the grandchildren.'

'I didn't realise you had grandchildren.' Lexi smiled. She imagined Ray was a fantastic grandad.

'Yes, I've got two, Maisie and William. I'm sure you'll meet them. They'll be over at some point. They like spending time with their grandpa on the houseboat.'

Lexi smiled. 'I bet they do.'

'Mind you, Sarah says I'm a terrible grandad.'

Lexi was surprised to hear that. 'How come?'

'I give them too many sweets and let them watch too much television.'

Lexi laughed. 'Someone needs to tell Sarah that's what grandparents are for.'

He guffawed. 'I tell her that all the time.'

Despite their faults, mainly not wanting her to go to England, and always discouraging her from leading a life of her own choosing, her maternal grandparents had been much like Ray, totally indulging their two grandchildren. It was a wonder that she and Andrea hadn't grown up spoilt, entitled brats. But that was their grandparents' doing too; Andrea did not sit on the board just because her grandparents owned the company; she'd had to work hard for each position as she rose through the ranks, just like everyone else.

As with her job and life in New York, Lexi had had some time to reflect on her family too – especially her grandparents. They were not all bad. Not at all. She just wished they didn't have such a thing about her being here in England. Cutting her off was just so extreme. Not for the first time, she wondered what their problem was. *Then why not ask them?* she thought. *I might just do that.*

'Which reminds me ...' Ray cut across her thoughts. 'You had a visitor this morning while you were out.'

Lexi's smile disappeared in an instant. 'At the houseboat?' She stopped in her tracks.

'That's right.' Ray came to a halt too.

'What did they want? Did they speak to you? What did they look like?' The questions came tumbling out. She thought, *It couldn't have been Margot. Ray would have recognised her in an instant.*

'Oh, she was yay high . . .' Ray held his hand up to his chest. 'Blonde hair, blue eyes. Quite the chatter box.'

Charlie. Lexi breathed an enormous sigh of relief. 'She's the little girl next door. Her father is renting the houseboat next to you. We made friends yesterday.'

'She looks around my granddaughter's age ...'

'She's ten.'

'Maisie is eight. Perhaps when my granddaughter comes round next she can call on Charlie. They can sit together and watch YouTube or Twitter or whatever the youngsters do on their phones.'

Lexi thought that wasn't a bad idea, although she wasn't sure Charlie's father wouldn't approve. She got the impression he wouldn't want anything to do with his neighbours. Even so, Lexi said, 'Charlie hasn't got any siblings or friends her own age. I'll suggest it to her when I next see her.'

'That will be this evening, then.'

'Huh?'

'Sounds as though you've got a dinner date.'

'Pardon me?'

'It's lucky we got on to the subject of my grandchildren because I almost forgot. Charlie asked me to pass on a message if I see you.'

'What is it?'

'She says to tell you that her dad has invited you to dinner.'

Lexi looked at him in surprise. 'He has?'

Ray nodded.

'This evening?'

'Yes.' Ray grinned. 'It sounds to me as though Charlie isn't the only next-door neighbour you've made friends with.'

Lexi blushed. 'Oh, stop. I just chatted to Charlie and made her some lunch, that's all.'

Ray raised his eyebrows. 'If you say so.'

Lexi wanted to change the subject. They'd continued on their way and arrived at Ray's houseboat first. Lexi glanced at the houseboat where Charlie and her father were staying and decided she wanted to change the subject. 'Well, er, I'd best be going.'

'Are you off to Aldeburgh this afternoon then?'

'No, that was what I was intending to do. I was going to catch the bus there today, but I had a change of plan.' Lexi failed to mention she'd spent too long shopping.

'The bus?' Ray looked at her aghast. 'Do you know how long that takes?'

'Yes, I've got the bus timetable.' She knew it was too late to get the bus. By the time she arrived in Aldeburgh, bought some flowers, and spent goodness knows how long searching for her father's grave, she'd probably miss the last bus home. Or even if she didn't, Lexi didn't fancy a six hour round trip on the bus now.

'I was going to go this afternoon, but I think I will need a whole day.'

'Hey wait.'

Lexi reluctantly turned on her heel. 'Yes?'

'I bet you were really looking forward to visiting Aldeburgh, and ...' he trailed off.

'Yes, I was. It's been a long time since I've been back in England. Years. I ... I wanted to buy some flowers and pay my respects, you know.'

Ray nodded solemnly.

Lexi wasn't sure why she was telling him all this. For the last few days, since she'd arrived in England, although she'd found everyone incredibly kind, generous with their time, and prepared to help her out, she did feel lonely.

She missed her family, even though she thought they'd all been very mean – it almost felt they were ganging up on her, even though she had a perfectly reasonable excuse for her trip. She was still annoyed at Andrea for not having the backbone to disobey their grandparents just this once to help her out.

'I wasn't sure where my father was laid to rest until I found an obituary notice in an old newspaper online in the library.'

'Your family couldn't tell you where he was?' Ray ventured.

Lexi shook her head. 'Once we moved to America it was like my father and England had never existed. We weren't encouraged to talk about our life here either. Far from it. I would like to have known if my sister and I have relatives in England, but I couldn't ask. It was like our past here was taboo.' Lexi stopped. 'Sorry, you didn't need to hear all that.'

Ray smiled. 'There's nothing to apologise for. You know, I reckon you're not alone.'

Lexi frowned. 'How do you mean?'

'Well, every family has skeletons in their closet, secrets in their family history.'

Lexi stared at Ray. *Is that what he thought from what I just told him?*

'Did you join AncestryDNA yet? I remember you mentioned that you wanted to find your paternal grandparents.'

Lexi shook her head no. 'I haven't got round to it.'

'It's worth giving it a go to see if you can trace them or any long-lost relatives in England.'

'Did I mention that my sister joined that site?'

'I don't think so.'

'She didn't come up with anything.'

'When was that?'

Lexi stared into space trying to remember. 'Chad, that's her fiancé, bought her a DNA kit one Christmas.' Lexi shook her head. 'She did join, but nothing came out of it.'

'So, it wasn't in the recent past.'

'No, it was a few years ago now.'

'Is she still a member?'

'I don't know. She hasn't mentioned anything about it recently.'

'Ah, well in that case, I recommend you join. There might be family member who has joined in the meantime.'

Lexi looked at him sceptically.

He shrugged. 'It's worth a try. And I'll tell you something – you're not the first person I've suggested it to who has given me that look and then found someone they never thought they would.'

33

Lexi was about to step aboard Margot's houseboat when Ray called out, 'Would you like a lift to Aldeburgh?'

'You'd drive me to Aldeburgh?' Lexi was surprised by the offer, although there was no way she could accept. How would he feel when he found out she was a liar and a fraud, and she'd taken advantage of his sweet, kind nature? She knew how *she* felt about it. *I'm a terrible person*, thought Lexi.

'I couldn't possibly accept, Ray.'

'Don't be silly, Lexi. What are friends for?'

Oh, god. Now we're not just neighbours – we're friends. He really was going to feel so let down at the end of the summer, when she left and he found out about her little charade. What would he think of her then? And what about her job in the library? She was trying to keep that under wraps because she was meant to be houseboat-sitting – as far as Ray was concerned, that was her job.

'My car is just up here in the car park on the quay.'

Lexi followed him to the car park.

'Well, this is me.' Ray tapped the bonnet of a blue Volkswagen Golf. They both got in and set off along a street of cottages in Walberswick. So far, Lexi had only crossed the bridge into Southwold. She hadn't set foot in the village of Walberswick. 'It's very pretty,' she said. 'It feels quite different to Southwold.'

'Yes, it does, doesn't it?' Ray agreed. It's much smaller and quieter than Southwold, that's for sure, but it's still worth exploring on foot. There's an art gallery, which I've visited on many occasions.'

'I like the style of the cottages.' As they drove through the village, Lexi admired the red-brick properties. Some were three-storey houses with wooden sash windows and shutters.

'It's a Georgian village. Do you know that it sits in a designated Area of Outstanding Natural Beauty?'

Lexi shook her head. 'No?' She wasn't surprised though.

'Tourists come to have a traditional seaside holiday and see the unspoilt sand dunes.'

Lexi decided that at some point she would walk into Walberswick to explore the village and see the dunes.

They passed a set of old wrought-iron double gates, beyond which was a detached cottage in gardens.

'Wow, that's a lovely old house, isn't it? I wonder who lives there?' She looked at Ray.

He took his eyes off the road for a moment and glanced in the direction of the house. 'Hmm … no idea, I'm afraid.'

Lexi caught a glimpse of a weeping willow tree in the front garden as they passed by. Andrea came to mind. It brought back a memory of the two of them playing hide and seek in a garden with a weeping willow when they were children.

At the end of the street, Ray took a right turn by the pub on the corner and started up a country lane. 'Once we reach the main road, it's about half an hour by car, so it's not far at all.'

'Perfect. I don't remember Aldeburgh, apart from the cemetery.' She didn't add that she hadn't even realised until recently that her father was buried there, and had assumed the cemetery was in London.

'Did you live in Suffolk before you moved to America?'

'We lived in London. My dad worked in publishing.' It was the reason she had pursued a career in publishing too. 'My dad was an illustrator.'

'An illustrator?'

'Yeah, a book illustrator. He was very artistic, apparently.'

Lexi wished she had inherited his artistic talent. Although she had never really tried to discover if she had. Pursuing a career in the arts had never been encouraged while she was growing up.

'Ah, a man after my own heart. Was your mum an illustrator?'

'She was travelling at the time, and happened to get a temporary typing job at a publishing house. That's how my parents met.'

'Did she continue working in publishing?'

'No. When we returned to America after my father died, she joined the family business.'

'The family business?'

'My grandparents started a real estate company.' Lexi really didn't want to get into that.

'Does she sell property?'

Lexi pursed her lips. She knew Ray was just making conversation. The problem was that she hadn't told Ray about her mum. 'She passed away a few months ago.'

'Oh, forgive me. I'm so sorry.'

'Yeah, well … that's life, isn't it?' Lexi frowned. *Do I sound bitter?* If so, she thought she had good reason. She'd lost her mum far too young. And now all she had left was the letter from her, which she still hadn't opened.

'Did you visit the publisher in London where they met? I'm assuming it's still in business.'

Lexi looked at Ray. 'No.' It was a nice thought, but she wouldn't have a clue what the name of the publisher was. She'd been so busy with her life in New York, and then her mum had got ill. All the things she wished, in hindsight, she'd asked her, the conversations she could have had about her and Dad, and their life in England, were lost forever.

Ray spent the rest of the journey pointing out the scenery – the bright yellow oilseed rape fields interspersed with lush rolling green fields, little cottages lining some of the route, and English church spires nestled amongst little villages in the rolling countryside in the distance.

This was the coastal road, but Lexi noticed that it didn't hug the coast with a view of the sea like some of the coast roads in Connecticut. She had taken a shoreline road trip in New England with Brandon when she was in college. Although the Suffolk countryside was quite different to Connecticut, that didn't mean she liked it any less. She was enjoying the drive and the scenery immensely.

Ray flicked on his indicator light and took a right turn down a country lane. The straight road stretched ahead for some distance.

'This road takes us to Aldeburgh and the coast. Not far now.'

'Can we stop off in the town first? I'd like to visit the flower shop you mentioned in Cobblers Yard.'

'Of course. I'll park on the sea front and we can double back into town. It's only a matter of walking down one street and we're in the high street. I'll point out the church, you'll see it on the way in. It's literally a five-minute walk from Cobblers Yard. You know the church overlooks the sea?'

Lexi nodded. She remembered that Jill had mentioned it.

'While you are at the church, I am going to pop along and surprise my wife.'

'Are you going to buy flowers too?'

Ray took his eyes off the road for a second to glance at Lexi. He grinned. 'What a marvellous idea. I haven't bought her flowers in a while.'

'I bet she'll love them.'

'Let's hope so.'

Lexi gave Ray a sideways glance. She imagined he was thinking about the time he had bought Sarah flowers every single day, annoying her. She hoped her suggestion didn't backfire.

'Ah, we are entering the outskirts of Aldeburgh now. Does anything seem familiar?'

Lexi noticed a couple of grocery stores on the right – a small Co-op and a Tesco just before a roundabout.

Lexi shook her head. 'I'm afraid it doesn't.'

'Not to worry. Perhaps the town will jog your memory.'

Lexi doubted it. She had only been six years old, and that horrible day had been a blur of cars and the hearse and people in black, tears, and a cemetery filled with old grey headstones. Lexi shivered. Was it really a place she wanted to be? She suddenly thought that it might be a bad idea. She hadn't long lost her mother. Did she really want to revisit another loss?

'Now, I could turn left, which takes us straight to the seafront, but I want to point out the church, which is down the street ahead. Don't worry, the little detour won't take us out of our way.'

'Okay.'

Ray carried on across the roundabout and along a residential street lined with cottages and detached houses. Towards the end of the street, they drove up an incline. 'We're coming up to the church on your left. Look, there it is.'

Lexi saw a red-brick wall, a wooden gate, and an impressive church. It was much bigger than she had expected for a small coastal town.

'I could park in the church car park just there.'

Lexi saw the entrance to a rough gravelled car park surrounded by trees as the car slowed at the brow of the hill.

'But we want to visit The Potting Shed, so I'm going to park on the sea front, if you don't mind.'

'Not at all,' said Lexi gazing up at the impressive church steeple.

'It's a lovely church. You know that Benjamin Britten, the famous English composer, is buried here. It's worth a visit inside to admire the splendid window in his memory.' Ray groaned. 'Sorry, that was really insensitive. You're not here for that.'

'Oh, Ray, don't apologise. I'm glad you told me. I'd like to go into the church too and see the window.'

'It's a wonderful church inside,' Ray added. 'Very homely, not like some churches, which are quite austere.'

Just beyond the church, the road sloped gently down to an intersection. Ray brought the car to a gentle stop and looked both ways. 'There on the corner is the cinema.'

Lexi craned her neck and looked out of the passenger window. She saw an impressive detached building on the corner that looked like a large cottage. It was painted white, and she could see dark wood criss-crossing the exterior. The building looked very old. 'That's a cinema?'

'Oh, yes. It's an independent cinema. We have a few of them in Suffolk. There's one in Southwold and one further afield in Woodbridge. A bit quirky, but worth a visit to catch a movie. It's been modernised over the years, so you'll find a modern auditorium inside with comfy chairs and the usual snacks and popcorn.'

Lexi decided that she must tell Charlie. Perhaps she could ask Scott if she could take Charlie to the cinema one day.

'There's the town centre.'

Lexi turned to look at Ray, who was pointing down the street in the other direction. 'You can't quite see it from here, but this street opens up into a wide shopping street with shops on either side, and cottages further along. Rising up behind the town are streets with houses and cottages. There's some steps up to those streets with lovely views over the rooftops of the town to the sea.'

Lexi loved it already.

Ray headed down to the seafront to park. There was a small green, and then the promenade where people were walking alongside a low wall behind which was the shingle beach. Ray found a parking space alongside the green. When Lexi got out of the car, she spotted some large wooden huts on the beach and even a couple of small fishing boats right on the beach. 'Oh, wow.'

Ray locked the car. He smiled. 'That's where you can buy fresh fish of the day. There's even a little outdoor restaurant where you can sit and have a seafood platter.'

Lexi saw people queuing at one of the huts, and others sitting at wooden benches under an awning right on the beach, eating seafood and looking out to sea. It reminded her of some similar places along the Connecticut shoreline. But surprisingly, that thought didn't make her feel homesick.

Ray turned to Lexi. 'How about we meet up at my wife's place later? I'll take you to The Potting Shed in Cobblers Yard to buy flowers. I just thought you might want to visit the cemetery alone to pay your respects. You can call for me when you've finished.'

Lexi smiled. 'Great idea. So, where will you be?'

Ray grinned. 'Come with me. Let's take a little detour. We can walk a little way along the promenade. I'll show you where Sarah lives, then we can cut down a side street into the town.'

Lexi followed Ray across the green, passing a little hut that sold takeaway tea, coffee and ice cream. Turning right, they walked along the promenade with the shingle beach on their left.

'It's not far. Aldeburgh is quite small, but I find the town and the beachfront very cosy, intimate even – and quite undiscovered. Why Londoners flock to Brighton and Bournemouth, which are huge, I have no idea. Doesn't appeal to me.'

Lexi didn't know Brighton or Bournemouth, but she nodded nonetheless.

'East Anglia is still relatively undiscovered. I'd like to keep it that way.'

'Oh, these are so pretty,' commented Lexi, surprised to see a mixture of properties fronting the promenade, from little two-storey terraced cottages to three- and four-storey Victorian townhouses painted in pastel shades of blue, pink and yellow. Although Ray owned a lovely houseboat, she wasn't surprised that his wife was reluctant to move out of Aldeburgh and move in with him. She didn't know the reason they still lived apart, but she imagined this might be it. She looked at Ray. 'Does Sarah live in one of these?'

'Oh, yes. Little wonder she can't be persuaded to move in with me. These places are wonderful.'

'They certainly are,' said Lexi, admiring the facades.

Ray came to halt outside the front door of one of the townhouses. Lexi noticed there were two doorbells. 'This is where she lives. There are two apartments here. She lives on the top floor with the most marvellous views. Hopefully, she's in. You can see the views when you pop in later.'

'Oh, I wouldn't want to intrude.' Lexi didn't expect to be invited in.

'Nonsense. She'll put the kettle on. We'll have a cuppa before we set off home.'

'Oh, okay.' She looked at Ray, wondering why he didn't ring the doorbell.

'Ah, I don't want to turn up empty-handed. I haven't got the flowers. Let's nip to Cobblers Yard first.'

Lexi had forgotten all about her suggestion that he should buy Sarah a bunch of flowers.

Before they left, he looked up and down the promenade. Lexi wondered what he was looking for. 'Ah, there it is.' Ray pointed at a small car parked a little further along the promenade. 'That's her car. She's definitely around. If she's not in when I return with the flowers, I can always text her. She'll probably be in town.' He turned to Lexi. 'Why don't we walk back the way we came?'

Lexi readily agreed. She was enjoying the stroll along the promenade. Although they were not alone – there were teenagers, young couples, and families with children and grandparents – it wasn't as busy as she would have expected for such a pretty seaside town. Perhaps it had something to do with what Ray just said – that it was relatively undiscovered.

It was Saturday, so she imagined the people were mostly locals with a few holidaymakers too, and that some of the cottages in the town were holiday lets. Even so, to get parked right by the beach at the height of summer would have been unheard in the coastal resorts along Connecticut's shoreline. It was quiet here for high season; very sedate – and very English. Lexi adored it.

For some reason, her anglophile ex-boyfriend came to mind. He'd love it here to. Thinking of Brandon reminded Lexi that her visit here was not meant to be a day out, enjoying herself, but a pilgrimage to find her father's grave and lay some flowers.

'It's such a beautiful day – seems a shame not to meander along the promenade,' commented Ray.

Lexi agreed. She stopped to watch some children outside a small single-storey concrete building on the beach with a sign saying it hosted artwork inside. There was a trestle set up on the beach with paints and brushes, and large pebbles for children to paint.

'I don't know if they do this in America, but over here it's become a bit of a thing, painting artwork and messages on stones and leaving them all over the place for people to find.

'What a lovely idea,' said Lexi. She'd heard of people leaving them in public parks for others to find, but had never come across one herself in Central Park.

'Would you like to give it a go? It's not just for children, you know.'

Lexis started shaking her head, reminding herself she wasn't there to have fun. Besides, she imagined she'd be a bit embarrassed with her efforts. But then she had a thought. 'How much does it cost?'

'It doesn't cost a thing.'

'It's free?'

'Of course.'

Lexi noticed three concrete steps that led up to the beach. She stepped up to the trestle table. A little boy was busy painting his stone. He showed Lexi what he'd had done.

'That's very good,' commented Lexi, smiling at him. She looked over at his mum, who was at the end of the table, busy helping a younger boy who looked like his brother.

Feeling self-conscious, Lexi chose a large stone and picked up a paint brush and chose a colour. It didn't take long to paint. There wasn't an awful lot of room to do anything too complicated. *Not that I'd have the skill to paint an intricate design*, thought Lexi.

After choosing another colour, writing her message, and surrounding it with a heart shape, she blew on the stone to dry the paint as she joined Ray back on the promenade.

They fell in step again. Ray pointed out that the promenade continued up ahead past a large grand hotel called The Wentworth Hotel. Lexi could see that the wide promenade narrowed to a path which continued alongside a large car park. Beyond the car park, the path ended, giving way to the shingle beach.

Ray came to a halt near the little pop-up takeaway café that they'd passed at the start of the walk.

'We won't be going as far as the hotel, but if you come back to Aldeburgh, I'd highly recommend walking along the path until it ends. Then if you continue along the beach for a good fifteen, or twenty minutes, you come to Thorpeness. It's a very popular walk. You can't get lost. There's always people on that walk.'

Lexi wondered what was so special about Thorpeness. 'Is it nice there?'

'Oh, yes, very much so. It was built as a holiday village back in the nineteen twenties. It's very picturesque. That's where you'll find the House in the Clouds.'

'The House in the Clouds?' *Why did that sound familiar?* 'Has it got a boating lake?'

Ray turned to her. 'Yes, it has.'

'Really?' Lexi looked at him in surprise. 'How did I know that?'

'You've been there before.'

'Have I?'

'You must have, otherwise how would you know?'

'I do remember a house really, really high up. And taking a boat out on a lake. But I didn't know if that was a dream or a childhood memory from where I grew up in Connecticut.'

Ray shook his head. 'Nope, that will be Thorpeness. Look, can you see it?'

Lexi put her hand up to shield her eyes from the sun and looked towards Thorpeness. 'What's that?' She could see a red house remarkably high up. She pointed. 'Is that it?'

Ray nodded. 'The House in the Clouds was originally a water tower disguised as a house. Did you know that the author of Peter Pan, J.M. Barrie, was good friends with the wealthy Scottish barrister, Stuart Ogilvie, whose vision it was to create an olde-worlde village and playground for the well-to-do. The mere, or lake, with its creeks and islands, was inspired by J.M. Barrie's Neverland. Apparently, the writer named the islands. Pirate's Lair, Wendy's Home, and Captain's House are some of the ones I can remember. I'm sure there are others.'

Lexi shook her head. 'I didn't know that.'

'I read somewhere that the mere is only three feet deep. It's so tranquil. Ogilvie's original idea was that children, even quite young children, could go out on the lake safely and learn to sail or row.'

Lexi wondered if Charlie would enjoy taking out a boat on the lake to find Pirate's Lair, Wendy's Home, and Captain's House. Wouldn't it make a wonderful day out, to go to the beach for fish and chips and an ice cream in Aldeburgh? And then on to Thorpeness for some fun on the lake, followed by a movie at the old cinema back in Aldeburgh.

Even if Charlie couldn't join her, Lexi rather fancied doing it herself. But there was a huge fly in the ointment; Ray had been so kind to drive her there, but she couldn't possibly ask him to take her again and pick her up at the end of a day out. The bus trip would be too long, and a taxi would cost too much. *I would need a car, or someone else who had a car,* she thought as they passed Ray's car.

'Everything all right?' Ray asked.

Lexi guessed he'd noticed her go quiet. 'Oh, yes – fine, thank you.' The day out had been a nice idea while it had lasted.

'So, here we are, back on the street we came in on. I thought I'd bring you back the way we came so when I show you the way to Cobblers Yard, all you have to do is retrace your steps to here. It's just one long street. You won't get lost. And up there is the church.' Ray pointed across the road, up the street they'd driven down on the way here. 'You can't miss it. You can see the church spire from here.'

'Thanks, Ray.' Lexi looked at the large stone in her hand. She tested the paint and discovered it was dry already. Lexi popped it in her handbag.

'Now, let's find The Potting Shed.'

34

Lexi followed Ray into the high street. There were small, expensive-looking boutique clothes shops interspersed with a grocery shop, a pet shop, and two fish and chip shops, one on either side of the street.

There were also several cafés. One caught her eye because it had an unusual name – The Two Magpies. Lexi glanced in the window as they passed by. It looked like a bakery, but there were tables too. It was obviously popular; there were no free tables. Lexi was disappointed. The sandwiches and scones on the customers' plates looked really appetising. She had fifty pounds burning a hole in her pocket and felt like taking Jill's advice. She hoped Ray wouldn't mind if she stopped for lunch before they set off back to Walberswick.

When she turned to Ray to ask if that was okay, she was surprised to discover that he was nowhere to be seen. He'd been right beside her a moment ago.

'Lexi – I'm here.'

She looked about her and for a split second didn't see him, until he stepped out from the shadows, appearing from a small gap between the shops. 'Cobblers Yard is down here.'

Lexi peered down a little, narrow cobbled walkway. 'Well, I would have missed this, for sure.'

Ray smiled. 'Everyone says that. There is a sign.' He pointed to an old sign. It said *Cobblers Yard* and had a small arrow.

Lexi frowned. 'I would never have spotted that!'

'Yes, I know. The shop owners in the yard have been lobbying the local council for years to remove that sign and put up a new one that people won't miss.'

'I totally agree. They should.'

Lexi followed him down the narrow lane and was surprised that it came out into a decent-sized cobbled yard with old-fashioned shop fronts on three sides. She spotted the flower shop immediately. The Potting Shed was hard to miss, with its beautiful display of flowers in the window and an array of pots and bouquets outside, enticing the visitor in. Lexi couldn't imagine they got a lot of passing trade, though.

'The shops here do very well with local people who know them. I think it's the tourists and day-trippers that miss out.'

'And the shop owners,' added Lexi. She glanced around the yard. She recalled what he'd said. *It's like something out of The Old Curiosity Shop.* Lexi thought he'd been right when he'd said that Cobblers Yard was straight out of a Dickens novel, with its old-fashioned Victorian store fronts and bow-fronted leaded windows.

'Right, let's go and buy some flowers, shall we?' Ray said, turning on his heel and heading across the cobbled square, past the old-fashioned lamppost that Lexi thought looked like something out of a forties film noir – or the famous scene in the movie, *Singing in the Rain*, where Gene Kelly danced in the rain.

Lexi remembered watching old black and white movies as a child; she thought perhaps it might have been with her parents, but she couldn't remember. She knew it wasn't with her maternal grandparents – they were so busy running the business they never really had the time to lounge on the sofa glued to the television.

Ray opened the door to the flower shop, and Lexi heard the bell tinkle above the door.

'Ray! What are you doing here?'

Lexi walked up behind Ray and smiled at the young woman behind the counter.

'Lexi, this is Lili – a good friend and my son's fiancé.' He paused. 'Lili, this is Lexi, a houseboat neighbour of mine.

Lexi could feel her face flush. Now another person knew.

'Lili runs her own landscaping business too. She visits clients and looks after their gardens.'

Lexi thought of the garden she'd seen behind the gates of the old property set back from the street in Walberswick. It seemed extensive, from what she had glimpsed through the gates. The detached house sat in gardens that she imagined extended from the front right around the side. She wondered how large the garden was at the back of the house. She imagined a place like that would need a gardener.

'So, do you visit properties in Walberswick?'

'Oh, yes. You'd be surprised how many large properties there are with gardens that the older generation are finding hard to manage.'

'We don't have that problem – do we, Lexi?'

Lexi offered him a weak smile. She really hoped he did not bring up the fact that she was houseboat-sitting for a neighbour, and which neighbour that was. What if Margot had visited here and bought flowers, or was a good friend of Lili's? Lexi avoided eye contact, although Ray was right: who needed a gardener on a houseboat? Lexi relaxed.

'And Sarah doesn't have that problem either, living in a flat.'

Lili laughed. 'That's very true. Now, what can I do for you today, Ray – and Lexi?'

Lexi felt relieved when the conversation veered away from the houseboats.

Ray turned to look at Lexi. 'We're here to buy some flowers.'

She stepped up to the counter. 'Yes, I'd like a bouquet.'

'Great.' Lili got out a pen. 'Now, what is the occasion?'

Lexi hesitated and exchanged a glance with Ray. He turned to Lili. 'Lexi has come here to lay some flowers at her father's grave.'

'Oh. I'm so sorry.'

Lexi repeated what she'd said to Ray. 'It was years ago. I've returned to England and I wanted to pay my respects.'

'Of course. Are you American?'

Lexi wished people would stop asking her that. 'My father was English. I was born here but left for America when I was still a child.'

Lili smiled. 'Well, welcome home, Lexi.'

Lexi stared at her. 'Thank you.' Lili had been the first person to say that after finding out she was born there. Lexi knew that England was where she would have grown up if her father hadn't died. Although there had always been that question in the back of her mind: *why couldn't we have just stayed in England after Daddy died? Why did Mum have to return to America?*

It wasn't really a mystery. Lexi knew it boiled down to money. Her mum had two young children to support and no husband. And her parents in Connecticut had money – but Lexi imagined Nana and Grandpa would not have supported their daughter or their grandchildren unless they returned.

'So, Lexi, I would suggest this bouquet.' Lili looked up from a book she was flicking through and pointed a photo.

Lexi smiled. 'That is gorgeous. How long will it take to make up?'

'Now, let me see. If I put it in my order book, I'm sure it will only take a few days.'

Lexi glanced at Ray.

Ray caught her look of disappointment. 'Lexi was hoping to take the bouquet today – like now.'

'Oh, I see. I'm sure we will have something to your liking.'

Lexi glanced around the shop; she noticed that it was full of flowers, potted plants, wreaths and climbers, but that there were no bouquets. 'I don't really want to take a wreath.'

'Okay, look.' Lili beckoned her to follow. 'If you come with me, I have lots of flowers for various bouquets my assistant and I are in the process of making in our little studio.'

'Can I come too?' asked Ray.

'The more the merrier.'

As Ray followed, Lili said, 'Are you here to buy flowers for Sarah?'

'Yes – how did you guess?'

Lexi saw a knowing smile pass between them and guessed that Lili knew all about Ray bombarding his ex with bouquets.

What she said next just confirmed that. 'Are you sure that's a good idea, Ray?'

'Yes, why not?'

'Because last time—'

'Last time I was the biggest fool, now I'm a little wiser. Besides, it's been an age since I bought her flowers.'

'That is true.'

They walked into a little studio at the back of the shop. 'Oh, wow!' exclaimed Lexi when she saw a trestle table strewn with flowers, and lots of small buckets filled with flowers, their stems in water. 'I don't think I've seen so many flowers in one place.' The scent of flowers in the air was amazing.

Lili smiled at her reaction. 'Okay, so if you guys just want to go along and choose whatever you fancy. Here . . .' She picked up two empty baskets and gave them one each.

'You're going to make up a bouquet for us now?' Lexi asked.

'Of course.'

'But have you got the time?' Lexi looked about her at the number of bouquets they were in the process of making.

'Don't you worry about that. Now, take the basket, and choose whatever you like.'

Lexi stood there with the basket in one hand. So did Ray.

'Whatever you like,' Lili repeated. 'I'll be just out there. Call me when you're done.'

Lexi watched her walk back into the shop. She turned around and sighed. 'Where to start . . .?'

'Yes, that's what I was thinking.'

'Remember, Sarah likes chrysanthemums,' Lili called out.

Ray grinned. 'That's right!'

Lexi watched Ray set to work, picking from the selection in the buckets and lying on the table. 'Now, that wasn't too bad. I'll just take these over to Lili and she can put the bouquet together. Are you okay?'

'Oh, yes, fine,' Lexi lied. She watched Ray take his basket out to the counter and join Lili in the shop. She could hear them chatting as Lili worked on his bouquet.

Lexi turned back to the abundance of flowers and frowned. 'How hard can this be?' Unfortunately, Lexi *was* finding this hard. It made her realise how much she didn't know about her dad. What were his favourite colours? Did they have anything to do with football? She'd heard how much the British liked their footie. Had he even wanted flowers at his funeral? Lexi tried hard to remember if there were flowers.

Lexi suddenly felt a hand on her shoulder. She whirled around. 'It's only me,' said Lili, smiling at her. 'Just take your time, trust your instincts. You may not know what he would have liked, but you know what *you* like. Just remember, you are your father's daughter, so whatever you choose, he would have loved because it's something from you, from your heart.'

Lexi thought of what she had written on the stone she had painted on the beach. She smiled at Lili. 'Thank you.'

'Now, remember, choose whatever you want, and I'll set to work making it up. But if you would like a suggestion ...'

Lexi looked at her eagerly.

'Roses. As you can see, we have a lot of varieties. Red roses are very popular for sympathy. And I would suggest rosemary.'

'Rosemary?'

'We always put some rosemary in flower arrangements for loved ones who are no longer with us. It means remembrance, and because it's evergreen, it's available all year round.' Lili fetched some sprigs of rosemary. 'Would you like some?'

'Oh, yes.'

Lexi took them and put them in her basket. 'Thank you.'

'You're welcome, Lexi. Now, take as long as you need, and I'll make up the bouquet when you're done.'

Lexi smiled as she walked over to the roses. She was just going to choose one colour, keeping it simple, but then she thought of her dad, an illustrator, an artist. She guessed he would have loved a variety of colours. She picked up a rose in every variety they had. It wouldn't be a huge bouquet, but that wasn't what she was after; she just wanted something uncomplicated, simple but heartfelt.

When she'd finished and she looked in her basket, she thought of a paint pallet of colours. She smiled, thinking, *This would have suited him perfectly.*

Lexi walked out of the small studio up to the counter, where Lili was just putting the finishing touches to Ray's bouquet. They were still deep in conversation.

'Excuse me. I've chosen my flowers.'

Lili turned around. 'Wonderful. Oh, I love these. They will make such a vibrant, colourful bouquet.'

Lexi smiled. 'That's what I was after.'

'I won't be long – I'm just putting the finishing touches on these, then I'll start on yours. Would you like a little card included for a message?'

'No, thank you.' Lexi smiled to herself. She had the stone she'd hand-painted with a message. She looked at Ray and Lili. She felt a bit awkward. They'd been chatting until she'd interrupted them.

She sidled off to look around the shop, leaving them to continue their conversation, but the shop was quite small.

She glanced at the door. 'I'd like to go outside and have a wander around Cobblers Yard while I wait. Would that be okay?' It wasn't just an excuse to leave Ray and Lili to their catch-up; she did want to have a look in the other shop windows.

Lili looked up. 'Oh, sure – I would if I were you. There's a nice little charity shop if you're into vintage clothes and a bit of gossip.'

'Gossip?'

'Oh yes, it's run by two sisters, Mabel and Marjorie. They've been running it for years. They're both widows now.' Lili smiled. 'We call them the Gossip Girls. They do like to know everyone's business.'

One to avoid, then, thought Lexi.

'Apart from the old bookshop, though,' added Lili. 'The one that's closed. They never talk about that.'

'Yes, it's very strange,' commented Ray. 'The antique store is worth a little browse around just for the fun of it. It was run by a father and son for years, but it's changed hands recently. They sell the most amazing amber jewellery.'

As well as chatting to Ray, Lili had been busy putting his bouquet together. She looked up. 'Ray!'

Ray rolled his eyes at Lili. 'Oh, all right, I'll admit I'm biased.' He looked sheepishly at Lexi. My ten-year-old granddaughter started the little amber jewellery business. Her creations are displayed in that shop. They sell really well. It's worth a look – you might like them.'

Lexi said, 'Thanks, I'll check it out.' She walked to the door and heard the tinkle of the doorbell as she stepped outside into the cobbled yard.

She had a wander around, peeking in the shop windows. She discovered a music shop next door. There were guitars and violins displayed in the window. An older man, around Ray's age, with long dark hair was sitting on a stool by a desk near the window. He looked as though he was mending a violin. He looked up, smiled and waved. Lexi waved back. He beckoned her inside, but Lexi declined, shaking her head but smiling all the same.

Next up was the charity shop. Lexi quickly walked past. The last thing she needed was to get into a conversation with the Gossip Girls, as Lili called them.

Across the cobbed square opposite The Potting Shed was the arts and crafts store that Ray had said he used to run. It was no longer an arts and crafts store but a solicitor's office. There was a sign in the window offering free legal advice. Lexi steered clear of that one too; they'd advise her that she was squatting, it was illegal, and that she could be arrested. She didn't need a lawyer to tell her that.

She stopped outside the old antique store. In the window was a display of handmade jewellery. Although Ray was biased – understandably, he'd love anything his granddaughter had made – the amber necklaces and bracelets were lovely, and would make a perfect gift.

Lexi glanced across the cobbled square. She could see Lili in her stop, still busy flower-arranging, and Ray chatting away as she worked. Lexi smiled. She still had time for a bit of shopping.

35

Lexi stepped out of the shop and smiled at Ray. They were both holding their bouquets of flowers.

'Aren't they marvellous?' commented Ray.

'Oh, yes! Gorgeous.' Lexi had been a little overcome when she saw hers. She thought the arrangement was just exquisite. 'Lili is very talented.'

'That she is.'

'Right, this is where I leave you.' Ray stopped in the high street. 'I'm going to cross the road and head down that lane over there to the sea front.' He looked at the flowers. 'I am feeling strangely nervous.'

Lexi looked at the beautiful flower arrangement in Ray's hands. 'Don't be. She is going to adore them.'

'I hope so.'

So did Lexi. After all, they were her suggestion.

'Are you sure you don't want me to accompany you to the church?'

'No, thank you, Ray. I know my way.'

'I'll see you at Sarah's place later. Just ring the doorbell when you arrive. We'll have a brew ready.'

Ray looked at the flowers. 'Well, wish me luck. She's not really one for surprises.'

'She'll like this one, I'm sure.'

'Right, well, I'm off.'

Lexi smiled as she watched him cross the road. He turned around and gave her a little wave before disappearing down an alleyway.

Lexi took a deep breath, looked at her flowers, and turned in the direction of the church. Some people passing her on the street threw appreciative glances at the beautiful bouquet.

A few hundred yards down the street, the shops gave way to cottages. She could see the impressive Tudor building up ahead that housed Aldeburgh's independent cinema. Lexi turned left up the street they had driven down, and immediately saw the church up ahead on the other side of the road. She crossed the road and entered the churchyard through a wooden gate.

The church was a few paces along on her right, the door open. She wanted to lay her flowers on her father's grave before going inside, but she couldn't resist poking her head inside first, just to take a peek.

Ray had been right when he'd said the church wasn't austere inside like some. There were light wooden pews with cushions. In one corner of the church she could see little chairs and tables for children. She guessed they ran a Sunday school here.

Lexi stepped back out of the church and looked about her. She hadn't told Ray that she didn't know exactly where her father was buried. She'd thought it wouldn't be a problem. She'd imagined that in a small town like Aldeburgh, the church graveyard would be ... well ... small. She'd just have to locate the more recent gravestones and start searching from there. It wouldn't take long. But now she had entered the grounds of the church and realised that this was not a small church, or a small graveyard.

As she walked along the path, she realised that the gravestones stretched right around the impressively large church; and not only that – there were several different parts to the graveyard too. It was organised not unlike a walled garden, or several gardens, the different sections separated by hedgerows.

As she walked on, she discovered that the graveyard had incredible views across the rooftops of the town to the sea. She'd passed the gravestones in the oldest part of the cemetery near the church, but these were more modern, and there were a lot.

Lexi sighed as she made her way down a path separating two grassy areas filled with headstones. Up ahead was another hedgerow. She walked between the hedgerow to another area laid out just the same, with headstones either side. Lexi counted them; they were at least eight deep on both sides.

She'd spotted some plastic beakers and a tap, which she intended to use to clean her father's gravestone before she organised the flowers. Although the bouquet arrangement was beautiful, she hoped there was a little grate that she noticed some gravestones had so that she could take the roses from the bouquet and place them inside the metal holes, and fill the container underneath with water, so that they could stand up by the headstone. The trouble was that Lexi couldn't keep Ray waiting all day. She'd have to find it soon.

Lexi stopped just past the next hedgerow and looked about her. Where should she start? He could be anywhere.

Lexi thought of the church. Would they have church records with a map showing which plot her father was buried in? Quite possibly. But would somebody be around to show her? And would they keep those records in the church, or were they kept somewhere else?

When she'd popped her head into the church it had been empty. Even though there were a few cars in the church car park, there was no one around but her.

On the left, under a tree tucked in the corner of the cemetery, she spied a wooden bench. Lexi left the path and walked past a row of headstones to the shady tree. She sat down on the bench, holding the bouquet, and stared at row upon row of headstones. She lifted her gaze to the sea view. *At least I found out where he is*, she said to herself. Even so, she was still immensely disappointed that she had come this far but couldn't lay the beautiful flowers at his graveside.

She decided it was time to leave. It was no good trying to find it. What were the chances that she would just happen upon it?

Lexi had just stood up when something hit her on the head. 'Ow!' She looked up at the tree, then down at the floor. She leaned down and picked up a conker off the ground. She looked around her and discovered a couple more. She didn't think conker season really started until the autumn – September or October – although she knew it wasn't unheard of for the season to start in August, depending on the weather.

She looked up at the horse chestnut tree. Lexi remembered the conker game she'd played when they'd lived in England, finding the biggest conker to win a conker fight. She looked at the conker in her hand, feeling its smooth surface between her fingers. That was when a memory resurfaced. She was standing by her Dad's grave, feeling something between her fingers; something round with a smooth surface.

She recalled that her mother had been cross with her for some reason. Was this the reason? Had she picked up a conker or several off the floor when she was meant to be standing solemnly by the graveside? Lexi turned around and looked at the bench. There was an inscription. It was dedicated to a lady who had lived in Aldeburgh all her life. Lexi didn't know if the bench had been there when she'd attended her father's funeral, but the horse chestnut tree obviously had. And that memory suggested she had been standing at her father's graveside close to this tree.

She whispered, 'You're here, aren't you?' Lexi looked along the row of headstones, her eyes settling on the back of the gravestone nearest the bench. 'Surely not!'

Lexi took the flowers and stepped in front of the headstone she'd been sitting just a few feet away from on the bench under the chestnut tree. She smiled. 'Hello, Dad.'

36

'So, I see you laid your flowers.'

Lexi nodded. On her arrival, Ray had immediately noticed she no longer had her bouquet. He had answered the door and led her up two flights of stairs to Sarah's light and airy apartment on the top floor of the Victorian townhouse overlooking the sea.

Sarah had introduced herself and warmly welcomed Lexi into her home before nipping out of the lounge and down the hall to put the kettle on.

Lexi glanced around Sarah's cavernous lounge-cum-dining room. She loved it. The walls were painted white, as were the floorboards, and there was a low wooden coffee table on a colourful rug between the two large, comfy cream-coloured chenille sofas. The furniture was a bit sparse, but it made the place appear even more roomy. The top floor was in the eaves, so the high ceilings, although heavily beamed, accentuated the feeling of light and space. Lexi wandered around the room, looking at the framed art works on the walls. Ray had already told her that some were painted by him, others by Sarah, and a few had been given as gifts by visiting artists who stayed with Sarah and worked in her studio, where she ran a summer school and retreat for artists.

Her two visiting artists, students, were out on the beach with canvases and paints. Although not an artist herself, Lexi could just imagine the draw of sitting at one of these large Victorian sash windows with an easel. The trouble was that she'd probably spend so much time just drinking in the views and watching the people down below that she wouldn't get any painting done. *I wouldn't have the patience*, thought Lexi, although she had enjoyed painting the stone, which had surprised her – and she thought she'd done a rather good job of it too.

She could see people walking by on the promenade below, and there were still children decorating stones at the trestle table on the beach.

Lexi turned from the window. She could hear the chink of china coming from the kitchen next door. She glanced at the door. 'It's very kind of Sarah to make me a drink before we set off, but I wouldn't want her to go to any trouble on my account.'

'Oh, it's no trouble at all.'

It was certainly no trouble for Ray. He slouched on the sofa, looking so at ease in his surroundings that anyone would be forgiven for thinking that he lived here. Lexi imagined that although they lived apart, and she wouldn't be surprised if they continued to do so, they spent so much time in each other's company, and in and out of each other's dwellings, that Sarah's place felt like a home from home to Ray.

'So, how did it go?' asked Ray.

Lexi walked over and sat down on the sofa opposite. 'It was ...' Lexi's brow furrowed. 'It wasn't what I was expecting.'

Ray sat forward in his seat. 'The graveyard was different to how you remembered it?'

Lexi nodded, although her memory was sparse from that day. Perhaps it was her subconscious protecting her from the hurt by blocking the memory of her father's death and his funeral. Try as she might, she could never really get a grasp on the memories from that time here in Suffolk, where they'd obviously come to lay her father to rest.

She told Ray her surprise at discovering the graveyard was so large, but she had found a bench under an old chestnut tree – something she did remember. She told Ray about the conker that hit her on the head.

'Ah, the old horse chestnut tree. It's a bit early for conkers, but not unheard of in August, I'm afraid.' He looked at her, his expression one of concern. 'Are you all right? Those things can be blessed hard, I can tell you. I've had fair few run-ins with conkers falling from trees. They seem to choose the right moment just as I walk underneath their branches.' He frowned. 'It's not the best when that happens.'

'It certainly isn't, but it did bring back a memory.' Lexi proceeded to tell him what happened when she'd picked up the conker. She'd remembered she'd found one on the ground during the ceremony by the graveside.

'I'd given up on finding my father's headstone when it dawned on me that it must be quite near or even under the old chestnut tree. I remembered a carpet of conkers right where he was buried.'

Lexi explained how she had stepped forward just a pace or two and found it. She'd had an old cloth to hand that she'd found near the bottles of water provided in the graveyard to wipe any dirt and debris from gravestones. But she hadn't needed it.

Lexi had been surprised – stunned, even – to discover that her father's headstone was spotless, the grass around it weeded, and most surprising of all, there were already fresh flowers arranged with care in the little grate, with its container full of water.

Lexi had spent several moments double-checking she hadn't got the wrong grave. Perhaps if the spelling of the name were different, the date of birth or death, the mention of being a son, a husband, a father. But no, all the details about her father tallied with the headstone she'd been standing staring at, which had quite clearly had a recent visitor – so recent, in fact, that the flowers were almost as fresh as hers.

Lexi had stood for some time in shocked silence, totally unprepared for what she had found; all these years later, two decades in fact, someone was visiting her father's grave and laying flowers – but who?

Lexi sat and told Ray all about her visit. She didn't voice her thoughts about the conker. She'd looked at the conker and thought, *Is this a sign?* She'd just been about to leave when it had fallen from the tree. She didn't believe in the afterlife – at least, not until that had happened.

She'd sat for some time on the bench, looking out to sea with one thought going through her mind: someone else was visiting her father's grave, and she had no idea who it could be.

'So, you left your bouquet.'

'Well, no.' Lexi hadn't wanted to lay the bouquet down at the base of the headstone. What if it blew away in the wind? That would be such a shame. And she didn't have the heart to remove the fresh flowers and replace them with hers. Someone had gone to the trouble of visiting her father, cleaning his headstone, and put together a lovely little flower arrangement. Lexi had glanced at the gravestone next to her father's. That headstone was in exactly the condition she had been anticipating.

Lexi had looked at her damp cloth in one hand, and her lovely bouquet in the other, and suddenly felt so sorry for the young woman called Billie. Whoever she was, however she'd died – she'd died young, before she had a chance to marry or have children, as far as Lexi could surmise from the epitaph – she'd clearly been forgotten. Perhaps all her relatives were dead, or they just couldn't be bothered to visit, or more likely, with the passage of time, the memory of her had disappeared into oblivion.

Lexi remembered thinking that no one deserved that. So she had bent down and spent time cleaning a stranger's grave, making several trips to the water containers to rinse out the cloth and douse it with fresh water. When she was satisfied, Lexi had spent time cutting the flower stems and arranging them in the little metal container, which she'd also filled with water.

Her father's grave next door had simple white and pink carnations, which were lovely, and suited the grey headstone. Billie's headstone was jet black with gold lettering. The brightly coloured roses stood out against the dark background.

When Lexi had finished cleaning the headstone, she'd discovered that it was not one grave, but three. It explained perhaps why nobody had visited in many years, for her parents were also there, together for eternity with their only child.

'How sad,' Lexi had commented. Their young adult child had died first, and they'd chosen to be buried with her when they passed away.

Before she left, Lexi had placed the conker and her painted stone on the granite base of her father's headstone. It was only a simple message, but she hoped that as an artist and illustrator her father would appreciate it, wherever he was. She'd drawn the outline of a heart on one side of the stone, with the words *Always in my heart*, and had written a simple message on the other side – *Luv you, Dad. Miss you.*' Lexi had taken a photo on her phone to send to Andrea, wondering even as she was sending it whether it was a morbid thing to do. Would Andrea appreciate it? What would she think when Lexi told her that someone else had visited the grave in the recent past?

The flowers are so fresh, whoever left them could still be here. That thought had crossed her mind as she'd retraced her steps down the path towards the church, but disappointingly she was the only person in the graveyard, besides those who had long since passed.

Lexi finished recounting her visit to Ray. 'What do you make of it?'

'I think someone up there is looking out for you.'

Lexi frowned. 'I'm not talking about the conkers – if that's what you're referring to.' She still didn't think she believed in that sort of thing, although she felt she could quickly change her mind if she chose to read too much into things like a conker falling right on her head, reawakening a memory of the funeral that led to her finding the grave.

'I'm talking about the fresh flowers that were already at his graveside.'

'Ah, yes. Of course.'

Lexi fixed her gaze on him. 'What does it mean?'

'What does it mean?' Ray scratched his head. 'Well, it's certainly a turn-up for the books.' Ray quickly rephrased, 'What I mean to say is—'

Lexi cut in. 'I understand. That's a bit of an old turn-of-phrase, but my grandparents, who are well into their seventies, say it all the time.' Lexi realised too late that she had made a gaffe.

'You're making me sound ancient.'

'Sorry.'

'Mind you, I probably do seem quite old to someone in their early twenties.'

'I'm twenty-six.'

'Ah, pardon me. I'm afraid that when you get to my age, it seems to get harder to discern the younger generations' ages. Everyone looks a youngster of twenty-one to me.'

Lexi smiled. 'In the US, I still get asked for identity when I buy alcohol. It is *very* annoying.'

Ray smiled ruefully. 'I bet. I'm afraid that you won't escape that over here, if that's why you decided to return here.'

Lexi and Ray exchanged a smile at the joke. she said, 'But about the flowers ...'

'Did someone say flowers?' Sarah walked into the room carrying a large vase filled with water and a beautiful arrangement of flowers. *It wasn't as lovely as the bouquet I bought*, thought Lexi, knowing she was biased. Of course, Ray's bouquet was just as gorgeous.

'Aren't they just the most beautiful flowers?' commented Sarah, her eyes lighting up.

Lexi looked at Ray, who winked at her as he mouthed, *Thank you.*

She mouthed back, *You're welcome,* feeling so happy that her suggestion had worked. She watched Sarah put them down on the deep windowsill in the bay window. 'There now, I can admire them from anywhere in the room.'

Lexi caught Sarah turn around and smile at Ray before her eyes settled on her new guest. 'Do you know that he used to buy me flowers every day?'

Lexi acted as though she had no clue. 'Really?' She furtively glanced at Ray. His worried expression gave him away; he was probably wondering what Sarah was going to say next.

'Oh, yes. It annoyed me, I can tell you. But then when he stopped buying them, I missed them dreadfully. I'd told him to stop, then I wished I hadn't.'

'You never told me that,' commented Ray in surprise.

'Well, I'm telling you now, you silly fool.' It might have sounded rude, but there was no malice in her voice. Although Ray and Sarah were living apart, Lexi could tell they were just as much a married couple as anyone living together.

Lexi smiled at them, but it was bittersweet. She thought of her relationship with Brandon. Although they'd had their spats, as anyone in a long-term relationship did, she'd always thought they'd grow old together.

Sarah stood back and admired the flowers before she turned around and said, 'Now, I'm going to bring in the tea – or would you prefer coffee?'

'Tea would be lovely, thank you.'

'Of course, Lexi. Do you like scones?'

'Oh, yes.'

When Sarah walked out of the room, Ray turned to Lexi. 'So,

the flowers on the grave ...'

'Yes?'

'Now, there's even more reason to join that website and trace your English relatives, because after all these years, although it could be a jolly good friend of your father's, I think it's more likely that a person who is still leaving flowers after two decades is a relative.'

'You think so?'

'Oh, yes.'

'And, talking of fresh flowers ...' Ray grinned at Lexi. 'I'll be paying a regular visit to The Potting Shed from now on.'

Lexi understood. He was going to become one of Lili's regular customers again.

'Perhaps you'd like to come along again when I go next? You could buy some flowers, and visit your father again.'

'I'd like that very much.'

'And perhaps while you're there you might bump into the other visitor who is leaving flowers. You never know.'

Lexi grinned, catching his drift. 'You never know ...'

'And right now, you've got the advantage.'

Lexi tilted her head to one side, interested to know what he meant by that comment. 'How so?'

'Whoever they are, they won't be aware that someone else is visiting.'

Lexi pursed her lips and thought of the hand-painted stone she'd placed at the base of the gravestone.

37

'Do you mind if I call my sister? The mobile reception is not great back at the houseboat.'

Ray took his eyes off the road for a second. 'Of course, go ahead.'

Lexi got out her phone. It wouldn't be a private conversation, but Ray knew all about what she was going to tell her sister. She'd sent her the photo of the grave. She had planned to text her again, but she decided she would prefer a quick chat, if Andrea answered her phone.

'Andrea? It's Lexi. Did you get the photo?' She'd told Ray about that too, although she hadn't mentioned that Andrea hadn't responded to her text. It was mid-morning back in Connecticut, so she hoped her sister was just at work and hadn't had time to respond. Or was it something else? That was the other reason Lexi was making the call; she had a feeling there was more behind it than her sister simply being too busy to reply.

'Oh, Lexi – you didn't catch the flight.'

Lexi sighed heavily. *So that's what it's about.* Lexi gave Ray a sideways glance. This was awkward. She hadn't expected her sister to get straight into that, especially after she had sent her the photo.

'Are they cross with me?' What Lexi wanted to ask was, *Do you think they're really going to cut me off?* She didn't know if the monthly allowance had been deposited in her bank account as usual. Perhaps she could ask Andrea if she'd check. Then again, Lexi didn't think it was a good idea to hand over her bank details and password over the phone.

It wasn't that she didn't trust Andrea; the trouble was that she imagined that there were all sorts of sophisticated ways people could get hold of those details, perhaps even by using technology to listen in on phone conversations.

She glanced at Ray. 'Hold on, Andrea, I just want to ask Ray a question.'

'Who?'

Lexi lowered the phone. 'Ray, you know I had my bank card stolen? I wanted my sister to check my account. Do you think it would be okay to give her my bank details and passwords over the phone?'

'As long as you trust the person you are giving the details too, it should be fine. But once you do, then you release the bank from any liability.'

Lexi was pleased she'd asked Ray. It gave her an idea. 'Thanks, Ray.'

'Who are you talking to?' Andrea asked down the phone.

'It's a neighbour where I'm staying.'

'You sound as though you're in a car. Are you in a car?'

'Yes.'

'With a man called Ray who you barely know!'

Lexi breathed a heavy sigh. This was not how she envisaged the conversation would go when she phoned. 'Look, I'm perfectly fine. Ray is an ex-cop, police officer, retired. He drove me to Aldeburgh, it's a lovely little town on the Suffolk Coast not far from London. That's where I am right now, and where I just visited Dad's grave. I had tea and a lovely scone with him and his wife.'

'Oh, okay.'

'Look, this isn't the reason for my call, but I need you to get online on to my bank account and check if, er …' She glanced at Ray.

'You want me to find out if your allowance has been stopped.'

'Yes.' Lexi breathed a sigh, thankful that she didn't have to spell it out in front of Ray. She didn't want to get into the story about her grandparents and allowances. Besides, it made her feel embarrassed that at twenty-six years old she was still living off handouts and was not independent.

She'd never felt that way in New York – perhaps because she wasn't actually living off the money but was pretty much using it to fund Brandon's dream. Despite defending Brandon when anyone suggested that his dream to become a rock star was just a childhood fantasy, and that he should get a *proper* job and stop sponging off her, in hindsight Lexi thought they were right. *What a joke*, thought Lexi, *that now I need the money, they'll probably cut me off.*

'There's a file I left along with some of my clothes at the cottage.' Lexi had only packed clothes and essentials for her trip. There was no reason to bring along passwords or anything like that. She didn't think she'd need to access her bank online while she was away; after all, she'd had her bank card. She had no way of knowing it would be stolen. 'When I rang the bank to report my cards stolen, they said they'd issue me with a new card.'

'I haven't been to the cottage since you left. Did you change your address with the bank?'

'No, I didn't inform them of my new address. I should have done that.' Lexi shook her head and caught Ray glancing at her.

Andrea said, 'I can't possibly fly to New York to collect them.'

Lexi looked at Ray and apologised for swearing. 'Sorry, just trying to sort things out regarding my bank. I moved house before I came to England and didn't give my bank my new address.'

Lexi hadn't had a chance to change her address details before she flew out to England. *Why would I?* she thought. She wasn't moving back to Connecticut permanently – she knew that.

Ray nodded. 'If your sister has your bank account number and passwords, then I imagine with the same bank account number you should still be able to access your account online.'

'What did he say?' asked Andrea.

'That shouldn't be a problem, Andrea. If you can just pop into the cottage, my bank details and passwords are in the file in my suitcase. Will you do that for me? Will you go online and check?'

'If I give you your bank details, you could get online yourself.'

Andrea had a point, but she didn't have access to the internet. Lexi looked at Ray. He had kindly offered for her to use his laptop on the boat to join AncestryDNA, which reminded her of the reason she had called Andrea in the first place. But Lexi didn't want to ask him for another favour. He'd been so helpful already.

He really was the best neighbour, but she just felt she was taking advantage, especially as she'd led him on and she was on Margot's houseboat under false pretences. She felt bad enough as it was, without relying on his generous nature any further. The other option was the library, but it might not be safe using the internet to access her bank on a public network.

Lexi had a further thought. 'Look, I'm going to open a bank account over here, so if there are funds in my account, I can give you my new account number and you can transfer the money.'

Ray said, 'Sorry to butt in, but would you like me to drop you in Southwold to pop into a bank to open an account?'

'Oh, would you? That would be great.'

When Lexi put her phone back to her ear, she thought she'd been cut off. 'Andrea – are you still there?'

'Yes.' She went quiet again, before she asked, 'Why are you opening a bank account in England?'

'Well, I got a job.' Lexi gave Ray a sideways glance. She really, really didn't want to get into the nature of her job. She could hardly tell her she was working in the public library when she was meant to be houseboat-sitting.

'What does that mean? You're not coming back?'

'No, not necessarily.' Lexi frowned. It really depended on her getting that allowance, so she could leave the houseboat and rent a place. Lexi thought it best not to tell Andrea that just yet, though.

'So, will you do that? Check my account?'

Andrea sighed down the phone. 'Of course. I'm at work at the moment. You'll have to wait until later.'

'That's fine.'

'It's going to be quite late. I'll have to sneak into the cottage and try and avoid Grandpa finding out. They've been on at me about whether I've heard from you.'

Lexi rolled her eyes. Why couldn't Andrea just keep their conversation a secret? She had it on the tip of her tongue to say that, but she knew how Andrea would respond – *You mean lie?* It wasn't in Andrea's nature to do that; besides, she knew what else she'd say – *That's not our family; we don't lie to each other or keep secrets.* That meant Grandpa would find out about this conversation eventually.

'Talking of which,' said Andrea. 'Have you heard from Brandon?'

Lexi stared out of the front window. They were now on the main road heading back to Southwold. She looked out of her window at the rolling countryside and sighed. 'Yes.' She'd received voicemails she hadn't bothered listening to, and texts she hadn't bothered reading. What was his problem? Why was he so concerned about her? They were no longer together. She didn't give a fig about him.

Even as she was thinking it, she knew that wasn't true. Frustratingly, she still cared for Brandon a great deal, and missed him terribly. That, she knew, was the reason she couldn't read those texts or listen to those voice messages. He'd already broken her heart – why couldn't he just go away and leave her alone?

'He's been leaving *me* voice messages and texts. I won't speak to him. I'm not bothering to reply.'

'Good.'

'Have you spoken to him or replied to his messages?'

'No.' Lexi didn't admit that she hadn't even read them.

'He said it's really important that you get in contact with him.'

'Is it?' Lexi said flatly. 'I don't care.' She changed the subject. 'Look, the reason I called was about the photo I sent you. Did you get it?' She was surprised Andrea hadn't texted back a response.

'Yes.'

'Well?'

'It's a grave, Lexi. I mean I don't know what to say. I'm glad you found it, but ...' she trailed off.

Lexi understood. Andrea didn't have the same memories of their father that she had.

'Okay, well, the thing is that I didn't just find the grave.' Lexi glanced at Ray, who looked at her and smiled.

'I found something else, too.'

'You did? What is it?'

'Well, it's not a case if *what*, but *who* ...'

'Huh?'

Lexi didn't tell her all about trying to locate the grave in the large graveyard, and how she had eventually found it by way of a conker from a chestnut tree. Instead, she cut to the chase. 'When I arrived, there were fresh flowers on his grave.'

'Really?'

Lexi hadn't let on in her text. She had wanted to tell Andrea herself.

'Oh, my god, Lexi. Do you know what that means? There might be English relations still alive that we don't know about on Dad's side.'

Lexi smiled. She couldn't remember the last time Andrea had spoken to her about their father. When she said *Dad*, she was normally referring to Mitch.

'Exactly!'

'You might have passed them in ...' she paused, 'Where are you again?'

'A place called Aldeburgh, a little town on the coast.' They weren't in actual fact in Aldeburgh anymore, but turning off the main road that took them along another country lane heading towards the coast – this time to Southwold. Lexi hoped her phone battery didn't run out or that she lost reception, as she still had a question she wanted to ask her sister.

'You could have passed them in the street, Lexi, you never know.'

Lexi hadn't thought of that. Perhaps when she was walking to Cobblers Yard, or along the promenade, the person who had laid the flowers had walked right on by. 'Andrea, I just want to ask you a question. Have you been on AncestryDNA lately?' Out of the corner of her eye, she caught Ray glance her way.

'No, it's been an absolute age. I remember getting it for my birthday – or was it Christmas? – one year. Nothing much came out of it, though.'

'Yes, I remember you saying, but people join all the time. I'm going to join too. Perhaps something will come up this time.'

'When I've finished work I'll see if I can find my user credentials and sign in.'

'You won't forget my bank, though, will you?'

'I won't forget, I promise.' Andrea asked, 'What are you going to do about your return flight? You've still got one booked – haven't you?'

'Yes, I have. I'm sure I told you it's a flexi return. I want to find the person who visited Dad's grave, but staying on here really depends on—' Lexi glanced at Ray and stopped abruptly.

'Whether you're still getting your allowance?'

'Yes, otherwise ...'

'You'll have to come home?'

'That's right. Let's just say my new job isn't overly well-paid, not like what I used to do.' Lexi hadn't mentioned to her sister that she was also squatting. At least if she knew she still had the allowance, it meant she could find somewhere else to live if Margot suddenly returned.

'Oh, okay.'

Lexi looked ahead. They'd driven down the long straight road, bordered by fields and farmland on either side, that led into Southwold. They'd just passed the sign for the private girls' school on the right. Lexi could see the outskirts of the town up ahead.

Ray said, 'Lexi, sorry to interrupt ...'

Lexi lowered her phone for a moment.

'I'll park in the town centre so you can nip into the bank.'

'Great – thanks, Ray. Andrea, I have to go.'

'Look, before you do,' said Andrea. 'If I've lost my password, do you want me to re-join AncestryDNA?'

'Yes, why not. We can put our heads together and see what we come up with – or *who* we come up with. Oh, wouldn't it be amazing if we could find an English relative!'

What Andrea said next caught Lexi a little off-guard. 'Do you think that whoever laid the flowers, assuming it's a relative, is the reason our grandparents have always been so dead-set against us returning to England?'

Lexi frowned. 'What makes you say that?'

'I don't know, but it's odd, isn't it?' replied Andrea. 'They must have a good reason.'

Lexi didn't want to admit it, but she was wondering that too.

38

'There's Lloyds or Barclays Bank.' Ray pointed the two banks out from where they were parked outside the Co-op in the high street.

'Thank you so much, Ray.' Lexi was about to get out of the car when she had a thought. 'I must give you something for the petrol.'

'Absolutely not.' Ray shook his head. 'I wouldn't hear of it.'

Lexi didn't think he'd accept the offer. She put the money back in her purse. She hadn't spent any money on lunch either. Sarah's fruit scones with jam and cream had been delicious, as had the finger sandwiches she'd made. Lexi hadn't expected to stop there for lunch too.

'Are you sure you don't want me to hang around and wait? I could drive you back to the quay in Walberswick?'

Lexi shook her head. 'I'd quite like to walk back, but thank you, Ray, for driving me to Aldeburgh. I had a really nice time visiting Cobblers Yard and meeting your friend Lili, and Sarah.'

'You're welcome, Lexi. You must let me know how things go with AncestryDNA and if you find a long-lost relative.'

Lexi forced a smile. 'I will.' She couldn't help thinking about her grandparents and why they didn't want her to be there.

Andrea had said that she felt they must have had a good reason to discourage them from returning to England.

As Lexi got out of the car, she thought *I want to be the judge of that*. Lexi shut the car door and gave Ray a little wave as he set off in the car down the high street. A moment later, he did a U-turn and was heading back in her direction. He had to drive to Walberswick, where he would park his car on the quay. It meant doubling back through the town to the main road that led out of Aldeburgh, and driving the mile or so to the next village.

There was no way to cross over from Southwold to Walberswick by car. There was the footbridge and a little passenger boat ferry that ran in the summer. Lexi had discovered a leaflet about the ferry in the library.

Lexi was looking forward to making her way back towards the quay and crossing the river. It would be a lovely walk if it didn't rain, although straight away she felt a raindrop on her cheek. She glanced up at the dark clouds that were gathering and wondered if she should have taken up Ray's offer to wait for her.

Lexi waved at Ray as he passed by again, deciding not to flag him down and ask for a lift instead. She stepped into the bank. As she approached a cashier, she hoped that Andrea would soon get in touch with good news about her allowance – that would mean some decent money hitting her new bank account very soon. She still couldn't really believe her grandparents would cut her off just over her flying to England. It was ridiculous, and quite petty, thought Lexi, just because she had disobeyed them. She wasn't a child anymore. *Then you need to stop acting like one and depending on their money.*

Lexi frowned when that thought entered her head. It was unwelcome but true. The problem was that she was in a bind. She wanted to be independent, but she needed their money. It was only now that it really hit her – the fact that she had never really broken free of the family money and, ipso facto, the family business.

As Lexi stepped into the bank, thinking about the paltry income she would be receiving from the apprenticeship role at the library, the lady at the publishing house in London came to mind. Could she persuade Margot to write another book? That finder's fee was still in the offing. But how could she go about that? Lexi thought of the letter. It was the perfect introduction – something personal, something from Margot's past. Something she'd travelled all the way here to give to her, in person.

Lexi sighed heavily at the thought that it would have been a perfect introduction if she hadn't been squatting on Margot's houseboat. How she thought she was going to conceal that, she had no clue.

Besides the fact that she shouldn't be living there, Lexi knew she was making a huge assumption that Margot would be happy to receive a letter from her mother; she had no idea what was written in the letter or whether they were indeed friends.

Lexi's own letter from her mother came to mind – its contents still a mystery until she opened it.

'So, open it,' Lexi said under her breath, catching the eye of a woman ahead of her in the queue, who had obviously overheard her talking to herself, as she had turned around and given Lexi a look.

Lexi avoided eye contact, feeling embarrassed. Fortunately, the orderly queue moved along swiftly. *What is it with the British and queuing?* thought Lexi, smiling. Everything was so much more orderly and polite in England.

When it was her turn, she stepped up to speak to a young man behind a counter. She eyed the clock on the wall. The flight Grandpa had booked for her had long gone. Grandpa never made empty threats; everyone knew that. Lexi was trying not to think about that as she handed over her passport and five pounds to deposit in her new account. She had no choice but to give the houseboat mooring as her home address.

Lexi thought that perhaps Grandpa wouldn't follow through and stop her allowance. Stranger things had happened; like the letter that had turned up unexpectedly and that she had to give to a woman she didn't know, and those flowers she'd discovered on her father's grave. Someone was out there who knew her dad, who possibly had attended the funeral years ago and had met Lexi and her sister.

She had thought of leaving a note somewhere on the grave for the visitor to contact her, but she'd had second thoughts. What if she scared them off, and they stopped visiting? Or what if she left her mobile phone number and someone else came across it and contacted her? That was a scenario that she would rather avoid. She decided against the idea of leaving a note, but she was still determined to find the person.

39

'Hey, Lexi?'

Lexi had just arrived back at the houseboat from Aldeburgh when she heard Charlie, who had come out on deck next door. Lexi was about to open the cabin door. She looked up, surreptitiously glancing about her, hoping no other neighbours had spotted her on the houseboat, or heard Charlie calling her name.

'You're not in trouble again, are you?' Lexi asked.

'No, not this time.' Charlie grinned at her. 'Did you get my message? I knocked on your door but you weren't in, then I saw our neighbour and I told him he must give you the message if he sees you. He's around a lot. Our neighbour is retired.'

'Ah, you mean Ray?'

'Yes.'

She was relieved it was Ray that Charlie had spoken to and not another neighbour who had no idea she was there. Of course Lexi remembered the message: *She says to tell you that her dad has invited you to dinner.*

Lexi had been surprised by the invitation, considering that Charlie's dad seemed to keep himself to himself; it was odd. Charlie didn't go to school, and they moved around a lot. What was that about? She got the impression he wasn't really that keen on making friends with the neighbours, so why the dinner invitation?

She imagined it was a thank you for spending a bit of time with his daughter on Friday.

By the sound of things, Charlie didn't have any friends or female company. That wasn't good, not having girlfriends her own age. That thought brought to mind Ray's mention of his granddaughter, Maisie, who was around Charlie's age. Perhaps if she went to dinner, she could mention that to Scott, and he might be able to arrange a playdate with Maisie.

Although it seemed like a good idea, when she thought of Scott, she couldn't imagine it. She wondered why he was being sociable towards her. *Perhaps it's got nothing to do with Charlie, and he likes me.*

Lexi blushed at the thought, trying to quell the feeling in the pit of her stomach – she fancied Scott, there was no denying it. *But he's not my type. I know my type – it's Brandon.* Lexi frowned. *Perhaps it's time to re-examine that assumption*, she thought. Was she up for a date, so soon after Brandon had cheated on her? Not at all. But she was lonely in the evenings. She fancied a bit of adult conversation, and if it was in the company of a very good-looking, albeit slightly mysterious guy, then all the better. At least there would be no awkward silences. She had chatterbox Charlie, who was sure to diffuse any that arose.

I'd have to change first, put on a bit of makeup, do something with my hair, thought Lexi. *It's not a date*, she reminded herself, *just a thank you meal for looking after his kid.*

But you'd like it to be a date, wouldn't you? another internal voice said. Lexi rolled her eyes. Where had that thought come from? She nodded at Charlie. 'Yes, I got your message.'

'Good. Daddy is cooking dinner now. It will take a bit of time, though, as he makes everything from scratch.'

Lexi looked past Charlie to the cabin door. Even though he was busy cooking, she was hoping that Scott would poke his head out the door and say something like, *Do you mind eating such and such a dish? Do you have any allergies? Are you sure you want to come?* But there was no sign of him; just Charlie delivering the message. 'My dad says that I can come round yours again, if you like.'

Lexi smiled. 'I'd like that very much.'

'I tried to call on you earlier, but you were out.'

'Yes, I was at work in the library, and then I went out with Ray to lay some flowers at my dad's grave.'

'Oh, okay. How did he die?'

'It was a long time ago. Heart attack – I think.' Lexi would have preferred to spare her the details, but she had asked. There wasn't any way of sugar-coating death, even though Charlie was only ten.

'Okay.'

Lexi saw she had a question. Lexi hoped it wasn't about death, or something like that. She'd rather Charlie saved the difficult questions for her dad. That was what parents were there for; to help you fathom and navigate the difficulties that life inevitably brought.

For some reason, Lexi thought of the letter from her late mother. Would there be words of wisdom in that letter, showing her the way to get through the big things in life that she might have to face without her mum – like breaking up with her boyfriend; something she had never, ever thought would happen? Six months on, she still missed her mum every single day.

'Can I come over and visit now?'

'Sure, why not. Is it okay with your dad?'

'Yes.'

'Great, because I've got something for you.'

'You have?' Charlie said excitedly, 'Is it a present?'

'Yes, I suppose it is. When I was in Aldeburgh, I visited a lovely little place called Cobblers Yard to buy some flowers, and I bought something else too.' Lexi grinned, thinking of the two amber necklaces she'd bought in the antique store – the ones that Ray had said his granddaughter Maisie made. She'd bought them one each.

'I can't wait to see what you bought me from Aldeburgh,' Charlie called out.

Lexi was about to walk down the stairs when she felt a heavy plop of rain on her shoulder. She glanced at Charlie, who was about to exit her houseboat down the gangplank. She called out, 'Just be careful. It's starting to rain, and it might be slippery.'

'Yes, I'll be careful.'

As Lexi bent down to get the key from under the flowerpot – she still left it there so there was no chance she'd lose it – she smiled as she heard Charlie's footsteps running down the gangplank. She was just thinking that she should have been a bit more explicit and told Charlie to walk, when she heard a splash. Lexi stepped away from the door and looked up.

'Charlie?' Lexi frowned. She wasn't on the gangplank or running the short distance along the path towards Margot's houseboat.

Lexi did just what she had not wanted Charlie to do; as the heavens opened and it started to lash down with rain, she ran along the gangplank and threw open the gate.

'Charlie!'

As she ran towards the houseboat next door and looked along the gangplank, she could see something in the water.

'Oh, my god! Oh, my god!' Lexi ran frantically towards Charlie, watching her spluttering in the water, her arms flailing.

'No, no, no!' Lexi threw herself to her knees, screaming, 'Scott! Help!'

She got on her stomach and reached out her hand towards Charlie. Then she froze. A memory hit her of a little girl, younger than Charlie, and it was dark, so very dark. And she was drowning.

'Charlie!' Scott came thundering down the gangplank and threw himself in the water.

Lexi sat up and stared into the murky water. She sat there, with her arms wrapped around her legs, her chin on her knees, rocking back and forth, thinking, *I did this – it's all my fault she fell in.*

Charlie and Scott came to the surface, both taking an enormous gulp of air. Scott somehow managed to get Charlie up on to the gangplank before he pulled himself out too. He looked at Lexi. 'Why didn't you help us?'

'It was all my fault, all my fault,' Lexi said over and over.

'It wasn't Lexi's fault that I fell in, Dad. She told me to be careful, but I ran and then I slipped.'

Lexi stared into the water, rocking back and forth. 'All my fault.'

Charlie looked at her dad. 'What's wrong with her?'

Scott stared at Lexi. 'I don't know.'

She was shivering even though it wasn't her who had fallen in the water and got soaking wet.

He turned to Charlie. 'Go and fetch me a blanket. And don't run!'

Charlie walked very quickly back to their houseboat, then ran into her bedroom and fetched a spare blanket from the wardrobe in her room.

'Is she going to be all right?' Charlie asked when she returned. She watched her dad gently wrap the blanket around Lexi's shoulders.

'I think she's in shock.'

'But I'm the one who fell in the water.'

'I know, sweetheart.'

'How do you know she's in shock? Is it because you were a medic in the army?'

'That's right.'

Scott put his arms around her shoulders. 'Come on, let's get up and go inside. Everything is going to be all right.'

Lexi slowly turned her head to look at Scott. 'I … I'm sorry, I just ... I couldn't go into the water.'

'It's okay, Lexi,' Scott said in a soothing voice. 'Charlie is fine.'

Charlie looked at her dad. 'Is she going to be okay?'

Scott offered his daughter a reassuring smile as he helped Lexi to her feet. 'Put the kettle on, Charlie. We're right behind you.'

Charlie stepped on to the houseboat, throwing them a backwards glance to check they were following before she darted inside and put on the kettle.

A moment later, Scott steered Lexi on to the houseboat, and settled her down on the sofa in the cabin. He crouched down in front of her for a moment to pull the blanket around her shoulders.

'The kettle's boiled,' said Charlie. 'Shall I make some tea?'

'Good girl. Make Lexi's extra-milky and sweet, would you?'

'Yes, Dad.' Charlie made Lexi's first and brought it straight over, being careful not to spill the tea. She had made it in the biggest mug she could find and had added lots of sugar.

Scott perched on the sofa next to Lexi and held out his hand for the mug. 'Thank you, sweetheart, Now, you're soaking wet, so go and get yourself dried off. Just leave your wet clothes in the shower cubicle. I'll sort them out later.'

Charlie looked at Lexi and hesitated.

Scott glanced at his daughter. 'Everything is fine. Just go and get out of those wet clothes. Go on, now.'

Charlie left the room as Scott handed Lexi the mug.

'Thank you. I ... I don't know what came over me out there,' she said in a shaky voice.

'It's okay. Drink this. You'll feel much better.'

Lexi sipped the sweet tea. She looked at Scott. 'You need to get out of those wet clothes too.'

'I know.' Scott didn't budge from his spot, perched on the sofa, looking at her, his face full of concern.

'I'm okay, really I am. I wouldn't want you to catch pneumonia. I'll just sit here and drink my tea.'

'All right.' Scott stood up. 'Just ... just stay there. I'll be back in a minute.'

Lexi offered him a smile. 'I will.'

❖

Charlie ran out of the room and saw the empty mug of tea on the coffee table, the blanket draped on the arm of the sofa, and Lexi heading for the door.

'Where are you going?'

Lexi turned around, looking like a rabbit caught in headlights. 'Oh, Charlie, that was a lovely cup of tea, but I must go.'

'Why? Aren't you staying for dinner?'

'I'm really not all that hungry, Charlie, but it was so kind of your dad to invite me over. Another time, perhaps.'

'What was that about dinner?' Scott walked into the room, took one look at Lexi standing at the door, and said, 'Where are you going?'

'Lexi's leaving. I don't want her to go.'

Lexi said, 'I was saying to Charlie that it was very kind of you to invite me over for dinner, but I'm not all that hungry.'

Scott furrowed his brow.

Charlie stood there biting her lip and avoiding eye contact with her father.

Lexi shifted her gaze from Scott to Charlie. 'Oh, oh … this is really embarrassing. You didn't invite me over for dinner, did you?'

Charlie said, 'I told him that he should after you were so nice to me the other day and made me lunch.' She looked at her dad. 'You said that you'd think about it, didn't you?'

Scott smiled at his daughter. 'I did. And I have thought about it. And I want you to stay for dinner, Lexi.'

Lexi was already shaking her head, no. 'I'm really not hungry.'

'I bet I can change your mind. I make quite the curry.' He paused. 'You do like curry, don't you?'

'Yes. But as I said, I'm really not that—'

'Hungry.' Scott smiled. 'But you haven't tasted it. If you're still not hungry when you smell the aroma from my homemade curry, then by all means, go. But I'd much prefer that you stay and at least have a taste and give me your verdict.'

Scott exchanged a glance with Charlie, and winked.

She grinned at her dad. Charlie knew her dad's curries were the best.

Scott looked at Lexi. 'Is it a deal?'

Lexi sighed. She took her hand off the door handle. 'Oh, all right.'

Charlie ran over and took Lexi's hand. 'Can I show you my bedroom? It's very small, but it's cool.'

Scott intervened. 'Charlie, let Lexi sit on the sofa and relax while I cook.'

Lexi looked at Charlie's pleading face. 'No, it's fine. I'd love to see your bedroom.'

❖

Charlie sat on the easy chair, staring at Lexi and her dad sitting together on the sofa. She had her hand on the little amber necklace around her neck that Lexi had given her. It was the best present ever. She felt so grown-up wearing it. But best of all, Lexi had a matching necklace. They'd helped each other put them on when Charlie had shown Lexi her bedroom.

Charlie sat fingering the little stone on the end on the necklace, her eyes moving from Lexi to her dad. She stood up. 'I'm getting an early night.'

Scott looked at his daughter in astonishment. 'Are you feeling unwell? Come over here and let me feel your forehead.'

'Is she running a temperature?' asked Lexi.

Charlie stood there while her dad placed the back of his hand on her forehead. He then felt her cheeks. 'You seem okay.'

'That's because I am. I'm just really, really tired.' Charlie faked the biggest yawn.

'Oh, okay.'

Charlie avoided eye contact with her dad, but she did look at Lexi. Lexi was fun. She made Charlie laugh. She smiled at her dad as she walked past the sofa. He'd made the best curry ever, even better than he normally did. Lexi had said she wasn't hungry, but when she'd tasted his curry, she'd wolfed down the meal, and had even asked for seconds. Charlie and her dad had exchanged a knowing smile across the table as they ate.

Lexi said, 'Goodnight, Charlie. Sweet dreams.'

Charlie walked over to her and put her arms around her. 'Sorry I scared you.'

'Oh, that wasn't your fault, Charlie. You slipped.'

Charlie caught her dad shaking his head. She understood. She wouldn't mention it again. She stepped towards her dad. 'Goodnight.'

'Goodnight, sweetheart.' She could tell by the look on his face that he was still surprised she was taking herself off to bed without a fuss – and so early. Charlie normally liked to stay up late, and always, always complained when it was bedtime.

She pursed her lips as she headed for the door to her bedroom. She didn't like telling her dad a lie, but it was for his own good. Her dad was no fun. He didn't laugh. He hardly smiled. It had been like that since Mum had walked out and he'd left the army and his posting overseas to look after her. But today, this evening, she had sat up at the dinner table and watched her dad and Lexi chatting, and seen him smiling a lot.

She opened the door to the little inner hallway and turned around. Her dad and Lexi were talking. Lexi had made her dad laugh. Maybe Lexi would make a good girlfriend. Maybe she'd make a good mum. Maybe they could stop moving around and settle down, and be a normal family with a mum and a dad, and a home. She wouldn't even mind staying living on the houseboat if it meant they could all be together, just like this.

Charlie caught her dad edging closer to Lexi on the sofa before she closed the door. She smiled to herself. This could work.

40

Lexi shifted her attention to LC, who was lying on the keyboard. She imagined that if she picked him up and put him down on the floor, he'd just jump up again. She had an idea. She stood up, moved her comfortable office chair back from the desk, and then turned to LC. She gently lifted him off the keyboard and placed him on the chair. She watched him sniff the chair for a moment and then settle down, curling into a ball of fur. He closed his eyes.

Lexi felt like closing her eyes too. She wasn't meant to be working on Sunday, but Jill had texted her and asked if she could possibly come in today as the other library assistant had called in sick. The previous day, Lexi would have jumped at the chance to have something to occupy her time. But after her eventful evening, she felt differently. Now, she would rather be spending the day with Scott and Charlie.

They'd talked about going out for a day together. She had thought of making up a picnic lunch and inviting them to go for a walk into Walberswick to see the sand dunes and have lunch on the beach. Unfortunately, that plan had been scuppered.

She could have said no to the work, but Jill had mentioned overtime money, which on a Sunday wasn't something Lexi could afford to turn down. However, it wasn't just the money. Lexi had only just started her new job, and she wanted Jill to feel confident that her new employee was committed and flexible. She was both those things; she just wished she didn't feel so tired after the stress of Charlie falling into the water the previous evening. What a nightmare. But it wasn't just the accident that had kept her awake when she finally returned to Margot's houseboat after the amazing curry and the evening spent with Scott. She had kept trying to put her mind to things, but all she could think about was Scott. Why was that?

She smiled at the sweet black and white cat looking very at home and comfy. She wished she could curl up and join him for a nap. She sighed and turned around to find an older lady, who she guessed was in her seventies, standing by the desk with some books. Lexi asked, 'Checking those out or returning them?'

'I'm returning these.'

Lexi took the two books and scanned them to return. The lady's personal details briefly popped up on her screen. Her name was Meredith. Lexi caught her date of birth – 1946.

She put the books on the trolley beside her desk.

'I'd like to check these out please. Now, these two are mine, but my friend has ordered two books – that's why I'm not using the self-service over there. I thought I might as well do it all in one go.'

Lexi glanced behind her. There were two self-service computers with trolleys beside them, where the public could check out and return library books themselves.

'She ordered them online. Are they ready to collect? I have her library card.'

'Let me see.' Lexi turned to the bookshelves behind her, which were full of books, with white cards placed in the books like bookmarks, each with the name of the person who had ordered them. 'What is the name of your friend?' Lexi asked over her shoulder.

'Margot Dorey.'

Lexi froze. She slowly turned around and stared at the lady.

'Did you just say *Margot Dorey*?' Lexi enunciated the name. It couldn't be her, could it? She was in London, or somewhere, but she certainly wasn't here. Lexi would know. She was living on her houseboat.

'Yes, I have her library card here.'

Lexi looked at the card.

'Did you find them?'

'Oh, er … hold on, I'll have a look.' Lexi looked at the bookshelves behind her. She found two books, each containing a white card with the name *Margot Dorey*. She turned around, eyeing the lady who was collecting them on her behalf. She was dying to know if the books were for the same Margot Dorey she had come to find. What were the chances there would be another lady in the area by the same name? Lexi thought it was doubtful. Perhaps she wanted them collected for when she arrived back from her trip. But Lexi knew that wouldn't be for another month, at the end of the summer. She was aware that you could only check books out for three weeks at a time. Unless her friend was going to visit her and hand them over.

Lexi had all these questions running through her mind. She turned around with the two books and put them on the counter. 'So, are you going to give these to your friend?' she asked as she took the library card and checked out the books.

'Of course – why would I get them out if I didn't intend to do that?'

'Oh, yes … silly me.'

'You're new here, aren't you?'

Lexi nodded.

'Are you American?'

'Yes, I'm here on—' Lexi was going to say *vacation*. But this wasn't exactly a holiday.

'You're a student?'

Lexi nodded again. She guessed that was kind of true. Jill had mentioned the librarianship course again. 'I'm here on an apprenticeship. I'm considering getting a professional qualification.'

'Do you want to be a writer?' the lady asked. My friend loves books. She started as a librarian, years and years ago, but all she wanted to be was a writer.'

Lexi stared at her. 'And did she?'

'Did she *what*?'

'Become a writer?' Lexi held her breath in anticipation. The older lady nodded her head, but quickly said, 'Well, I must be off.'

Lexi wanted her to stay and chat so she could find out more about the elusive author friend. 'That's really nice of you to collect her books. Do you have far to take them?' Lexi asked, wondering if she might mention she was off to London to visit her friend. Lexi wondered when the lady would get suspicious of all the questions.

'No, she's just round the corner from where I live in Walberswick, so it's no bother to drop them round.'

'In Walberswick?' Lexi said with a start.

'Yes.'

Lexi tried to mask her surprise. 'I bet she's keen to start reading them,' Lexi went on, hoping the nice lady would continue the conversation.

'Oh, yes, I expect she'll start straight away – I mean, it's not like she's spending her time doing anything else.'

'What, this evening you mean?'

'Oh, yes, I expect so.'

Lexi stared at her. *Margot was in Walberswick?* It couldn't be the same person, surely.

'Everything all right?' asked Meredith.

Lexi caught her looking at the computer.

'They're not double-booked or anything, are they?'

Lexi realised that the woman standing in front of her, who was not much younger than Nana, had mistaken the reason for her hesitation. 'Oh, er ... no, it's fine. I've checked the books out. She will have plenty of time to read them.'

'Good, good. She'll be glad to hear that.'

Lexi looked at the time. Her shift wasn't over just yet. Unlike Saturday, when the library closed at one, today the library's opening hours extended until four. She had five minutes to go.

Meredith followed her gaze to the clock on the wall. 'Well, I'd better get going. You close in a few minutes, and I expect you'll be keen to get off home.'

Lexi wanted to stall her just for a couple of minutes. 'Wait!'

Meredith had just turned to go. She turned back to the front desk. 'Yes?'

'Um, we are just double-checking people's details while you are here. Have you just got a moment?'

'Well, of course – if *you* have.'

Lexi had an eye on the clock on the wall across the room, ticking down until four. 'It won't take a moment. Can I have both of those library cards please?' Lexi furtively glanced about the library, looking for any sign of Jill, worried she'd ask her what she was doing. There was no need to check any details on the computer system, unless you had a personal reason to find out someone's home address.

Lexi was interested to see if there was another address on the system different to the houseboat on the quay. Lexi took Margot Dorey's card first and quickly pulled up her personal details – it was an address in Walberswick, but it wasn't the houseboat. Perhaps there were two Margot Doreys – was that possible in a small community such as this? Lexi frowned. She wanted to visit the address, but she didn't know the town very well. It would be much easier if she followed Meredith.

Lexi said, 'Can you confirm your friend's address?' She looked up when she didn't get a response.

'What have you got on the system?'

Lexi stared at her for a moment before reeling off the address in Walberswick. 'Is that correct?'

'Yes, that's the one.'

'Good.' Lexi glanced at the clock on the wall. It was three minutes to four. She handed the card back. 'Thanks.' If she wanted to follow her, she'd have to stall for a bit.

'Don't you want to check my address too?'

'Oh, yes, of course.' Lexi took the lady's card. She punched in the card number and pretended to read her details, her thoughts elsewhere. She knew that if Meredith left now, she would soon disappear into the town, and Lexi probably wouldn't have a hope of catching up with her, let alone following her to her destination. 'Well, let me see ...' Lexi pretended to access her records. 'Oh, would you believe it? The computer has frozen.' Lexi made a show of sighing in exasperation. 'Always the way,' she added. There really was no need to access her record, but she eventually did it anyway, with one eye on the clock. 'Can you confirm your address for me, please?'

Meredith reeled off her address.

'Excellent. And do we have the correct contact phone number?'

Meredith confirmed that this was correct too.

'Great.' Lexi smiled. She'd already covered the important bit – Margot Dorey's address. *Am I barking up the wrong tree?* she thought. Margot Dorey might be a completely fictitious name. She stared at Meredith. What if *she* was Margot Dorey?

Lexi blurted, 'So, you don't live on a houseboat?' Her eyes went wide. She really, really wished she hadn't said that. It was a completely ridiculous thought. In any case, they had two different library memberships. And she'd seen a photo of Margot Dorey. Although it had been taken years earlier, the lady standing in front of her looked nothing like her.

'No, no – I gave you my address. You wouldn't catch me on

one of those things. Well, not to live on, in any case. Definitely not my cup of tea. I prefer bricks and mortar.' She peered at Lexi. 'Why do you ask?'

Lexi let out a little high-pitched nervous laugh. 'I don't know. I guess because there are houseboats in the area and I thought you might live on one, that's all. Sorry.'

'Oh, there's no need to apologise, young lady.' Meredith looked at the books in her hands. 'I can assure you I don't live on a boat, so there's no fear of these ending up going overboard – if that's what your concerned about.'

Lexi could tell that was meant to be a joke. She was about to laugh when she caught the look on Meredith's face. Her expression was turning to a deep frown.

'Have we finished? It's nearly four and the library shuts very soon. I've got errands to run, and shopping to buy.'

Lexi handed over the two books that Meredith had come to collect for her friend. 'So, she's at home now, to receive the books?' It was very forward of her to ask that question, and she was clearly repeating herself, but Lexi wanted to know. If it was the writer, Margot Dorey, was she here, in Walberswick?

'Well, yes.' Meredith threw her a questioning look, suggesting she found the question a little odd. 'I did say that she'd be reading them straight away, didn't I?'

'Oh, yes, of course. Silly me.' Lexi smiled when she caught the time. 'Well, thank you very much. It's closing time.'

'Good.'

Lexi watched Meredith scoop up the books. As soon as she turned her back, Lexi grabbed her handbag and summer coat. Jill appeared within seconds of Meredith leaving.

'I'll be going.' Lexi rounded the desk. 'See you tomorrow.'

'What was that about?' Jill asked, glancing at Meredith's back just before she disappeared out of the door.

'You were a long time serving that customer.'

'Oh, er …' Lexi was heading to the door too, as she spoke. 'Just, you know, being friendly.'

'All right … well, have a nice afternoon.'

'Oh, yes, right.' Lexi felt guilty for using her position to look up a home address with the intention of following a lady who had just popped in to collect some books for a friend.

41

Lexi ran out of the door. She glanced right and left, looking for the lady who had just left. She frowned. 'Seriously!' she said under her breath. The lady appeared to have vanished. *If only I had the bike that Margot left on deck of the houseboat with me right now,* she thought, *I'd soon catch up with her.*

Every time she saw the bike, Lexi was tempted to take it out for a spin around the village of Walberswick. She'd even been tempted to cycle into work. There were railings outside the library where other people left their bikes. She had looked round the houseboat but couldn't find a bike lock. She'd have to buy one.

But it wasn't just the lack of a lock that had put her off using the bike. It was the thought that someone might recognise it or a neighbour might notice it missing from the houseboat. What if they reported it stolen, and the police found it padlocked outside the library and inquired within who had ridden it there?

Lexi thought that the police had far more important issues than a stolen bike, if it was reported. Then again, this was a sleepy Suffolk market town, full of holidaymakers, second-homers and retired people. She couldn't imagine there was an awful lot of crime here – not like New York, which seemed to have wailing police sirens at every time of the day and night.

Lexi heaved a sigh and dismissed the bike. She didn't have it, and it was no good wishing she did. She stood at the entrance, scratching her head and wondering where Meredith had gone. Then she spotted her a little distance down the street, emerging from a butcher's shop. Lexi's frown turned to a grin. 'There you are,' she said under her breath. Meredith clearly hadn't been lying when she'd said she had some shopping to do.

Lexi had the presence of mind to follow at a discreet distance. She looked at her watch. Although she had Margot Dorey's address, and could have followed the directions on Google Maps on her phone, she wanted to follow Meredith and actually see if she handed over the books to Margot. Besides, rather than relying on Google, in case she lost her phone signal, she thought this was a much quicker way to find the place.

Half an hour later, she realised it wasn't quick at all. Meredith was still in and out of the shops. 'Is she going to shop all afternoon?' Lexi said under her breath, getting ever-more impatient.

She was relieved to discover that they had reached the end of the street, and it looked as though they'd finally run out of shops. The high street trailed off into a row of cottages on one side, and a pub and a hotel on the other. Lexi saw the path that ran along the clifftop where she'd walked when she'd first arrived in Southwold. It led down to the beach. Beyond that was a rough path heading to the quay and the little bridge into Walberswick.

Meredith was heading that way with her shopping bags. She crossed the green beside the hotel and aimed for the path. They left the town centre behind. Lexi knew how long it took to walk to the houseboat from here – ten minutes if she didn't dawdle and look at the lovely views of the beach and the sea. She hoped Meredith didn't have any more stops before Walberswick. Lexi had got tired of standing, gazing into shop windows, pretending she was interested in what was inside, while she waited for Meredith to emerge from another shop. Now she felt she was getting somewhere.

She followed her to the footbridge, but rather than taking the towpath which ran alongside the houseboats, which Lexi normally did once she'd crossed the river, she followed Meredith straight on, past the car park on the quay where Ray's car was parked.

Yesterday, on the way to Aldeburgh, Ray had suggested that she walk into Walberswick and explore the village. Lexi thought of that conversation. She shook her head. Although she had intended to do just that at some point, she hadn't expected to be following a lady she didn't know through the village the very next day. As she continued up the street, passing a row of pretty terraced cottages, Lexi remembered admiring the Georgian seaside village as they'd passed through in the car. This was the first time Lexi had ventured into the little community of Walberswick on foot.

She passed a little village shop and could see the pub up ahead on the corner. She wondered if there were rooms to rent. Lexi fancied staying in the old thatched roofed pub when she had to leave the houseboat. Although how she'd afford it on one hundred pounds a week, she had no idea.

Lexi brushed that thought from her mind, along with the call or text she was anticipating from Andrea to tell her whether her allowance had arrived in her bank account or not.

She was still following Meredith at a discreet distance. Lexi hoped that she didn't glance over her shoulder. With no one else around, she would be sure to spot her.

Meredith suddenly stopped in front of a cottage. She turned and opened the gate.

Is this it? Is this where Margot is living at the moment? Lexi thought. Then her inner voice said, *What am I doing here?* Margot, the writer, was supposed to be in London, wasn't she? And even if she wasn't in London, why would she be there, a stone's throw from her houseboat? It didn't make any sense. *And neither does lying to her houseboat neighbours on the quay.*

She saw Meredith looking in her bag before she got out a door key. She shook her head. Perhaps Meredith had popped home first, to get the dinner on. It only occurred to her now that Meredith might decide to take the books round to her friend later. She was just thinking that she'd had a wasted trip when Meredith emerged from the cottage again, coat still on, two library books in her hand. She turned and closed the gate and continued along the street.

Lexi stared after her. She was going to her friend's house. Lexi hurried after her and saw Meredith stop a little further up the road in front of a pair of wrought-iron double gates. Lexi waited a few moments for her to open the gates and walk into the grounds of the property. She caught a glimpse of the house, an old ivy-clad two-storey detached cottage, surrounded by gardens, as she quickly walked by. It was the cottage she'd been admiring, with the weeping willow tree in the grounds; the one she had fleetingly seen when they had passed by in the car the previous day.

Lexi stood just the other side of the gates, hoping no one had spotted her passing the cottage. She took a peek through the gates. She caught sight of the woman standing at door, taking the books from Meredith. Lexi hastily got out her phone and found the photo on her phone of Margot that she'd taken in the library.

She looked older, but there was no mistaking that she was the woman in the photo – the author who had visited the library to read her book to schoolchildren.

'What the hell?' exclaimed Lexi. Realising she'd said it out loud, she clamped a hand over her mouth. She'd just managed to step to one side of the gates in the nick of time as she saw Margot turn in the direction of the double gates.

'What's the matter?' Lexi heard Meredith exclaim.

'I don't know. I thought I heard something.'

Lexi stood stock still, wondering why she wasn't running away. If Margot hurried down the drive, she'd see her standing by the wall beside the gates.

The house looked big and expensive; just what Lexi imagined a writer would live in – not that she was under any illusion that all writers were rich, but she knew that Margot Dorey had had a best-selling trilogy. Now that she thought about it, it did seem odd that someone who had probably made a pile of money from her books would live on an old houseboat.

She recalled the conversation with Ray, when he had seemed surprised to learn that his neighbour was an author, even though she hadn't published for some years.

Perhaps Margot Dorey's other houseboat neighbours had no idea who she was either. It seemed they had no idea of her whereabouts, and would be quite stunned to learn that she wasn't spending the summer in London, but was right here, in this house.

Lexi stole one last look at the house, risking a glance through the gates as she quickly walked by. That was when she noticed a house sign on the brick pillar by the gate – *Willow Tree Cottage.*

42

Lexi hurried back along the street towards the quay, still shocked to discover that Margot was right there, in Walberswick, just up the road from the houseboat. Even after she'd decided to follow Meredith, she still hadn't quite been able to believe it until she had seen Margot with her own eyes, outside Willow Tree Cottage.

Lexi was walking at such a pace that she was nearly breaking out in a run. She had to get her suitcase and things out of the houseboat before …

She suddenly slowed to a stop. What was she thinking? Margot lived but a five-minute walk away, ten minutes tops. She could turn up at the houseboat at any time. But why would she? It was that question that had stopped Lexi in her tracks.

Think about it, Lexi told herself, glancing over her shoulder up the street where Meredith lived in one of the small terraced cottages. Margot had sent her friend to fetch her library books for the simple reason that she wouldn't be caught dead in the town; she was meant to be a hundred miles away in London. So why would she venture to her houseboat?

Lexi relaxed. She set off again, this time at a much more leisurely pace. Margot was not stopping by any time soon. Once Lexi's heart had stopped racing, something occurred to her. She knew where Margot was. There was no reason for her not to knock on her door and hand her the letter. But how would she explain where she had got her address? It was not as though any of the houseboat community knew where she was.

Lexi slowly shook her head from side to side. She didn't understand why Margot would lie to her friends and neighbours about going away every summer to see her grandchildren in London when she was right there, a few hundred yards away, living in an old country house. Was that the reason? Was she embarrassed to tell them about her lovely cottage? And why didn't she live there all year round? Why live on a small, cramped houseboat when you had a beautiful home just up the road?

'None of this makes sense,' Lexi said aloud.

She had the letter in her handbag. She knew that she could turn right around, head back to the house and knock on the door. So what was stopping her? It was the thought that Margot would ask where she had found her address. It clearly wasn't written on the envelope. It crossed her mind that she could say she'd made enquiries in the library, and that was how she'd found the address. But even as Lexi was thinking it, she knew she wouldn't want to get Jill or any of the other staff into trouble. She wouldn't want to risk them losing their jobs.

There was an alternative; she could just admit she had started a job there and found out her personal details; then surely no one would get into trouble but her. But she couldn't guarantee it. Jill was her boss; she might get into trouble too. And besides, Margot wouldn't look too favourably on Lexi if it appeared she had just got that job in order to access her personal details. Any which way Lexi thought about it, there was not a good outcome.

So put it through her letter box and be done with it. It would be better than leaving it in the post box by the houseboat where a nosy passer-by might open it.

Lexi didn't turn around and head back with the letter. Her mother's express wish was for her to hand the letter to Margot in person. If she wanted it put through her letterbox or into her post-box, then she might as well have dispatched it from America. Lexi knew that. It had occurred to her before.

As she walked along the street, heading for the quay, she smiled. She realised that the discovery that Margot was right there actually worked in her favour. She didn't know the exact date she'd return to the houseboat, but it would be some time at the end of the summer. But that didn't matter now. She no longer had to wait for her arrival to hand her the letter. She just had to walk up to the house when she'd thought of a good enough story as to how she had come by Margot's home address.

Lexi frowned. She knew she was really stalling. What did it matter how she had got the address? Lexi was thinking about her new job, and the friends she'd made – Ray, Sarah, and even Lili, who'd been so kind and helpful. Lexi imagined that in time, she and Lili might become close friends. Time. That was her enemy.

In the back of Lexi's mind, she knew all this wasn't real. It would take months to get the qualification in librarianship she'd need to progress to a senior librarian role and the decent salary that came with it. And even if she persuaded Margot to write another book, which was a ridiculous thought, the finder's fee would only last so long.

Deep down, Lexi knew she'd most likely be on a flight home, returning to face the music in the shape of her grandparents, who for some totally absurd reason had something against their grand-child returning to England. *What are they afraid of?* she wondered, then raised her eyebrows. *What a peculiar thought.*

As she neared the bridge linking Walberswick to Southwold, Lexi decided that she was determined to enjoy it all while it lasted. The flight home and the first-class ticket that her grandparents had organised, along with the limo that was going to whisk her to the airport, were long gone. And so were any thoughts that she was getting her allowance. Andrea had just texted. Lexi had paused to read the text. Her sister had logged on to her bank account and discovered the standing order depositing the funds into her bank account from Grandpa had been stopped. Not only that, but she'd confronted Grandpa over it. He'd said it would be reinstated as soon as Lexi returned. One phone call, and he'd rearrange the flight home.

But she didn't want that. In fact, she didn't need it. Lexi had her flexi return ticket; she just didn't want to use it. *I want to stay here, in my job, with my new friends, and have another dinner date with the lovely Scott and his daughter next door.* For the first time in her life, Lexi felt free. Free to make her own decisions, to live the life that she knew had always been waiting for her – and that life was here on the beautiful Suffolk Coast in England. But she knew it would come at a price.

You wanted your independence – so here you are. Lexi was already contemplating whether she could get a second job so that she could afford to continue in her new life in England. *If only I could stay on the houseboat by the quay.* She'd only been there a short time, but strangely it already felt like home.

Just then, Lexi decided she would enjoy the time she had left on the houseboat, and her new job, and try to avoid neighbours and any awkward questions – apart from her next-door neighbours, Scott and Charlie, and Ray, of course. He'd kindly offered to take her to Aldeburgh again. She couldn't wait to return – Lexi was still intent on finding out who was laying flowers on her father's grave.

And when she felt the time was right, before the end of the summer, she knew she would hand-deliver the letter, just as her mother had requested, to the lady who was living in Willow Tree Cottage.

The Sunrise Coast Series continues in

Return to Willow Tree Cottage

Paperback and Kindle eBook available from Amazon

I hope you enjoyed *The Houseboat by The Quay* and would be grateful if you wish to leave a review on Amazon.

To find out more about my books or sign up to my newsletter please visit my website.

www.elisedarcy.com

Printed in Dunstable, United Kingdom

81129658R00184